Cerebrante Trilogy: Book One

By

Andrew John

Copyright and Disclaimers Notice

Dedication

To my beautiful Wife and Children.
(My light in the darkness)

Table of Contents

CEREBRANTE TRILOGY: BOOK ONE -THE SACRED BALANCE   1

COPYRIGHT AND DISCLAIMERS NOTICE   2

DEDICATION   3

TABLE OF CONTENTS   4

MAP OF IMPARTIA: YEAR – 5000   6

PROLOGUE   7

CHAPTER ONE: A FATEFUL MEETING   11

CHAPTER TWO: THE SANCTUARY OF DARKNESS   32

CHAPTER THREE: INTO THE DESERT   52

CHAPTER FOUR: LAKE TINOMAR   73

CHAPTER FIVE: THE CAVERN OF ETERNAL WATERS   94

CHAPTER SIX: THROUGH THE EYES OF INNOCENCE   116

CHAPTER SEVEN: THE POOL OF INSIGHT   135

CHAPTER EIGHT: THE TRIAL OF ETERNAL FLAMES   156

CHAPTER NINE: THROUGH FORSAKEN EYES   180

CHAPTER TEN: ABOVE CLOUDS AND BENEATH THE STARS   201

CHAPTER ELEVEN: THE ASYLUM OF ETERNAL LIGHT   225

CHAPTER TWELVE: BETWEEN THE DARKNESS AND LIGHT   242

CHAPTER THIRTEEN: THE SACRED BALANCE   263

CHAPTER FOURTEEN: A CHAOTIC RESURGENCE   279

CEREBRANTE: THE FORGOTTEN GUARDIAN   295

APPENDIX: NAME PRONUNCIATIONS   296

ABOUT THE AUTHOR   298

Map of Impartia: Year – 5000

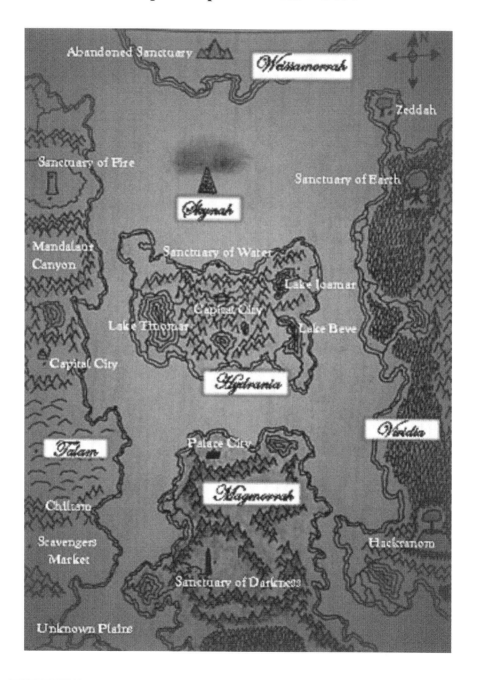

Prologue

Impartia has suffered many conflicts over its short existence; some proving necessary to protect *The Sacred Balance*, a spiritual force that acts as a bastion of harmony within this small world. From time-immemorial, Impartia has been governed by its Celestial and Elemental Spirits; each unified to prevent chaos from spreading across the lands and their mortal inhabitants.

The greatest Celestial Spirit was known as Cerebrante – The Spirit of Balance, then there were the Spirits of Light and Darkness – Alaskia and Kufiah. Together, these formidable beings embodied Impartia's *Sacred Balance*, though they constantly struggled to bond with one another. The Elemental Spirits, respectively, shared the sole purpose of sanctifying Impartia's physical powers. Each one had their own divine duty; be it to control the ocean waves, air currents, magma flow or even the minutest grain of sand – all held accountable to Impartia's ultimate survival.

Over the course of five-thousand years, Impartia's Spirits dwindled in their control over humanity. The only means of salvation, was for the Celestial and Elemental Spirits to bond themselves within a physical host - a mortal whom would be worthy of their gracious presences. The Elemental Spirits found a great ease in choosing their mortal vessels, even being able to transcend their powers through various adornments or selfless acts of sacrifice.

The Celestial Spirits, however, soon discovered that their powers could only be contained within mortals whom displayed mighty auras of their own. On selecting a physical vessel, Cerebrante would create a distinct mark upon their flesh to signify a connection between them – the Mark of Cerebrante, a symbol of one's ability to harness the unlimited power of Impartia's strongest being. However, Alaskia and Kufiah were lost in being able to choose their own hosts; a result from constantly struggling against each other, and so could only take the form of Cerebrante's.

As chaos began to once again flourish, a newly-willed malignance arose. Impartia's mortals grew weary from their futile wars and conquests, their wrongful actions woefully going unchallenged by Impartia's protective Spirits. All hope seemed to fade, and its place festered a darkened mind – one that would forever leave a dire impact upon this fragile world. In the Ash Lands of Magmorrah, the nation's tyrannical ruler - King Kanaan Til-Magmorros, had become Cerebrante's chosen host from birth. Kanaan from a young age had grown lustful for more power and immortality, eventually using his heightened connection with Kufiah to spread a cruel dominance across his own nation and the other lands surrounding it - without any mercy shown.

Prophetic whispers soon travelled throughout Impartia; they spoke of a risen light that could quench the sordid darkness that had inflicted it, though also spoke of how the evil that had been allowed to strengthen, could one day render all life into an eternity of penance. The *Hymn of Alaskia* was one of these prophecies: It envisioned the Spirit of Light's eventual resurgence, though the Elemental Guardians and few other followers who performed these verses, did so within a vain hope of them ever coming into fruition...

Teach us with your isolation
Free us with your love.
Cast aside the fear and pain
Sleep beneath the stars above
Teach us with your adoration
Grant us purest peace
Hear our prayers and through your graceful light
Bring to us our soul's release

The *Hymn of Kufiah*, however, mockingly mirrored Alaskia's own enlightened verses. The Spirit of Darkness' foul prophecy portrayed a tainting hold over life and was performed only by Kufiah's Dark Acolytes - servants who devoted themselves towards seeing their Master Spirit reach an infinitely destructive level of existence...

Teach us with your immolation
Cleanse this world of love
Gather forth the shadows of pain
Bring fear beneath the stars above
Teach us through your aberration
Through your hate's release
Into the endless void relinquish light
Render mountains to the seas

King Kanaan's diseased obsession, to become Impartia's only ruler, eventually became his own undoing. A great uprising took place in Magmorrah; where the citizens from its Metropolis all marched to Kanaan's Royal Palace, in want of dethroning him for his heinous acts. Kanaan learned of this dissent, his malice grew and by using his possession over Kufiah, he decimated the once advanced nation into a landscape of ashes and ruin. Despite his ruthless nature, Kanaan bore two daughters; each so vastly different in comparison to their sibling – Princesses Cara and Cera Til-Magmorros. Kanaan's children, unlike their wicked father, were radiantly beautiful with their longing-flowing, blonde hair and piercing amber eyes - that entranced any whom looked upon them. The youngest daughter – Princess Cera, proved to be Kanaan's proudest achievement; equal to her father in cruelty and evermore lustful, once she had matured, to seek further dominance.

Kanaan's firstborn child – Cara, showed no likeness nor promise in being worthy enough to take the crown from him; for she was kind, sympathetic towards others and sought no further rise in her regal role. Princess Cera came to learn of her father's malicious acts against their nation and others, whilst also discovering the true purpose behind his most-treasured possession; an amulet that completely controlled the will of Kufiah. Magmorrah's youngest princess conceived a plot to usurp King Kanaan from his throne, thus too ensuring her own immortal reign as the Spirit of Darkness' puppet-master.

Princess Cera, at the tender age of sixteen, had managed to deceive her father and take reign over Magmorrah; imprisoning him deep within Kufiah's Sanctuary of Darkness as punishment, and publicly branding him as a lunatic to their devout citizens. Now as ruling Queen of Magmorrah and owner of Kanaan's cursed amulet, Cera promised her subjects that she planned to return their nation to its former glory, and to destroy any who would oppose them in fulfilling this wanted destiny.

Princess Cara, along with her infant daughter - Sophilia, eventually fled the Royal Palace in fear of the increasingly jealous Queen's threats to their lives. In close pursuit of them, was Queen Cera's closest ally and General of Magmorrah's Army - Nira, who along with an elite taskforce searched tirelessly for the two fugitives. Cara and Sophilia found refuge as exiles within the wild landscapes of Viridia; a nation where great forests stretched out for hundreds of miles, separated only by towering mountain ranges. Viridia's remote landscape provided the perfect cover for Cara and Sophilia, as they hid themselves away from Queen Cera and General Nira's reach on their eventual journey northwards – far away from Magmorrah.

Queen Cera continued to reign on high for many years, despite her failure to capture Cara and Sophilia – now Magmorrah's most-wanted enemies. Cera callously invaded the other nations by harnessing Kufiah's brutal power and General Nira's devout army; succeeding with every step taken to fulfil her twisted schemes, as none dared to defy them. The mass resources and wealth Cera had gained through her numerous conquests, gradually fuelled an obsession to dominate all life within Impartia even further.

Magmorrah's Queen sought to ultimately end Cerebrante's sacred cycle, hoping to do so, by eradicating their influence over the other Celestial Spirits. Cera reasoned, that by doing this, Kufiah would forever be her own personal weapon, and soon she constructed a new abhorrent plan - that would take exactly ten years in the making. To fulfil her evil desires, Queen Cera came to reason that the only way they could be achieved was by finding Alaskia's hidden Sanctum - to wilfully destroy the benevolent Spirit; being that they had been incarcerated secretly by King Kanaan many years prior.

Thankfully, King Kanaan had only shared with Cera some cautious details of Alaskia's whereabouts, mainly that he had managed to imprison the Spirit of Light within a fortified space; allowing for him to truly harness Kufiah's powers within his accursed amulet - which Magmorrah's Queen now aptly wore. News reached Cera from the Acolytes of Darkness – Kufiah's subservient followers, that the only way to enter Alaskia's Sanctum was to receive individual passwords; each only granted by Impartia's Elemental Guardians. The prominent issue being with this to Cera, was that these passwords were bestowed only by the Elemental Guardians upon a worthy mortal that bore the 'Mark of Cerebrante'. Cera clasped her hands together in a sickening joy as she looked upon her chest, where the very same mark bore itself - though only faintly.

Magmorrah's Queen, who suffered greatly from extreme paranoia and compulsions, acted on this information without question; in knowing that Cara too had this distinct mark. Cera ordered for General Nira and her forces to search yet again for the elusive princesses, hoping to track them before they could somehow intervene with Queen Cera's ultimate plan.

General Nira quickly gained word herself, from the many clandestine sources at her beckoned call, that a woman of Cara's description had been seen travelling within Viridia's northern forests. Magmorrah's General reasoned, from what she had been reliably told, that it could only be Princess Cara that was being described to her. With her Elite Guards and advanced war-machines at hand, General Nira immediately set out to hunt down the evasive fugitives in Viridia...and so too began a quest to save *The Sacred Balance*.

Chapter One: A Fateful Meeting

Peace and tranquillity. For the last ten years, this is all Cara and her young daughter Sophilia have known. Together, they had survived within Viridia's ancient forests in forced exile, though were still being tracked down by the tyrannical Queen of Magmorrah – Queen Cera, and her most-devoted servant – General Nira, for crimes which neither could truly justify or comprehend.

"Don't stray too far!" Shouted Cara over to Sophilia, as the child briskly left her mother's side to collect some flowers for her. "You don't want to be eaten by a bear - do you?" Sophilia frowned back in return.

"Mummy! I'm ten years old now, I'm a big girl…and bears don't scare me!" A gleeful smile swiftly arose on her face. Just ahead, lay some Jasmine flowers – Sophilia's favourite. "Look, Mummy! Aren't they beautiful?"

"Yes, Lia…but *please* be careful!" Sighed Cara wearily, ever cautious to the threats that still lingered over them. "Whether your ten or one-hundred years old, you will always be my baby. I don't mind you wandering off…just not where I can't see you, okay?"

"Yes, Mummy." Smiled Sophilia contently. "I want to make you a new necklace, it won't take long." She hastily reached down for some of the flowers that had already fallen, always mindful not to disturb any still alive. "They're perfect, Mummy!"

Cara leant herself against a nearby tree to rest, whilst continuing to observe Sophilia's present whereabouts. Impartia's midday sun was at its height now, and the rising heat was becoming almost unbearable within Viridia's humid forests. Cara could feel her eyes slowly closing, then soon she started to drift off into a wakeful sleep. In her dream, Cara saw herself standing in the middle of a vast ocean, she was surrounded by nothing else and was completely alone. A faint voice began to whisper through the passing breeze; it sounded like a small boy, and they were begging for Cara to return home – to Magmorrah.

"Mummy!" Screamed Sophilia, instantly waking Cara from her disturbing vision. "I heard a bear! *Honestly*!" The child appeared frantic and fearful, expressions she would never normally need to display. "Mummy…now I'm scared!"

"Your imagination, Lia…" Chuckled Cara dismissively. "Bears only roar when they feel threatened, have you done anything to scare one lately?"

"Mummy, I *heard* a bear roar! It sounded like…" Sophilia was suddenly halted in her explanation, as a terrifying growl echoed nearby. "…That!" Cara's eyes immediately flared with terror, their amber colour radiant in a knowing apprehension.

"That is *not* a bear, Lia!" Gasped Cara, she then quickly grabbed at Sophilia's arms to tear through the trees that lay ahead together – away from these horrific howls.

"Mummy…are the bears going to catch us?" Whimpered Sophilia anxiously. "Will they eat us?" Her heart raced faster, this was the first time she and her mother had ever needed to flee like this. More howls and beast-like cries aimed towards Cara and her daughter, their reach seemingly close now.

"I *know* that howl and what creature makes it," panted Cara, as she hastened her and Sophilia's sprint through the dense woods. "Magmorran Tracking-Hounds…"

"Magmo-what?" Questioned Sophilia in perplexment, she had little knowledge of her true homeland. "Are they Wolves? That doesn't sound like a wolf to me, Mummy!"

"No, they're far worse than wolves *or* bears!" Spoke Cara sporadically, desperate to preserve her breaths. "They are wicked, evil dogs and they won't stop chasing us…not unless their master commands it." The abhorrent image of General Nira instantly appeared in Cara's immediate thoughts to her bitter dismay – Queen Cera's own lap-dog.

"Mummy!" Screamed Sophilia, her own amber eyes sodden from the tears flowing from them. "I don't want to die! I don't want you to either!"

"Keep running, Sweetheart!" Cara, through her blinding fear, had lost any sense of where she and Sophilia now were. A powerful gust of wind suddenly struck at the fleeing pair, it forced them further off track, deeper into the more mysterious parts of Viridia's ancient landscape.

"Why are we going this way?" Despaired Sophilia, as she tried to break free from Cara's tightening grasp. "It's getting darker…I hate the dark!"

"We don't have a choice, Darling!" Assured Cara, she somehow felt a calming presence in the guiding breezes; they were taking her towards a deeply spiritual dwelling – and she knew it. "We have a Guardian Angel watching over us, Lia…Keep running, and follow the air current!"

More howls sounded in the air, their piercing cries now joined by loud crashing noises that also came from behind where Cara and Sophilia fled. The guiding breezes intensified, urging the mother and child forwards, and within them a benevolent feminine voice began to speak, just enough to be heard:

"Spirits shall protect you…Reach the Sanctuary…Daughters of Magmorrah."

"Did you say something, Mummy?" Asked Sophilia with a pleading expression. She felt no fear from the angelic voice, though it did leave her slightly uneased. The Magmorran Hounds could still be heard and their demonic howls seemingly intensifying with each step taken. As Cara and Sophilia started to lose hope, they suddenly found themselves out in the open, yet the day's sunlight could not reach them. A large clearing now stood before them and towering above it was a gargantuan tree; the natural wonder stood thousands of feet high and was supported by three equally massive roots, with a strange-looking stone circle at their centre.

"I told you, Lia…" Stressed Cara forcefully, though her daughter was not as enthusiastic in response. "We have a Guardian Angel looking after us! I've read about this place years ago, long before you were born…it is the Sanctuary of Earth." Sophilia took in some laboured breaths and then looked to her mother in beleaguerment.

"Our Guardian Angel…she mentioned a Sanctuary!" Exclaimed Sophilia, her spirits now lifting. "You were right, Mummy! We'll be safe now!" The child's innocent joy however, was very short-lived. Three snarling Magmorran Hounds burst into the clearing with their mouths foaming, their monstrous teeth bared and their bodies twice the size of an average wolf and far more intimidating – all too much for Cara and Sophilia to bear.

"I don't want to die, Mummy…" Grieved Sophilia, as she rested her head into Cara's loving arms. "Make them go away!"

"Stay absolutely still, don't move an inch…they will attack us if we do so." Cautioned Cara, as she gave a resentful look towards the imposing beasts. "What was safe-word…" Mumbled Cara to herself nervously. Then, in a harrowing moment of realisation, Cara and Sophilia watched on helplessly as several obsidian tanks from Magmorrah tore through the trees towards them; leaving a wake of destruction behind to the immediate delight of General Nira - who proudly took lead at the helm.

"I've got you now…TRAITORS!" Rejoiced Nira, as she focused on the cowering fugitives lain ahead. The malignant General soon alighted from her tank and was laughing sadistically as she did so at the success of this mission. Nira then slowly walked over towards Cara and Sophilia, where on reaching them she looked down upon both in a malevolent judgement over their supposed treachery.

"What do we have here?" Taunted Nira cruelly, whilst glaring at Cara with a hate-filled stare. "…*Princess*…" Cara wrapped her arms around Sophilia defensively and then glared back to Nira in defiance; she had prepared herself for this moment over the last decade, though it still wrought so much pain and sorrow.

"No curtsied today, Nira?" Replied Cara, with a sarcastic smirk. Her smile swiftly diminished on seeing the General's infamous blade; it had slaughtered countless innocents and was supposedly cursed.

"Not to YOU!" Countered Nira viciously. "You hold no title or power over me now, Wretch!" She clasped onto her sword's hilt, instantly removing Cara's defiant demeanour.

"How did you find us?" Questioned Cara meekly, her fingers tremoring upon Sophilia's shoulders. "Ten years is a long time to be searching for someone, such a great deal of effort must have been made?" Magmorrah's General cackled louder and with more resonating anger; every moment Cara suffered, brought so much pleasure to Cera's greatest warrior.

"Why…you left Queen Cera a trinket to remember you by!" Nira hastily ripped a small, silken doll from the hands of one of her Elite Guards. "See? This horrid thing still has your daughter's scent all over it!" She moved callously to feed the precious doll to one of her hounds; the beast ripped it asunder instantly, signifying what would happen to Cara and Sophilia – should Nira will this.

"Your sister is waiting for you, Cara…" Whispered Nira to her in a threating manner. "Luckily for yourself and the child, we have only come here to this *disgusting* land so that I can bring you both back home…taking your lives will just have to wait - it seems."

Sophilia cautiously tore her face away from the shielding protection of Cara's bosom, held in a curious reluctance in wanting to look upon Nira's malevolent figure for herself. Cera's General looked to be around the same age as Cara, though her own features were far less appealing and disturbingly more masculine. Nira's skin appeared deathly pale in colour and was littered with scars from the numerous battles she had fought in; wholly protected by scale-like obsidian armour that contrasted itself with the General's shaven head. The most daunting feature however, which Sophilia soon noticed to her immediate revulsion, were Nira's piercing black eyes that continuously looked as if they were staring in your very soul – no matter where the evil warrior glared.

"Do you think that *I'm* pretty…little girl?" Snarled Nira to Sophilia, as she ran her sharp fingertips across the child's tremoring face.

"You *will not* touch my daughter!" Cried back Cara fearfully in response, whilst at the same time swiping Nira's hand away from Sophilia. "We'll go back to Magmorrah willingly, there is not going to be a need for any violence…which I know greatly disappoints you, Nira."

Without any warning, several acolytes from the Sanctuary of Earth thankfully appeared to counter Nira's ambush. They swiftly left from the light of their Sanctuary's entrance Seal, the strange stone circle, to surround Cara and Sophilia in defence of them, also patiently awaiting the arrival of their Guardian and hoping that his further protection could save the two helpless victims from an uncertain fate.

"INFIDELS!" Screeched Nira. "I will make short work of destroying you all!" She cackled in assurance to herself, knowing that there was no further place for Cara and Sophilia to hide. Nira proceeded to snarl through her rage, she then violently tore from its sheathing an obsidian sword that had been nestled safely against her waist. The General taunted her pitifully-outmatched opponents; coldly describing to each of them how they would die slowly by her skilful hands.

The air around grew eerily still within a haunting silence, leaves upon the surrounding trees fell unnaturally still and the earth beneath tremored through a coursing power that remained yet, unseen. Nira glared inquisitively towards a peculiar-looking stone seal that was placed within the centre of the Sanctuary's entranceway, far below its towering trees where an eminently-robed stranger now stood; looking back sternly upon her.

The person was that of a tall, muscular-looking man with bronzed skin that glistened radiantly in the light of Impartia's risen sun. Dark, dread-locked hair fell far beneath his broad shoulders and the stranger's eyes radiated with an emerald light as green as the ancient robes that clad him. The figure's eyes suddenly released this transient light that shone itself far from within them, creating a mysterious power to close the gateway between the entrance seal and Sanctuary far above.

"How *dare* you defile this holy site with your war-machines!" Declared the prominent figure sternly. "You have no authority here…General Nira!"

The Acolytes of Earth gave a unified cheer; they instantly recognised the cloaked figure to be that of their mighty Spirit Guardian – Ven. He stared upon Nira and her soldiers in utter detest and then, whilst motioning towards them, he slowly began to raise a crude wooden staff above his head. Ven hastily slammed his staff into the earth with a tremendous impact and hate-filled cry. Nira's beleaguered soldiers each cowered and lifted their weapons in uncertainty, as a proceeding wave of massive tree roots now broke out from the ground beneath; their presence summoned by the powerful spiritual connection Ven ultimately shared with his element. The thick roots lashed violently against their unsuspecting enemy; crushing some of them with a merciless force, swiping others away and easily relinquishing the Magmorran Hounds from this horrifying scene.

"The shadow of Magmorrah and its cursed ashes have spread far enough already!" Cried out Ven angrily at Nira. "This…I will not permit for any longer!" The Guardian used this moment of onslaught to swiftly reach one of his followers – Jenayan, in now seeing that she had Sophilia held protectively within her arms. Ven frantically commanded Jenayan, that the stranger's child be taken into the safety of their Sanctum, whilst he searched in vain through the waves of clashing roots to locate Sophilia's mother.

"Make haste, Jen!" Commanded Ven with a heavy heart, his voice desperate in tone. "Do not concern yourself with my fate…save the child!" To Ven's instant dismay, he soon found that the enraged General had somehow managed to take a cruel hold over Cara from behind. Nira moved cautiously through the aggressive tree roots and their swiping blows, the whole time resting her cold blade against Cara's throat in an apparent threat against the princess's life.

"She is MINE, weakling!" Roared Nira, through her sadistic laughter. "Make *one more* step, and I will slit this wretch's throat…I swear it!"

Now held within a remorseful state of sorrow, Ven acknowledged his unwilling defeat in failing to save Cara, though reassured in the knowledge that her child would come to no harm within his impenetrable Sanctum. As the Guardian reluctantly cast aside his staff in surrender it returned to the form of a shrivelled tree root, which surprised both Cara and Nira alike as they curiously studied its unnatural transformation. The towering roots slowly sunk back beneath the earth of their Sanctuary and with her captives now attained, Nira rejoiced.

The General proudly signalled for her remaining soldiers to make haste back to Magmorrah, where Nira's precious monarch waited impatiently to receive her most-prized enemies.

"You will regret this," muttered Ven in resent to Nira, on being escorted by her. "You and your Queen...the Spirits of Impartia are not blind to such abhorrent acts."

Forced against their wills, Cara and Ven were thrown violently into the cells of a foreboding Magmorran tank; much to the immediate pleasure of General Nira and her devout soldiers. The heavy cell doors loudly slammed shut as Nira's tank fire up its engine with a deafening roar, signalling the start of an arduous journey back to Magmorrah's ash lands and the uncertain fates of her captives. Cara barely managed to breathe as she became increasingly anxious, mostly through the troubling thoughts relating to her daughter's own safety.

Nira's soldiers had secured the cells meticulously, fully incarcerating their unfortunate victims within the dark carcass of the tank without any sign of escaping. The soldiers themselves were celebrating with Nira outside, unaware of a gentle hand that moved gracefully towards one of Cara's flailing arms as the Guardian in the adjoining cell willed to start a meaningful conversation with her.

"Please, forgive me...I had no choice but to surrender." Whispered Ven to Cara remorsefully, his voice trembling through despair. "I could not risk her, or those soldiers, killing you... at least for the sake of the child." The Guardian sighed, then looked again towards Cara's mournful expression. "I hope, that you understand my actions were taken with both of your interests at heart, and not through an act of cowardice?" The Guardian continued to stutter over his painful and guilt-ridden words, each one highlighting the terrible loss now inflicted.

Cara raised her sore eyes to meet with the stranger's and soon smiled back to him in reassurance, herself slowly moving a hand through the bars to lay it upon his.

"It's okay...I really appreciate how you and the others risked your lives for me and my Sophilia so selflessly back there." Sighed Cara heavily, as she took in another laboured breath. The flashbacks from their recent kidnap persisted in penetrating her immediate thoughts, as she struggled greatly to rid herself of them. "It was inevitable anyway, I always knew that Nira would eventually catch up with us. She and the Queen of Magmorrah have been trying to track us down for the last ten years or so, ever-since I escaped from them when Sophilia was only a baby." Cara recounted, as she glared over the shaking hands of Ven. He in turn, lowered his head empathetically towards her.

"Queen Cera has wrought so much pain and uncertainty to so many unfortunate souls just like yourself, through her reign of terror…" Sympathised the Guardian mournfully. He then glanced with shock at Cara's right facial cheek, duly noticing the distinct birthmark which bore itself upon her – an unmistakeable feature which he had not yet observed. Ven studied the mark intricately; for he knew the significant meaning behind its purpose, forcing the Guardian to tremble more in this harrowing realisation.

"Are you okay?" Asked Cara nervously, on noticing the stranger's keen interest in her mark. "What a stupid question to ask in such circumstances…sorry."

"Yes, I am alright…may I introduce myself?" Motioned the Guardian politely to Cara, she thankfully nodded her head back to him in acceptance. "Thank you. My name is Ven, I am the leader of Viridia's Earth Acolytes and Sanctuary. May I ask your name, if that is alright with yourself?" The Guardian said hopefully; wishing to know as much as he could about this mysterious stranger now sat beside him. Ven attempted to make further eye contact with Cara, who was still deeply lost in contemplation over her daughter's current fate; the child's present safety yet still unknown. "You seem so familiar, if you don't mind me saying, perhaps…we have crossed paths before?" Cara forced a slight grin to emerge through her present melancholy towards the seemingly-gentile man, sensing that it would be rude not to address him - after what he had just done for her.

"Maybe? It *is* a small world that we live in - isn't it?" Cara jested, though she in truth struggled to recall any previous meetings with Ven, as he continued to stare upon her accursed mark intently. "My name is Cara and the mark on my face, which you keep looking at," she snapped disapprovingly. "Is the reason why the Queen has hunted me down for so long…ten years to be exact." Explained the princess sternly, whilst caressing the peculiar birthmark with her fingertips. "It has a special meaning - supposedly. Cera told me, that it somehow made me a traitor and a pressing threat to her rightful reign over Magmorrah. I couldn't understand any of what was being said to me at the time, it's not like I wanted to be born with this mark and it was never an issue before she came to the throne…" Ven steadied himself as best he could against the bars of the shifting tank, realising that his previous suspicions had been now worryingly justified.

"I apologise unreservedly if I was being rude to you, Cara." Muttered the Guardian bashfully. "I mean for no personal intrusion, but may I also ask…" Ven said, as he hesitated momentarily. "You are Cara, first-born princess of King Kanaan - aren't you?" He held his breath in anticipation to her reaction, given such an invasive question and fearing that he may cause some further upset. Cara merely nodded to him silently in confirmation to this impressive observation, despite her hatred towards this painful reminder.

"Yes, at least, I *was* a princess." Moaned Cara. "Now my little girl and I are nothing but unwanted exiles - fugitives to be erased from Cera's ever-growing list of enemies." She dwelled sadly, whilst rolling her eyes back towards Ven.

"Did your father ever explain to you what significance this mark really has, Cara?" Questioned Ven, praying that she may at least hold some knowledge regarding her spiritual link, though the princess only returned her sights to him with a blank expression. "The mark on your face *does* have great meaning, but not as Cera would make it out to be. It is a sign that you have a great connection with a very powerful Celestial Spirit, one who is meant to watch over our world - Cerebrante.

Cara showed no obvious awareness to this sacred name. "Cerebrante…I've never heard of them before." At this moment, the Spirit's Mark seemed to react by burning slightly upon flesh. "This scar has brought nothing but heartache to me…I hate it."

"Your birthmark proves that Cerebrante, at present, has a strong bond with you." Said Ven assuredly. "I know that all this must seem strange, Cara…but what I am telling you *is* the truth!" He immediately regretted revealing such privileged knowledge to the already beleaguered princess, herself still sat silently in deep-thought beside him.

A new mixture of raw emotions flowed through Cara. Most of the memories from her past were indefinitely sore and she fought hard to keep them at bay, though a curiosity slowly began to take a hold in her from what Ven was saying. Cara was undecided initially with wanting to know more behind the purpose of her sordid mark and the link it had with Cerebrante, feeling unmoved by what difference it could possibly make now in this futile situation.

"Father and I weren't exactly close, he always made it very clear to me that Cera was the prodigal child - not his '*pathetic*' first-born. I was nothing more than an inconvenient embarrassment to my him, and for this crime he hid me within our palace walls away from public view for most of my childhood. Father also prevented me from bonding with Cera as we were growing up, apparently so that my little sister could never be influenced by me… his worst failure." Recounted Cara in a harrowing tone. "I often wander to myself, what if Cera had been able to spend some time with me… would she have become a different person or even return a similar love?" Cara then lowered her head into the support of her tremoring hands, the princess strove hard against an amounting sorrow that now began to forge several tears in her eyes. "The possibility still pains me, to an extent, Cera *is* my sister after-all and is the only 'real' family Sophilia and I still have." A solitary tear ran steadily down Cara's birthmark, she then allowed for her long hair to fall freely in a pitiful bid to hide herself away from the Guardian's yearning look. Ven allowed a further moment for Cara's grief to flow, he was disturbed greatly by what she had shared and remorseful for having not intervened against Kanaan's rule any sooner.

"Do not permit these sad memories to affect you so, Cara." Whispered Ven in sympathy. "Queen Cera has become the evil person she is only by the faults and corruption of your father's actions; nothing could have prevented this." Cara quickly leapt towards the bars of her cell facing Ven, momentarily angered by his ill-conceived insight into her past and by the previously hidden emotions which she had now so carelessly revealed.

"You know *nothing* of what Cera and I went through with Father!" Snapped Cara abruptly. "My sister is *not* evil - only lost!" More tears now coursed down Cara's face through her rising contempt, though this anger was really directed at her own recollection rather than at Ven himself. After pausing initially, Ven reached out to Cara again in an understanding of her feelings and was also desperate to comfort her in some-way if possible.

"I honestly do know, Cara…" Breathed Ven, as he exhaled a laboured breath. "As Guardian of the Earth Sanctuary, it is my duty to assist…" He hesitated awkwardly. The Guardian knew what he was about to reveal to Cara strictly broke the sanctity of his vows; primarily in keeping his identity secret from strangers unless, that is, in times of great need. "It is one of my duties to assist Cerebrante's mortal host, in carrying out their purpose on this earthly plain - to right the balance between darkness and light within it. For Cerebrante to carry out their own purpose, they must create a strong bond with their physical host; that being a mortal who bears the Spirit's distinct mark upon their bodies." Ven stared knowingly into Cara's eyes with a solemn and radiant expression.

"In all honesty, I am reserved to share with you this most-secret wisdom…though I feel you need to know this now. Cerebrante currently resides within your father, using him as their host… meaning… he must still be alive." Ven silenced himself cautiously as he held his head down, feeling that his words would be too unbelievable for Cara to trust; she had never heard of Spirits such as Cerebrante before, so how could she possibly accept that what Ven was saying to her was indeed the truth? The likelihood of her famously-wicked father being this all-powerful being perplexed Cara even more now than anything else that had troubled her.

"What are you saying, Ven… Spirits *do* exist?" Replied Cara in astonishment. "I thought that they were just fantasies; told only to young children, so that they could be scared into obedience? Father had his servants tell me such tales as a child to keep me quiet…" Deep within her own reasoning, Cara knew that Ven would not have any purpose in lying to her as he had nothing to truly gain from it, though her curiosity began to grow even more now regarding these peculiar revelations.

"I have no doubt that Kanaan would have told you such stories, Cara." Said the Guardian woefully. "You too bear the same mark of Cerebrante as he does... and also Cera." He muttered reservedly. "I remember Kanaan's mark being plainly situated upon his forehead; the King constantly wore his crown for this reason, perhaps in shame. If Cerebrante's host cannot achieve *The Sacred Balance* its control over Impartia's dark and light powers, then the mark upon them eventually fades and the Spirit would then ultimately wish to reincarnate itself using a new body. The only problem with this connection, is that Cerebrante uses the lifeforce of its original host to complete the spiritual transfer; sometimes killing the unfortunate mortal in which they had chosen to reside in." Ven persisted with his daunting lecture, despite Cara's deafly silence in return to him. The Princess duly absorbed what was being shared and despite how far-fetched they may have seemed, felt for an instant a pity towards her father's fraught burden.

"What shame," sneered Cara, "that this Cerebrante didn't kill Father years ago...Impartia would have been far better-off." The Guardian shrugged back with a neutral smile.

"Well, Cara...Kanaan came to learn of this fatal hold that Cerebrante had over him, and soon discovered a way in which to cheat the Celestial Spirit out of fulfilling their holy cycle. Kanaan achieved this, by using dark magic to entrap the Spirit of Light - Alaskia, within a prison that only a select few may enter. Kanaan had also possessed the Spirit of Darkness - Kufiah, for his own selfish purposes, using his newly gained powers to decimate your nation and those around it. Your father managed to prevent his own death through Cerebrante's severance by committing these blasphemous acts, he obviously sensed that they were preparing to move onto a new host...perhaps you, Cara?" Ven sat himself uncomfortably on the floor of his cell, looking back cautiously at Cara who now stood in awe over her father's clandestine actions.

"My mark...it began to fade years ago though, Ven. It began to fade even before I left Magmorrah with Sophilia, it's barely visible now!" Shouted Cara in shock. "I'm sorry, but... I think that you're wrong in believing that this 'Cerebrante' would choose me." Cara gasped fearfully as she held a hand against her face, in a purpose of hiding the mark away from Ven's repetitive viewing of it. "How did Father manage to cheat this Spirit in such a way? He was ruthless, but certainly not the wisest of rulers." Cara queried hesitantly, in a dread that she already knew the answer to this.

"Kanaan had created a powerfully cursed amulet, born through the darkest spiritual magic and willed by Kufiah's Acolytes of Darkness." Recounted Ven bitterly. "When worn, the amulet allows for its bearer to fully control Kufiah and their abilities, it is now in the hands of Queen Cera - a fact of which I presume...you know." Cara again turned away from Ven in embarrassment towards her apparent naivety, though she proceeded to mutter in agreement with the Guardian's keen observation.

"It all makes sense to me now; why Cera took the throne from Father." Replied Cara with a beleaguered expression. "I wish that there was a way to destroy it, then maybe, I could save my sister from the same fate?" She contemplated sincerely. The tank then abruptly came to a shuddering stop, jolting the two weary prisoners trapped within it violently. Cara and Ven sat still in a wary silence, awaiting patiently for their captor's unwelcome presence as they could now hear many heavy footsteps passing by outside.

The doors to the tank's rear opened and slammed harshly against the sides of General Nira's monstrous machine. The light of day seemingly had begun to fade under the thunderous clouds across from Cara and Ven in the distance, they had now reached the sea which lay between Viridia and Magmorrah towards the south; the very same strait of water that sat ahead of Cara now, was the same one that she and Sophilia had only just managed to cross with their live many years prior.

"Magmorrah…" whispered Cara in a terrified voice. "I never thought that I would see the Ash Lands ever again." Cara felt a strong compulsion to look away from the agonising site, though soon a newer threat stood itself before her upon the ground outside. The dominating figure of Nira now lingered towards Cara and Ven, proudly inspecting the sorrow upon their faces which wrought a sadistic satisfaction to the General's innate cruelty. Nira had a small woven sack held tightly in one of her hands, she it violently in the direction of Cara to land just within reach of Ven.

"Well, it didn't take long for these new tanks of mine to make it back here through those primitive forests of yours…*Guardian*." Nira mocked to Ven coldly. "We've made a new road from here that leads straight back to your Sanctuary, it should make travelling there far easier; should the time come if we must do so… *pathetic scum!*" Nira taunted the Guardian further and then cackled incessantly as she observed Ven's disgusted look; a justified reaction to what within the crude sack held within his hands.

"What are these?" Questioned the grimacing Guardian to Nira. "Whatever they are, take them away with you!"

"Why, these are your rations for our short journey back to Magmorrah." Cackled the General. "It won't be long before we reach there, as these machines can now cross oceans as well, thanks to our Queen's magnificent insight… she is *truly* an inspiration!" Nira then closed her eyes as she gladly imagined the glory of which Cera would now bestow upon her, giving that she had finally caught the Queen's most sought-after enemy.

"There are few within Impartia who would say that Cera is an inspiration!" Mocked Ven in return. "The Queen will not reign forever, and neither will Cera's need to keep you by her side - once your ill-purpose is spent."

"It's a great pity that traitors like yourselves cannot appreciate such a gifted foresight," seethed the General hatefully. "Nevertheless, you *will* learn to love and respect Her Majesty… or instead at least face her wrath; which I strongly pray you both do!"

The tank doors once again slammed shut as Nira swiftly left her captives to dwell on their forthcoming judgements. With the returning darkness in their cells, a smell of burning ash now filtered inside that forced Cara and Ven to flinch defensively. It only meant that they were a step closer to Cera's unforgiving presence, making Cara reason that it would be wise to learn more of what Ven had been teaching her regarding the powerful spirits who watch over Impartia.

"How do you know so much, Ven?" Questioned Cara with an innocent smirk. "With all respect, I thought acolytes were nothing more than followers of an ancient religion, who only sit about all day praying to some unseen power. You appear to know so much about my family and these other spirits…how?"

Ven merely looked upon Cara sickeningly in response after discarding the rotten sack that Nira had burdened them with, the mouldy bread and decayed fruit from inside it scattered far across the floor of his cell; revealing a smile to slowly form upon his face. Ven humoured to himself the sweet thought of sitting around all day praying as Cara had innocently suggested, knowing that his divine duty as a Guardian was far greater and more meaningful than this supposed theory.

"You may be right, Cara… from a certain point of view." Stuttered the Guardian humorously. "Acolytes, whom reside within Impartia's many Sanctuaries, do follow in the ways of an ancient belief - as do their Guardians. Our sacred ways of life have been mostly forgotten and corrupted by those who would choose to serve in their own misgiven purposes over recent years - mostly by your father and sister's inherent rule… I'm afraid to say." Ven noticed as he spoke to Cara the initial reluctance in accepting her family's discordant influence had now thankfully dwindled; forging a stronger bond of trust between them.

"I know of these truths because as an Elemental Guardian myself, I am sworn to protect the balance of this world also…though with your father as Cerebrante's host it has become almost impossible to do so. It seems as if your sister is in the process of planning something terrible against us spirits through her present actions, which we Guardians and the other world leaders fear more than anything else that has threatened us before…even Kanaan."

Further disbelief entered Cara as she tried to take in as best she could these morbid words spoken by Ven, all the time fleeting back remorsefully to the concerns over her daughter; a distraction which the Guardian quickly noticed.

"As the Spirit of Earth incarnate, I am keeper of its eternal Sanctum and ethereal powers upon this earthly plain. The sanctum itself can only be only accessed by an ordained Acolyte or Sanctuary guard with my own given blessings, I tell you this Cara, because Cera's increasing interest over our sacred dwellings has been duly observed, and I want to reassure you again that your child is certainly safe protected within mine". Ven looked promisingly to Cara as a faint sense of relief re-entered into her. "I solemnly promise you, that no matter what Cera or her army throw at my Sanctuary, they *cannot* pierce the seal around my Sanctum chamber."

Cara wept joyfully on hearing Ven's comforting words to her, despite at this time remaining blissfully unaware of how deep she had now managed to get herself in between a spiritual war; which Cera had willingly started.

"I can't believe that it's come to this, Ven. I only wish, I could hold Sophilia again and comfort her just like I also need right now." Cara said pleadingly, as she looked deeper into Ven's radiant-green eyes. "Do you think that we will ever be able to escape from Nira and my sister; given how powerful Cera has become?" Ven softly placed a reassuring palm across Cara's hands as he granted some of his calming spiritual energy to flow into her from him, easing the resentful anguish taking a hold thankfully through the selfless process.

"Sophilia will be okay and you *will* see her again, I honestly believe this. It will take more than prison walls to hold a spiritual vessel such as myself and a brave fighter like you from freeing Cera's clutches!" Ven declared in resolve. "In Magmorrah at least, we may even discover what the Queen is really planning, her motives against the Sanctuaries remain both a mystery and grave concern to us Guardians."

A sharp and deafening crash hit the side of the tank with such a force that it swept Cara and Ven from their feet, throwing them again helplessly onto the floor of their cells. The tank had now descended into the strait of Magmorrah, as the machine pressed forward from the banks of Viridia its engines roared even louder and more imposingly. General Nira's squadron moved clumsily through the ocean waves at first as they struggled against a strong flow of ocean currents. The soldiers aboard could soon be heard jeering in ecstasy however, seeing that their war-machines eventually propelled through the crashing waters with ease. Cara held her head low despairingly within her hands once more, feeling both sick and disheartened by the nearing proximity of her forsaken homeland and with all hope of escape now seeming to fade.

"We will need a miracle to get out of this." Cara thought to herself, as the Guardian, who was now knelt in his cell beside her, fell silently still on entering a meditated state of composure. Ven occasionally opened his eyes to check on Cara through a growing compassion, which had steadily begun to rise in him. "How can you be so calm, Ven?"

Time seemed to pass by slowly upon the surging waves which tormented Cara even more, motion- sickness soon took its toll on the princess; something which she had never been able to accustom herself to. Cara gradually regained some of her more rational thoughts, she thought back again to Ven's teachings and now fully accepted that everything which she had come to know regarding her family were obviously just lies.

"I wish to know more," Cara muttered enthusiastically to the quiet Guardian, who remained held in his meditation though was also discreetly listening to every word she now spoke. "What do these spirits you speak of have to do with the lives of myself and my little girl, as it seems we've somehow gotten ourselves embroiled with them and Cera?" Cara held her hands as if begging through the bars towards Ven, wishing to snap him out of his trance and to gain some further insight.

"You *deserve* to know…" Replied Ven firmly. "It is only right." Ven opened his eyes towards Cara as if he somehow knew what kind of response would be given back to him, granting the emotional magnitude now being placed on her. "You must have suffered so much already, though, we are now involved in a war that has secretly been taking place for a long time… I'm afraid, that this is something we must accept." Ven placed a hand upon his heart and the other across Cara's arm tenderly, he was preparing himself for the next lecture that would delve deeper into the regretful history of Cara's family's ancestry and their desolation. "This machine, which we are both trapped in, lies as testimony to the advancement of Magmorrah's recent evolution. It is however, quite crude to what technology your homeland once boasted; long before Kanaan's dark influence upon it. Do you even know of the time when Magmorrah was Impartia's mightiest civilisation?"

Cara nodded dismissively as she acknowledged this unfortunate truth to Ven. The nation of Magmorrah which she had known from being a child, was one swept in both misery and austerity, its people poor and forsaken, their hopes unfortunately surviving on the lies and twisted promises of their tyrannical King and his usurping successor. The palace city which Cara and Cera were raised in, was surrounded by vast man-made walls of ashen rock with a towering mountain plateau south to them, shrouding the southern lands in mystery to all its citizens. To the north across the ocean and lying upon its horizon, were the fertile water lands of Hydrania that were only just visible to see; hiding their natural beauty and peaceful inhabitants far away from sight. Cara had a secluded life, which her father vigorously kept the princess locked under, that was, until the day she and Sophilia fled from Magmorrah into exile.

"There was a mighty city that lay in the southern plains of Magmorrah; serving as its ancient Capital and where your royal ancestors once ruled. Towering structures reached into the sky and were countless in their numbers." Said Ven gladly as he reminisced over these distant memories with Cara. "There was no poverty or strife within this city, or its borders. Every citizen had a role to play in feeding the splendour of their great nation and all lived in a mutual harmony; without suffering any wars or famine."

Cara found a peaceful solace in imagining this heavenly place, wishing also that she could have seen it with her own eyes. The city that Ven was describing to Cara was far different from the one she had been born in, most of Kanaan's subjects struggled to survive daily in wake of the king's desolation and wars; a legacy which Queen Cera callously allowed to endure.

"It sounds beautiful," Responded Cara vacantly. "Whatever happened to it?" The Guardian's expressive joy seemingly began to dwindle, as a faint and rising sorrow now replaced it in response to Cara's anticipated question. Ven reluctantly brought into his immediate thoughts more scenes from Magmorrah's past, though these were from its not-so-distant and far-graver events.

"In the last few years of this magnificent city's existence, Cerebrante was bonded to an Acolyte who served in Hydrania's Sanctuary of Water - Levia." Ven recounted this memory fondly as he shared in this name with Cara. "Levia was very loyal to his Sanctuary, though as the Spirit of Balance incarnate, he also ensured that Impartia's darkness and light flowed freely; just as the magnificent waterfalls which surround Hydrania's Capital still do." Ven's smile suddenly fell again, with painful memories instead filtering into the Guardian's mind.

"I've always wanted to visit Hydrania, to see its great lakes and mountains… a pleasure which Father would never permit for me." Said Cara in frustration. "What happened to this… Levia?"

"Well… as time gradually passed," Continued Ven wearily. "The Sanctuary's Guardian 'Jendoro' fell under a mysterious illness that eventually led his untimely death. In an act of true devotion to his beloved Guardian, Levia willingly severed the bond he shared with Cerebrante; doing so to take his mentor's place as their Sanctuary's Guardian and thus did not perish through committing such a selfless move…" With each word Ven was saying, Cara's interest in Cerebrante grew even greater. The humble, exiled princess excitedly envisioned these spiritual figures; believing in a way that they were somehow rekindling a hope deep inside of her.

"After their severance with Levia; Cerebrante wandered Impartia merely as a lost spirit, desperate in search for a new host and this would unfortunately take an expected turn. In Cerebrante's absence, a perilous discord swiftly rose through the surrounding nations; they fought against one another over such meaningless quarrels that only served to fuel as a bastion of hatred and fear. Queen Karolheid of Magmorrah, your grandmother, made a great amount of wealth from supplying these warning nations with her far-more advanced weaponry - supporting as well as manipulating each fighting side to further her own selfish gains." Ven's reminiscence of these unpleasant events revealed an apparent draining effect on him, the Guardian's breathing deepened, and his calm demeanour changed drastically to reflect in the dark nature of these tormenting moments.

"I know very little about my Grandmother," Replied Cara coldly. "She can't have been any worse than her son, though?" Ven looked to Cara in sympathy of her ignorance, the princess's sheltered upbringing was far worse than he had first reasoned.

"A relentless wave of fatigue created by the many wars fought, left Impartia's other lands broken and vulnerable against Queen Karolheid's increasing influence over them. Her sovereignty slowly spread across each nation, with little resistance granted in return." Ven continued glumly. "In celebration, Karolheid chose to bear a child whom she wished would one-day rule as well over their vast domain; some months later the Queen's son was born and instantly became Magmorrah's new king in-waiting... Prince Kanaan." Cara noticeably grimaced, just the mentioning of her ill-gotten father's name wrought a foul disgust to the princess.

"What a wonderful gift to bestow on her people... a monster." Seethed Cara angrily, though Ven surprisingly shook his head at this notion.

"Believe it or not, Magmorrah's citizens were joyful and celebrated the birth of their new prince," Replied Ven cautiously. "They saw Kanaan and keenly believed that the Prince could one day perhaps better their shattered world. Your grandmother however, was not so content."

"Maybe Grandmother realised just what an evil creation she had made?" Snapped Cara back sarcastically, Ven held his tongue towards the princess's anger however to focus back on the wisdom he felt needed sharing.

"A dire concern manifested itself in Karolheid, understandably as a very distinct and strange birthmark lingered upon her young infant's forehead. The Queen had never seen such a strange symbol before and this troubled her greatly; not knowing its meaning also eventually forged an obsessive compulsion to discover more about the Spirits within Impartia." Ven hesitantly glared at Cara, he wanted to establish whether this information brought a greater insight to her or merely an unwelcome vision into the exiled princess's sordid family history. Cara sat in repose thankfully, these given secrets of her father's past granted a desirable though small sense of closure; despite their disturbing nature.

"Queen Karolheid eventually fought against her reservations; in seeking further advice regarding Kanaan's embarrassing and obvious birthmark. She at first sought the wisdom of her royal advisors, though none of them dared to answer their Queen's questions regarding the peculiar mark's origins and all pleaded ignorance towards it - resulting in them losing their own lives ultimately. As a last resort, Karolheid turned to the Elemental Guardians for our ancient wisdom; despite the initial doubts she held against us." Ven started to shake nervously now, as if struggling through an unseen strife held far within his soul.

"You helped her?" Gasped Cara in surprise. "After what she did to the other nations?"

Ven shook his head sternly and then stamped his feet in frustration; dismaying against Cara's dire judgment upon himself and the other Guardians.

"The Queen was very careful and secretive in her motives... we had no reason at all to deny Karolheid from visiting our Sanctuaries." Ven explained solemnly, whilst struggling to contain his own obvious shame. "The closest Guardian to Magmorrah, whom Karolheid strangely chose to speak with last, was my dearest friend and spiritual brother – Levia the Guardian of Water. He naively gifted the Queen with his own personal knowledge regarding the connection to Cerebrante which Kanaan now had, mostly its purpose in serving as a powerful unifier between the Celestial Spirits of Light and Darkness... Alaskia and Kufiah."

Cara placed a hand gently upon Ven again; seeing how overwhelming these painful memories were for him to cope with, though hoping too that they would not deter her new mentor from revealing even more.

"Levia still admits to this day that he was foolish in bestowing so much sacred knowledge on the Queen, especially in relation to how Cerebrante could at any time kill their host; if the Sacred Balance could not be maintained within them. Levia had, albeit unwittingly, instilled a compelling fear in the Queen for her infant son's life. There-after, Karolheid disregarded any further teachings from us Guardians and instead sought a more absorbing form of intervention from more darker souls; in a desperate attempt to find a way of preventing this fatal possibility from ever happening to Prince Kanaan. The Queen's royal household allowed for these twisted souls, who would eventually be known as Dark Acolytes, into their lives and they searched tirelessly for ways in order to control the fate of Kanaan and his connection with Cerebrante. Finally, after Queen Karolheid's own death and during Kanaan's eventual reign, his Dark Acolytes discovered an ability to harness Kufiah's will; forcing it into a cursed amulet using powers I daren't even speak of. Through the cursed amulet's power, they found that King Kanaan could then fully harness the power of Kufiah and with it abuse the Spirit to further Magmorrah's dominion..."

Cara now understood why her father had become the wicked soul whom she had come to both fear and despise – also to what menacing force truly lingered within him and to how he had gained so much untameable might and cruelty.

"Kanaan perversely abandoned his duty with Cerebrante and by possessing Kufiah, he became the most powerful ruling figure this world has ever been forced to witness. The citizens of Magmorrah however, were not the mindless fools their king had thought them to be and soon they plotted to form an uprising against him, which would serve in the aim of removing Kanaan as their monarch and in his place they themselves wished to create a land only governed by a democracy. Kanaan somehow learned of this uprising, he then used Kufiah to reduce the once great city and his most of his own people into the ruinous ashes they now still lie in as a 'divine' punishment."

Cara started to weep softly through the disbelief in learning of her father's unforgiveable actions, she was also pained by her lack of understanding as to how Kanaan could have committed such a horrific act against their people - despite knowing what kind of brutality her father was famously capable of achieving.

"How could he have done such a thing?" Cara grieved aloud. "How could Father commit something that evil and to so many innocent people… without showing any kind of remorse afterwards?" Cara toiled as she wiped her tears away with trembling fingers, still fighting to hold onto the previously unbroken attention which she had placed upon Ven. The Guardian halted his lecture as he hesitated to delve any further into the morbid history of Cara's homeland and bloodline, instead forcing himself back into a meditating state to hide away from the overpowering helplessness he now felt.

"Why are you telling me this, Ven?" Asked Cara profoundly as she looked to silent Guardian. "What have my father's past crimes got to do with *our* current situation?"

"I wanted to tell you that story," Replied Ven in an eerily calm manner. "Because I am presuming the prison which we are now heading to lies far south of the palace city where you once dwelled, it is situated within the remnants and at the heart of this lost capital - which I spoke of to you. The only structure which now serves any meaning there is the Sanctuary of Darkness, within it, the very Sanctum of Kufiah himself." Ven despairingly shook his head upon the restraints which bound the Guardian's wrists together, seeking to mask out the anxiety which he now felt on mentioning the Kufiah's imposing residence.

"I thought that place was a myth…" Replied Cara in shock. "There were rumours that Nira once fought against another soldier there to claim her right as General, I just assumed it was Cera's way of making Nira seem more intimidating to others – it's not like she needed to."

"Kufiah's Sanctuary does exist," Said Ven woefully. "I know that Cera incarcerates her most feared enemies there, Cara. I only told you about the surrounding city and its fate, so that if you were to witness the remains there, no greater suffering may come to you by its harrowing sight - I just wanted to prepare us for what we may see."

Cara fell to her knees in melancholy, she had now submitted herself to the fact that she could not escape and for the first time in her life prayed, desiring that she may receive some form of divine intervention that could inertly return Sophilia back into her loving arms.

"Have faith, Cara." Muttered Ven assuredly. "This torment will not last." Suddenly, a deafening roar coursed by the two captives from outside that rocked the entire tank they were sat within violently, almost forcing it out of control as the soldiers aboard each raised their panicked voices in response. Cara held tightly onto the bars of her cell; fiercely scared by what unnerving events were now transpiring around herself and Ven, who himself, had swiftly leapt to his feet in want of deciphering the frantic calls as best he could.

"Hydranian warships!" Exclaimed the Guardian joyously, after hearing a few of the anxious words being screamed repeatedly outside. "Hope, I believe Cara… has arrived!" General Nira's frantic commands soon grew to echo throughout the walls of her tank, it now dawned on Cara that they were under a co-ordinated attack.

"Hydrania… are you sure, Ven?" Gasped Cara. "Don't they have the greatest naval force in Impartia?"

"Yes. I believe they said it was a Hydranian vessel, it's hard to tell…" Said Ven now in an uncertainty to what he had heard. "The soldiers seem scared out of their wits though, maybe they will call for a ceasefire?"

"There's no chance in Nira surrendering… you don't know her like I do." Countered Cara in dismay. A deathly silence settled momentarily within the cells as a second, thunderous roar shook the tank and its occupants aggressively - this time followed by a piercing explosion.

Positioned north of Nira's fleet and nearing itself to them now across the ocean strait, emerged a single Hydranian warship that aimed itself against the Magmorran convoy - who hastily turned their own weapons against the imposing vessel in defence. Placed at the bow of this Hydranian ship, was a unique cannon that stretched out right upon the front of the gigantic vessel. A powerful blue light suddenly streamed from it that created a powerful hydro pulse-wave, which sliced effortlessly through some of Nira's tanks to shatter two of them clean in half with its deadly precise beam of energy.

"INFIDELS!" Screamed the Magmorran General at the enemy ship. Nira understandably, had now reached beyond her normal level of rage and took to the central cannon atop the tank herself, verbally displaying a tirade of disgust against the elite soldiers at their apparent failings to protect their Queen's valuable assets. With an unearthly cry, the General fired a single blinding ray of crimson light from her cannon, violently dismissing the incoming pulse-wave from the Hydranian vessel and on contact vaporised part of its hull within a second of impact.

Some of the few survivors left remaining from Nira's strike threw themselves over the stricken ship's railings into the cold sea below, only to be greeted by a second ray from Nira's cannon that vaporised them all into ashes - leaving only minute remnants of themselves to float upon the ocean waves for Nira's perverse enjoyment. The engines from the Hydranian warship soon fell into an eerie silence, which was floating aimlessly now as an empty and broken shell. Cara and Ven looked to one another in an oblivious fear to what true events had unfolded outside of their confinement, they then sat visibly shaken by the disturbing noises which continued in the distance.

"There goes our hope then, Ven." Said Cara glumly to the quiet Guardian. "If a Hydranian warship can't stop these tanks… then nothing can." Nira swiftly returned below to scold her soldiers further over their seeming cowardice, the General then delightfully informed them of her single-handed victory in overcoming their enemy's warship.

"Fools!" Seethed the General at her lowly warriors. "You are meant to be elite soldiers... now prove your worth or instead face a swift execution - once we reach Magmorrah!" Nira proceeded to order for a full search of the stricken Hydranian vessel; ordering her soldiers to look for any survivors who could possibly prove of some use to her, as well as perhaps adding more trophies for Queen Cera to savour upon the General's victorious return. The fleet of Magmorran tanks hastily rattled back into full throttle again as they moved forth through the surging waves towards the stricken ship, which at this moment appeared to show no apparent signs of life on it.

As the tanks reached their target, eight mechanical arms with bladed fingers raised from each of their carcasses to numerously puncture at the Hydranian vessel's side. With a surprisingly swift speed, the tanks then clambered upon the ship's deck as if they were some form of abhorrent arachnid until they finally rested upon it, raising themselves over with such a force that the impact knocked Cara and Ven back off their feet again.

"What is Nira doing now?" Sighed Cara through discomfort. "She's relentless!"

It was not long before Nira and her soldiers were met with a last resisting force from the surviving Hydranian soldiers aboard, though they were easily dispersed by Nira's own cold-blooded strikes as she tore through them sadistically with her cursed blade. The elite force of Queen Cera now triumphantly approached the ship's main quarters as a severe bloodlust flowed itself steadily through Nira, herself still ecstatic from the merciless killings she had committed as adrenaline continued to course violently through her pulsating veins.

"This is too easy!" Cackled the General excitedly. "Are there no worthy opponents to face me on this accursed ship?" Two Hydranian officers now stood defiantly alongside their captain before Nira, being the sole survivors from the General's cruel massacre, though not submissive in their surrender to her as she had presumed they should have been.

"Are you not going to beg for your lives?" Jested Nira coldly. "It would please me greatly for you to do so!"

Nira approached the three officers alone with an unsurprising scorn, scanning at their pristine uniforms and laughing at how inferior their weapons were compared to her own. One of the officers bravely stepped forward to confront the intruding General, only for them to be hurriedly restrained by one of his concerned comrades that stood in caution beside of him.

"Your friend is very wise," Taunted Nira as she aggressively raised her obsidian sword towards the ocean view outside. "Look out there, your men now lie upon the ocean as ashes! Fish bait to be consumed and excreted; being as such the waste of life they all were!" She now raised her blade from the horizon back towards the captain in aim against his throat, who merely looked upon Nira with an expressionless counter-response.

"You're wrong... 'General' of Magmorrah." Replied the Captain in defiance. "Impartia's free nations will never bow down to you or Cera!"

"You *dare* oppose me and defy the just will of our Queen!" Screeched Nira to him with such a pure and disdaining hatred, the officer however remained unmoved and in a resolve by his actions back towards her.

"No… I am afraid that *you* are mistaken, Nira!" Responded the Captain again bravely. "The valiant men and women who fought against you today, will *forever* be revered as heroes by our people… their legacy will live on far longer than your sordid acts will!" The hate-filled General viciously glared back at the Captain and then as she smiled coldly upon him, actioned her narrow blade against his throat; slitting it - following this with a merciless strike against that of his protecting officer to canvas the floor beneath them with their callously spilled blood.

"Beautiful…" Laughed Nira to her fellow soldiers. "Red is a far more attractive colour for these white uniforms… don't you all think?" The General relished in her murderous euphoria as she then turned towards the last remaining officer, surprisingly sheathing her weapon as she did so which remained coated in the blood from his friends. "Consider yourself extremely fortunate, boy… I only have one cell left!" Nira remarked in a regretful tone, she then turned to her elite guards who themselves stood in shock of how ferocious their General's actions were towards the Hydranian captives. "Throw this pitiful creature in with the other rats, I will spare his life…for now."

The lone officer wept as he looked upon his fallen comrades, whispering discreetly to each of them on passing by for their forgiveness in the guilt of knowing that he now was the only survivor from Nira's massacre. The General's new prisoner willingly held out his arms to meet with the iron restraints which were to adorn him, then without resistance he obeyed Nira's commands as they made their way back to the cells of her leading tank.

"It's happened again," Thought the officer sadly to himself. "I lived yet my friends had to die." Cara and Ven shielded their eyes from the foreign light as the tank doors opened again, though this time with a newer shadow faintly emerging from outside. The officer took to his cell more freely than they had, he merely bowed himself submissively to linger in his incarceration without speaking a single word - dismissing Cara's initial attempts to speak with him.

"The poor fellow," Commented Ven to Cara, in sympathy with Spero's suffering. "I dread to think what he has just been through…" The Magmorran tanks hastily propelled themselves back overboard by using their powerful limbs; back into the turbulent ocean waves below and after a further command from General Nira, they sped hard against the forging currents in aim of their homeland – now only a few miles away.

"Cera will be so pleased with me," thought Nira boastfully, whilst scraping off the dried blood from her father's cursed sword. "Ten years its taken us to reach this point; there's no turning back from it, no Spirit or Mortal shall stand in the way of our Divine Reign…our Immortality!"

Chapter Two: The Sanctuary of Darkness

Nira's tanks came to an abrupt halt after they took to land again from the ocean. Beneath them, the earth sunk slightly under their heavy obsidian carcasses, though it did not take long for these great war-machines to hasten in their moment over it. An all-too familiar, burning smell now reached Cara; instantly forcing her to feel nauseous whilst she fought against the putrid stench.

"Magmorrah... that didn't take long at all." Said Cara nervously to Ven in want of some comforting words. The Guardian however, remained silent in response - choosing instead to remain focused on how they would deal with Queen Cera; once they arrived at the Dark Sanctuary. General Nira's powerful tanks soon made fast ground over the ash-laden deserts of southern Magmorrah towards Kufiah's Sanctuary, even faster than Ven had woefully predicted. Cara begrudgingly examined her cell to discover where the sickening aroma was coming from, only to find a small elongated vent placed above as a possible source.

"I wonder if I can close it?" Pleaded Cara to herself as she stood carefully on her seat to reach the vent, though in doing so, had inadvertently managed to peer outside of it upon a truly distressing scene. The Hydranian officer who was sat opposite to Cara and Ven kept silent as he reflected on his present grief, however occasionally looking over at the exiled princess with a hesitant curiosity as she fumbled to gaze outside.

"Remember what I told you, Cara." Said Ven in caution. "The southern plains of Magmorrah are a distant vision to the grandeur they once were... you may not be ready yet for what is out there?" The wise Guardian had hoped to discourage Cara from looking upon the desolate landscape any longer, but despite his caring words she continued to stare over the decimation outside - despite an overpowering reluctance to.

"I didn't believe you at first, Ven... I couldn't." Cara sobbed to the Guardian. Ven tenderly reached out in a vain attempt of comforting her over this haunting discovery, as before Cara's eyes now, lay the ashen ruins of Magmorrah's once great capital city – just as he had so clearly described. The towering skeletons of numerous skyscrapers merely sat there as tombs, spreading far across Magmorrah's horizon as a sorrowful reminder to the evil that had once been committed there. "How could Father have done this?" Screamed Cara in disbelief to Ven. "One selfish man destroyed an entire civilisation!"

"Mankind alone did not achieve this evil, Cara." Replied the Guardian duly. "Only by using the power and influence of Kufiah... could such wanted destruction be achieved on this scale. I fear now, with Cera in control of the Dark Spirit, that this world too will likely fall into its own ruinous existence just as this once-great civilisation did under King Kanaan.

"There must be a way of stopping her?" Replied Cara frantically. "I know there is still some good left in my little sister…"

"Without the guidance and light of Alaskia… this fate will too be ours." Replied Ven frankly and within this moment he now constructed an unlikely plan, one that had little chance of being successful. "…There is always a hope." Nira's tank halted again violently, the General and her soldiers had now reached Kufiah's Sanctuary within Magmorrah's ruined city; where it stood in dominance over them as its dark and festering heart. The three prisoners were quickly removed from their cells, only to be then thrown upon the ash-laden ground outside by Nira's guards. Cara and Ven raised their heads fearfully, whilst the Hydranian officer lowered his, to look upon the obsidian monolith that rose itself high above them in shock and despair.

"The source of Impartia's darkness," Muttered Ven anxiously. "Kufiah's Sanctuary." The captives wearily wiped away the ash that was steadily forming on their faces as they slowly made progress towards Kufiah's imposing Sanctuary. They were soon greeted by six Dark Acolytes that were clad in black, golden-laced robes; each giving off an unceasing presence of death as they approached their cowering guests. General Nira swiftly clasped at Cara's hair with a violent, forceful grip from behind so that she could whisper cruelly to her.

"Behold your new palace, Princess… *this* is your home now!" Taunted the malicious General. "You will never again know freedom, nor see your *bastard* child… which is what I know you desire more than anything else in your rotten heart!" Nira then joyously released Cara from her torturing grip to address her soldiers once more. "Assist the Dark Acolytes with placing these vermin in their secured chambers at once!" Ordered the General sternly. "Her Majesty will be here soon enough to grace them with her divine presence… make sure they're uncomfortable!"

Cara understandably felt an overwhelming wave of mixed emotions flow through her, as she and her fellow prisoners made their way unwillingly into the cold entranceway of Kufiah's Sanctuary. The knowledge of soon seeing her sister in person also brought with it a tormenting possibility to Cara; that she may be given a chance to alter Cera's feelings towards her and to also avert the tyrannical Queen from committing whatever wicked act she was now planning. The Dark Acolytes swiftly marched their prisoners through the Sanctuary's narrow hallways, eventually reaching a small, darkened chamber where they would indefinitely be incarcerated. The walls of this chamber were decorated with monstrous, obsidian shards that hung like swords precariously over Cara and her fellow captives. The intimidating appearance of their current housing remained as a constant reminder of their unwelcomed stay and a repulsive smell of rotten flesh mixed with sulphur also filled the air - choking them incessantly with its sordid aroma.

"I hope they're not going to keep us in here for too long?" Thought Cara to herself as she pried away at her crude restraints. After quickly discovering that there was no use in trying to remove her handcuffs, Cara turned inquisitively towards the young Hydranian officer sat beside her; whom yet had not uttered a single word back to herself nor Ven. He was around the same age as Cara, slim-built with hair as golden as her own though his eyes seemed empty in despite of their attractively-unique turquoise colour. The officer's eyes met momentarily with Cara, though soon returned to their previous position held against the ground in front of him as she carefully moved herself closer towards him – in a keen desire to learn why he was being so withheld.

"Hi, my name is Cara and my friend here… is called Ven." She said excitedly. "We are both from Viridia. I know that you're from Hydrania, but do you mind me asking who you are?" Cara then stubbornly moved her face into the officers, hoping to break him out of his catatonic state. "We may as well introduce ourselves, now that we could be here for some time… there is no need to be so defensive with us!"

"Spero… my name, is Spero." Whispered the officer sadly back to Cara. "I am… or at least I was… a Hydranian naval officer until Nira destroyed my ship and killed everyone else aboard." Ven turned to Spero with a perplexed expression on his face, the Guardian himself understood what it was like to lose someone close and how helpless it could make you feel afterwards.

"Well, that certainly explains the commotion Cara and I heard back there." Said the Guardian carefully. "I must say, from what we did hear… you are lucky to be still alive my friend." Spero politely acknowledged Ven's kind gesture by tilting his head towards him, though inside was screaming as he felt that he should have died in place of his friends - some of which who had their own families to support, unlike him.

"The 'commotion' you probably heard was most likely from my ship's pulse cannon…" Replied Spero plainly. "It can tear through waves and metal like a blade through silk, the most powerful hydro-weapon ever created… yet it still didn't help us against General Nira and her laser, did it?" Further angered by his failings and guilt, Spero turned himself away in shame from his fellow captives to dwell again over his unfortune capture. Cara now edged herself more discreetly into Spero's personal space, she defiantly placed a tender hand upon the officer's shoulder; in the hope that she may help him in some way as well as take her own mind off their foreboding situation.

"It's not your fault, Spero…" Said Cara sympathetically. "Your friends who died back there, they did it while doing their duty… just as you were." Spero gently dismissed Cara's hand from him and then stood to move further away her, still heavily overcome by his painful loss. "Why did Nira let *me* live?" Responded Spero angrily. "If I'm just the same as my friends, whom she killed so coldly, then why was I spared and not them? I honestly don't understand what she hopes to gain from keeping me as her prisoner." Spero paused in his tirade for a moment to look back upon Cara, hastily giving her an apologetic glance as he walked back to where she and Ven still sat within the centre of their chamber.

"I know you're hurt," muttered Cara in compassion to Spero. "Blaming yourself for Nira's actions will not help you though." Spero stared into Cara's entrancing amber eyes thoughtfully, her face now seemed so familiar to him in some way - he however reservedly dismissed this as a mere and impossible fantasy.

"Where *was* your ship going to… when you were attacked?" Questioned Cara blatantly. "We were nowhere near Hydrania." She shook her head in perplexment.

"*We* technically attacked Nira first." Jested Spero, who was now starting to feel slightly more relaxed in Cara's gentle presence. "My Captain had noticed a convoy of strange-looking vessels that were travelling across the strait of Viridia, that's when he ordered for our approach to investigate them. It quickly became clear from their dark designs, that the 'ships' were without question from Magmorrah; with the threat of further invasion by Queen Cera, my Captain decided that a pre-emptive strike would be justified in halting any further attacks on Hydrania by her." Ven listened close to what Spero had to say regarding this unfortunate incident, unknowingly, he had instilled a greater fear in the Guardian's mind.

"You said 'further' attacks… I was unaware that Magmorrah's Queen had already committed an atrocity against your homeland." Said the Guardian anxiously. "When did these attacks happen, Spero?" The reserved officer felt that he had not yet come to understand who Ven really was and didn't know if it would be wise to divulge any further knowledge to him; regarding Hydrania's current hostilities which Cera had wrought. Cara stood herself between the two awkwardly-silent men, smiling to both reassuringly as she did in wanting to learn more about these secretive events.

"Spero, you can trust us." Said Cara exhaustively. "We are in the same hopeless position that you are, we only want to know a little more about you and if we can… maybe help?" On moving even closer to Spero, Cara again noticed the innate attraction of his eyes which grew an instant fascination in her - much to the immediate amusement of Ven who sensed their hidden feelings.

"Please stop staring at me." Said Spero coyly to Cara. "I'll tell you what's been going on, okay? The Queen herself was observed acting suspiciously at the Sanctuary of Water only a few weeks ago, though how she managed to reach it undetected, remains a mystery to our high command and it appeared also that she could not gain access to it - at the time. Our Regent was unaware of any planned visits by Queen Cera and when he later questioned her through his messengers about it, found that instead of an apology she sent a covert task force to attack him and his family at the royal palace. His Excellency, by pure luck, suffered no harm from Cera's assassination attempt, but Hydrania has been placed on high alert ever since and that is why my ship was stationed so close to Magmorrah in patrol of its waters." Spero's eyes unwittingly met with Cara's once more and the two quickly shared in a unified sense of serenity with one another.

"Acting *suspiciously* at Levia's Sanctuary, was she?" Muttered Ven to himself under his breath, whilst also keeping a watchful eye over the door in case any guards may be nearby to possibly listen in on their private reflections. "Our concerns are truly justified then…we *must* reach the other Guardians to speak with them as soon as we can!"

"What's wrong with him, Cara?" Questioned Spero, who was genuinely confused by Ven's sudden interest in Hydrania's affairs and at the distress which his words had caused. "If you're from Viridia, Ven… why would an attack on Hydrania worry you?" Cara was also troubled by the Guardian's sudden change in composure, she instantly marched towards him with the same look of annoyance that would be given to Sophilia - if the child had upset her.

"What *is* the matter with you Ven, and how do you expect us to get out of here to see these other Guardians, bearing in mind the current predicament we're all in?" Snapped Cara bitterly in frustration.

"For some time now, my brethren have noticed Cera's spies loitering around our Sanctuaries, seemingly trying to gain access. The Queen's sudden interest worries us greatly, we *must* speak with my kin to try and discover what they think Cera be maybe up to now."

Spero joined with Cara after he cautiously approached Ven, gently moving her aside thereafter so that he alone could confront the mysterious figure – whom until only moments before was presumed to be a vagabond or just some crazy wanderer.

"So, you are a *Guardian*… a keeper of the Elements." Said Spero with an awkward smile. "To think that I thought you were all just a myth, you're rarely ever seen by us mere mortals after-all." Cara laughed for the first time in a long while at Spero's comments, they had relaxed her slightly in proving that she alone was alone in her ignorance towards these Spirits and their protective hosts.

"You're not the only one, Spero!" She jested heartily. "I don't believe Ven will mind in me telling you, that he is indeed *the* Guardian of Earth. Ven and his acolytes saved me and my little girl Sophilia from death at the hands of Nira; they are the bravest souls who I have ever had the pleasure of meeting." Cara then smiled appreciatively to Ven, who returned her gesture with a shy nod.

"I am honoured to finally meet a Guardian," chuckled Spero sincerely. "Why though could the Queen's spies not enter these Sanctuaries… are they all heavily defended?"

"In a way… Yes." Replied Ven assuredly. "Though, not with the sort of artillery or similar show in force as you might be imagining… my innocent companion." Mused the Guardian as he patted Spero's shoulders in an empathetic disagreement with him.

"How are they fortified then, if there are no soldiers guarding them?" Queried Spero further, now increasingly growing curious to learning more about Impartia's spiritual watchers.

"The Sanctuaries are each held within their sacred grounds and are all linked together as one - through the divine power of us Elemental Guardians. An impenetrable seal lies over them and their inner Sanctums; only some chosen few can be granted access therefore the use of weapons is unnecessary." Ven paused suddenly in his discussion with Cara and Spero, within a daunting moment of realisation he had unwittingly broken his sacred vows by revealing the secrets of Impartia's Guardians, though he did not truly believe that Spero nor Cara could hold any immediate threat to them.

"Oh," responded Spero in disappointment. "I thought that you were going to say they had an elite force of trained monks with advanced weapons… that would have been far-more exciting!" The three prisoners then shared in a precious moment of laughter together, each savouring this desirable release as time slowly continued to torture them within the dark chamber.

"What is that?" Gasped Cara in terror. Scraping noises were coming from outside their chamber's door and soon the rustling of keys could also be heard. As the door gradually opened, two heavily armoured Magmorran soldiers entered themselves, holding staunchly in their grasps a set of drawn swords aimed towards the fearful captives.

"Don't move!" Commanded one of the soldiers aggressively. "Stay silent!" Behind the cold warriors stood a single Dark Acolyte who was observing the prisoners intently; hidden behind a grotesque iron mask that only revealed a small eye socket for which the wicked creature could peer through. "You have been duly summoned by Queen Cera for investigation; regarding the treasonous acts which you have made so *wilfully* against our great nation!" Seethed the Acolyte as they motioned for the prisoners to be escorted.

"How can we be traitors… if Cera is not our Queen?" Countered Spero mockingly to the embittered Acolyte, now feeling a newer sense of bravery and determination enter him. Spero by now felt ready to confront the abhorrent Queen; regarding the atrocities she and General Nira had committed against his homeland, and for also how Cara and Ven were both being treated so unfairly - despite their obvious innocence.

"Silence!" Screeched the Acolyte as they shook in an instant anger against Spero. "You *will* show our Queen the respect she deserves, and you *will* bow in servitude to her before this day's end… this I can assure you!" The Acolyte then turned towards Cara's now trembling body and instantly gasped in shock as they noticed the unique mark of Cerebrante, which still faintly bore itself upon her face. "Her Majesty will *indeed* be most pleased to speak with you… Princess. I believe, she will have a splendid surprise in store for such a special occasion!" Laughed the dark servant sadistically; held in the knowledge of Cara's impending treatment by her long-lost sister. "Come now to meet with your rightful destinies! Any attempts of escape from this Sanctuary will be futile… these chambers are sealed by our master Spirit's eternal powers, if you choose to run from us you shall only come to a slow and painful death by the hands of our soldier's cursed blades!"

The Acolyte callously turned away from their worrisome prisoners to then guide them along a lengthy obsidian passageway, which was so much more intimidating in its appearance compared to the claustrophobic chamber that they had been presently trapped within.

"I don't know where they are taking us Cara, but I *do* know that when we see the Queen, she will have a lot to answer for!" Declared Ven sternly. "Remember… I am a Spirit incarnate, it will take more than her cruel words and threats to break me and I promise that no further harm will come either you nor Spero!"

The daunting passageway somehow abruptly came to an end, Cera's prisoners were now met with the tall, imposing doors of Kufiah's inner Sanctum. Placed above the door, were the ancient seals of Impartia's Elemental and Celestial spirits – which Ven in an instant recognised as he bowed respectfully before them. The Dark Acolyte held an armoured palm firmly against the centre of the door and on doing so, the seals above it emanated in their collective lights of green, blue, red and silver - which soon opened it. Before the prisoners now lay a narrow causeway of ash that formed as a bridge, itself appearing to be formed by what seemed like charred human remains; leading to a circular platform at the vast chambers centre which was cascaded eerily over an endless pit of darkness below.

"I'd like to say that I've honestly been in a worse situation than this… but that would be lying." Muttered Spero despairingly to Cara, in trying to make light of their current morbid surroundings. Cara keenly observed the ancient chamber and felt a strange recollection to it as if she had been here before, though in her heart she reasoned this could not be feasibly possible.

"There is something awfully familiar about this place…" Cara whispered to Ven. "I have the strange feeling that I've been here before." Ven remained silent whilst looking to Cara in response. The Guardian motioned his eyes in a cautious suggestion to her, hinting discreetly that remaining quiet would ultimately be wise, though this only made Cara even more nervous - if a mighty Spirit Guardian was anxious in this place then surely, so should she be. The central platform which they were now standing on had within it a set of spiritual seals, the very same as those sat above the doorway leading in. Cara wanted to ask Ven about the connection between the seals and what relation they had to the Sanctum but was to be only met by his closed eyes, as he forcefully fell back into a meditating state.

"Why is he so calm?" Pondered Spero aloud to Cara whilst they both shook their heads in confusion to the Guardian's tranquil disposition.

Kufiah's Acolytes gradually encircled the Sanctum platform around their captives, with one placing themselves upon a seal at its centre. Suddenly, a fiery beam of light flowed into the dark servant from the seal beneath as they raised their arms away from it, gesturing them agonisingly behind where the prisoners knelt in anticipation.

"Let Her Majesty, come forth!" Fiercely declared the surrounding acolytes in unison, whilst the lone servant writhed within their illuminated seal.

Everything around Cara now froze within her fearful thoughts, she had not seen her younger sister for almost a decade and having left on such grievous terms, dreaded this forced reunion between them. The exiled princess woefully considered how Cera could react on seeing her again after so long and if there would be any remorse held in her – despite their differences and turbulent history.

"Enlighten us with your gracious presence!" Commanded one of the Dark Acolytes enthusiastically. "Enchant us with your divine beauty… Queen Cera!" Cara unreservedly knew that the Queen's hesitant arrival was nothing more than a deliberate attempt to exacerbate the torture she and her fellow prisoners were presently enduring, each second passing to them felt like a lifetime in waiting for Cera's unwanted company.

The Magmorran Queen finally entered Kufiah's harrowing Sanctum, surprisingly notable in her regal movements and without any word of initial scorn towards the unfortunate guests held within it. Cera could have easily been mistaken as a twin to Cara, though her golden hair fell thinly in comparison and the Queen's body was drastically gaunt through its willed malnourishment. She wore a long, flowing crimson dress that had countless precious jewels adorning it, including the accursed amulet that Ven had spoken of which was secured tightly around Cera's thin neck to lay upon her chest.

"Finally," Whispered the malicious Queen in relief to herself. "It's taken ten years… but now, you are mine." Cera carefully inspected the prisoners in judgement over them, particularly taking a lengthy time to look upon her despised sister.

"Insolence…bow before Her Majesty!" Ordered the leading Dark Acolyte to their captives fiercely, though they found no avail in this command with them. "Kneel before the divine presence of our *gracious* Queen… at once!"

"There is no need for such formalities here… my dearest servants," Dismissed Cera frankly to the Acolytes. "I am here not as a mortal Queen but instead a being with a far greater, spiritual purpose…" Cara felt as if the air suddenly left from her lungs on hearing her sister's familiar voice, so many conflicting emotions then ran through the exiled princess as she desperately wished in truth to speak with Cera - despite the pain she had caused to herself and Sophilia. Cera however, leant in firstly to examine Spero and immediately waved her hand against him in an apparent distaste.

"I hear that you were involved with the destruction of some prized tanks, which I had only recently commissioned myself…" Sneered Cera to the cowering officer. "How-ever shall I repay such a dishonourable act against my nation?" Spero desperately attempted to move his vision away from Cera, yet a compulsive beauty in her which was very similar to Cara's, drew the officer reluctantly back to look upon the vicious Queen.

"I'm not the monster with devil horns that your people would make me out to be, slave of Hydrania!" Laughed Cera coldly to Spero as she reached in closer towards him, seeming to offer the beleaguered officer a teasing kiss, though her demeanour soon changed within a foreseeable hatred that was more familiar to the bitter Queen. "Your *precious* lands will soon feel my wrath for the cowardly attack you and your crew actioned against my elite force - in *our* sovereign waters!" Cera then spat distastefully at Spero, striking him thereafter with the back of her hand to tear violently across his face. Spero shook off the pain that Cera had inflicted on him without uttering a word, the Queen then stepped away from his side to now confront Ven - who remained focused on the Dark Acolyte's sacrificial actions ahead of him.

"What is this… a common altar boy from a fairies' forest Sanctuary?" Taunted Cera in delight. "You hardly emanate a threatening stature, of which my General so fearfully told me about. Nira also informed me about the ambush you held against her and my elite troops in Viridia which was so… un-spiritual!" As Cera focused on Ven's unfaltering eyes she screamed out in an intensified rage, then sharply turned her attention back towards Kufiah's Dark Acolytes who were still stood around their Queen in anticipation upon the central platform.

"Explain yourselves swiftly to me, *servants*!" Scorned the Queen angrily. "How could such devoted Acolytes miss the obvious fact that they have… in *their* possession… a Sanctuary Guardian?" In a swift response, the Acolytes bowed ashamedly to their Queen as she returned her enraged vision back against Ven. A shared thought soon entered them, that it was actually Nira to blame for their lack of knowledge – a grudge they would hold always against the malevolent General afterwards.

"There is no mistaking it!" Cera declared ferociously. "His eyes radiate with the tell-tale green light, even in this dark Sanctum don't they… Guardian of Earth?" The Queen soon calmed her anger against all natural and hateful intuitions, replacing it instead with a renewed, sadistic realisation. "This is surely fate; you were brought here by destiny, to help fulfil a greater purpose in this life…"

Ven felt greatly uneased by Cera's sudden change in interest towards him and was concerned by what scheming thoughts may now have entered her demented reasoning.

"I have such an honourable duty for you to perform, Guardian… a duty that far outweighs your own miniscule role within Impartia - whether you will it or not!" An increasing ecstasy coursed through Cera now with each passing word as Ven stood himself visibly more awkward. He struggled at first to respond with her, though many answers needed to be gained and quickly - if he were to escape and reach his fellow Guardians.

"What task do you have in mind for me, Cera… dare I ask?" Asked Ven defiantly. "is it an act of contrition on your behalf?"

"I have already redeemed myself, Spirit…" A twisted and self-righteous smile crossed Cera's face now. "In ridding this world of Father's incompetence and his lack of will, I will renew Impartia in a way that should have been done many years ago…" Cera now perversely caressed Ven's face as she placed her skeletal hands upon it. "For too long now, these lands have been ruled under the chaos of their Spirits, their lesser Guardians…I have found a way to right this wrong and plan to bring a true balance in this world!" Ven aggressively moved his head away from Cera's cold touch, disturbed in a great concern of what she was implying to him by this supposed decree.

"Do you not have enough power and control already, Cera?" Snapped the Guardian in defence. "How could you possibly wish for more and at what price would you deem necessary to enact your merciless will?" Cera violently latched a hand against Ven by his jaw, her eyes stared into his now like a wild animal hunting down their prey to will a hatred deep within him.

"Such is the way of you Guardian…so narrow-minded and dogmatic in their views of how this world should truly exist!" Cera slowly released her grip from Ven to place her hands upon the golden amulet adorning her neck in nurture of it. "With the power that has been gifted to me, I have brought peace to the warring lands of this torn nation, wrought by such devastation and despair by my Father's own hands! If I can achieve this with Magmorrah… why should I not allow for the rest of this world to benefit from my divine reign?" Cera snarled as she turned her head now across from Ven towards Cara, who herself could not yet find the courage to face the Queen's delusion.

"Are you really so blind?" A sharp anger mustered now in Ven of which he had never felt before. "Your 'benevolence' has brought *nothing* but further despair this nation that you claim to have brought peace to… Usurper! Do not be mistaken by such self-worth, you will never reign eternally over this world as you obviously wish to do so!" Ven had only left himself vulnerable to the Queen's arrogance as she merely moved away from him without any further reply. Cera excitedly savoured in in the tormenting moment of her much-awaited reunion with Cara, she proudly positioned herself before the withdrawn figure of her sister who shook in fear on seeing the devastation that the Dark Spirit had inflicted through their unnatural connection.

"Are you not pleased to see your little sister after such a long time in exile… have you not missed the royal life that you so cowardly fled from?" Taunted Cera as she gradually forced her face upon Cara's in dominance over her. "Why would you betray your own flesh and blood, Cara… do you think as well that I am the monster whom our ignorant peasants detest?" Cera noticeably tremored through her hatred towards Cara as she interrogated her sister further in a wanted cruelty.

"No," replied Cara anxiously. "I don't at all." She sighed mournfully. "You should be *proud* of me! I have redeemed our homeland from the ruins that Father left it in!" Said Cera in a pleading voice. "I am about to redeem this world also, will you co-operate with my plans, *beloved* Sister?" Cara now found enough strength within her to finally look at Cera, finding only in a painful reluctance that The Queen's once beautiful features had been faded and corrupted by Kufiah's malicious power.

"Cera…" Gasped Cara in dismay. "…What has happened to you?" She whimpered, seeing how far her sister had fallen was all too much for Cara to bear with.

"What has happened to me?" Requited the Queen in amusement. "I must say, you're not aging very well yourself! Life in the forests must have been very difficult, it is evident upon your own completion!" Laughed Cera bitterly as she looked at her ugly reflection within the seal beneath where she stood.

"Why do you want to kill me… what threat do I or Sophilia pose against your reign?" Questioned Cara sorrowfully. "You have the throne… and I don't want it!"

"Do you *really* not understand, Cara?" Replied Cera in a sarcastic tone whilst she opened her arms as if to offer an embrace. "I have done all that is necessary in restoring harmony to this broken world and you are all that stands in my way of fulfilling this righteous purpose!"

Cara cautiously moved in to accept her sister's surprising, though desired, loving gesture to her; only to be wickedly dismissed by Cera as she moved herself away to focused instead on the lone Dark Acolyte centred within the Sanctum's core seal. "Such a naive fool… love has truly weakened your senses!" Cried out Cera scornfully to Cara. "It is what has made you into the pitiful creature you have now become… kneeling before me just like a child begging for scraps - you make me sick!" Cera then held lovingly onto the amulet lain upon her chest to quickly sense the evil energy that coursed through it.

Cara held her tongue despite Cera's mockery; she instead observed the accursed amulet to find that it was nothing more than a crude-looking golden disc, that had at its very centre Cerebrante's now-familiar mark.

"I may as well indulge you all with my grand design for Impartia's Rebirth." Boasted the Dark Queen, though she was merely met by a wall of silence in return. "I have found a way to end the imbalance within Impartia - once and for all! I alone will achieve what Father had failed to do… I will destroy Alaskia the Spirit of Light *and* break Cerebrante's cycle and thus making me a God!" The chilling sound from a monstrous heartbeat eerily began to echo in this moment within Kufiah's Sanctum. Where the lone Acolyte stood trembling at its core in an unimaginable pain, a scarlet beam rose powerfully to then surround them within its imposing radiance.

"You will *destroy* us all, Cera! Are you completely mad?" Cried out Ven, whilst furiously trying to be heard over the ever-increasing heartbeat that reverberated through Kufiah's chamber. "You will *never* rule over Impartia… you *cannot* destroy Cerebrante!" Ven silenced himself as the Sanctum suddenly fell into an instant, deathly repose. Behind the three prisoners, Cera's Dark Acolytes now gathered themselves as if in prayer with their heads bowed obediently.

"Cerebrante will be nothing more than a distant memory; a remnant of a time when Impartia rose from its chaotic existence!" Rejoiced Cera hastily. "The Spirit of Balance will die…I shall vanquish it along with Alaskia from this plain to linger forever in the Void!"
The Dark Acolytes jointly started to sing Kufiah's hymn, in a joint effort aimed in summoning Impartia's most repulsive presence.

"What is wrong with you?" Cried Cara to Cera, as she rose herself defiantly against the Queen. "Must you make this world and its people suffer more than they already are?"
"You wouldn't understand," Replied the Queen coldly. "My destiny lies plain before me… unlike yours."

A thick, disturbing air now consumed the Sanctum chamber, rendering each prisoner helplessly into submission. The demonic heartbeat raced faster in depth and aggressive tone as the Acolyte's hymn echoed its words relentlessly, matching against Cera's captives as she laughed towards the fierce beam blaring before her.
"You can't do that to the Spirits, Cera… it's not natural or right!" Pleaded Cara to her sister. "Please don't… please, listen to me!"

"You *will* understand my actions… one day, Sister." Replied the Queen calmly. "It is too late to turn back now from my divine path. I have spent the last ten years in planning for Alaskia's destruction, nothing can stop this from happening now." Cera gasped in excitement as an unearthly, terrifying voice bellowed from within the beam, its spiritual power surged into the Dark Acolyte centred to swiftly cause their willed-for immolation. "My malignant protector…" Whispered the Queen intently as she savoured in the Acolyte's slow demise. Ven in contrast, turned away on seeing this distressing sacrifice to look upon Cara - who herself shook in dismay beside him.

"Have faith!" Commanded the defiant Guardian. "No power on this earth is strong enough to commit such a hateful act, Cera's plan will fail!" Ven suddenly fell to the ground in exhaustion from his emotional exertion. Spero sympathetically leaned in to him and Cara as he tried tirelessly to support their mental fatigue.

"We won't let her get away with this," Whispered Spero angrily. "Let's take her down now while we have a chance!" In this moment, the suffering Dark Acolyte was thrown violently from their immolation after releasing a set of haunting cries. Their lifeless, charred remains landed before Cera, scattering immediately, much to the Queen's preserve enjoyment. Now burned beyond any recognition, the ashes from the Queen's fallen servant flowed hauntingly over the ground from where they now lay towards Kufiah's prominent seal.

"Come forth, my great darkness!" Commanded Cera lustfully. An unnatural dark mass quickly formed from the fusing ashes to tower above all who stood within the Sanctum. Within the black mass, two burning lights grew as if they were amber jewels that were set ablaze - piercing their wicked vision into the souls of those who dared look upon them.

"Ven," Spoke Cara in a nervous desperation. "What is going on?" Inhuman roars suddenly reigned high above the dark Hymn Cera's Acolytes were performing, soon finally silencing their malignant chorus in a terrifying display.

"Behold! My greatest weapon and harbinger of peace!" Screamed Cera in a twisted delight, entranced by the fear this disturbance had noticeably brought to the petrified captives. "Rise, my darkness in the light…Rise…Kufiah!" The amassed ashes formed into a tall, imposing, beast-like figure - clad in torn, ash-ridden robes that flowed freely upon the ground around it and through the air as if immersed in water. Their fiery pupils sank deep within the dark sockets which formed as eyes, looking across each startled face surrounding them with a menacing glare. Kufiah, despite their forced servitude, stood proudly over Cera who herself knelt in reverence before them The Dark Spirit's large hands twisted their elongated fingers to meet with their shaven scalp, relishing the physical vessel of which they now controlled.

"This can't be good," Responded Spero anxiously as he inspected the demonic creature stood against him. "We may need to reconsider attacking the Queen… at least for now."

Cara froze in fear upon witnessing Kufiah for the first time, she screamed in pure fright at the horror that now faced her within the daunting realisation of Kufiah's true existence. Ven tried gravely to defy the Dark Spirit and Cera by standing in confrontation against them, only to be dismissed easily from a powerful wave of ashes from within Kufiah's robes.

"This is only a fleeting glimpse of what punishment will come to any who would oppose me!" Ridiculed Cera as she stared intently upon Ven's weakened body, then the Queen turned to Cara who sat in comfort of him by his side. "I will end this futile cycle and with it, rule as supreme empress of Impartia… no more Light… no more Darkness… only *my* New Order! I will become Empress of Impartia!" Cera's declaration was by rapturous cheers from her Guards and Kufiah's Acolytes.

"You will only meet with the same fate as your father," stuttered Ven through his passing pain. "My brethren will stop you and if *we* don't…"

"Guardian of Earth…" Spoke Cera in a softer tone, almost sympathetic. "You *can* redeem yourself, I shall permit it. Help me to find Alaskia, and I will spare you *and* your kin; should you choose to turn down this gracious offer, I will ensure that your own eternal demise is met by the hands of Kufiah himself!" Roared Cera to Ven, her face now grimacing on giving him this merciful absolute. The Guardian vehemently shook his head in dismissal, as he fought still against the pain Kufiah had inflicted on him.

"I will *never* help you, Cera…" Ven stammered. "As long as I still hold breath in this mortal body, your plan will be doomed to fail!" A harrowing roar came from Cera and Kufiah in response, both united by their hatred against the Elemental Guardian and his stubborn resolve. The Queen then eagerly moved to address the Dark Acolytes, in wake of her failure to turn Ven, to reaffirm what authority she still held over them.

"Return this stubborn fool to his holding chamber, he shall be dealt with accordingly by my divine judgement… soon enough!" Cera now looked to Cara and Spero as she simpered. "For you two, I have such a gracious gift to grant…take them both to the Vault of Loss so they can suffer for their sins against me!" The echoing voices in the chamber fell into a distant whisper as the acolytes led their captives away to their separated dwellings. Cara's sight did not leave Cera, only until the doors of Kufiah's Sanctum were sealed heavily behind her. She accepted that there would be no possibility of truly redeeming her sister and saw Cera now as a sad reflection of their father's evil legacy.

Ven was led reluctantly back to the chamber where he had been previously incarcerated within. Once alone, he sat in a saddened mediation to dwell on the revelations Cera had willingly shared with him. Ven had finally come to learn of Cera's destructive obsession with Kufiah and the fact that the she wanted to end a Celestial Spirit's existence, greatly began to torment him, his thoughts pressed desperately to somehow inform the other Guardians of this most heinous act.

The Vault of Loss in which Cara and Spero were now being taken to by Cera's acolytes, lay far deeper within Kufiah's Sanctuary. Through many distorted catacombs, layered with images of ancient demons and evil acts upon the world, the Acolytes silently guided their two prisoners further into the Sanctuary's bowels - as if through an endless, nightmarish maze. Cara and Spero found to their surprise that no door secured the Vault of Loss once they reached it, only a line of etched symbols stood above the open passage as its seal.

"What is this place?" Questioned Cara nervously to one of the acolytes standing beside her, though no answer was returned by the malicious figure. Another acolyte then raised their arm to direct Cara and Spero into the entranceway, remaining still to them as the doorway's seal returned through an unspoken curse.

"What kind of holding cell has no door?" Asked Spero nervously whilst moving closer towards Cara.

"What a horrid place this is," Responded Cara in an equally anxious tone. "It's like we've walked into a morgue." Kufiah's Acolytes swiftly vanished into the darkness outside, leaving the two captives alone and uncertain of their fates within this new horrifying environment. Cara and Spero eagerly attempted to walk back through the open doorway, however finding that its invisible seal continued to prevent them from crossing over.

"What is going on, Cara... why can't we get through?" Despaired Spero in frustration. "I never knew before of any magic and now I'm surrounded by it!"

"An ancient and evil power is keeping us here," Muttered Cara cautiously. "For some reason, I want to venture in further... something is drawing me there." Cara vacantly moved herself away from Spero and walked on as if under a possession, stepping blindly into the only narrow passageway that at its end lay an even darker spherical room.

"Cara!" Shouted Spero in fear. "We don't know what's down there... Stop!" Spero reluctantly followed Cara's footsteps as he continued along the narrow passageway in a frantic search for her, that was, until they both finally reached Kufiah's 'Vault of Loss'. Scattered around the imposing spherical chamber knelt several woeful figures of men, women and children who all rocked manically to and thro. Some murmured to themselves in some form of indecipherable language whilst others merely stared ahead into nothing.

"Is this what will become of us?" Asked Cara in a profoundly sorrowful voice. A relief was soon found in her however as she eventually managed to find Spero, who himself had moved towards the chambers only source of light – a red beam cascading down within its centre. Now reunited, Cara and Spero lingered around the crimson ray of light to hide away from Cera's demented figures situated around them.

"Cara, what do you think happened to these poor souls?" Commented Spero, who in truth could not bear an answer to this dreadful scene. "Most of them are catatonic..."

The two companions wearily sat themselves upon the cold obsidian floor beneath, both desperate to block out the melancholy around as they held onto to one another and hoping for an absolution – one that could rid them of this newly inflicted nightmare.

"We'll never get out of here!" Cried Cara in defeat. "I can't bear the thought of us existing like these unfortunate people are…" She then grasped onto Spero's torso in a ferocious desire to seek his comfort - a gesture willingly returned by him.

"Think of somewhere or someone that makes you happy, Cara." Whispered Spero tenderly to her. "Try to remember a happy memory or a person you love, you have a young daughter… don't you?"

"Yes, her name is Sophilia… though she likes me to call her *Lia*." Responded Cara tearfully, still immersed in the shock from her current surroundings.

"That's great!" Said Spero in ecstasy. "Please, tell me about her… perhaps it will help keep our spirits up in this awful place?"

"Well…Lia has just turned ten years old, though, she acts a lot older in some ways which even surprise me!" Cara began to laugh faintly, now feeling a reassurance in picturing her daughter's infectious smile. "She loves to sing and has *such* a beautiful voice, I could listen to her all day!"

"She sounds like a right character… tell me more." Replied Spero as he smiled back to Cara, diligently taking in every detail that was sharing with him.

"Sophilia loves to go walking with me through Viridia's forests, mostly so she can pick flowers to make jewellery from them... which she's really good at it!" Continued Cara as she steadily became overwhelmed with the innate love she felt towards her precious child. "When Lia was just a baby, we both had to flee from Magmorrah so that I could keep her safe from Cera and General Nira. Even at the young age she is, Lia knows somehow that something terrible had happened to us back there and she'll ask sometimes if we'll ever see 'our family' again?" Cara's voice noticeably faltered as she tried hard to focus on the happier times, though the remnants of her troubled past persisted in haunting the exiled princess's current thoughts.

"Sophilia's father, he didn't manage to escape from the ash lands with you…did he?" Spero instantly chastised himself for asking such a personal question to Cara, she though seemed unmoved by his curiosity and instead remained surprisingly emotionless in response.

"In all honesty, Spero… I genuinely can't remember who Sophilia's father is." Said Cara frankly. "I don't know why, but I can't picture him in my head... I can easily block out any memories - if they're too painful for me to recount." Spero quickly lost his desire to reach further into Cara's past on hearing this, his plan to help relax her was unwittingly beginning to backfire so he instead moved himself away in an awkward restraint.

"Honestly, don't worry yourself… it's never been an issue for us before." Replied Cara calmly. "To Sophilia, I am both her Mother *and* Father; she knows that I would do anything to keep her happy and safe… that's all that matters." Cara then affectionately scuffled Spero's hair to diffuse the obvious embarrassment he had felt from his invasive questioning.

"You're right, Cara… that's all that should matter!" Declared Spero passionately. "My family were taken from me when I was very young. The Sanctuary of Water's Acolytes took me in and raised me as their own; even though they didn't know who I was, and it didn't concern them that I couldn't understand their beliefs… I still don't! It's funny though, I never actually met the Sanctuary's Guardian… I always thought that Levia and his powers were just a myth that the Acolytes use to scare people away." Both captives smiled sympathetically to one another and the oppressive chamber around them grew to be a more tolerable discomfort, learning these intricate details from their pasts now seemed to forge a strong bond between Cara and Spero.

"You'll be with Sophilia again, Cara." Spoke Spero in defiance against her sadness. "Soon, you'll be wandering the forests of Viridia again together and I will be back sailing the many oceans of Impartia with my comrades…we can't afford to die in this place... we still have so much of our lives to live!" Spero and Cara embraced one another tenderly. Though they were mere strangers only days before, the two now felt a loving and unified bond in struggling through this current ordeal grow - despite the rising malignant darkness that was enslaving them. In their immediate distraction, Cara and Spero had failed to notice a hooded man who now stood within the Vault's entranceway. The mysterious figure cautiously peered in and, after hesitating for a moment, called out to echo their voice in reaching the two prisoners.

"Hey!" Shouted the figure hastily. "I have come to save you, come to me… quickly! I can break this seal but only for a short time, my Master Spirit will notice and the Queen herself soon enough…now… come to me!" The rescuer then rigidly held out their hands towards Cara and Spero's presence, hoping to usher them towards his phantom voice.

Unsurprisingly dazed by the figure's unclear motives, Cara looked beyond them to thankfully notice Ven's familiar smile in the faint light that streamed outside - who himself was ushering the captives towards the entranceway.

"Please do as he says!" Commanded the anxious Guardian. "He *is* a Dark Acolyte, but one who has bravely abandoned Queen Cera… we must trust him!" Ven inspected the catacombs behind in caution, checking them for any unwanted persons who may have followed him and the treacherous Acolyte on their journey down to this wicked place.

"Okay… we're coming!" Replied Cara, as she reached for Spero. "Wait for us!" Now finding that they could step over the entranceway's threshold, Cara and Spero in a shared relief both felt their drowning oppression swiftly leave from them. The redeemed Dark Acolyte remained fixated as he motioned for Cera's captives towards himself and Ven, occasionally fleeting his own glance back towards the catacombs in a nervous disposition – in knowing what predators would soon be hunting.

"Any longer in that chamber and you two would have both become lost within your own madness…" Said the acolyte morbidly. "Follow me back into the catacombs, there is a secret tunnel further down that leads out of this Sanctuary… we must make haste there before my fellow brethren realise that we've gone!" Cara saw that Kufiah's Acolyte had discarded their grotesque mask; revealing the face of a young man no older than herself though greatly paler in complexion and with a long, black beard that contrasted well with his sunken eyes.

"My name is Moah, you must trust me now… please?" Pleaded the acolyte pitifully. "I am risking everything to save you all from the wrath of Queen Cera and my Master Spirit, please… you must follow me!" Moah swiftly led the way through, what felt like, an endless maze of catacombs, using his expert knowledge of them to escort the escapees deeper into his Sanctuary's foundations. "It won't take us long to reach the hidden port."
After a short while of traversing through the Sanctuary's bowels, Moah's unlikely party finally came across a secret river that flowed through an earthly cavern. Floating atop this river, were several Magmorran military boats that were each heavily armed and anchored along its path.

"This river is safe to drink from," Explained Moah to his doubtful companions. "You can replenish yourselves quickly before we begin this journey of ours. Am I correct in understanding, that none of you have had any sustenance since your arrival?" Asked the acolyte whilst taking a handful of purified water for himself, wishing to reassure the thirsty onlookers who themselves soon followed in his actions. Moah then quickly filled a small canteen that was previously hidden within his black robes, though he also offered a mouthful to Ven - who was stood intrigued beside him.

"He's not lying!" Exclaimed Ven to Cara and Spero as he took several large gulps of water from Moah's canteen, unwisely wasting some across his severely parched lips that still burned from the ash that had scorched them. "Please… drink… we've got a long journey ahead of us." Spero accepted a few subtle sips of water first with Cara's safety in mind, despite initially being unsure from the disgusting taste, he soon assured her that it was indeed safe to consume and then offered Moah's canteen to Cara – who herself quickly indulged a few mouthfuls.

"This is vile!" Spluttered Cara to Spero, as she forced herself to take a few more mouthfuls of the bitter replenishment. "It's better than nothing... I guess?" In the distant catacombs, angered voices could now be heard reverberating through them as General Nira and several of her elite soldiers encroached on the escapee's current position. The fleeing companions clumsily threw themselves into one of the nearby vessels on hearing Nira's scornful voice.

"They've found us!" Gasped Moah in an instant panic. He released anchor and then ignited the boat's engine into full power, swiftly motioning his newly-acquired vessel to speed off downstream whilst the terrified passengers aboard looked on anxiously behind.

"She's going to capture us again!" Screamed Cara in dismay. "Nira's relentless!" Her entire body tremored in anxiety.

"Have some faith in me," reassured Moah. "I know these caverns well... don't worry!" The Dark Acolyte accelerated harder along the flowing current, seemingly into an unknown abyss which lay ahead.

"Are you sure we can escape, Moah?" Asked Spero dismissively. He now held a tight grip upon Cara, who herself looked behind in a reluctant anticipation of Nira's unwelcomed appearance.

"Yes, I'm certain!" Responded Moah quite angrily. "I know these caverns better than any other... especially that dozy General!"

Moah's boat swerved perilously through the meandering passages, barely missing their walls as he forced his vessel into full-speed. The hopeful Acolyte, unlike his fellow crew members, remained calm despite the increasing desperation to reach an exit and ultimately freedom.

"We're almost there!" Rejoiced Moah. His joy though soon dwindled, as behind in the darkness an artificial light suddenly emerged, followed simultaneously by Nira's vicious taunts.

"I'm coming to get you... *TRAITORS*!" Screamed the General in hatred. "You can't escape from me!" Spero clambered quickly to reach an armed mini-gun that was placed at the rear of Moah's vessel; in a blind determination he quickly aimed then fired its cannon, back towards Nira's incoming screams. The enraged General and her soldiers however, soon made fast ground against their fleeing captives, approaching them with their own returning gunfire that tore out sporadically across the rapid water.

"Just DIE... you evil bitch!" Screamed Spero, as he squeezed the trigger of his weapon harder. After some more futile bursts, the mini-gun suddenly failed to fire as its mechanisms jammed. "No... Moah, the gun's jammed!" He then punched furiously at the useless piece of machinery - wishing for it to be Nira's face instead.

"Keep your heads down!" Replied Moah forcefully. "The exit's not too far away now!"

Nira was now painfully visible through the light of bursting gunfire to Cara and her companions. The General smiled sadistically towards her prey and laughed with each bullet being fired at them, several of which ricocheted off the cavern walls to send a barrage of small rocks into Moah's struggling vessel.

"Like Moah said… have faith!" Said Ven calmly whilst he lowered his hands to retrieve a piece of fallen earth beneath him. After inspecting it, the Guardian's eyes radiated green as he faced his hands towards Nira - who was at this point fearfully close. "We will soon be free from this twisted creature's malice!" The piece of rock left from Ven's tremoring hands as if it were an arrow released powerfully from a bow. The wily Guardian had deliberately missed Nira, instead he had aimed it against the area of cavern ahead of where she was positioned. Instantaneously, a wave of boulders fell hard into the river, forcing a sudden halt to the General's wanted path.

"INFIDELS!" Screeched the General agonisingly. "I *will* find and kill you all!"

Nira's ranting cries echoed eerily throughout the cavern, after-all her vessel had only just managed to avoid colliding with the large rocks which Ven had skilfully cascaded before it. Soon the piercing sounds from the General's voice faded as Moah sped on towards the Sanctuary's exit, itself revealed by the suns warming light from outside.

"You did it, Moah!" Rejoiced Cara heartily. "We're free!" The companions spared a moment to embrace each other in euphoria, despite being blinded at first by the rising sun's glowing rays. Across the distance from them, a golden haze faintly emerged from the desert lands lain westwards of Magmorrah - Talam.

"Where *are* you and Moah taking us?" Queried Cara politely to Ven, who himself was still slightly shaken by the chase they had only just endured. "Isn't Hydrania to the north?"

Ven carefully sat himself beside Cara and Spero to speak with them. The Guardian's focus had returned on fulfilling a divine mission of which they all were, albeit unwillingly, a key part of.

"Our only option at this point is to travel west." Said Ven in a firm resolve. "The desert lands of Talam are far closer to us than Hydrania is. There I believe, we should make a safer passage across the seas further north to reach Levia's Sanctuary!" He shouted coarsely over the loud rattling noises that resounded from their ship's aged engine.

"How can the Guardian of Water help us?" Asked Spero in beleaguerment. "What use will he be against Queen Cera and General Nira… who I bet are still after us?

"I *must* speak with Levia so that I can warn him and the rest of my kin about Cera's plans!" Pleaded Ven sincerely. "We *cannot* allow for her to find Alaskia, if she has found a way to destroy the Spirit of Light… then Impartia truly is doomed!" Cara nodded in an assured agreement with Ven, she strongly desired to be as far away as humanely possible from her sister's clutches - despite this meaning they may be stranded within a scorching desert landscape. Cara also discreetly yearned for a return to Viridia in hoping to be reunited with her young daughter once again, regardless of Ven's claims that his Sanctum could not be breached.

"I agree with you, Ven." Muttered Cara boldly, to Spero's vacant expression of surprise in return. "Southern Talam won't be that far from where we are now."

"We'll reach shore by midday!" Shouted Moah back eagerly. "This boat may be old… but she's still fast." Magmorrah's lingering ash clouds soon faded away as the fleeing companions met with an increasing heat, which was steadily flowing from Talam's nearby desert landscape. The waves from the ocean strait below crashed against Moah's boat, though thankfully, they did not diminish its speed and a welcoming feeling swept through the unlikely group of friends – a sense that a greater, unknown destiny was now arising.

Chapter Three: Into the Desert

The risen sun cast its penetrating rays warmly upon Moah's boat and its occupants, as they travelled in due-haste towards the beaming shoreline of southern Talam – The Desert Lands of Impartia. Radiating with a crimson hue, the reigning sunlight held a natural beauty that Cara could not remember witnessing before; it silenced both herself and Ven – though he observed this rare natural occurrence with far less enthusiasm.

"What a beautiful colour the sky is," Muttered Cara in awe to Ven. "It's quite a haunting site though, isn't it?"

"Yes, it certainly is." Ven whispered back hesitantly. He boded the crimson atmosphere as if it were a dire warning to him, for a red sunrise was indeed a rare occurrence that had previously proven to be an omen of some forthcoming ill-event. Ven remained strictly vigilant in his observing of this strange sight, only looking away from it to scan the strait behind for any signs of Cera's army - who may have managed to track down their current whereabouts.

"Try and get some rest," Pleaded Spero, who had fallen into an exhausted daze upon the uncomfortable deck of Moah's ship. "If we've got a long journey ahead then this may be our only chance to." He focused on Cara and in delight now found, for the first time since their meeting, she appeared somewhat more content within her surroundings as she talked pleasantly with Ven.

"Thanks, Spero. We're fine… honestly." Reassured Cara to him as she moved her eyes towards Moah. "How far *are* we from Talam would you say?"

"We are making good speed, don't worry yourselves!" Said Moah in a frustrated tone. "We should reach Talam sooner than I first thought, that is, as long as nothing else happens to us!" The Dark Acolyte held firmly onto his accelerator, pushing the worn vessel into its physical limits whilst a burning excitement continued to grow in him.

"You better be right," Snapped Spero back distrustfully to Moah. "Queen Cera won't let our escape go unpunished… her devout General will without question be after us all now." He had managed to shake himself free from the daze that had encapsulated him, only so that he could manoeuvre himself closer over towards Cara.

"Sit down next to me and relax, Spero." Laughed Cara to him nervously. "We'll be alright, we have a Spirit Guardian with us after-all and I would really appreciate the extra company."

Spero obediently moved to seat himself beside Cara, though before he had a chance to calm his nerves as she had wanted, the wary naval officer noticed a foreign glimmer of light that now lay north to their boat's position.

"We're not anywhere near Hydranian waters are we, Moah?" Questioned Spero reluctantly as he continued to examine the blinding light across the distance.

"We are *nowhere* near Hydrania, my 'learned' friend!" Mocked Moah in response. "That is exactly why we are heading to Talam… I presumed, that having been in a navy you would have known this obvious fact?"

"Okay, if that is so… then why is there at least one Hydranian warship moving towards us from the northern horizon?" Spero stuttered in fear, he suddenly remembered some vital information that the Captain of his forsaken vessel had shared with him - shortly before his unfortunate passing. "After the assassination attempt on our Regent, Hydrania's naval fleet were ordered to patrol further south in anticipation of any further attacks from Queen Cera. A contingency plan was made that if any other aggressive acts were to be carried out by Magmorrah, then an immediate counter-invasion would be authorised…" The timing of the mysterious ship's arrival was too coincidental for Spero and his friends now within this grave sense of realisation. Suddenly, more Hydranian vessels appeared from behind their leader - only confirming the officer's worst suspicion. "They're coming right for us… we're heading into a trap!" Screamed Spero as he desperately tried to gain Moah's complete attention through his panicked voice. "We can't go this way anymore, we *must* return to Magmorrah… it's our only chance to save ourselves!" Cara clasped onto Spero in bewilderment to force him back into a seated position, his outburst was the last thing they needed at this already stressful time.

"Spero, what *are* you saying?" She asked reservedly to him. "We can't possibly go back to the ash lands… Nira will be waiting there for us!" Moah begrudgingly reduced the boat's speed on listening to Spero's desperate plea, he then turned his head in confrontation against such an outlandish suggestion - as the Acolyte felt was made.

"I think that the sun is getting to you, Spero." Dismissed Moah in a polite manner. "Going back to Magmorrah is out of the question… Cera's forces will kill us on first sight, that is, if they don't drag us back to the Sanctuary of Darkness for Kufiah's own judgement." Moah now looked to Ven for some kindly support, though was only to be met with an uneased expression from the Guardian as he trembled terribly in anxiety.

"Are you sure of this?" Asked Ven fearfully to Spero. "Are you certain that these are Hydranian ships we are now seeing in the distance? Talam's heat *can* play tricks on one's mind…" The Guardian then duly awaited Spero's response to him.

"Why won't you all just believe me?" Exacerbated Spero angrily as he leapt up to force his way past Ven in reaching their boat's steering wheel, only for him then to be wrenched away by Moah - whose rage against the officer had swiftly grown during this short time.

"Have you gone mad?" Shouted Moah as he restrained Spero upon the deck in an unnatural display of strength. "You'll get us killed… is that what you truly want?" Ven gracefully moved over towards Moah so that he could calmly place a hand upon him and Spero. The Guardian's powerful spiritual energy coursed into them both, somehow relieving their present tense emotions – much to Cara's own wanted respite.

"I trust in what Spero is saying, Moah." Spoke Ven in authority over the Acolyte. "He has sailed the oceans of Impartia for a long time and his eyes will be more accustomed to any undoubted trickery, which these seas can create in their mirages." The Guardian then slowly looked across to Spero with a reassuring smile, despite his own hidden concerns. "What is this trap which you believe we are now heading into, Spero?"

"Look, it would not take long for Hydrania to become suspicious of one of their vessel's suddenly vanishing without a trace…" Said Spero in a rising angst. "As I've *just* explained, in any event of attack from Queen Cera's forces, we were given strict orders to enforce an immediate counter-attack… which means a surprise invasion of Magmorrah."

The companions each looked back over towards the northern horizon, finding that the ships which Spero had rightly identified now became clearer to distinguish and were in fact from Hydrania.

"The Queen would not be so blind to such movement within her own sovereign waters, would she… Moah?" Jibed Spero to the Dark Acolyte, in still feeling some uncertainty over the suspicious disloyalty he had made against Cera and Kufiah.

"Yes, I hate to admit it… but you are right." Responded Moah coldly. "Queen Cera has spies scattered throughout all the lands within Impartia… including her own. I believe you are correct, in that she would not be unwise to such a provocative and predictable manoeuvre…" Moah briskly returned to the steering wheel of his ship to force the vessel back into full acceleration. "Reaching Talam is our only hope now." The nearing Hydrania warships shone like purest silver, their sheer size and might were evident in the immensity of their pulse-cannons that stretched out upon their bows – a sight which was truly terrifying to behold for anyone unlucky enough that lay before them.

"Where is Cera's counterstrike… shouldn't we be seeing some Magmorran ships by now?" Asked Spero as he scanned across the Magmorran waters spanned out behind them, their emptiness surprisingly brought no relief to him. "Maybe I was wrong about us being caught in a trap?" Just as Spero finished speaking these words, a sudden and deafening siren rang out from the leading Hydranian ship. "That's a warning siren, it signals an incoming attack but there's nothing here though… apart from us!" He swiftly reached over to Cara in protection of her, wanting to grant some sense of security in knowing what fate may soon meet with them.

"I wonder," Spoke Ven sternly. "What can the Hydranian radars see that we can't?" The Guardian then looked to Moah for a possible explanation from him. "You know of what I speak… Dark Acolyte?" Moah defensively kept his sight away from Ven's penetrating gaze. The dark servant remained in determination to reach Talam's nearby shoreline, though getting there safely would obviously mean cutting across the Hydranian fleet and their apparent phantom enemy.

"Let's just focus on making it to Talam… shall we?" Moah said as he secretly despaired to himself, in being wise to what renewed monstrosities from Magmorrah's past Cera was now unleashing against them. "We'll need a miracle to get out of this situation." The surging waves thrust against Moah's ship suddenly with an intensified force, knocking his vessel into the encroaching path of the Hydranian warships. Another warning siren blared out from the leading Hydranian vessel, though for a longer duration this time and its deafening noise vibrated within the unwilling ears of those aboard Moah's boat.

"This can't be good!" Screamed Cara as she attempted to shield her ears from the painful sound. "What's going on?"

"I'm sorry, but I don't know." Replied Spero to her in uncertainty. "Hydranian radars are rarely mistaken."

"What…What *is* that?" Cara released a further sickening cry, as she observed in the murky depths below a rising, gargantuan object. "There's something huge down there and it's definitely not a whale!" Spero and Ven both stared intuitively at the strange mass, soon finding also that several other dark bodies gradually became visible around it.

"Queen Cera has been busy in restoring Magmorrah's historical weapons over the past decade, it seems." Said Ven intently to Moah. "This can mean only one thing…" His train of thought was abruptly halted however as the horrific shapes below shifted in unity with a rapid pace, to then ominously break through the ocean's surface in a terrifying display of glory. The nose of the leading Magmorran submersible leaned high into the air as it lifted then slowly fell, crashing with a violent burst into the waves beneath to send Moah's ship further into the path of Hydrania's waiting armada.

"I can't believe this, we're in the middle of battle!" Despaired Cara frantically. "Is there any way that you can help, Ven… can you use your spiritual powers to save us all?"

Ven rolled his eyes apprehensively to Cara in response. He then placed a hand over his face to wipe away the cold sweat forming on it, then shook in frustration against this foreboding predicament.

"I am the Spirit of Earth incarnate… Water is not exactly a speciality of mine, Cara." Without further word, Ven motioned Cara and Spero to lie upon the deck of their ship in attempt to spare them from any incoming cross-fire.

"We can't take down two naval fleets," Responded Moah in anguish. "Especially if our only weapon is beyond any use, all we can do now is pray." Ven wrapped his arms tenderly around his cowering friends as they sheltered themselves in obedience, the Guardian himself had not yet accepted such a pitiful fate.

"Moah, do what you must to spare us from this onslaught…" Commanded Ven. "The shores of Talam are close, I will do what I can to bide us some time!"

"I will," said Moah, plainly in response. "Though I must tell you, Cera has made significant changes to these submersibles in comparison to their predecessors… I can't guarantee that we'll make it to Talam in one piece." The lead Magmorran submarine now echoed its own warning call in a challenge to Hydrania's fleet, followed instantly with a barrage of incendiary bombs that aimed towards the opposing warships. Countless missiles seemed to fly from the Magmorran aggressors into the ocean nearby Moah's boat, lifting it helplessly into the air within a flurry of random explosions.

"I don't want to die." Whimpered Cara to Spero, as she raised her head in observation over the harrowing scene. "What will happen to my Sophilia - if I do?" The Magmorran missiles had thankfully missed their mark upon Hydrania's armada, Cera's obsession with readying her new weapons had ultimately paid a heavy price in the accuracy of them. In return, a beaming blue ray of light began to emanate then increase in its contrast from the leading Hydranian ship's pulse-cannon.

"Stay Down!" Ordered Spero in fright to his friends whilst holding protectively onto Cara, who he had forced into a prone position beneath him away from the daunting cannon's sight. "They're going to return-fire any moment!" The Hydranian pulse-cannon strangely drew in a great volume of water within it, like the waves from an ocean that were surrendering themselves just before a Tsunami. After a tense moment of silence, the lead warship released an immense energy from its cannon with a powerful roar that sliced towards its enemy vessel – sending a towering fountain of water countless feet into the air in its wake.

"So that was the noise we heard after leaving Viridia!" Commented Ven in awe as he looked to the unleashed destructive power. He never imagined such a weapon could have existed, even after all the years he had spent living himself. "This is going to be close!"

The attack from the Hydranian pulse-cannon did not however miss its intended mark. With a sheer display of endless force, the surging beam tore past Moah's boat and then through the leading Magmorran submersible - rendering it clean in half to float asunder. This small defeat signalled an instant parry of cannon-fire from the remaining Magmorran submersibles, which themselves were followed by counter pulse-waves fired in precision from the Hydranian warships in an embittered exchange between them.

"We're almost at Talam!" Cried out Moah bravely who continued to ride on through the ensuing chaos around, his sights still lay firmly on the desert landscape ahead that was now closing in evermore gradually. "Why did I get myself into this mess, again?" Several more explosions reverberated around Moah's boat from the opposing fleets. Two of Hydrania's ships had suffered fatal blows, they began to sink slowly where they once stood along with four of the Magmorran vessels which themselves were torn apart by the relentless pulse-beams that had been shot accurately against them. A metallic smoke soon coursed along the ocean's surface to smother the fleeing companions, which sent Moah back into a previously withheld panic.

"There must be *something* you can do, Ven… anything would be good right now!" Moah screamed to the Guardian as he defiantly carried on in his personal struggle towards Talam - despite a crushing impact that could be soon brought on them by the incoming ships from either side. Ven stiffly raised himself to scan across a small peninsula that lay just ahead now, finding his hopes swiftly rekindle from sensing its hidden earthly structure lying beneath the sea waves.

"Aim for that peninsula, Moah" The Guardian instructed. "I may yet be able to prove of some use in this futile battle!" He rubbed his hands together, as if preparing to fight.

"But that will draw us closer to the Magmorran vessels!" Snapped Moah back. "Aren't we near enough to them already?" Ven quietly meditated his emotions to focus on the earthly vibrations nearby, which when fused with the Guardian's own spiritual power forced a set of huge boulders to shift away from their foundations.

"Are you all still holding on tight to something?" Ven asked as he inspected his companions' whereabouts. "I doubt either army have ever witnessed something like this before…" Ven stretched out his arms towards the peninsula and then motioned his hands as if he were clasping onto some unseen object held within them. A radiant, emerald light shone mightily from within his eyes thereafter and his voice deepened to empower the Guardian's forthcoming spiritual herald.

"Arise, mighty earth… protect us from the decimation theses armies now threaten ourselves with!" Ven's arms shook furiously on saying this, like if he were suffering from some agonising form of pain. - with each word the Guardian spoke, sweat also began to draw endlessly away from his flesh. "Rise… Rise!" The possessed boulders rose in a thunderous appearance from their ocean dwellings to drown out the ceaseless crossfire by each opposing army, neither side could fathom what it was they were witnessing and all halted in their pressing advancements.

"I can't believe it, Cara!" Gasped Spero, who at this point had fallen back into his seat in astonishment. "Is it really Ven doing that?" He implored.

"Yes," She replied with a loving smile. "He *is* the Guardian of Earth." Cara now selflessly leant into Ven, attempting to support him as she noticed his obvious exertion in raising these large earthly boulders through the air above. She held tightly onto her tiring friend, then with Spero's aid tried to ease Ven's suffering further as the gargantuan rocks lifted towards them through his impressive skills.

"End this pointless slaughter…come to me!" Ven commanded passionately as he elevated both of his arms greater, despite struggling under the immense spiritual connection he was sharing with these monstrous boulders. The Guardian's companions then looked on in horror at what appeared to be an insane act of suicide wrought by Ven's current actions.

"What are you doing?" Stammered Moah nervously. "…Ven!" The weary Guardian parted his arms violently in a seeming response to Moah. His tremendous boulders, without any apparent warning, separated themselves within the air then reunified to form two structured walls of earth - miraculously landing directly in front of each opposing army situated either side to Moah's vessel. Before avoiding their imminent collisions with this newly formed peninsula, both navies unwillingly silenced the engines and weapons aboard them in an uncertainty of what unnatural force had now revealed itself.

"That was certainly something!" Laughed Moah in relief to Ven. "Never have I seen such a spectacle before… you were the miracle we needed!" Ven uncontrollably lowered himself to the deck of Moah's ship in exhaustion, from being both physically and mentally drained by the spiritual act he had committed, and of which left him with a desperate thirst.

"Water…" The Guardian pleaded desperately. "I need… water." His skin looked pale, and the green light in his eyes seemed weaker now.

"Are you alright?" Asked Cara to Ven in concern. "You looked like you were in so much pain there, Ven?" She quickly handed over Moah's water canteen to the weakened Spirit, in sympathy and appreciation of his draining ordeal.

"My connection to Impartia's earth is strong - spiritually." Whispered the Guardian faintly. "Though such a use of my power and being so far from my Sanctuary has a great draining effect on the body… I just…feel so weak." Ven only took a single mouthful to quench his fierce thirst; in feeling the intense heat of Talam's midday sun now he knew what rations they had left were to be a precious resource, preferring instead to save their only source of pure water instead for the impending desert journey.

"It's not over yet, Ven." Requited Moah anxiously. "You're protecting walls best hold out for us." A startling thunder from Magmorrah and Hydrania's remaining weapons once again filled the air, both armies now waged war against the new peninsulas which Ven had created to continue in their campaign of needless slaughter – eventually resulting in no ship to survive from this. Spero looked on in disdain at the sinking vessels around him and grieved in realising that he had now lost even more of his friends, people of whom he had most likely trained with for so many years - all gone within minutes of taking part in such a pointless charade of dominance. It was this very observation that drove Spero into a deeper desire to protect those who he now called his 'friends' particularly Cara, who the lonely officer had grown so fond of over their short time spent together.

"We were lucky to make it through that alive, weren't we?" Spero asked Cara as he helped to calm her. "We'll be free of Cera and General Nira in no-time."

"Do you really think so?" She replied to him in beleaguerment. "I don't believe they'll ever stop hunting us." Moah finally anchored his battered vessel against the shoreline of Talam, just as its last few drops of fuel spluttered away from the overheating engine inside. All aboard leapt joyously onto the scorching sands, their freedom and recent survival suddenly began to set in with its warming touch upon them.

"We made it... we've actually made it to Talam!" Cara shouted excitedly as she scooped up a handful of sand to throw it into the passing breeze, creating a cloud of shimmering particles which instantly satisfied her child-like euphoria. "It feels so good." Moah returned promptly to the broken vessel from which the friends had been granted their liberty, wishing to retrieve what rations may be left as he intimately contemplated his own fate - having never left the Sanctum of Kufiah's Sanctuary before. Ven and Spero however, were intently observing a range of mountains far to the north where they knew Talam's capital city now lay.

"We must find some shelter first," Cautioned Ven as he looked over the surrounding arid landscape. "The heat here at midday can quickly drive a person mad and, I dread this in saying so that, we are dangerously low on our water reserves."

"Great..." Sniped Spero in reply to the Guardian. "We leave one Hell-hole just to land in another!" He was from a nation that boasted numerous lakes and waterfalls, so the desert plains of Talam were far too foreign and dry for any current liking.

"Not necessarily, if we stay calm and logical... surviving our journey over the desert plains should be fairly straight-forward." Said Ven back in an unsettling tone. Around them appeared to be nothing less than endless miles of searing and unforgiving sandy plateaus, with no obvious water source evident in plain sight. The companions each sat hopelessly upon the shoreline's banks in frustration, whilst taking any such relief as they could from the ocean spray that filtered in.

"We can't just sit here to wait for General Nira and her army to catch us." Muttered Cara in want of breaking the silence that had befallen her and the others. "What *are* we going to now... does anyone have an idea whereabouts we are in Talam?"

"From my reckoning, I would say that we are less than one hundred miles away from the capital city." Remarked Moah glumly. He was surprisingly learned in these foreign fields, despite having such a solitary life within the Sanctuary of Darkness. "Further to the south of us lie the *Unknown Plains*, where Talam's precious ore mines are hidden, Queen Cera would give anything to learn of their true locations." Moah then continued to digress in his knowledge of Talam's geography, much to the boredom and weary looks of his fellow companions in return. "She had always hoped that Talam would provoke Magmorrah into all-out war, only so that we could milk dry the natural reserves from these lands…" Spero halted Moah, wishing to end his torturous teachings and the time that they were spending under Talam's midday sun.

"It's settled then, we head north to the capital… I don't know how much more of this heat I can take!" Spero ranted further. "If you know so much about these deserts, then how long should it take for us to reach the capital, Moah?"

"It'll be at the least a twelve-hour trek from where we currently are… that is… if we had a decent supply of water and rations to hand - which we don't!" Sneered Moah back angrily. "In our present dire state, we could possibly crawl there in under twenty-four hours… should we not all die from heat exposure in the process."

"In that case, we'll make a shelter for now and then travel at night when the desert is cooler." Declared Ven in authority to end the childish bickering going on. "I can see no sign yet of Cera's army, so we should at least be safe here for now until any of us can come up with a decent plan." The Guardian carefully made his way back over towards the grounded vessel beside Moah, in an unexpected move he then tore away some tarpaulin from its supports to crudely fashion a tent.

"You're doing it all wrong, Ven." Humoured Spero to the Guardian, who was increasingly becoming agitated with his struggle to erect their tent. "Here, I'll show you how to do it."

With Spero's military knowledge it took no time at all for him to help Ven in perfecting the make-shift canvas. Shortly afterwards, the bonding pair went in search nearby for some dried-up driftwood to prepare a fire – which they hoped could bring some greater protection as the freezing desert night now gradually drew in.

"Thank you," Whispered Cara to Moah, as they watched over Ven and Spero's bickering from a safe distance. "No-one else may have said this yet, but we do appreciate what you did for us back there in Magmorrah."

"The pleasure is mine, Princess." Replied Moah shyly. "Queen Cera has corrupted my Master Spirit for too long now, it is time for their reign of terror… to end."

The sun soon lowered fully in the sky above, though time for the companions filtered on with a seemingly slow pace as each were succumbing to dehydration. As the day's light vanished into the western horizon, Talam's vast desert shone like thousands of diamonds that lay scattered across its endless landscape under the pale moonlight – a scene Cara swiftly treasured.

"It looks so pretty doesn't it, Spero?" Commented Cara happily, despite now shivering from the cold night air. She huddled herself into Spero in seeking his warmth, then together they looked upon the small fire centred within their exposed camp.

"It's pretty *worrying*, Cara." Laughed Spero, in a nervous response. "I honestly wish that I could see things the way you do, this desert to me is so uninviting and infamous for bandits."

"You just need to look past the darkness and instead see what beauty it draws out from within it." Said Cara sternly. "That is how I take each day, otherwise this world would drive me insane." Moah and Ven had placed themselves further away from the other two, talking together as if in some secret discussion with one another. Cara could not help but to enquire of their clandestine conversation as she cautiously moved over to them, whilst wrapping her arms around her torso to preserve what heat remained.

"Is everything okay?" She keenly asked, whilst gesturing for Spero to come over and join her. "What are you talking about?" Ven rose himself to greet Cara and Spero with his now-familiar reassuring smile, though his body language displayed a more conflictive emotion.

"I have been asking Moah why he chose to turn away from his servitude at Kufiah's sanctuary, and what caused him to betray Queen Cera so lightly." The Guardian explained in honesty. "Such a brave act… though it could regrettably cost Moah his life." Moah knelt himself before his new friends, an overwhelming feeling of loss and terror entered him as he looked back across the ocean towards Magmorrah – the homeland he had only just forsaken.

"Why *did* you help us escape from Kufiah's Sanctuary, Moah." Questioned Cara sincerely. "I know that you have lost faith in Cera, but what *really* made you aid us – my sister's most despised enemies?" The Dark Acolyte looked with an assuring grin to Cara in response, he could sense a calming presence radiate from her and was truly grateful of the fact that she had referred to his home as a Sanctuary - not a prison as many others would have.

"Before I explain my reasons," Stuttered Moah anxiously. "I must tell you that no matter what treacherous act I have made against Queen Cera, I continue to be an Acolyte of Kufiah."

Spero grimaced on hearing these genuine words come from Moah, the thought of having to journey with this obviously conflicted person was casting many doubts in his troubling mind.

"You say that like it is something to be proud of!"

"I am proud!" Snapped Moah defensively to the naval officer. "Being a servant for one of Impartia's Celestial Spirits is truly an honour; it means more than just obeying a random set of given commands, it is a calling to protect this world's divine rule. I heartily respect the Dark Spirit, just as I am *also* bound to do with all the others – be they Elemental or Celestial."

"I think that is very noble of you." Interrupted Cara, with a widened smile. "When the Queen said that she planned to find Alaskia and end their existence, it created a conflict in my own loyalties and morals. Though *I am* a citizen of Magmorrah and subject of Queen Cera, my allegiance will always lie in serving the Spirits of Impartia first." Moah then carefully moved his vision across to Ven who was still stood over him, who himself nodded confidently in agreement to the vulnerable acolyte's confession.

"Wouldn't a servant of Kufiah be more inclined to wish the demise of this *Alaskia*?" Sneered Spero furiously. "The other Dark Acolytes were pleased with Cera as she revealed her plan back there… how are you not any different?"

"My Brethren follow their Queen blindly, under her promise of a greater power being granted to them… if Alaskia were to be destroyed." Muttered Moah in detest as he recounted this memory. "She made a solemn vow that their connection with Kufiah would increase infinitely, thus empowering them with inhuman powers – which in truth, is what Cera desires only for herself." Moah rubbed at his sore eyes, struggling to focus them whilst looking over the firelight centred before him; he actioned his hands again though only to mask the tears that he was faintly shedding in remorse.

"Is that what made you turn?" Said Cara frankly, with a curious tone. "I don't think anyone could blame you…"

"I could not allow for myself to be enslaved under such a false spell, not even if it would mean forcing myself into exile – *especially* if it were to spare Alaskia's divine existence."

Ven stepped himself in front of the firelight before Moah's weeping figure. The Guardian's mighty shadow cast itself far upon Talam's glistening desert and his eyes now radiated again as they focused on the kneeling Acolyte.

"*The Sacred Balance* shall never perish, my good friend." Declared Ven gladly. "Though if even one Spirit were to be lost from us, then an unstoppable chaos would ultimately take a hold over Impartia…this, we will not allow!" Ven endearingly scoured his vision over the concentrated faces of his friends that all now knelt around him. He had for so long hidden away in the safety of his own Sanctuary and realised that if this world were to survive Cera's evil, he would surely need to take a more physical role in protecting it from her.

"The Queen of Magmorrah only wishes to prove that she is a worthier ruler than her father was, so much so that she blatantly cares not for how her evil schemes will bring about an irreversible annihilation across these lands!" The spiritual light within Ven's eyes shone even greater in its intensity, his emotions flared with each passing word to enforce this dire lecture. "If Cera *does* succeed in reaching Alaskia's prison, then through Kufiah's power I am afraid that she will be able to achieve this sordid act of decimation. We *must* reach Alaskia before she or General Nira do, we alone are the only force now that can oppose them!"

"How can we stop her?" Asked Cara reservedly. "Cera doesn't know yet where Alaskia is hidden, and neither do we."

"You are correct in one sense, Cara." Said Ven dismissively. "In truth, I do know of Alaskia's supposed whereabouts, though we can only gain access through a set of passwords that are willingly granted by us Elemental Guardians; a powerful seal lies over the Spirit of Light in concealing them from Cera and her army, our mission now is to reach my Kin so that they can bestow their knowledge and rite of passage on us." Cara in reluctance, knew from what Ven was saying that she and their other friends now had to venture across Impartia in seeking these passwords. Her more pressing thoughts however, lay on the uncertain welfare of Sophilia - whom at this moment could still be in danger from Cera.

"We must return to Viridia and save my Lia before we do anything else!" Commanded Cara. "My child needs her mother, and no man here will stop me from protecting her."

"Please, try to stay calm." Responded Ven anxiously. "There is no doubt that a threat may still be present against your child, though if we are to truly save Sophilia we must stop Cera from reaching Alaskia; It is not certain whether through Kufiah, that the Queen may be able to breach our Elemental seals." He sighed.

"You didn't say that before!" Countered Cara to the remoreful Guardian. "So, there *is* a chance that Cera can reach Alaskia by using Kufiah. In that case, what is stopping her from breaching your own Sanctum to take Sophilia?" Spero leant himself over to Cara in sympathy, wishing to provide her with some much-needed reassurance though to little avail as her despair had grown far too strong now.

"All that matters to me is my little girl, my only child! I'm sorry that I shouted at you Ven, but I want to go back so that I can be with her again...to know that she *is* safe." Cara cried as she collapsed suddenly to her knees, within an expelling effort to drain the negative emotions now coursing on through. Ven lowered himself before her to gently wipe the tears away from Cara's eyes, expressing his own sorrow in unison.

"Permit me, but I do understand what it is like to lose someone whom you love with all your being." Ven stuttered in agony. "I too had a family that were taken from me by a Magmorran Queen: my wife Natara and three children, whom I love still with all my grieving heart. I did all I could to save them, but it just was not meant to be… the thought that I could have perhaps done more is a burden which I now must learn to live with for an eternity." Ven tremored through the painful memories as they entered back into his thoughts, of which he had blocked away for so many countless years. He remained strong in his composure in wishing to bring a determined strength to Cara, that she would undoubtedly need on their quest which lay ahead of them.

"I'm so sorry, Ven." Said Cara sorrowfully. "I can't imagine what such a loss must feel like?" She thought of how her own family was robbed from her, albeit they never saw eye-to-eye.

"There is no need for an apology, my dear Cara." Whispered Ven tenderly as he stroked at her hands in reassurance. "My desire to reach and free Alaskia, is because I too am concerned for your daughter's wellbeing; Our only means in ensuring Sophilia's long-term safety is to stop your sister and General Nira's reign of tyranny…"

"Ven is right!" Remarked Moah abruptly. "There would be no logic in Queen Cera using her resources to pursue a helpless child…" He pondered for a moment, reasoning that there was something truly evil at work here.

"That is very true, Moah." Said Ven in assurance. "I myself cannot fathom a need for Cera to trouble herself with such a wasteful exertion, her will is set solely against destroying the balance in this world… not to kidnap a child." The Guardian's rationale was coarsely interrupted by a dreaded gasp that left itself instantly from Cara.

"Cera is determined to kill Alaskia and stop the cycle of that other Spirit you spoke of… Cerebrante." Mumbled Cara almost incoherently, whilst Ven stared to her in an uncertainty of where she was going with this train of thought. "It's obvious why Cera hates me so much, because I also bear the mark of Cerebrante like she and Father do." Spero and Moah looked to the named mark upon Cara's face in a risen dread. It was merely a set of interlocking lines on first glance: two arrows pointed in opposition against one another, their ends signifying the four elements and situated within their centre were two small speckles which represented Impartia's Celestial Spirits.

"If Cera wishes me dead because of the mark on my face, then how would you say she feels about my Sophilia's… did you not notice this at your Sanctuary, Ven?" Said Cara knowingly to a shocked response in return from her friends. "Sophilia's birthmark rests on her right hand and is far clearer in its appearance than mine, does that not make my her a greater threat to my sister?" Ven breathed heavily as if he were winded on hearing this unfortunate revelation from Cara, he could not at all find any words of comfort to counter this horrifying reality.

"No, I did not." Mourned the Guardian. "Please forgive my ignorance, everything happened so fast back there when I was confronting Nira; I didn't have time to notice Sophilia's mark before my acolytes took her away into safety." Ven gently lowered his forehead against Cara's in anguish, Sophilia sharing a connection to Cerebrante was an unexpected twist and this left him questioning as to what path they must rightfully need to take now.

"Do not share in this burden alone, Cara." Said the Guardian sorrowfully. "We are all here to help you, and we *will* rescue your Sophilia... it is only a matter of time." Moah stared inquisitively at Cara and Ven while they dwelled in this intimate moment of grief; the Dark Acolyte had never himself experienced such a pain as losing a loved one before, nor the pleasure they could bring into his life.

"If your child also bears the mark of Cerebrante," said Moah nervously to Cara. "Then I can guarantee you that Cera *will* endeavour to find her. The Queen is obsessed with gaining immortality and will not allow for any such threat to exist, regardless of how miniscule they may seem to others...." Cara howled and covered her ears to shield herself from hearing any more of Moah's honest words, her mournful fears had without question become an unwanted reality.

"I'm just being honest with you, Cara... I didn't mean to cause further upset." Responded the naïve Acolyte in regret to his ill-thought actions. "Once we reach Hydrania, we can then head eastwards across the ocean strait to Viridia where you can be reunited with your child... it should not be difficult to achieve this."

"That's what we'll do okay, Cara?" Said Spero in a sensitive tone, he brushed away a lining of course sand from her clothing and face and then handed to Cara their last rations of drinkable water. "Drink, you will need it more than we do if you are to get out of this desert and reach your Sophilia..." The stagnant drops of warm water trickled quickly down Cara's throat, calming her shaken nerves slightly with its short-lived replenishment. Ven at this moment gazed up to the night sky and noticed that its moon had not risen as he had anticipated, making only a few metres of land visible at a time before him. The thick web of darkness, despite being useful in shrouding the companions and their footsteps, also brought a foreboding sense to Ven that someone or something was observing in secret.

"The plateau that lies before us is renowned to be a haven for rogues and exiles, we must tread carefully and stay as quiet as possible if we're to avoid an ambush – which is likely." Heeded the Guardian as he attempted to shield himself from Talam's forceful desert winds. "Be on your guard at all times... let's go now." The four companions gathered themselves hesitantly, with some hope remaining, that they could make it alive through the cold night. They followed along Talam's nearby shoreline which glistened softly under the dim moonlight above; each step taken felt as if they were several through the shifting and sinking sands beneath them, annoyingly resulting in their progress taking even longer than they would have wished.

"Stay by my side, Cara." Ordered Spero as he moved closer to her. "The last thing we need is for any of us to get lost out here in this wilderness; I've heard some pretty worrying stories about the callous nature of these so-called bandits…"

"Keep your voices down!" Strained Ven in a whisper-like command. "They will carry easily over the pacing wind current, and I doubt you both wish to be kidnapped again?"

"Ven needs to seriously lighten up, doesn't he?" Laughed Spero to Cara nervously, knowing the Guardian held some truth in his fears. "The atmosphere out here is already bad enough!"

"He's only trying to protect us, Spero." She replied with a disappointed expression. "Let's just stay quiet like Ven asked us to, this desert is terrifying in the dark…" Out on the ocean, several flickering lights slowly appeared and seemed to be moving southwards; they were parallel to the shore line though far away enough not to pose any threat.

"Ships, in these dangerous waters?" Pondered Spero as he slowed down his and Cara's pace to watch over the strange movements. "Surely they're not more Hydranian warships?

"If they are, then they're just as stubborn as Queen Cera is…" Responded Moah, who had by chance overheard Spero's conversation with Cara. "You would have thought after their recent loss, that they would not pursue such another futile move as to attack Magmorrah again - it will only end in their destruction." Spero turned to lunge angrily at Moah, he was enraged by such ignorant words against his home-nation and soon the Dark Acolyte was dragged helplessly to the freezing ground.

"If it would mean stopping *your* Queen from invading *our* lands, we would risk a *thousand* ships to end her wicked reign - servant of darkness!" Screamed Spero into Moah's face. "You know nothing of the pain your precious monarch has brought to Hydrania… *nothing!*" Ven swiftly placed himself between the two; he tore Spero away from Moah without any sign of exertion and then stared to both in fear of their positions being unwittingly given away.

"This bickering is of no help to any of us and it is what Cera would want!" Said Ven in dismay. "Did we not agree to stay quiet on this perilous journey… do you want us all to be killed or enslaved?"

"Forgive me, Ven." Muttered Moah in a pleading voice. "I was only being truthful in the knowledge I know of Cera's mindset and capabilities to Spero." Cara stumbled clumsily over the uneven terrain to stand amongst her three disgruntled companions, now pointing a finger worryingly towards a new light within the southern horizon.

"That *can't* be a ship…" Reasoned Cara whilst she positioned herself behind Ven, who was the tallest out of the friends, in feeling a greater protection from him. "What do you think it is?"

"Bandits!" Snapped back Ven fearfully. "Stay low to the ground, if they find us… let me do the talking." Ven cautiously stepped away from his companions to confront the incoming light. His options however were limited, despite being a Spirit of Earth incarnate, as manipulating sand was a far trickier feat for Ven to manage - having this been a skill he had not practised for a great length of time.

"I can deal with this," repeated the Guardian anxiously to himself. "I've been through worse…" Ven's breathing became more rapid through his racing heartbeat as the foreign light grew in its size, bringing with it also a peculiar rattling noise that now became quickly apparent over the silent evening air. A flurry of sand and piercing wind blew against the companions as the light neared, stinging their skin and blinding them at first from identifying the strange intruder. When the dust began to settle around them, it revealed a crude hovercraft that had been adapted to travel across the desert sands. In control of this craft was a lone driver, his face and other features were hidden behind numerous layers of thick cloth that were wrapped tightly around them in protection.

"Oh, so there is *four* of you?" Humoured the driver as he dismounted from the vehicle. He removed a single torch from the front of his craft, which proved to be the growing light of which had been seen travelling over Talam's southern plain towards Cara.

"Who are you… and what do you want from us?" Questioned Ven defensively to the imposing traveller. The stranger merely ignored Ven's question and instead scanned his torch across the startled faces placed before him, laughing smugly as he did so.

"You *do* know how well sound travels out here, don't you?" Said the mysterious figure as he scratched away at his itchy garments, removing some so that he could speak clearer with the studious onlookers. "You lot must be mad, what were you thinking by walking through this desert at night and without any weapons?"

"We don't exactly have a choice…" Replied Spero in defiance. "Don't try anything funny, I don't need a weapon to handle a bandit like you." The Stranger hastily placed his torch into the ground beneath and then removed what shrouding cloth remained from their face, in the fickle light was now revealed a youthful man: his face was battered and worn by an obvious length of time spent living in the desert, his raven-black hair was knotted and littered by many grains of dusty sand, his eyes eagerly opened wide to meet with Spero - showing no evidence of any threat in them.

"I'm *not* a bandit, and by the looks of it, neither are any of you… am I correct?" He asked whilst showing some hint of concern towards the group of friends. "You all look strange enough to be though…" Ven calmly signalled for Cara and their other two companions to stay behind as he walked closer towards the seemingly amicable stranger, who continued to laugh at them whilst observing their differing dress senses – much to his own amusement.

"What do you mean by that?" Asked Ven, who too gave a whisper of a laughter on realising what the stranger meant by his rude remark. "I can assure you that we're not bandits, though we are technically exiles…"

"Well, just look at you all!" Cackled the traveller more loudly. "You my good sir, are dressed in some old green robes… he is wearing black robes… this other fella is wearing, what looks like, a Hydranian naval uniform and you have one woman travelling with you - very suspicious!" Cara herself was dressed in the common peasant garments that most Viridian women would normally wear, she quickly pulled them closer together over her chest and then looked to the stranger with a disapproving glance.

"I am not what you are suggesting," Said Cara proudly. "It would be appreciated if you would stop staring at me, as well."

"There are a lot of slave traders in these parts," Responded the traveller awkwardly as he lifted his arms up in repent to Cara. "I meant no insult, I'm just curious as to why you are travelling with these weird-looking men… I've never seen such a sight!" A needful laughter then erupted between all present, it was a welcome escape from the harsh surrounding environment and this stranger did make a valid point – at least in Cara's eyes.

"I'm so sorry if I've caused any offense to any of you…" Remarked the cloaked figure sincerely. "I am Firin, one of many unfortunate exiles who roam this plain and a scavenger also. For you all this fine evening, I shall be a mode of transport… if you so wish?" Cara smiled gladly to her friends on hearing this, their own reactions however we more reserved.

"Your offer is greatly appreciated, but we hardly know you…" Responded Ven. "We are wanted fugitives, not exactly people whom you would wish to be associated with."

"That doesn't bother me," Chuckled Firin to the reserved Guardian. "I would hate to think that you all actually ran into any *real* bandits out here, especially while taking such a leisurely walk over these dangerous plains… plus… you will probably die of hypothermia!" Firin suddenly clambered back onto his hovercraft after replacing his torch into its rightful setting. "Are you getting aboard or not? My driving isn't too bad, and I can get you to wherever you are heading quicker than at your current pace." Cara leapt onto the craft excitedly without any further thought, oblivious also to any dangers that could have met with her in trusting Firin so freely.

"Come on!" She ordered to her hesitating associates. "You can all freeze out here if you want to… but I'm not!"

"Do what the lady wishes, Gentlemen." Sniggered Firin contently, he loved watching their awkward reactions. "My rates aren't too expensive, you all look light enough for my hovercraft to hold the extra weight!" Firin laughed again as he reignited the spluttering engine back into power. Ven stepped onto Firin's craft first, feeling that the dangers around them could be possibly far worse than travelling in such a flimsy death-trap. Cara herself, laughed unashamedly at the struggle her new friends had in trying to find some comfort when seating themselves whilst Firin slowly turned his head to address them.

"Please forgive the lack of amenities my vehicle has," Mumbled Firin, as he pretended to brush away some dust from his craft. "Luxuries wouldn't exactly be practical for me and they would most likely draw unwanted attention from the *real* bandits out here. So; where is it you were heading to?" He asked with a sense of excitement.

"We are trying to reach Talam's capital city in the north!" Shouted Ven, who was straining to reach his voice over the drowning noise from Firin's large swirling fan placed behind him. "There, we will find a way of crossing over the sea to Hydrania... is that too far for you to travel?" Firin shook his head to the Guardian with some uncertainty, the very mention of Talam's capital raised many old and painful memories within him.

"No can do, I'm afraid." Said Firin begrudgingly. "The capital is a no-go zone for me...being an exile an all. I can however, take you to *Port Station* which lies on the eastern shoreline; there is a new train service there, apparently, which travels far under the ocean across to Hydrania through an underground system of tunnels – clever, isn't it?" The three companions seated within the back of Firin's craft looked to him in confusion, having never heard of such a feat.

"An undersea trainline..." Replied Spero with a bemused smirk. "Are you sure it exists...I've never heard of it before?"

"Certainly!" Shouted Firin back in assurance. "The king of Talam and Hydrania's Regent officially opened it only last week, due to all the recent naval activity from Magmorrah..."

"I don't understand," whispered Spero to Cara nervously. "I've been stationed on a Hydranian warship for the past few months now, Firin... never once was there any mention of there being attacks on our western coast."

"What I told you there is top-secret information, mind...shared with me by my friends in the Talamite army!" Replied Firin, he quickly restrained himself however from digressing any further into whom these 'friends' were. "The King doesn't want to concern his subjects with such concerns."

"Firin," Said Cara in a desperate voice. "I'm starving, do you have any food aboard?"

Firin smiled to her then motioned a stiff level from beside him, releasing a compartment that had inside of it a small, woven sack.

"Please feel free to help yourselves... those are my rations and there's plenty to spare, I've just returned from the Scavenger's Market!" Shouted Firin enthusiastically to the hungry passengers aboard. Moah hastily reached over to grab the large sack, he frantically ripped away the seal from it to find numerous fruits and bread within.

"Thank you," gestured the Dark Acolyte, as he fumbled to swallow a large mouthful of flat-bread. "It has been a while since we last ate." Scoffed Moah.

"We should reach Port Station by sunrise," Said Firin, as he leaned around again to speak with his new companions. "Now would be a good opportunity to get some rest, that is, if you can on this rickety craft of mine." Firin had unwittingly moved a heavy sheet away from behind him, underneath it was a large rifle with several boxes of ammunition situated alongside that Spero, initially, felt tempted to take. This instinctive thought soon passed though in Spero; he reasoned that if Firin was really a threat to them, then he would have already done something by now.

"Get some sleep," requested Cara to Spero politely. "We've still got a long way to go."

The night passed by, thankfully, without any issues. Impartia's morning sun soon began to rise again, though this time without the foreboding crimson glaze witnessed the day before. Cara awoke from an uncomfortable sleep, aches flew throughout her body as she moved from the awkward position she had lain within next to Spero in Firin's craft.

"That was the *worst* night's sleep I have ever had, and I used to live in a forest!" Yawned Cara in dismay. She could tell from her companion's equally drained faces that they themselves had not rested well either, their own expressions noticeably drawn and haggard.

"Good! So, I'm not the only one!" Laughed Spero to Cara. "I can't feel my legs from all the shaking this craft is making."

"Be grateful that we did not encounter any vagabonds," Said Ven sternly to Spero as he awoke himself in agony. "It must be mid-morning?" He pondered.

"Good Morning my fellow travellers... how are we all feeling?" Firin gleefully called out over the noise from the crafts engine, he then glanced back briefly to look across the weary faces of his passengers; they stared back to their enthusiastic chauffeur, unenthusiastic themselves however and praying that sometime soon they would finally reach their destination at Port Station.

"We're fine thanks, Firin... just a little cold." Said Cara as she huddled herself back into the warmth of Spero beside her. "Have we far to go still?" She then asked through juddering teeth.

"Yes, we're nearly there now!" Shouted Firin in delight. "It's a good job too... we're almost out of fuel!" Though Firin was laughing again to himself, the thought of being stranded did not go down well with the still-nervous passengers aboard; they quickly inspected what rations they had left for themselves - should such an unfortunate situation befall them. The sun now began to course fully over Talam's desert plains around them, only masked slightly by some distant dust clouds that gathered from the western horizon. Firin merely shrugged them off as a 'natural disturbance', caused by the unpredictable gusts that travel regularly through the open plains. Spero however, felt an unease against them and swiftly reached for the high calibre rifle that was stashed in front of him - soon noticing upon it a high-resolution sniper scope.

"Hey!" Shouted Firin angrilly, as he observed Spero grab his most-prized possession, though he felt no real threat from this impolite intrusion. "You be careful with my weapon... it's one of a kind; that rifle there is the reason why I was exiled, I spent a decade serving in Talam's army as a lead sniper and was fully decorated with it... only to be cast aside after they felt I had fulfilled my services with them! I thought, that it would be a good idea to take it as a souvenir - since the final pay check they gave me was so poor and that didn't go down exactly well with my superiors..." Spero held a fist into the air, clearly hinting at Firin to silence his reminiscent ramblings.

"Those dust clouds... they are moving pretty fast towards us and against the wind!" Cried out Spero, he suddenly felt the imposing weapon being snatched back by Firin who had brought the craft to a stop now on hearing this. Firin peered through his rifle's scope across the western plains and, to his horror, found that Spero's concern was well-justified.

"They are... aren't they?" Stammered Firin knowingly. "We best make a move now... and fast!" He hit the accelerator lever hard back into its full throttle, sending his craft almost uncontrollably forwards again to escape from this new danger. Through the growing dust clouds several hovercrafts, which were similar though far more advanced to Firin's, abruptly emerged into plain sight. They boasted heavy armour with, what appeared to be, harpoon-like attachments which were obviously in aim of Firin's vehicle.

"This is bad," Said Cara in a trembling voice. "This is all we need!" The ensuing crafts soon caught up to Firin, who was now only half a mile or so away from them. Firin threw his beloved rifle back at Spero for him to catch, hitting it hard against his chest in the process and winding him by the forceful impact momentarily.

"Right, my friend... do you know how to fire a weapon like that?" Commanded Firin with an air of authority to Spero, who in turn gave back a puzzled look as he cocked open the weapon from its safety setting - ensuring that it was armed and ready for use.

"Of course, I do..." Replied Spero arrogantly. "Who do you think they are... those other crafts?" He steadily aimed Firin's heavy rifle towards the incoming aggressors, trying desperately to fix his sights on any possible target.

"Could be bandits... could be slave traders..." Firin responded, as he shrugged his shoulders dismissively. "They're more than likely the folks I took those rations from, gaging from the kind of crafts they are using. I didn't exactly pay for those things, being so poor myself, it's survival of the fittest out here and I get hungry quick; I didn't think for one second that they would miss a few items here or there – this is a total overreaction on their part!"

"You've *got* to be joking, Firin?" Remarked Cara despairingly, she looked beside to Ven for some sane form of intervention in aiding them through this new nightmare. "Can you help us again, Ven?"

"I'm still weak from yesterday," responded Ven in a regretful tone. "It is Spero's turn to save us now...may the Elements preserve us." He laughed faintly. Spero prepared his finger over the trigger of Firin's rifle; he fired a single warning shot against the incoming crafts, hitting one accidently to send it coursing through the air into another craft racing beside.

"What are you doing?" Quailed Firin in shock as he snapped his head back towards Spero. "They're my friends that you're firing at... who else am I going to trade with if you wipe them out?" Spero moved his eyes slowly away from the gun's scope to roll them at Firin, utterly in disbelief to his selfish plea.

"Those *friends* of yours obviously want to hurt us, Firin!" He said firmly. "I doubt they want to trade with you anymore..." Spero returned his sight to the rifle's scope, ignoring Firin's further requests to halt in his deadly shots. A second bullet, which Spero had fired, just missed its mark and was swiftly countered by an enemy harpoon; Cara quickly hid herself beneath Ven's lengthy robes in wanting to escape from this terrifying ordeal. "I *told* you they aren't friendly!" Reiterated Spero to Firin. "They're firing harpoons at us now!" Spero cocked his rifle weapon once more, this time aiming for a craft centred within the convoy in presuming it to be the leader; his strike hit true and sent the enemy vehicle flying into the air against two others - leaving only four more left in pursuit.

"Come on, you *Bastards*!" Snarled Spero as he gripped the lengthy rifle tighter, though he had unwittingly knocked a switch that was located upon the weapons side in doing this. As it fired again, Firin's rifle sprayed out a rapid-fire of powerful bullets towards the hostile convoy - forcing them to flee in several directions over the many dunes lain further south.

"Was there *really* any need to use the rapid fire on them?" Laughed Firin in disbelief, now accepting his loss in business and feeling a relief, in the fact that they had escaped from their would-be captors.

"That's some weapon you have!" Remarked Spero as he reluctantly handed the rifle back to its rightful owner. Smiling back in response, the ex-sniper proudly sheathed it then gave a suggestive wink to Spero.

"Why do you think I went through the bother of stealing it... well worth being forced into exile, wouldn't you say?" Said Firin smugly. "Speaking of which, my fellow exiles... Port Station is now only a few miles away!" The group of unlikely friends instantly erupted with a raucous cry of jubilation at this news; only Moah remained silent as he looked intently upon a small obsidian tablet held within his palms, which was hidden away from sight in caution.

"Can you see me?" Whispered the Dark Acolyte into it. "Can you sense my thoughts?"

"What are you doing?" Enquired Ven curiously to Moah. "What is that you have there?"

"It's nothing," replied the Acolyte bashfully. "...Just a souvenir from home"

Chapter Four: Lake Tinomar

Firin's battered craft choked on the last few drops of fuel left in its engine, thankfully just he managed to reach Port Station. The travelling companions each looked in awe upon a set of great golden gates that lay before Talam's major harbour town; spanning from them was a sandstone wall that stretched out in surrounding the valuable port, supposedly to protect it from any foreign threats.

The town itself was a large complex of homely structures, also made from sandstone, that clearly displayed a vast difference between the richer and more poverty-stricken citizens who inhabited it. In the harbour, stood a long modern-looking pier that trailed out easterly towards Hydrania, alongside it stood numerous cargo ships that had been quarantined as none were permitted to leave the port at this time – in wake of Magmorrah's current aggression.

"I've never seen a place like this before!" Declared Cara excitedly to Spero, as Ven and Moah counted what little currency they had to compensate Firin. "I once read about Port Station in my father's library, *'Talam's Epicentre for Trade and New-Beginnings'*; it definitely lives up to that, from what I can see." She gasped in awe.

"There doesn't seem to be much trade going on," Commented Spero whilst he observed the many ships docked in the harbour. "Times have obviously changed since that book was written… and not for the better." Firin grimly dismounted from his craft with less enthusiasm than he had held before, having lost his live-hood in an instance and a great level of uncertainty suddenly dawned on him about what future he may now have within these turbulent lands.

"Here we are…" Firin said as he glumly looked to the travellers. "You can reach Hydrania now, don't worry about paying me though as I can't exactly return to the Scavenger Market…" He then turned away from them to linger over what possible price may now be upon his head.

"It is only right for us to pay you for your services," Said Ven in a firm resolve to Firin, as he reached into his robes to search from something of value. "Though, what we have is not much…Sorry."

"Do you honestly have enough to make the crossing over to Hydrania, by any chance?" Asked Firin wearily to the Guardian. "From what I have heard, it costs five silver coins to use this new train system… do you have that amount?" He lifted a single eyebrow curiously.

"No," interrupted Moah glumly. "Not even close…" The Acolyte scoured through his robes, finding only two silver coins, which strangely enough weren't there previously.

"Well, that's no good!" Firin grinned sympathetically to his new companions, then without any reluctance he removed the hovercraft's ignition key from his pocket in a withheld sadness. "I'll just have to sell it to help you all, I should be able to get a good price and if my rifle is also included… we'll have plenty of silver to buy some tickets!" Cara joyously leapt into Firin's arms to embrace him with all her sincerest appreciation, thankful beyond any words towards his selfless act in aiding this new quest of theirs.

"Thank you…Thank you so much, Firin." Whispered Cara passionately into his ear, as she reached her arms around him. "Such a kind gesture, we will repay you…somehow."

"There's nothing for me here now, Cara." Muttered Firin back to her plainly. "I've become an exile of exiles… if there is such a thing?" He chuckled. "May I travel with you and your friends to Hydrania; perhaps I can make a new start there?" Cara smiled in return to Firin and then turned her head across towards Ven, seeking his own decision regarding this pleading request as the journey they were about to undertake was beyond any rational explanation.

"I say, more the merrier!" Laughed Ven heartily to Firin. "I hope that you will understand though, there may be worse perils ahead of us than desert bandits where we are going to?"

"Trust me," humoured Firin in response, though with a serious expression. "I've survived some pretty harrowing things in my life… I'm ready for a new challenge."

"Have you ever needed to fight against a Celestial Spirit before?" Mumbled Moah anxiously. "A gun won't be much use against one of those…"

"What was that?" Countered Firin hastily. "I couldn't hear what you said there…" He leant into Moah's personal space, glaring at him humorously as he did so.

"Nothing," groaned Moah wearily. "Let's go and sell your only belongings… shall we?" He silenced his tongue now on noticing Ven's increasing glare, which was aimed directly at him now. The companions swiftly made their way through the large harbour town, eventually finding themselves within its main bazaar. Firin managed to sell his craft and rifle, though for far-less than he had hoped for, then made his way slowly back through the dense crowds to meet with his new friends.

"We should have enough coins here to buy our tickets for Hydrania's western coast," Said Firin woefully, whilst playing with the few coins he had in his hands. "So much for a long-term investment!"

"Thank you, again." Said Ven endearingly to Firin. "We will find some way of repaying you… eventually." Firin handed over what little currency he had accumulated to Ven, then afterwards the peculiar party struggled further through the uncomfortably-crowded streets towards Port Station's Grand Train Terminal; they waited there for what seemed like hours to obtain the correct tickets, Cara toyed with hers and repeatedly looked over the text which was stamped upon it reading:

Single Adult: One-way payment accepted - Depart: Talam Port Station. Destination: Tinomar Lake. Price:5.00 SP. Non-Refundable.

Cara shifted across the station platform in perplexment over to Ven. He, along with Moah, had sat willingly in isolation away from Spero and Firin, who themselves were engrossed by discussing their military pasts and numerous sagas – within a tedious arrogance.

"Where *is* Tinomar… I've never heard of such a place in Hydrania?" Asked Cara naively to the wise Guardian. "The countless books I read made no mention of it."

"I am surprised to hear you say that, Cara." Said Ven in a sympathetic tone. "Tinomar is the largest lake province in Hydrania's western region, King Kanaan would famously frequent its shores as his desired place of rest…" He paused, as a swift thought occurred to him. "Which he must have done in secret, judging by your expression? I presume, King Kanaan had Lake Tinomar wiped from Magmorrah's Records?" Cara had only ever known the choking ash lands of Magmorrah during her youth, and Viridia's ancient maze-like forests when exiled. Kanaan had never allowed for his first-born to leave the 'safety' of their palace and now Cara wished to learn more of this idyllic setting from Ven.

"I always wanted to visit Hydrania," She said solemnly. "Please, tell me more about it. I bet it is a wonderous nation to live in." Cara drifted into a daydream, imaging the picturesque Hydranian landscapes.

"Certainly!" Replied Ven with an eager smile. "East of Lake Tinomar, and over its vast mountain ranges, is Hydrania's central province where the capital city and Levia's Sanctuary are situated. The capital itself, is held within a crater of magnificent waterfalls and rivers that boast ancient marble households… I am very much looking forward to you seeing this beauty for the first time!" He nodded excitedly.

"So am I…" Thought Cara as she closed her eyes, desperately wishing to imagine such a magnificent nation, and of how Sophilia would love to see it for herself – something they could perhaps manage when all their present troubles ceased. Ven and Cara both jolted as a resounding voice echoed throughout the station; it signalled their train's arrival and with it wrought a sense of relief in the companions.

"Finally!" Exasperated Firin, who had quickly grown impatient in waiting for this train to appear. "I thought we were going to be stuck in this place forever!" Cara examined the long length of their train's carriage in delight. It was decorated with a separate flow of blue and gold paint to signify the union between Hydrania and Talam, several exhausts also ran along the sides which bellowed out many bursts of steam to power this technological marvel.

"That's something you don't see every day…" Remarked Spero as he stepped into the train first. He held out a hand to assist Cara onto it, then together they clambered slowly through the crowded carriage to find their designated seats. It soon became obvious to the travelling party what effect Cera's threats were having, on the ease of travel between the free nations, being that the train was well over its safe capacity.

"I hope our journey to Lake Tinomar doesn't take too long," Panted Cara through the rising heat. "I can barely breathe in here!"

"This *is* pretty bad, but still more comfortable than Firin's hovercraft." Humoured Spero to ease their unwanted nuisance, Firin however was not so amused. "Hydrania's western shore isn't that far away… don't worry, we'll be cooler in no time." A deafening whistle coursed from the train's many vents, then it swiftly accelerated into a tunnel that would lead far beneath Talam's ocean waves – away from the sight of Queen Cera's motioning war vessels above.

"How do you feel, about meeting the Guardian of Water?" Questioned Ven with a hidden purpose to Moah. "Levia is a close friend of mine, and I believe that you will find no ill-bearings from him when we reach his Sanctuary." Moah shrugged at Ven dismissively in response; his thoughts were dwelling instead on Queen Cera whom he had seemingly betrayed, in knowing of what true horror she still desired to unleash. The train moved at a surprisingly fast speed through Talam's immersed tunnel network, spanned deep under the ocean waves upon its seabed to Hydrania. The tunnel's protecting walls were fashioned entirely out of reinforced glass that revealed an underwater kingdom outside, itself littered with strange fauna and relics from previous wars fought above.

"Even down here, we can't escape from being reminded of how violent Impartia's history has been." Said Firin with an ominous expression. "People… they never learn, do they?"
Patrolling the train's causeways were several heavily-armed soldiers, respectively from both Talam and Hydrania's armies - a morbid sign of the hostilities which these two lands were now embroiled in against Magmorrah. Spero glanced discreetly to the passing Hydranian soldiers in a vain hope of perhaps recognising one of them.

"Three years of harsh military training," He uttered to himself. "Only to be stationed on a civilian train as babysitters… what a let-down that must be?" Cara noticed Spero's frustration by his twisting facial expressions, she immediately decided to cheer him up by using the serene views outside as a needful distraction.

"Isn't this exciting?" She exclaimed to her mindful friend. "It's amazing what Talam and Hydrania have done by making this passageway... don't you think?" In one hand, Spero now firmly held a small tattered photograph which he then carefully removed from his waistcoat for Cara to receive. He vacantly turned from her to look across a graveyard of many sunken warships outside as she studied it, seeing them as fallen remnants of previous wars left to fall into ruin and sadly be forgotten. Spero greatly hoped that the lives his own friends, who had so selflessly sacrificed themselves for their nation, would not be lost in a similar and undignified way.

"Tinomar province was where I was born, Cara." Stuttered Spero hesitantly. "I haven't been back there since I lost my family when I was younger, just the thought of its great lake is enough to rekindle so many awful memories of them..." Cara saw in Spero's photograph two young boys who were sat hugging one another upon a long wooden jetty, it faced out over a noticeably vast lake that stretched far over the worn image in her hands. The smiling children in it looked so happy and carefree to Cara, she quickly distinguished a similarity with one of them to Spero who himself wallowed in an apparent state of grief beside her.

"Is that you in this picture?" Chuckled Cara awkwardly. "You've barely aged, just look at your long hair!"

"This picture is all that I have left... of my family." Replied Spero in a sorrowful tone to Cara. "My younger brother Stevian and I would play for hours on the lakeshore... it only feels like yesterday and I can still sometimes hear his voice." Cara nestled her head sympathetically into Spero's shoulder, she herself had felt the impact of losing family members and could sense what anguish this too wrought in her new friend.

"This is a lovely picture of you and your brother," She sighed to him. "I know how hard it can be... not seeing them ever again." These words struck hard with Cara, she had spent so much of her life trying to forget her painful memories.

"After my family died, I left our small village to start a new life in the mountains... that was where Levia's acolytes found me." Continued Spero, his demeanour now lightened with this fonder recollection. "I wander how much Lake Tinomar has changed since then?" He then gently removed the precious photograph from Cara's hands to place it back securely within his waistcoat, wishing also that he could do the same with some his more bitter memories.

"We'll just have to see... won't we, Spero?" Replied Cara in an aspiring tone. "We're all here for you now anyway... we'll support you." Cara savoured the following moment when Spero tilted his head into hers to rest upon it, the shared comfort meeting between them eased their tensions – especially now as the journey to Lake Tinomar was coming to its closure.

Hydrania's motioning sea waves above appeared eerily calm to the companions as their train made for its tunnel's exit, they regrouped outside on the station platform after alighting in a determined sense of reprieve from their previous anxieties. More Hydranian soldiers greeted them in the train station of Tinomar and once again Spero could not recognise anyone amongst them, his mind now resolute in the fact he stood alone from the friends who had signed up to serve alongside with him.

"It *does* feel good to be home," said Spero in relief to Cara. "You certainly can't beat the fresh air here." He took in a deep breath, then exhaled for just as long. "Perfect…"

"I said that you would be fine, didn't I?" Smirked Cara. "Hydrania is just like I imagined from the books I used to read…beautiful." Before the companions now lay an awe-inspiring landscape of snowy mountain ranges and several lakes, with many villages spread over the grassy plains that surrounded them. The most dominating feature was Lake Tinomar, its clear waters glistened within an air of ancient wonder that shone majestically under the golden sun rays above. Moah shifted awkwardly where he stood from seeing such a natural beauty for the first time, having him been so accustomed to the desolate, bleak landmass of Magmorrah and its choking atmosphere.

"This place…it looks like it was conceived from a heavenly dream." Commented the Dark Acolyte in astonishment to Ven. "I can envision the endless realm of Eternamorrah to be just as tranquil." He contemplated with a hopeful expression.

"You are full of surprises…particularly for an Acolyte of Darkness!" Jested Ven in response, then his mood swiftly turned sombre. "I pray however, that on this noble quest of ours we do not end up in Eternamorrah."

"I don't believe we will," Whispered Moah, whilst he secretly tinkered with his hidden obsidian tablet. "There will be no chance of that… for me at least." He despaired.

"Spero!" Shouted Ven sporadically. "You are a man of Hydrania, how far is it to the capital from where we are now positioned?" The Guardian shrugged his shoulders for an answer. He received a quick response, albeit a melancholy one.

"We can cross Lake Tinomar on one of its ferries, that is, if they are still running." Replied Spero in resentment. "Then, we will have to trek over Hydrania's western pass to reach the capital city lain beyond. That route has a fairly-high incline and, to be honest, we're not exactly dressed for hiking as we will need to be."

"Very good, my friend!" Laughed Ven heartily. "You can lead our way then…" Spero reluctantly took lead in guiding his friends along Lake Tinomar's southern shoreline; it was undoubtedly a far more pleasant journey than their trek across Talam's scorching desert, which they were still recovering from. Eventually, after a couple of hours walking, the party reached a solitary jetty that sat peacefully within the lake's calm water, docked against it were some rusty-looking ferries that each swayed gently upon the passing current.

"I recognise this scene…" Thought Cara as she reimagined the image from Spero's photograph, she then looked to him with a curious expression. "This is where you and your little brother had that picture taken, wasn't it?" Spero appeared emotionless in his response to Cara, though within he was holding back the tears that were fighting against his restraint.

"Yes, Stevian loved coming here… it was his favourite place." Stammered Spero. "It hasn't changed a bit and neither have the ferries." He then gestured for his companions to board the ferry, once on deck they found several other sight-seers who were eagerly admiring Tinomar's magnificent lake - none seemed to notice the unlikely group of friends arrive.

"You can all make the most of these lake views, I'm going below deck to find the bar…" Said Spero in a frantic voice. "We've got a few silver coins left, should be enough for a few drinks?" He looked across to Cara with a hopeful expression, wishing that she may also join him, though she only continued to immerse herself within the grandeur of Tinomar's innate beauty.

"I'm sorry, Spero." Replied Cara begrudgingly. "I've waited my whole life to see Hydrania's lakes and mountains… I'll see you later, okay?"

"It may be wise for you to take some time alone," said Ven sympathetically to Spero, sensing his obvious remorse. "Get some rest and *please* don't drink too much… we will need your further guidance over the western pass, remember?" Muttered the Guardian sternly.

"I'll make sure he behaves!" Laughed Firin, he and Spero then swiftly made their way onto the steps which led below-deck towards the bar. "See you all in the morning…"

Cara loitered now in a solitary appreciation of the picturesque views around her, finding a gradual flowing release of her tensions in them of which she had not enjoyed for a long time. She made a fleeting glace over towards Ven, who himself was admiring the foreign surroundings, and the Guardian appeared to her as if he had fallen under some form of trance again.

"Have you visited this lake before, Ven?" Cara asked quietly in attempt to re-awaken him. "Are you even meant to leave your Sanctuary?" She observed happily at Ven's returning smile, which he made in response to her questioning of his spiritual duties. The Guardian scanned their tranquil surroundings once more and then made his way slowly over to Cara, placing a hand warmly upon her shoulder on reaching her whilst he allowed for more pleasant memories to flow back through him.

"I have been here before numerous times, though… very long ago now." Ven twisted his body to face eastwards, looking across the mountain range of Hydrania's western pass with an endearing grin. "Levia, the Guardian of Water, is my most-dearest friend and spiritual brother… we would often visit Tinomar together during the times of peace. I helped guide him in the ways of being an Elemental Guardian, shortly after his mentor Jendoro's untimely passing. I became both a teacher and consoling presence to Levia, but we also formed a unique friendship that has traversed the duty of our kin and has remained close ever-since."

A glint formed in Ven's eyes that Cara instantly understood, she could see that what Ven and Levia shared together in their relationship was something that she had dreamt for over most her life.

"You're talking about Levia like you haven't seen him for ages," Said Cara curiously. "Do neither of you spend time together anymore?" She whispered softly.

"Levia and I gradually discovered, that being away from our Sanctuaries over a lengthy period started to diminish the elemental powers within us…" Said Ven in a solemn tone. "We also found that the longer we spent in each-others company, the more we physically aged and our strength weakened. We still communicate through the Sanctuary portals in our Sanctum chambers, though, it is not the same as being with one another… I do miss those old days." Cara leant her head against Ven in empathy to his loss; she greatly wanted to know more about the friendship which he spoke of with Levia, and what it is truly like to be burdened with the gift of being a Spirit's host.

"I can imagine, that being a Guardian must be a very lonely task?" Openly contemplated Cara to Ven. She could keenly sense a strict similarity between their forced solitude, with her own being imprisoned within Magmorrah's royal palace years ago. "Despite the mighty powers you have, I get the feeling that they hold a control over your life, not the other way around."

"Yes, it can be hard at times." Replied Ven frankly. "I am afraid that I disagree with you though, about the elemental powers ruling over my destiny, for I make my own choices and paths to follow. Being a host to an Elemental Spirit is one of the highest honours that can be bestowed upon us mortals… a gift I freely give thanks to every day in appreciation."

"Does Levia feel the same way as you do?" Continued Cara, in her curiosity. "You said, he willingly chose to become a Guardian, didn't you Ven?" An eager look spread over her face, with each passing moment, Cara wished to learn more about the mysterious powers within Impartia.

"Levia willingly cast aside his material needs in loving memory of Jendoro, his predecessor, which also severed the divine duty he shared with Cerebrante to become Impartia's Spirit of Water incarnate…" Ven suddenly began to hesitate, he did not often dwell on these thoughts and felt no need in delving further into his or Levia's past – fearing Cara's reaction if she learned more regarding Cerebrante's recent history.

"What about the other Guardians as well, the ones we must eventually visit, are they as pleasant as you and Levia?" Asked Cara nervously, she felt reserved in meeting these other hosts and now wished to know more about them – for her own peace of mind, if anything.

"Far to the north of Talam, and held within a lake forged by molten lava, resides Impartia's Spirit of Fire at her monolithic Sanctuary – Pahoe. If I'm going to be honest, she is not as friendly nor understanding to outsiders as myself and Levia are…" Replied Ven cautiously to Cara. "Pahoe is a deeply private individual, and because of this, her Sanctuary is extremely hard to access on foot. She once had a bad experience with a prince from southern Talam and after their last confrontation together, Pahoe forged a surrounding plain of magma that now protects her Sanctuary and divides the north and south with towering mountains and a vast gorge beyond them; these were created only to deter any further pursuits this prince may have led against her… it was a sad tale for all involved that had so many dire consequences."

Cara felt a strange sympathy towards Pahoe, despite having not met her yet, as she knew all too well the stress such unwanted attention wrought with it. Also, the more Ven divulged into his brethren's individual characters, the more Cara came to understand that they were not the mysterious deities she had first envisioned but mortals after-all with faults and feelings of their own.

"Pahoe sounds quite feisty," Humoured Cara in a polite manner. "But, if her Sanctuary is surrounded by a lake of lava, how are we going to cross over it?" Her curious expression now turned to one of dread.

"Don't worry about that, Cara." Responded Ven assuredly. "For one thing, I helped Pahoe to make her more-earthly defences and secondly, our Sanctuaries are all linked together with spiritual portals that one can travel through to reach any of them; they are kept hidden within the Sanctum chambers on their central platforms… only a Guardian or their acolytes can authorise their use." Cara gave a noticeable sigh of relief on hearing this; she remembered how Ven had instructed his acolytes to shield Sophilia within their own Sanctum, though how safe her daughter truly was continued to concern the fearful mother.

"Well, that *is* good to hear!" She said ambiguously. "I am looking forward to meeting this Pahoe… I think that we may have a lot in common." Cara then deliberately left a moment for herself and Ven to enjoy the passing scenery around them, though soon turned back to her pursuing thoughts in relation with the other Elemental Guardians. "Well, that only leaves the Spirit of Air for you to tell me about now…what are they like and where is their Sanctuary?" Ven's demeanour seemed to change as he anxiously scanned the ferry's deck for any unwanted listeners, seemingly the only other person within earshot was Moah who gave no apparent need for concern – though only just.

"The Spirit of Air incarnate is called Aira… she is hidden well within Impartia and sadly has a very withdrawn existence." Said Ven in an obvious dismay to this fact. "She was using an ancient Sanctuary platform upon the sacred mountain of Skynah as her acolytes' recent place of residence, though Aira's Sanctum itself constantly shifts in the skies above us; it is a mysterious dwelling of which many have never heard of and even far-less have visited." Ven noticed Cara's puzzled expression in return, which he felt was justly understandable, given that no mortal could yet fly. "Aira is a perfectly-innocent soul with no earthly what-so-ever, her life instead is fully devoted to her spiritual duty and in protecting Skynah's holy mountain from any outside threats."

Cara quietly traced her mind back through the books on Impartia's landscapes she had read previously in Kanaan's library, recollecting that not one made a single reference to this 'sacred mountain' and her intrigue swiftly enflamed in yearning to gain more knowledge of it.

"Have you ever been to Skynah, Ven?" Asked Cara eagerly. "I must say, I've never heard of this mountain before…"

"That does not surprise me," mumbled Ven, as he carefully glanced around his and Cara's surroundings again. "King Kanaan spread rumours across the other lands that Skynah was haunted by monstrous demons, which itself is peculiar, because he frequented the mountain often in his later years… just before Cera dethroned him." The Guardian wisely scoured around himself and Cara once more as Queen Cera had many spies scattered throughout Impartia, though thankfully only Moah remained and was continuing to observe Lake Tinomar's unique features - seemingly oblivious to the clandestine conversation taking place nearby. "Once in a generation, myself and the other Elemental Guardians meet at one of our sanctuaries to discuss any issues that may have developed, our recent gathering was held at Skynah and involved us discussing Queen Cera's sudden rise to power and the growing influence of Kufiah's darkness." Said Ven in an ominous voice, he then smiled on seeing Cara's obvious infatuation to Skynah's mentioning again. "The holy site of Skynah is a gargantuan mountain centred within this world, its summit is shrouded densely by encircling heavenly clouds that reaches high into the atmosphere – a place of which no mortal has ever set foot on…"

"I know so little of Impartia," Said Cara woefully. "All these Spirits and sacred places, none of which I've ever heard of before…" Moah slowly approached Cara and Ven with a reserved look on his face, he had listened to their conversation and now felt a sudden urge to enlighten them further through his own wisdom.

"Please, if you will, pardon this intrusion of mine?" Stammered Moah anxiously. "I could not help but overhear some of your conversation…" Ven stared back intently at the Dark Acolyte in response, he was unsure and concerned to how much of his secretive discussion had been truthfully heard.

"You are more than welcome to join us, my friend." Replied Ven in uncertainty. "Do you have something to say… yourself?"

"I noticed how you only mentioned the Elemental Guardians and, in a way, suggested them to be Impartia's main spiritual protectors." Moah swallowed painfully as he spoke, in being fearful of how Ven may react to this observation. "What of the Celestial Guardians... that also exist?" Cara gasped curiously in response to Moah at this new revelation though Ven, however, was taken back by it. The muscular Guardian towered himself above the meagre-looking Dark Acolyte in waiting for a justifiable explanation, making it clearly obvious to Moah that he was uneased by his words.

"Cerebrante is the *only* Celestial Guardian," Snapped Ven in resolve. "There are no others..." Moah shook his and grinned to himself, he realised at this moment just how well King Kanaan had hidden his evil actions from the Elemental Spirits' knowledge. For *true* balance to exist, the elements of Impartia must be bonded to both light and darkness, meaning, there must be Guardians for them also..." He paused momentarily to think, then continued with caution. "For a Dark Acolyte, you seem to know a great deal regarding 'The Sacred Balance' and did you not hear what I said... that there is only Cerebrante to watch over Alaskia and Kufiah?" Scolded Ven, though deep down he wanted to know more for himself despite hating to admit it. "If I am to be incorrect, then please... prove your words to me." Cara placed a sympathetic hand upon Moah's arm and then looked across from him towards Ven, she sensed no malice from the Dark Acolyte's and his honest teachings - only a sinner in search for an absolution.

"Please, Ven... give Moah a chance to tell us what he knows." She carefully pleaded to the doubting Guardian. "If he knows something about Alaskia that we don't, then wouldn't that help us on our quest to reach them sooner... don't let your pride take over."

"It is not that I do not trust you," Assured Ven as he turned back slowly Moah. "I am... afraid... I am afraid of what you may know that we Elemental Guardians do not." The three now stood alone, lost quietly in thought, within darkness upon their ferry's deck; evening had finally arrived and Tinomar's lake around them shone serenely by the reflection of starlight above.

"Queen Cera held many talks with me and my fellow Dark Acolytes, regarding the mysteries of Impartia's Sanctuaries and their Guardians." Continued Moah. "Her Majesty did confess that she feels threatened by you - Cara, though she also spoke of a Guardian that protects Alaskia within the Spirit's Sanctum." Ven gently raised a palm to Moah in silencing him; his words had revealed more than just Cera's unstable paranoia, which was already a well-established fact by this point.

"Are you sure that you chose your words correctly there, Moah?" Questioned Ven sternly. "Alaskia is being held in their 'Sanctum'... not prison?" Moah swallowed heavily at having unwittingly granted this knowledge to Cara and Ven.

"Cera has spent the last decade trying to decipher where Kanaan imprisoned the Spirit of Light, her forces have already scoured their known Sanctuary in Weissamorrah and found nothing there… in her twisted mind, that leaves only one place left to infiltrate…"

"The pieces of King Kanaan's puzzle are starting to unravel," Said Ven in a gleeful tone. "We must reach Levia, maybe he will know a way to find this 'Guardian of Light' since he was once Cerebrante's host himself… a connection could exist between them?"

"I'm sorry, Ven." Replied Moah in contrast to the Guardian's hope. "The Guardian, who Cera believes is watching over Alaskia, is an aberration of nature… a by-product of Kanaan's cursed amulet… I doubt any real connection would exist between them and the other Spirit hosts."

"All that matters, is us finding Alaskia before my sister or General Nira do!" Interrupted Cara sternly. "My darling Sophilia is still in danger… and she needs her mother to be there for her."

"Saving you child will be our greatest priority, Cara." Replied Ven sincerely. "Let us get some rest now, we will have a mountain pass to traverse in a few hours and I am concerned to how fit Firin and Spero will be - after such a long period spent in this ferry's bar!" Ven cautiously led his companions back to their cabins, the air outside was growing even colder now with each passing second and a strange presence seemed to dwell upon Lake Tinomar – like a shadow following the party's every move.

The companions awoke a short-while later from the call of their captain; he signalled that they had arrived upon the shoreline facing Hydrania's western pass with a raucous bellow of his voice. Firin hastily left his cabin to grab any morsels of food available before his friends could, much to Spero's nuisance as both were suffering from their frivolous evening in the bar a few hours before. "I must say," Laughed the Captain as he inspected the unlikely group of travellers. "You all have such a strange fashion-sense. If you are wanting to travel the Western Pass, it would relieve my nerves if you would accept these coats to wear… you'll be walking up a mountain after-all." He then presented the companions with a set of thick overcoats for their perilous trek, despite being obviously used many times before, they would be a small comfort that was greatly appreciated by all who received them.

"Right!" Commanded Spero to grab the attention of his weary followers. "If I'm leading this journey, you'd better do as I say!" he then laughed faintly to himself on seeing the surprised expressions of his friends in return. "The Western Pass isn't that bad to cross, to be honest, but we will need to stick together…" The road laid ahead of the party climbed high into a range of mountains, situated just west before Hydrania's capital city. Slowly, they began to traverse its steep incline, occasionally losing their footing upon the rocks that shifted beneath them; Spero made a close observation of this and looked back to ensure his friend's safety.

"The path will level out soon enough!" Shouted Spero in confidence. "The Regent has seriously neglected this route… I wonder why?"

"Possibly due to the threat of foreign invaders?" Replied Moah knowingly. "The city's port will be heavily guarded… the mountain passes would be a perfect route for foot-soldiers."

"Can we *please* get some rest?" Begged Firin, who was still suffering from the copious drinks he had consumed the night before. "I'm not used to climbing mountains anymore!"

"You're out of shape, *soldier*!" Laughed Spero in taunt to Firin. "Try and keep up with me!" He boasted.

"I could beat you to this mountain's summit, easy!" Sneered Firin in response. "Just you watch me!" Ven was sensing Cara's own inner struggle in coping with their paining ascent, he supported her with his arms and then began to sing to a song; which itself seemed so strange yet familiar to Cara.

"Teach us with your isolation, free us with your love…"

"What is it that song you are singing, Ven?" Asked Cara who felt calmed by the hopeful words, though also intrigued by its haunting tone.

"It is the 'Hymn of Alaskia', a song that brings great strength to us Guardians in times of need… I hope, that these words will bring some comfort to you too Cara - as they do so for me?" Cara repeated the words again to herself; she had heard many songs throughout her short lifetime from the lands outside of Magmorrah, though this piece Ven was reciting to her now seemed so different.

"I don't understand," Moaned Cara, whilst innocently staring to Ven. "It sounds like when you are singing this song… you are hoping for someone to return… it's so… strange." Ven patted against Cara's back and laughed faintly at this observation, it was the exact reaction of which the wantful Guardian had desperately hoped to gain from her.

"Yes!" Said Ven in excitement. "That is *precisely* the meaning behind those beautiful words… the hymn is, in fact, a prophecy of which we Guardians came to be aware of some years ago - long before Cera's reign. Since time immemorial, the Spirits of Light and Darkness have both opposed one another, though, are also eternally drawn together in just the same way; Cerebrante is the power which unites Alaskia and Kufiah to create our world's destined balance." Cara still felt ignorant towards what Ven was teaching her, despite her best efforts to understand. They climbed a few more steps then turned back upon Lake Tinomar in the distance, its beauty again reminded Cara of the hope she would need in fulfilling this new quest of hers.

"If the hymn you sung to me is a prophecy for Alaskia, then I'm guessing that Kufiah has their own too?" Muttered Cara reluctantly. "Does that mean the Spirit of Darkness has a prophecy to suit their own fate?" Ven motioned his steps closer alongside Cara's but was now also looking behind to Moah, who was keeping a noticeable distance between himself and the other travellers.

"You are correct, Cara." Responded Ven in a foreboding tone. "The Hymn of Kufiah is sung just the same as Alaskia's, only, it is performed by those who have solely devoted themselves to the Spirit of Darkness – Cera's Dark Acolytes; you may remember hearing some of its verses back in Kufiah's Sanctum where it was used to empower your sister's connection the Dark Spirit?" The sinister voices of the Cera's Acolytes played back suddenly in Cara's thoughts, she quickly attempted to empty them from her mind and looked in a reluctant towards Moah - who now appeared to be looking upon a small, obsidian mirror held in his hands

"Why is it, that the only way we can gain access to Alaskia is with using passwords you and the other Guardian's grant?" Said Cara with a confused expression. "If that is so, then how did my father imprison them?" Ven halted his pace and then took Cara aside to rest upon a near-by boulder, the Guardian checked more stringently this time to ensure that their conversation was indeed being held private – also himself noticing Moah and his tablet, though this did not deter him from continuing the lecture.

"Kanaan used his connection with Cerebrante to achieve that sordid act; he used Kufiah to incarcerate Alaskia, there-after, we Guardians placed our own protecting seals over the Spirit of Light so that they could come to no further harm. The passwords we grant enter your soul, thus allowing access to Alaskia's hidden sanctum – once the bearer finds it." Cara didn't know how to react on hearing this, a mixture of anger and disbelief now toyed against her rational emotions from the feeble knowledge being revealed by Ven. She continued to vacantly journey ahead away from him, leaving the Guardian to wallow over his brethren's own lack of resolve.

"Have I upset you in some way, Cara?" Said Ven in a pleading voice to her back. "What I speak of is the truth, if we are to reach Alaskia before Cera and Nira to end of all this unnecessary suffering…" Cara turned around swiftly; a frustration took over her rational thoughts as she moved to face Ven directly which took the usually defiant Guardian by surprise, being such an unnatural display of anger for her.

"It is because of *you* and of the other Elemental Guardian's why we have to go on this ridiculous quest to find Alaskia… why does it have to be *me* that has to gain these passwords?" Seethed Cara with a trembling stutter. "Why couldn't you just have killed my father, instead of forcing me and Sophilia to take part in this war?" Ven was immensely remorseful for having placed Cara into this burdening position, though his reasoning soon returned to confront her again with these necessary truths.

"We Guardians do not have the strength required, even if united, against the rising power Kufiah now holds through your sister's control... only a remnant of Cerebrante does." Ven whispered sorrowfully. "It is as simple as this Cara, either you confront Cera and defeat her plans to extinguish Alaskia's light from this world... or allow for Sophilia and your child's generation to suffer the consequences. Only you and Sophilia hold the mark born by the Spirit of Balance, you alone have this choice to make Cara as I will not force you nor will any other from my kin... though, would you see Impartia fall into the void of Kufiah's making so willingly?" Cara staggered breathlessly as she absorbed what Ven had been saying to her. The Guardian slowly paced himself to meet with her once more, with his arms opened and head bowed respectfully as a sympathetic gesture to her.

"I'm sorry," replied Cara in a sad whisper. "It's just so much to take in..." She rubbed at her eyes slowly, trying to ease their burning fatigue.

"I know what is now asked of you is such a terrible responsibility to bear, Cara. Know this, as long I as I still hold breath in my body... I will do everything in my power to aid you in fulfilling this daunting task... all of us will help you... even if it costs us our lives."

Cara wrapped her arms tightly around Ven, whilst their fellow companions looked back to them in beleaguerment to what had just secretly transpired.

"I know that you are all here for me, Ven." Said Cara joyfully. "I *will* face my fears and do what I must, especially if it means saving my Sophilia from more harm... I must stay strong for her!"

"There is a strength in you, that has not yet been fully realised." Said Ven as he gave a determined smile to Cara. "You are doing this for you little girl and you are not alone."

The companions reached their mountain's summit sooner than expected thankfully, as Impartia's afternoon sun burst across the surrounding landscape to create a golden veil over it. Ven suddenly felt a renewed energy course through him, he made his way easily past Firin and Spero who had become exhausted and then held out his arms towards the sky above – also absorbing some of the powerful earthly energy that penetrated him beneath.

"We've made it!" Declared Ven in ecstasy, his words echoed over the many surrounding peaks to coax his friends forward - despite their fatigue. "Hydrania's capital city... where my good friend Levia's Sanctuary awaits!" Along with Hydrania's capital, the companions could now see for many miles around them: To the west, lay just in sight the golden desert shores of Talam, radiating like flames beyond Lake Tinomar's green pastures. To the south, lingered Magmorrah's harrowing ash clouds that stretched far over the horizon as a daunting reminder to what still haunted the travelling group of friends. Due north, Cara now noticed a large, triangular shape appear through the ocean's mist; she swiftly moved herself to question Ven about it.

"Is that… Skynah?" Asked Cara with a look of awe upon her face. "It's huge!" Ven nodded in agreement then looked upon the distant mountain for himself; Skynah rose mightily from its ocean depths, reaching many miles into the atmosphere above – it seemed. The mountain's summit was surrounded by dense, encircling clouds that had an enticing and heavenly appeal – proving to be an obvious symbol of the holy secrets hidden within.

"Skynah… Impartia's most-sacred mountain, yet so little is known about it." Replied Ven with a studious expression. "Between you and I, that is where I believe Alaskia may be imprisoned, but we must speak with Levia first to discover his own thoughts on this." The Guardian then allowed for Firin and Spero to take the lead once again on their descent from Hydrania's Western Pass.

"What was that?" Questioned Cara fearfully to herself; in the corner of her eye she had noticed an intense, blinding light that was immediately followed by a heavy dust storm that rose high above Eastern Talam. Moah had witnessed this strange spectacle also, the Dark Acolyte abruptly took Cara by her shoulders and then guided them away from the rest of their party.

"Please do not mention what you saw to the others," Commanded Moah anxiously. "Cera spoke of corrupting Kufiah's powers further and I think we have just witnessed such an attack by the Spirit of Darkness on Talam's capital – stay focused only on reaching your daughter, let me and the Elemental Guardians worry about this troubling event."

"We must tell Ven!" Snapped Cara in response. "What if my sister attacks Hydrania the same way, shouldn't we go somewhere safer?"

"Nowhere *at all* is safe from Kufiah," whispered Moah knowingly. "That is why I am telling you to stay focused on Sophilia… *our* main concern should be on where General Nira is at this moment anyway; I am surprised that she has not tracked us down by now." Cara and Moah silently joined their friends again, neither uttered a single word of what they had seen occur in Talam - in wake of the Dark Acolyte's reasoned warning. The companions each gazed in astonishment at the splendid waterfalls now encompassing Hydrania's capital lain before them, a deafening rush of water reverberated heavily over the city landscape that flowed steadily along endless streams of canals within it.

"It's just how I remember it… isn't the city amazing, Cara?" Said Spero as he hastily stood her before the nearest waterfall, a cooling haze from it instantly cleansed their tired skin and was greatly welcomed. "We can reach Levia's Sanctuary quicker on a taxi-boat, they travel along these streams which run through the city… we've done enough walking, haven't we?" Spero again took lead to guide his friends down the mountain side, aiming them carefully towards the nearest taxi-boat station. The vessels themselves, were deliberately narrow so that they could travel through the winding canals within Hydrania's ancient city; for Spero and his friends they were also thankfully long enough to seat all of them. A lone driver who was sat smoking a lengthy wooden pipe greeted the strangely-clad visitors with a respectful bow as they neared him, then with an eager gesture he ushered them to quickly board his boat.

"Ladies first!" Shouted Firin in authority. He grabbed Cara to throw her, albeit gently, into the taxi-boat whilst its unsuspecting driver looked on in horror to her embarrassment. "Take us to the Sanctuary of Water please… we have a very important meeting there with Levia – the Sanctuary's Guardian!"

"Commoners are not permitted to visit the Sanctuary," said the driver smugly, as he rolled his eyes back to Firin. "At least not without prior consent from the Acolytes or our Regent… you will need to show me evidence that permission has been granted for such a visit." Cara looked despairingly to Ven beside her, every second being wasted would surely be giving Queen Cera a greater advantage in reaching her daughter before she could. The Guardian closed his eyes then opened both again to stare upon the taxi-boat's driver with a radiant emerald glow in them – displaying his spiritual might.

"What are you doing?" Questioned the driver nervously. "How are you doing that… with your eyes?" The emerald light strengthened to surround Ven's whole body, it then flowed gently towards the driver and on touching the wooden pipe nestled between his lips created a single jade flower, which steadily rose from where ashes once lay.

"I am an Elemental Guardian also and yes, we do indeed exist." Whispered Ven with a smirk on his face. "No permission is required for me to enter Hydrania's Sanctuary… please, take us there." The driver nodded in beleaguerment to Ven's display of power, then at a slow pace his boat then made progress upstream into the city's main quadrant. Cara observed how the stream they were travelling along flowed into several smaller canals, each spread like veins throughout the capital and all lead to numerous grand housings. The city itself had been fashioned entirely from marble stone, its buildings stood like monuments with gigantic pillars supporting them and every house looked as though they were royal palaces - all were adorned with statues of their owners with various types of fauna strewn amongst them that thrived in the water-rich valley.

"Have you never thought of settling down in a place like this one day, Spero?" Suggested Firin, who himself glanced upon the grandeur around them and was also considering this proposal. "It's like a different world here…"

"Maybe - one day, Firin…" Replied Spero. "I've spent so long at sea though… I find it so hard to sleep at night on dry land!" The pair laughed at one another from this remark, but soon grew silent as they noticed that they were now entering the royal district of Hydrania's city. The surrounding palace walls towered over the party along their narrow canal - shadowing its waters from any reach of sunlight.

"Where is this Sanctuary you spoke of, Ven?" Questioned Moah nervously, as he now looked upon a large flowing waterfall ahead of them that cascaded tremendously into their present pathway. "It looks like we're coming up to a dead end?"

"You are looking at it, Moah!" Said Ven in excitement. "Levia's Sanctuary lies far underneath the royal palace and beyond this waterfall, we may get a little wet though on entering… just to warn you."

"You Guardian's take protecting your Sanctuaries very seriously!" Humoured Moah to Ven, who laughed back in return. "To be fair, *my* home lies hidden within a ruined city… so I can't exactly talk." The taxi-boat's driver reached beside himself for a small, protective umbrella; he then proceeded to erect it carefully above his head as the vessel gradually passed through Levia's shielding waterfall. The unprepared companions were instantly drenched by the waterfall's endless supply of water, whilst their driver stood smiling smugly back at them.

"Levia obviously has a sense of humour, Ven!" Chuckled Cara as she assisted Spero with draining the cold water from his saturated coat. "Couldn't he have thought of a warmer way for his guests to enter?"

"Indeed, he does… Levia has fantastic humour!" Replied Ven, who himself felt no discomfort from the waterfall's freezing rapids. "On my previous visits to Levia, I had the luxury of my Sanctum portal to transport me here… a far-drier way of entry, I must admit!"

"Levia won't be laughing when I see him!" Snapped Firin, as he removed a copious amount of water from one of his desert boots into the canal. "His waterfall has *ruined* my clothes… and I smell like a wet animal now!"

"You stunk anyway!" Responded Spero eagerly. "It won't hurt for you to have a bath…"

Ven grinned discreetly as he looked over the expressions of displeasure in his companions' faces, all still attempting to dry themselves despite the growing darkness of the Sanctuary's entranceway now intensifying around them.

"It's getting really dark in here, this isn't very inviting…" Murmured Cara anxiously to Spero. "I feel like we're back in the Kufiah's Sanctuary, it's so cold and the air is so thick."

"It is meant to be that way, the intention being to put off any would-be intruders." Explained Ven in a frank manner. "We will be given a friendly welcome, trust me… I wouldn't be surprised if Levia knew we were already here."

"Will he be so kind towards a servant of darkness… such as me?" Asked Moah to Ven in an anxious tone. "I have heard of how powerful Levia is, even Queen Cera fears that Guardian… though she does not openly admit it."

"Do not be so concerned with how Levia will greet you," Assured Ven. "He is most understanding towards others and especially to one as brave as yourself - who has turned from their forsaken path… Cera though, is right to be afraid of him." Moah nodded in appreciation to Ven's show of empathy, however inside his own thoughts, the Dark Acolyte contemplated what move his tyrannical Queen would be plotting next - knowing somehow that soon their paths would once again cross.

Back in Magmorrah, far within the depths of Kufiah's dark Sanctuary, General Nira rose herself cautiously from where she had knelt before Queen Cera. She was becoming steadily conflicted by the peculiar orders being given to her, something of which the submissive General had never felt prior.

"Your Divine Highness, I beg of you!" Seethed Nira, whilst kneeling in subservience before her Queen. "Send *me* with our elite soldiers to kill your accursed sister... once and for all!" Cera was proudly seated upon the throne of Kufiah, her eyes deliberately kept away from meeting with those of the enraged General who was desperate in trying to unite them.

"I believe, the fugitives would have travelled to Hydrania as a most-likely place of refuge... my sources have informed me also that the Earth Guardian, who is travelling with Cara, is closest to his counterpart there more than any of the other Spirit rats... they are *all* a serious threat to your crown and *must* be terminated!" Nira swiftly cowered herself beneath Cera, who now rose sharply in response from Kufiah's throne to stand over her defiant General. With a sadistic grin, the wicked Queen placed a hand into her silken robes to retrieve a small obsidian tablet, afterwards Cera signalled for her loyal Acolytes to step closer in surrounding the fearful General - who herself remained fixed upon the centre of their Sanctum platform.

"Let me do the thinking, Nira." Sneered the Queen cruelly. "Firstly, Hydrania's Regent has finally dared to enter my sovereign waters and this act, I assure you, will not go unpunished. Despite your logic, my sister and her *friends* are not in the Water Lands as you suspect they are... I will explain shortly how I know of this truth for a far-more pressing task shall now be bestowed on you; one far-worthier of your valiant skills!"

"I am forever your humble servant," continued Nira, whilst she trembled fearfully. "I will carry out any duty without further question." The General then looked around Cera's Dark Acolytes as they mustered themselves into alignment, Nira despised each of them equally and saw now real purpose in them being there with herself or her Queen. "What is your bidding, Majesty...?" Cera hastily gestured for Nira to rise once again and then leaned herself into the General's personal space, clasping onto her father's accursed amulet which adorned her emaciated neck as she did so.

"My *dearest* Nira, Hydrania's imminent defeat will be child's play compared to this honourable mission you are now to accomplish!" Cackled the Queen in delight. "Take our elite warriors and return to the Sanctuary in Viridia *at once*, we shall kill two birds with one stone... I will destroy the Spirit of Light and finish Cerebrante's interference, whilst you are to retrieve my sister's child and bring her before me... dead or alive!" Nira motioned again to interrupt Cera; she did so in being wary of her Queen's increasing and unpredictable agitation that was rising with each passing moment between them.

"The Sanctuary… it… *cannot* be breached!" Exclaimed Nira in dismay. "No weapon we have can penetrate the protective seal which its Guardian has fashioned, we have already tried and failed to achieve this when capturing Cara…" Cera hatefully clasped onto Nira's jaw with her skeletal fingers, piercing the General's flesh painfully with her ill-kept nails that were more-alike to talons in their appearance. The evil Queen's patience was now growing thinner with each obstacle Nira was inadvertently throwing at her, she started to also feel that her loyal General had forgotten her place somehow within their inner circle. A fiery flame began to burn within Cera's darkened pupils that wrought a great terror in them, they were the eyes of Kufiah, a sign of her own imminent fall as she had delved far too deep in repeatedly summoning the Dark Spirit's powers.

"Do you take me for a fool, Nira?" Scorned the Queen as she violently shook her General's face. "I *know* of the Sanctuary seal and of its Guardians' protecting power, the forests that surround it however, do not harness this same defence… do they?" Cera then cast Nira upon the Sanctum platform's hard surface, whilst the Dark Acolytes now circled even closer in surrounding her.

"Forgive me!" Pleaded Nira in a regretful voice. "I serve only you and will do whatever you ask of me… my Queen!"

"Burn Viridia to the ground! Leave *nothing* but ashes… let us see how the treacherous Earth Guardian likes that!" Screeched Cera maliciously at the thought of Ven's looming despair. "The proceeding smoke should draw out anyone who dwells inside the Sanctuary and if that fails, though I highly doubt it, my Acolytes here have created a unique gift that they have especially made just for you… it will certainly aid in fulfilling your mission!"

Nira studied closely at a crude, golden pendant that was now being placed into her hands by Cera's leading Acolyte; she accepted it freely though looked back to her Queen with a further expression of rage and perplexment against this unorthodox item.

"How will this *trinket* possibly help me gain access to Viridia's Sanctuary…" Questioned Nira bitterly. "Should I bride one of the Acolytes with it, so that they will let me in?"

Cera unexpectedly laughed at Nira's sarcastic response, she then waved a hand to dismiss her Dark Acolytes away from Kufiah's Sanctum to leave only herself and the devoted servant within it.

"That *trinket* is imbued with the same dark magic which powers my amulet…" Sniggered Cera knowingly. "When worn, it will give you the ability to disguise yourself as Cara…her clothes… her features… everything down to the smallest vile detail!"

"I am to transform into that *wretch*?" Gasped Nira as she fought against a flow of rising vomit that crept into her mouth. "I hate her, more than any other!"

"It is a small price to pay, if we are to succeed in fulfilling our greater destiny!" Declared Cera sternly. "For a gallant warrior such as yourself, dealing with my sister's offspring will be easy... so stop complaining." The Queen smirked again at her sub-ordinate's obvious disgust, then after briefly staring upon the obsidian tablet she sat back down upon Kufiah's throne – resolved in her actions and malicious intent.

"I will do what you ask of me," Stammered Nira in return. "Before I leave for Viridia though, I wish to ask how Talam shall be dealt with... they *are* harbouring known enemies of our glorious nation, after-all?" Cera gave a wicked grin towards Nira's want of cruelty, it was a satisfaction of which they both enjoyed immensely. The Queen then gently coursed her fingertips over Kanaan's amulet to sense its dark energy within, as it gave rise to a demonic power which itself presently festered deep inside of her fragmented soul.

"Talam has already fallen, Nira!" Screamed Cera, as she clasped onto her amulet in ecstasy. "You have so little faith in me, its almost treasonous." She glared with intent.

"How, your Majesty?" Whispered the General eagerly. "We have no troops stationed there yet?"

"The Spirit of Darkness and I, our connection together grows stronger every day... we have created a cursed crimson jewel that harnesses Kufiah's ultimate power of mass destruction." Said Cera as she clapped her hands manically. "I call it... a *Kufian Shard*... with this new and terrible weapon the people of Impartia will bow before me freely, or instead bask in their total decimation! One of my Dark Acolytes infiltrated Talam's capital city, it now rightfully lies as ashes... one more Kufian Shard exists though it serves a different purpose." A sickening lust swiftly filled Cera's entire being as she joyfully contemplated what horrid fate had befallen the desert lands under her will.

"You did it," replied Nira excitedly. "Finally, after all these years of trying... you have mastered that Celestial Spirit!" The General then gave a discerning look as she inspected her pendant again. "Your plan is reaching its finale... but, it will take me days to reach Viridia's Sanctuary now with the amount of Hydranian warships patrolling our waters!"

"Ahhh, Nira." Sighed Cera dismissively. "I have left the greatest surprise for you until last... Magmorrah once boasted vessels that could fly as if they were weightless birds, though strong as the obsidian which forged this very Sanctuary. Hidden within the ruined city that surrounds us, now exists such an airship which I have named *Divinity*...it shall take you to Viridia's Sanctuary in no time, though I must warn you, your cousin Desirah has been chosen to be its Captain." Nira screeched despairingly on hearing her cousin's name being mentioned, they shared a conflictive past and one that the General felt could never be healed.

"Once I have brought the child to you, may I take Desirah's life?" Pleaded the General scornfully. "It would be a small price to pay in compensation for my utter devotion to you..."

Cera cackled almost uncontrollably at this show of malice from Nira, she then waved a hand at her General in dismissal with a teasing wink to part with.

"Use that hatred once you reach Viridia's Sanctuary…" Warned Cera cautiously. "It may be needed, if the Guardian of Earth should return unexpected."

"I do not fear that pathetic sprite," retorted Nira proudly, with her hands held firmly upon her General's sword. "If he does turn up somehow… my blade would soon meet with his throat!" She and Cera then cackled together, their haunting voices travelled throughout Kufiah's Sanctuary to disturb even the Dark Acolytes themselves.

Chapter Five: The Cavern of Eternal Waters

The entranceway to the Sanctuary of Water was held deep within an ancient, cavernous hall that was saturated with a mystical haze. The gloomy cavern itself was dimly lit by several torches, each placed strategically along numerous marble columns that stood as supports to a great doorway; on carefully stepping ashore from their taxi-boat, the drenched companions woefully tipped their driver with what silver they had left then made their way towards it.

"These look familiar," said Moah, as keenly observed some strange symbols which were etched upon the door's archway. "They look different to ones in my Sanctuary though…" The Dark Acolyte felt a residual remorse towards leaving his now-distant 'home', though this contemplation was suddenly disturbed as the massive door opened - seemingly without any obvious authority given for it to do so.

"These symbols describe Impartia's first Guardian of Water and their purpose to serve Cerebrante," interrupted Ven to share his wisdom. "That is why they appear strange to you… they did to me when I first saw them." The grandeur of Levia's entrance corridor was beyond anything the group of friends had expected, they entered along its pristine path which was adorned with further marble columns that lined along it. A long row of statues lay to either side that were each dedicated to the Sanctuary's previous Guardians and Acolytes; the realistic figurines spoke without any words of the immortal reign that the Water Spirit held within its earthly hosts and centred within them was a thin stream that flowed steadily towards another cavernous hall.

"Levia is greatly respectful to those who served this Sanctuary before him, these statues were lovingly made by none other than himself… with some help from me." Said Ven proudly. Cara stood herself before one of the life-like statues that she somehow felt a connection with, it was far grander in size and workmanship compared to the others and below was a silver plaque which read:

'Brother Jendoro: Our most beloved Guardian of Water and greatest mentor. Taken without reason, though never lost within our hearts. Rest on peacefully now in Eternamorrah.'

Ven noticed Cara's keen interest in Jendoro's statue as he too observed it for himself. He then sighed in a genuine pity at recognising his old friend who had passed away so sadly - the grief he felt for him remained just as strong as it did then.

"He was a good soul, was Jendoro." Stammered Ven sorrowfully. "He is sincerely missed by both my kin and Levia's older acolytes, I only wish, that we could have found an explanation as to what actually killed him..."

"Jendoro... was murdered?" Questioned Cara in shock. "I thought, Elemental Guardians were immortal?" She stammered apprehensively.

"Jendoro's death was unnatural; that is all we know." Whispered Ven in caution. "Please, do not mention him at all to Levia... he still grieves heavily for his fallen friend."

"Why does the plaque refer to him as being a 'Brother'?" Asked Cara, feeling it was a question that may not be too personal for Ven to answer in this solemn moment. "Are you all related in some way... such as my family seem to be with Cerebrante?" Ven folded his arms across his torso then walked away from Cara without a further word, he was held in a quiet reflection of what she had just asked and felt greatly disturbed by it.

"What's wrong, Ven... why won't you answer me... I was only asking a simple question, wasn't I?" Cara stormed herself in front of Ven to bar his path, feeling slightly angered by his restraint in answering her. The Guardian held his lips tightly shut and his mannerism swiftly changed to that of a nervous one when looking upon Cara - the question she had asked of him was not as simple to resolve as she hoped it would be.

"Spirit Gaurdians are not related, Cara. We only refer to ourselves as brothers and sisters out of a mutual respect to one another." Ven swallowed heavily as he struggled to continue with speaking. "The spiritual cycle of this world is not a hereditary one...and *shouldn't* be. Cerebrante's current cycle is something myself and the other Guardians cannot rationalise, as to how and why the Spirit's mark has travelled through one bloodline for so long... it can only be from your father and his agents of evil corrupting this primordial existence."

"I still don't understand," replied Cara wearily, with an intricate stare. "Was Father not chosen by Cerebrante?"

"The Spirit of Balance *does* have a free will of their own to choose a worthy mortal, I sense though, that this freedom has been manipulated in some-way... but by whom remains a mystery." Said Ven as he quickened his steps towards his awaiting companions. "There are many forces at work in this world... some are more discreet than others."

"Come on you two!" Commanded Firin impatiently to Cara and Ven. "Don't you want to meet up with this Levia character?"

"Sorry, Firin." Replied Cara sympathetically to him. "We're coming..."

At the end of the passageway, lay a grand hall which rose high in its splendour above the awestruck companions situated within. At the centre, was a crystal chandelier which swayed gently above a towering fountain that flowed endlessly beneath it. The fountain itself, sprayed several bursts of water from a set of statues that were skilfully fashioned into to it by the Sanctuary Acolytes – a sight Spero immediately enjoyed. Opposite the entrance and beyond the hall's magnificent fountain, stood another opening that led itself further into the Sanctuary's catacombs. Five figures gradually began to emerge from the opening, all dressed in deep-blue robes with silvered seams that ran across them; they were Levia's devoted Acolytes and each observed the fountain for themselves as they approached their unexpected guests – also removing their long hoods to greet them more personally.

"Welcome… to our humble abode." Said a lone female acolyte, who keenly stepped forward to inspect her guests more closely. "We are here to aid you in any way that we can during your stay… what is the purpose of your visit to our sacred halls, may I ask?" She then ran her eyes discreetly over the strangely clad strangers; on noticing Ven she broke her initial reserve to express a joyous smile towards him.

"My goodness, you look so much older now." Muttered the acolyte as she knelt herself before Ven in respect to him "Sorry, I was meant to say that… it is such a privilege seeing you again after so long." Ven merely laughed off the acolyte's rude comment and returned his own pleasantries towards her with a reassuring smile, he instantly recognised her to be Levia's most trusted student and follower - Lenya. For a leading acolyte, Lenya looked very youthful for her age and outwardly appeared very relaxed. She was unnaturally tall for a woman and her hair was a unique silver colour, that matched a reflective radiance in the acolyte's eyes.

"Greetings, Lenya." Said Ven humbly, and with a respective bow. "I am also glad to be back here in these beautiful halls… seeing you again has greatly raised my spirits." He extended a hand to assist Lenya to her feet from the knelt position she had been in, whilst the other acolytes remained unmoved as they still focused on the strangers stood behind Ven.

"Have you come to speak with Levia?" Questioned Lenya in a hopeful voice. "He has expressed his own wishes to meet with you and the other Guardians, particularly over the past few days or so." She then gestured for her fellow acolytes to assist the weary travellers along a descending passageway that led further into their Sanctuary.

"Yes… it is a matter of urgency that I see him as soon as possible." Said Ven with a sombre expression on his face, despite fighting against it. "Lenya, it is with ill-tidings that we are visiting your Sanctuary; the darkness of Kufiah and Queen Cera is spreading fast now over Impartia… what she is planning to do next is far worse than any of us previously imagined."

"I will take you to our Sanctum at once," relied Lenya anxiously, her eyes still firmly set on Ven. "Levia will be in there meditating, he has suspected recently that Cera has been plotting something terrible. The assassination attempt on Hydrania's Regent was a brash move, even for her…" Lenya then suddenly noticed the distinct mark of Cerebrante upon Cara's face, her eyes widened in fright and all around seemed to become a horrifying blur.

"Your Highness," whispered Lenya with an intrigued smirk. "You are King Kanaan's first-born… aren't you?" Cara grimaced in response to her father's name, though felt no ill-feelings against Levia's observant follower.

"My name is Cara… Kanaan *is* my father," said Cara in a regretful tone. "I am nothing like him though, and if you could not mention his name again it would be greatly appreciated."

"Trust me, I *hate* King Kanaan just as much as you do. How is Magmorrah faring under your sister's rule anyway?" Asked Lenya in an impulse reluctance, then as Cara moved to reply the acolyte raised her hand abruptly in dismissal. "Never mind, I'd rather not be told… please follow me and I shall take you to Levia." Sunlight faintly seeped through the passageway which Lenya and her guests now travelled along; its appearance confounded each of the companions as to how it could have reached such a far depth underground. The radiant light grew intensely as they entered, Lenya quickly actioned her hands to halt the other acolytes before an entrance to an outer cavern - which itself echoed with a deafening, roaring sound.

"You must pass this, the 'Trial of Eternal Waters'… if we are to reach Levia's Sanctum." Declared Lenya as she held out her hands toward a cavernous sinkhole; it was located outside within a syphon of waterfalls that flowed from surrounding mountains - the pummelling rapids coursed into the gaping hole making it seemingly impossible to reach. "We have needed to tighten our defences of late, which is why doing this trial is now necessary." Ven stepped away from his terrified companions towards Lenya, he looked at her with pleading eyes then shook his head against the horrifying scene lain before them.

"Is there *really* a need for us to pass such a trial, Lenya?" Questioned Ven sternly to her. "My friends are in the company of a fellow Sanctuary Guardian, are they not… I permit their entry and Levia himself will surely not mind me doing this?" Lenya lowered her head and then shook it disagreeably at Ven, she also showed no change in her stance afterwards regarding the drastic measure her Guardian had put into place and merely pointed again towards his violent rapids.

"Levia is never strict with anything, but he has insisted that *all* must take this trial in order to acquaint themselves with our most-sacred chambers…" Said Lenya firmly. "You said it yourself, Ven… a darkness is now spreading which we cannot allow here." Lenya suddenly noticed Moah, who until this point had hidden himself from view behind Firin and Spero, she took her eyes away from him for a thoughtful moment and then looked back with an obvious scorn upon her face.

"What is the meaning of bringing such a vile creature to our Sanctuary, Ven?" Seethed Lenya. "Is this some sort of perverse joke made on our behalf... do you not see a Kufian Acolyte stood amongst you, as I do?" Ven held an arm out to Moah with an open palm, inviting him over to join him; The Dark Acolyte placed himself anxiously beside his new friend as the Guardian smiled reassuringly to Lenya - who remained held in her own preservation of this unusual sight.

"This is Moah and yes, he *was* once in the service of Queen Cera though he has cast this shadow from him willingly... without any other's influence." Reiterated Ven keenly. "Moah aided us in escaping from Cera's wrath at a great cost, I trust this man with my life Lenya... please trust him as we do." Lenya shuddered noticeably in having to associate herself with the unwelcome presence of Moah; she however gestured to Ven that she acknowledged his words, though with a great deal of doubt, then led the Guardian and his companions closer towards Levia's whirlpool.

"I trust your judgement, Ven..." Whispered Lenya to him discreetly. "Though how Levia will react, I cannot guarantee... he is fearful of anyone who may be associated with Queen Cera."

"Do not forget your own past," countered Ven instinctively. "A person's nationality should not force them to be condemned in such a way..." A deafening roar echoed around Cara and her companions as they neared the violent water rapids, she stood alone in fixation upon Levia's vortex which itself seemed to fall into an endless pit below. The one consolation was the beauty created through an array of sunlight which penetrated the surrounding waterfalls – though this did not diminish her fear in any way. Spero and Firin by now, had become swiftly impatient with the 'games' which they felt Levia's acolytes were now playing with them.

"What kind of trial is this?" Questioned Firin angrily. "This isn't a test... it's suicide!"

"Do you honestly expect us to throw ourselves into that pit of death, willingly?" Said Spero in support. "You must think we're mad!" Ven made a futile attempt to calm Firin and Spero's frustration, though despite his best efforts they incessantly continued to whinge about their unfortunate circumstances. Without any effect gained in reassuring his stubborn friends, Ven turned again to confront Lenya in a disbelief towards Levia's obvious act of desperation.

"There must be an easier path, Lenya... do you believe that I would jeopardise Levia's Sanctum and forsake our Order?" Pleaded Ven in dismay. "I promise you, with all my being, that Moah here is of no threat to any of us... my companions are worthy and with each second wasted Queen Cera and her forces grow ever-stronger!"

"Please, Lenya... *please* end this charade and let us meet with Levia." Said Cara with an air of authority in her voice. "Cera has threatened to take my little girl's life and your Guardian may be the only person who can help us save her now... also, I have no doubt that General Nira will be the one who is charged with capturing my Sophilia." Lenya gave a knowing look of grave concern to Cara on her saying this, she placed her hands tenderly upon the grieving mother's and a surge of positive energy suddenly flowed between them.

"Nira is pure evil and dare I say it, even more malicious than your sister... in some ways." Said Lenya solemnly. "We cannot allow for her to take your child, I beg you, have faith and take this trial... you will all pass if you are pure and mean no harm to our Guardian." Spero stubbornly marched himself past Lenya in response to Cara's sadness, she looked over his approach towards the vortex with an intrigue and felt a pride in his resolute bravery.

"A leap of faith is it?" Boasted Spero to Firin. "Then I will go first... I have faith in passing this ridiculous test, especially if it means that we'll see Levia sooner!" Spero then threw himself heavily into the swirling rapids, much to Cara's horror, and was closely followed by Firin who dragged Moah in with him. Ven held protectively onto Cara as they followed pursuit of their companions into the perilous waters, the whole time he sang Alaskia's hymn as a means to strengthen their precarious actions.

"Nira..." Muttered Lenya to herself scornfully. "What I would do just to have just ten minutes alone with that monster." The rushing waters instantly compelled the helpless companions as they fought hard against a flurry of thrashing rapids surrounding them. Cara searched blindly through the swirling water for Spero though could not find him to her sorrow, she was still holding tightly onto Ven who himself panicked about their uncertain descent - Suddenly, the deafening roar fell into a peaceful silence as the friends landed in a pool situated within a vast cavern.

"That wasn't so bad," Laughed Firin in relief at having survived such a terrifying ordeal. "At least this water is warm..." He sighed happily.

"It *is* warm!" Rejoiced Cara, after taking in a great gasp of air. "This is so strange..." The companions gradually emerged themselves from the mysterious pool and all were thankful to find that they were unscathed from such a large fall, soon they each crept upon a marble bank and in amazement discovered that their clothes instantly dried. The cavern that they now found themselves within was noticeably different in comparison to the others; it was not laden with statues and decorated stone, but instead had been formed solely by a dense earth that had compacted naturally with many fossils of prehistoric life which were scattered throughout its walls. Ven could sense the strong earthly presence around him, he placed his hands carefully upon the cavern walls and instantly felt Levia's familiar presence flow back into them.

"The spiritual energy in here is... powerful." Said Ven quietly to Cara. "Levia's Sanctum is not far from where we are now, it will be only a matter of time before we reach him."

"I am more concerned about Sophilia's safety than meeting your friend," Replied Cara nervously. "The look on Lenya's face when I mentioned Nira has only made me worry more."

"I will be swift in discussing what needs to be done with Levia," Assured Ven, he then smiled gleefully as now in sight was a solitary stone door. "The true Sanctuary of Water lies beyond this..." He excitedly raised a palm upon the door, and without further delay Ven fed his spiritual energy deep into it. "Permit us to enter...Levia!" The door's lock released slowly from Ven's grasp, as it opened a strange noise resonated from far within.

"What is that noise?" Asked Firin whilst he shielded his ears from it. "It sounds awful!" Pleasant pipe organ music now echoed across the mirroring walls around Firin and his friends. As the company moved closer towards this heavenly sounds, the streams that travelled beside the path on either side of them moved back and forth as if they were waves upon an ocean. Cara felt a calming sensation fill her entire body as she watched the minute waves flow back and forth together, almost hypnotising her with their transient movements.

"Are you sure that it's a good idea, me being here?" Questioned Moah to Ven as he moved himself closer beside him. The Dark Acolyte was now fully conscious of his unwelcome presence within Levia's Sanctuary and the daunting thought of actually meeting a Guardian other than Ven now filled him with an uncertain sense of dread and foreboding. "I don't think it is..."

"You have nothing to fear, my friend." Said Ven wearily. "If you are respectful to Levia and his Sanctuary... no harm will come to you." Firin and Spero pushed at one another in jest as they attempted to knock themselves into the shifting streams beside them. Firin unwittingly lost his balance and placed a foot within the sacred stream, as he did a burst of water formed a whip which grabbed at his ankle and threw him back upon the narrow pathway - much to everyone else's amusement.

"What just happened to me?" Responded Firin jokingly, though in secret he felt unnerved by the phantom prankster's actions. Suddenly, a mighty voice travelled across the passageway in response; it came from a doorway set high above another chamber with a set of crystal-like steps leading up to it – evidently where the ethereal pipe music was coming from.

"I do not appreciate you soiling my purified stream with your filthy boots, son of Talam!" Resonated the haunting voice in a humorous manner. *"Please my honourable guests... come forth!"* The Organ music greatly rose in its pace and volume, lifting the streams around the companions so that their currents flowed even harsher into one another. Ven quietly gestured to each of his friends to remain within the centre of their pathway, hoping to avoid any further upset, as they made a slow approach towards the steep stairwell ahead.

"I'm more scared now than I was back at Kufiah's Sanctuary," Whispered Spero to Cara nervously. "I thought you said Levia was friendly, Ven... I'm not really getting that impression, so far."

"Out of us Elemental Guardians, I would say personally that Levia is the gentlest." Said Ven in dismissal to Spero's angst. "Do be respectful to him when we enter his Sanctum, though… Levia is a very sensitive soul." After traversing the narrow stairs, Cara and her companions found themselves entering a vast cavern that had several small rooms situated either-side to a gargantuan sealed door. Ven quickened his steps towards the great doorway whilst he clapped his hands ecstatically; just above were the now-familiar seals of Impartia's Elemental Spirits - one of which glowed faintly with a pale blue light.

"This is it…Levia's Sanctum!" Shouted Ven in a child-like excitement. "It's been so long…" Inside the ancient Sanctum were countless waterfalls that cascaded around its inner platform into a large whirlpool beneath in many varying colours. At the back of the sacred chamber, sat the small figure of man who was clad in blue robes; he was joyfully playing on, what appeared to be, a pipe organ and at first did not seem to notice the arrival of Cara and her friends. The instrument he was playing on was fashioned from precious sapphire gems; they reflected the surrounding waterfall's beautiful colours and by using their powerful rapids fuelled what eminent music was being performed.

"What took you so long…" Questioned the figure abruptly. "Was my trial *really* that hard to pass?" The figure then halted in their performance to greet his awestruck guests, all that remained now from the pipe organ's disuse were the rushing sounds of the Sanctum's clashing waterfalls to echo eerily throughout its vast chamber. A long, mimetic gaze quickly formed between the two Spirit Guardians as they stood themselves in front of one other; each were held gladly within this savoured moment of reflection.

"My dearest Levia… how I have missed you and your music!" Exclaimed Ven, as he walked closer to his estranged counter-part. "Your trial *did* take some courage from us to pass, I must admit."

"Brother Ven, how I have missed your kind compliments…" Replied Levia. "They never grow old, and neither do you, seemingly!" The two Guardians then embraced in a genuine show of affection to one another, having spent so long away from sharing in their close company. "I cannot describe what a pleasure it is to see you again in person, my oldest friend… I only wish though, that it were in more pleasant times." Cara keenly observed that Levia was much shorter in comparison to Ven, though no-less imposing to those who had not familiarised themselves with him. Levia's ancient blue robes were delicately laced with silver threads and he had rugged-red hair that fell just above his eyes and shoulders. The Guardian of Water's eyes glimmered with a similar light to Ven's; though his shone with a radiant azure colour that seemed even greater in their intensity from the waterfall's reflecting lights around them.

"Welcome to the Sanctum of Water… friends of Ven!" Rejoiced the Guardian sincerely to an awkward silence in response from his other, more reserved, guests. "I am Levia… Impartia's present Guardian of Water and this Sanctuary of mine, which you are so kindly gracing, shall protect you all from any outside threat." Levia then politely examined the strangers placed before him; he was greatly intrigued by their unique appearances and varying facial expressions. "I see the children of many nations here…"

"It is a long story," quirked Ven with a tired yawn. "I will gladly explain to you why we have come here…so unexpectedly." Levia suddenly fell silent and his manner grew rigid; a wave of anxiety coursed over him upon seeing Cerebrante's mark on Cara's face, though the Guardian thankfully managed to force himself against addressing this shocking realisation yet - feeling this could be taken up with Ven later and within a more private setting.

"Your explanation can wait for now, Ven… you must take some much-needed rest." Said Levia more calmly, then he turned towards the other weary travellers. "I'm looking forward to accustoming myself with you all, but for now, please enjoy my Sanctuary… and try to relax." At this moment Lenya, Levia's most trusted Acolyte, entered the ancient Sanctum with a more endearing expression towards her guests than before. She bowed to the Elemental Guardians and then strangely, Cara.

"What are you doing?" Asked Cara in dismissal to Lenya's peculiar gesture. "Please don't do that, there is no need." She replied awkwardly, sensing that Lenya knew more about her than she was letting on.

"I am only showing my respect to you…Princess." Replied Lenya in a frank manner. "It does not matter to me if you've been exiled; you are still a Princess of Magmorrah to me, to a fellow Magmorran who cannot stand that monstrous queen!" She suddenly snapped, displaying an anger so unlike what would be expected from peace-loving Acolytes.

"Get up, Lenya!" Humoured Levia in sensing Cara's awkwardness. "Can you please escort our guests to their chambers and ask the other acolytes to prepare this evening's meal?" He politely gestured towards the Sanctum's doorway.

"Yes, of course." Said Lenya as she righted herself towards the companions. "Your personal chambers are located to either-side of the Sanctum… follow me."

"In the meantime, now that we have *some* privacy, I would like to hear this story of yours…Ven." Muttered Levia with a knowing glance to his friend. "I believe that there will be much to discuss between ourselves."

"Yes… there certainly is." Said Ven in a foreboding tone, he was then discreetly motioned towards a hidden staircase by Levia which lay behind a wall of ivy outside the Sanctum.

"Lenya will take good care of your friends," assured Levia calmly, whilst he revealed the hidden entranceway to Ven. "We will be safe from any unsavoury listeners in here…" Spero looked back to the two Guardian's anxiously, noticing how secretive their departure seemed to be, then turned to Cara who was walking alongside him.

"What do you think they will talk about together, Cara?" Questioned Spero. "It must be something bad if they can't trust us to listen in on them."

"Who knows?" Shrugged Cara defensively. "There's so much about the Spirits and their burdens that we don't understand, and I don't think it is our place to interfere with them." She then turned away from Spero in trying to conceal her own doubts; he in turn moved to face her again and was slightly perturbed by this dismissive remark.

"I think, that that you know more about these Spirits and their Guardians than what you're admitting to…" Snapped Spero in frustration. "Just be honest and tell us, we're here to support you Cara… but you need to be honest!" The mark of Cerebrante suddenly started to fade more upon Cara's face, as did her affections towards Spero.

"I know just as much as you do!" Seethed Cara, her amber eyes intensified in their angry display. "What makes you believe that I'm hiding something from you?"

"Don't think that none of us noticed how Levia recoiled… when he looked at your mark." Replied Spero more delicately. "I may be wrong, but I believe the Guardians are actually scared of you and are only using us to serve their own purposes." Cara slapped Spero's face in response, with enough force to knock him onto his back; she had hit him hard both emotionally and physically by reacting this way. She then raised a hand again, though this time in aid of Spero as Lenya and the others moved in to intervene.

"I'm so sorry!" Cried Cara in disbelief. "I shouldn't have hit you…" Spero brushed aside Cara's hand away in dismissal as Firin and Moah aided him to his feet, they each looked to Cara in shock and were astounded beyond any words to her sudden change in character.

"Don't worry yourself," Said Spero woefully to Cara. "All I'm trying to tell you, is that something doesn't sit right with me when the Guardians talk about your mark, how the world's balance and our survival rest only on you; it's like… they're not giving you any choice!" Spero gave no further glance to Cara afterwards, he stormed past Firin and Moah back towards the Sanctum; leaving her to be comforted only by Lenya who had now began to understand what burden lay over the unwilling princess.

"Levia and Ven would not commit you to anything without your blessing first," Said Lenya softly as she leaned herself into Cara's side. "I understand, that you have a child who is being kept safe at Ven's Sanctuary in Viridia?"

"Yes… Sophilia." Whimpered Cara in response. "She is only ten years old, I must get back to her." She rose her voice sharply, it was obvious how much torment Cara now was under.

"I will make the necessary arrangements for you, Cara. Levia has a boat which you could use to travel in; it is fast and should get you to Viridia safely, though I think we should have supper first... you must be starving?" Said Lenya as she coaxed Cara towards her personal chamber. At this point, Moah had moved himself purposefully away from his other companions; the prejudice he had encountered whilst travelling with them began to fester steadily and his purpose in this supposed quest was becoming ever-more doubtful – the Dark Acolyte's only solace now was in holding the obsidian tablet which he had secretly kept within his robes.

"The time for our next move is at hand," whispered Moah cautiously into the dark keep-sake. "The Elemental Guardians are certainly not ready for what is about to occur..." Cara found a needful peace in her chamber, finding that the calming streams which flowed through it aided in her reflection of the harsh journey that she and her companions had been through together. Lenya politely made her exit and again reminded Cara that she had a will to choose which path she must take, though evidently felt that the Guardian's would not hold so much esteem in her so futilely.

"See you again soon, Cara." Stuttered Lenya, as if in knowing that they would not be doing so. "Get some sleep, our evening meal will soon be ready." Levia had led Ven far from the secret stairway to an exposed cavern outside, it faced onto the ocean plain northwards where Skynah's mountain lay and with the setting sun fading a golden hue lingered serenely over the near distance.

"I come here often to meditate, it's the only place where I can't be bothered..." Laughed Levia nervously to Ven. "Here, we can speak freely with one another without any interference." The mountain of Skynah rose in its divine magnitude before Levia and Ven, its surface shimmered like the purest flame over the clashing waves beneath it. The two endearing friends sat quietly at first facing this sacred realm, savouring their long-awaited privacy which they had not shared together for a long time.

"A change is happening across these lands, Ven... though it is a necessary one." Remarked Levia in a surprisingly serious tone. "The balance of light and darkness is shifting again; can you also sense this?" Ven stared thoughtfully upon Skynah in the distance, conflicted by his own thoughts in relation to what his friend was asking of him.

"All I know, Levia... is if Impartia's Sacred Balance is not righted then the lands you are speaking of will soon burn as Magmorrah once did." Replied Ven despairingly. "I have never felt so helpless before, things aren't as they should be thanks to Kanaan and we, along with Cara, are now left to deal with the chaos he left through his sordid legacy." Levia gently placed a hand across Ven's arm beside him, then gestured his head in agreement with his morbid reflection.

"It's funny you should mention Cara, I noticed that she bears the mark of Cerebrante like her father. I am curious to know if you have told her yet of its true meaning?" Asked Levia reluctantly as he took in a deep breath, also trying to calm his fragile nerves by focusing stronger on the ocean waves spanning out before them both. "Does the princess truly understand what burden she has been born with?" Ven had tried to prepare himself for a moment like this over many years, where he could perhaps hold a positive influence in righting the wrongs of this world, though they had now become so complex beyond his own comprehension. Ven's responding silence spoke more than words ever could to Levia, who himself had shared in the burden of being Cerebrante's host.

"She is aware of the mark's purposes, though not of its power." Said Ven anxiously. "Cara's greatest torment though, is in that her only sister – Queen Cera – continues to hunt down both herself and her young child… who too bears the Spirit of Balance's mark."

Levia gasped in a noticeable horror to this revelation, he rubbed at his eyes in disbelief then turned back towards Ven's equal look of dismay. "We cannot ask too much of Cara, my friend. Her spirit is already tortured by what she has been through over her short life due to Kanaan and Cera's malice… there must be another way of stopping the Queen from fulfilling her mission to kill Alaskia?"

"She means to… what?" Exclaimed Levia fearfully. "That would explain why her agents have been skulking around our Sanctuaries… she means to discover our passwords!"

"I do not believe Cera has come to know of our Elemental seals over Alaskia… yet." Muttered Ven in response. "My friend, can you think of any other way we can stop her which could relieve Cara of her unwilling duty?"

"Kanaan must still be alive… if Cera still has control over Kufiah?" Thought Levia out aloud. "As long as the king lives, Cerebrante's mark on Cara's face will remain but only as a faded remnant of the Spirit's hold over her, thus, our kin may have a chance to rectify this evil plot?"

"Kufiah is nothing more than a slave to the will of Cera, she only has control over the Spirit of Darkness by using her father's enchanted amulet!" Declared Ven in agreement. "For us to free Cerebrante and allow for their true cycle to endure, Kanaan's amulet must be destroyed… even if we must kill Cera to do so!"

"Guardians are *not* permitted to kill, Ven." Said Levia, in a staunch dismissal to this terrible proposition. "Please, do not say that this is what you are implying?" Ven looked longingly into Levia's eyes in a vain hope that he may be forgiven by him, though his words were said through an utter sense of desperation.

"No, of course not!" Snapped Ven defensively. "I would never wish death upon any soul, though, this option appears to be the only one if Cerebrante and Impartia are to survive..." The two friends stood together awkwardly in a reflective silence, both unsure of how to resolve their difficult conversation amicably. The sun had now fully set upon Skynah's ocean and its mountain stood only as a shadow beneath the celestial stars above. Levia placed his hands into Ven's, holding them solemnly with a welcome comfort to ease their pressing uncertainties.

"The real purpose of us being here, Levia... is for you to grant Cara with your password as we mean to reach Alaskia and free them from Kanaan's incarceration before Cera can destroy the Spirit of Light." Whispered Ven as if in remorse. "I know that it is such a risky move to make, but it is our only hope now. I discovered, whilst being held captive at Kufiah's Sanctuary, that Cera believes in killing Alaskia it will strengthen her control over the Spirit of Darkness and gain her immortality – I need your own guidance and any you have heard from the rest of our kin about how to deal with this abhorrent situation..." Levia looked upon Ven with a reassuring eminence, he then guided him back towards the cavern's stairway in want of leaving the cold night's air and daunting atmosphere.

"I have managed to speak with Aira and Pahoe; they have both reasoned that there may be an actual solution to Cera's reign, though, it may be one that could come at such a terrible cost to us all, I'm afraid." Said Levia sorrowfully, he and Ven then looked in one more precious moment across the countless stars which rained endlessly above, before they finally re-entered the ancient Sanctuary.

"What else did they say to you?" Questioned Ven eagerly. "I was hoping that they could enlighten us, being that they are far older and wiser..." He winked amusingly, trying to rid the growing tension between himself and his oldest friend.

"Alaskia is always with us, my brother." Replied Levia almost despondently. "The Spirit of Light will forever exist in the dark of this world, as does the Spirit of Darkness live on eternally within the light... just as they should."

"What do you mean by this, Levia?" Said Ven in frustration towards his friend's apparent riddle. "What actual solution have Aira and Pahoe come up with to end our current plight?"

"The solution that our sisters have suggested, is in allowing for the Celestial prophecies to come true... for the Hymns of Alaskia and Kufiah to be heard and resonate across this world." Said Levia. "Our purpose in this, I believe, will be realised soon enough...though it troubles me just as it does with you." Levia then slowed the pacing of his steps to move in closer towards Ven for his calming presence, keeping in mind the daunting words he had spoken.

"What they mean, is for Kufiah to reach Alaskia unchallenged... to allow for those Spirits to unite without the balance of Cerebrante?" Gasped Ven in disbelief. "This is a *dangerous* notion, who knows what outcome we may be faced with in permitting such a reckless move?"

Levia again embraced his friend as both were noticeably fearful; with a dwindling hope they reluctantly reasoned that what had been propositioned may yet prove to be the answer needed in righting Impartia's doom - despite their own reservations.

"We must trust in ourselves and the companions whom you have brought here with you, Ven." Said Levia endearingly. "Princess Cara is the key for this plan to work though, all we can do is support her as best we can. In the morning, I will make the arrangements for you all to travel to Pahoe's Sanctuary safely, though you know all too well how much she despises visitors."

"Yes…" Responded Ven with a knowing glance. "I did help Pahoe create the defences around her Sanctuary, after-all. I only pray, that she will lower them for our visit."

"You must prepare your friends for the dangerous task ahead of them, there is no doubt in my mind that Cera and General Nira will be after you now…" Said Levia as the two Guardians met with an equalled silence, gradually edging their way back to look upon the beauty of the cosmos once more - a shared pleasure which they had both been so cruelly denied previously.

"When this is all over… you should visit my Sanctuary again for a much-needed vacation." Said Ven to Levia with a risen smile. "How about it?"

"I would love to," grinned Levia joyfully. "It would be just like old times…as long as Jenayan doesn't play any of her tricks on me." He laughed at this precious reminiscence.

"Jen is not a child anymore, Levia." Chuckled Ven, he treasured in sharing with his friend's unique humour. "I was thinking…that it may be time for her to take the reins from me." Together, the Guardians lowered their heads solemnly.

"Do you not fancy being a Guardian for a few more hundred years or so?" Remarked Levia with a forced smile. "You haven't been a Spirit host for that long, not like your predecessor."

"No," Sighed Ven thoughtfully. "But, I think that Jenayan might be ready to take on such a duty…I can't go on forever." Levia placed a hand upon Ven's and together they sat for a moment or two in silence, contemplating all of what they had been through over their eventful lives.

Spero had now calmed himself against the cold treatment which Cara had given him, though he continued to play back through their unwanted confrontation together painfully. He had not meant to be so forward and callous, his concern was meant to come across as wishing to protect Cara - though it failed miserably in doing so. Spero mournfully lifted himself from the Sanctum platform where had had lain himself amongst its tranquil fountains to ease his current sorrow. As he took one last glance around the sacred chamber, he noticed a billow of dark smoke suddenly begin to rise from a seal which was set within the centre.

"What the Hell is that?" Exclaimed Spero in utter terror. "This can't be good!" Spero quickly made an exit from the Sanctum chamber and was panicking blindly at what he had just seen. He ran aimlessly to each of the personal chambers beside the Sanctum and called out frantically for Cara whilst doing so, she eventually stepped from her room and was in truth relieved to hear Spero's familiar voice - though still cautious to his current feelings with her.

"What's the matter, Spero?" Asked Cara in shock, fearing her own safety from his apparent outburst of madness. "What are you shouting like that for?"

"Levia's Sanctum…there's this weird light…it had smoke coming from out of it!" Spero gasped as he painfully tried to draw in air through his tiring lungs. Suddenly, Moah stepped out from the shadows with an air of authority that he had previously restrained from displaying.

"This smoke you saw, Spero…" Said Moah, trying to remain clear and calm in his thoughts. "Did it come from a seal towards the centre of Levia's Sanctum platform?"

"Yes! It was thick and dark, unlike any normal smoke I have ever seen…" Spero instantly halted in his thoughts as a harrowing realisation crept in. "It was like what we saw in Magmorrah's Sanctuary!" He gasped with an expression of terror.

"Did the smoke flow like oil through water, I mean…was it unnatural in its appearance?" Questioned Moah further to Spero intently. "Tell me!" He commanded.

"Yes… it scared the life out of me!" Shouted Spero to the Dark Acolyte, in now fearing Moah's inquisition more greatly than what he had witnessed.

"What's all the shouting about?" Interrupted Firin as he wearily left from his chamber. "I thought we were meant to be resting?"

"We must find the Elemental Guardians… now!" Commanded Moah forcefully. "Queen Cera is attempting to use Kufiah's powers so that she may penetrate Levia's defences…all of you quickly… follow me… now!" Moah swiftly led his shaken companions up the staircase that had been previously hidden from them towards Levia and Ven – who were themselves in the process of returning.

"My esteemed guests, why do you all look so troubled?" Asked Levia nervously, he then turned towards Moah through sensing the risen anger in him. "What grave news do you bear?"

"Levia, your Sanctum has been compromised!" Responded Moah frankly as he bowed himself before the two Guardians in respect. "The Spirit of Darkness is coming, Spero witnessed this for himself… he saw Kufiah's smoke emerge from the Dark Sanctuary's seal… we must leave here at once, including all of your acolytes if they are to survive!" Levia in turn, gave a merciful look to the redeemed Dark Acolyte knelt so lowly beneath him; the Guardian knew that Moah's words were true, though he could not honestly fathom how Queen Cera may have conjured such a power as to break his ancient seal's protection.

"This has never been achieved before," said Levia, as a terror swiftly swept through his radiant eyes. "We must reach the other Sanctuaries… before it's too late!" The stunned companions looked to one another, each plainly astounded by Levia's shocking reaction.

"You want us to go *back* to the sanctum… what if Kufiah is already there waiting for us?" Asked Cara, herself greatly exacerbated by the thought of this new threat. "What if it's a trap?"

"He is right, Cara… there is no other way for us now." Responded Ven. "If we are to save your Sophilia, we must reach the other Guardians first." Levia, with a heavy heart, guided the guests back into his Sanctum; he regrettably had no time to warn his acolytes however of the impending danger, though reasoned that they were most likely secure within their own personal chambers. As the party entered, they found to an immediate horror that Kufiah's smoke was indeed reaching out to them from within the Spirit's blazing seal - just as Spero had forewarned.

"No!" Cried out Cara, the demonic smoke filtering from Kufiah's seal swiftly reached her and wrought with a terrifying impulse. "Ven, you promised me that the Sanctums could not be breached!"

"Forgive me…" Stammered Ven in remorse. "This… cannot be!" Kufiah roared mightily and the Dark Spirit's mass appeared to grow, as did their voice throughout Levia's chamber. Without warning, the Sanctum's door slammed shut behind Cara and her companions, instantly sealing itself through Kufiah's powerful possession over it to trap them all inside.

"This is only a foreshadow of events that are yet to come, an insight into Cera's will!" Said Moah unnervingly. "She means to attack Hydrania, without the protection of its Guardian… this land and Sanctuary will fall!" Moah shuddered from the familiar dark energy which flowed through him from Kufiah's presence. Each of the friends looked to one another for a longing reassurance, and for answers that could not yet be found regarding this disturbing invasion.

"Come forth and be judged!" Commanded the Spirit of Darkness ferociously. "Hydrania… is dead!" The thick smoke emanating from Kufiah's seal moved like an aggressive serpent that was preparing to attack its unwitting prey, causing a further fear to rise in the group of companions.

"How do you know of this, Moah?" Countered Ven. "When General Nira attacked my Sanctuary, we had no such warning?" The Guardian was confused just as his fellow companions were, though Levia himself felt a grave awareness of Moah's words towards Hydrania's current fate.

"Are you all unaware of Talam's capital being decimated?" Remarked Levia as his face twitched against the painful sadness coursing through him. "Queen Cera attacked the city yesterday." Firin threw himself into Levia's personal space, filled with a rage and an equal despair towards the Guardian on hearing this troubling news.

"Your saying… she totally destroyed it?" Stammered Firin tearfully. "Talam has the largest army in this world, how could Cera destroy the capital… it's the most heavily guarded area?" Firin grabbed at Levia's robes to drag him in closer; the guardian did not fight back however, he instead allowed for this assault to play over in sympathy towards Firin's obvious grief.

"Cera used a new weapon… it was similar to what King Kanaan unleashed in Magmorrah." Replied Levia carefully. "There were few survivors… going off what Pahoe – the Guardian of Fire - has told me." Firin held his grip on Levia's robes even tighter, focusing all his energy on the dire words which the Guardian was now sharing with him. "The weapon turned the city and surrounding desert into glass through its immense heat… the shockwave from the blast could be felt as far away as Pahoe's sanctuary in the north of Talam." Firin fell into a deeper despair on hearing this, though exiled, he still held a firm loyalty towards his home nation. Ven now placed himself before Levia, he yearned for a swifter explanation - given the smoke from Kufiah's seal was now intensifying.

"Magmorrah's Queen has long attempted, against the interventions of us Elemental Guardians, to force Talam into handing over its resources… to fuel her might and control even more." Continued Levia more hastily. "Cera is moving towards her final goal… we have no time to lose!"

"Queen Cera will not stop in her hunt for power, we know this too well now." Said Ven. "The power Kufiah alone holds is no longer enough to satisfy the Queen!" Now looking to Cara, Ven saw in her a resolve that swiftly echoed back into his thoughts. "Make now for the Sanctuary of Fire, we can use Pahoe's seal here to transport ourselves there within moments… quickly… before Kufiah fully emerges!" Cara forced her way between the Guardians in aid of assisting Firin to his feet, he was knelt weeping and all transpiring around him did not seem to bother him anymore.

"I know all-too-well how my sister thinks," said Cara with a trembling voice. "She will make Hydrania suffer like Talam…then Skynah…then…" She suddenly paused, raising a hand to her mouth aghast in a horrific realisation. "Viridia! We *must* save my Sophilia first before reaching Pahoe!" She shook at Ven vigorously in a desperate attempt to sway his thoughts. Ven placed his hands upon Cara's firmly, forcing a spiritual calm to flow from him to relieve her coursing anguish.

"We *will* save your child, Cara… I promise you!" Said Ven in a tired voice. "We must reach Pahoe first though, if we are to stop your sister in acting out her plans against Alaskia…we will only have one chance!" Ven's words came as no comfort to Cara who now lost all care for their ill-fated quest, replacing this easily by the immediate need to stop any further threat towards her only child.

The walls of Levia's Sanctum tremored as if under a massive earthquake, whilst Kufiah's demonic roar echoed hauntingly once again. Outside, upon Hydrania's Southern Ocean, Queen Cera's naval forces began a bombardment against the capital city and surrounding landscape with their high-end explosives; echoing in their assault with a greater destructive power than what the group of friends had previously witnessed upon Magmorrah's strait.

"Go!" Commanded Ven sternly. "Go to the Pahoe's Seal!" The Guardian quickly ushered his frightened companions into the centre of the Sanctum's platform, while Levia frantically approached the precious pipe organ nearby with a radiant light rising in his eyes.

"What are you doing, Levia… you'll get yourself killed!" Exclaimed Spero, though the Guardian merely continued to ignore his pleas "Your lands are being attacked and you choose to sit and play on some old organ…what kind of *Guardian* are you?" Ven gave an anticipatory grin to both Firin and Spero, reassuring to both that Levia had a justifiable reason for doing this strange act.

"Have faith…" Said Ven, with a hopeful wink towards his Levia. "Queen Cera could not have prepared herself, nor Magmorrah's army, for this display of raw power!" Levia stretched out his hands and then proceeded to crack them as he placed each fingertip perfectly upon the organ's ancient keys. A thunderous chord suddenly filled the Sanctum chamber, shaking the surrounding passageways as the sound reached through them and far across the lands of Hydrania. The ocean waves outside drew eerily away from the main-land, rising hundreds of feet into the air to tower over Cera's incoming warships.

"How can playing on that old thing possibly help Hydrania from an invasion?" Seethed Firin. "You've seen how strong Magmorrah's fleet has become!"

"Levia's organ strengthens his connection to the waters of Impartia," Replied Ven smugly. "Cera won't know what hit her!" Levia continued to play diligently, the song being performed was the 'Hymn of Alaskia' which Cara instantly recognised. With each passing note and chord, further tidal waves forced themselves against the oppressing fleet that was situated in defiance before Hydrania's shoreline.

"Take your stations!" Commanded the Magmorran Admiral on his leading vessel. "The Guardian moves to attack!" The Magmorran warships fired a barrage of incendiary bombs and vaporising beams into the approaching tsunamis, though they only created a small pocket of destruction within the mass waves that were about to befall them. The terrified citizens of Hydrania's capital city rejoiced in the divine protection their revered Guardian granted them, as Cera's nearing warships helplessly rose into the monstrous waves and were soon swept far into the distance.

"That should do it!" Declared Levia triumphantly. "There's no way that Cera would dare attack these shores again…" Unbeknown to Levia and his new companions, Queen Cera was observing her army's predictable defeat from the safety of her palace balcony in Magmorrah. She had carefully gambled against Levia's most likely counter-attack and had planned to play this move against him. Cera devised that all Levia's spiritual might would have been focused in ridding Hydrania of the enemy warships, however, in doing so the Guardian would render his own defences over the Sanctum of Water - to the Queen's expected advantage.

"Did you not think I would have expected such a foolish move…Guardian?" Cackled Cera to herself in ecstasy. "You are only making Kufiah's power grow stronger within your own walls!" The Queen then held fanatically onto her accursed amulet as the Dark Acolytes stood beside started to perform the 'Hymn of Kufiah' - empowering the Spirit of Darkness further with each passing verse.

"The fumes…they're still growing!" Remarked Spero in anguish, as he attempted to shield Cara from Kufiah's sickening smoke. "The Spirit of Darkness… is breaking through!" Levia suddenly halted in his playing, he was also bewildered by the demonic figure that was now rising to greet him and felt that no further aid could come by using his own spiritual powers against Kufiah. The Guardian struggled hard against Kufiah's enclosing atmosphere to re-join the others within his Sanctum platform's centre. Then as all hope seemed to fade, the two Elemental Guardian's united their powers to summon a deterring force in wake of their evil intruder - something though seemed to be weakening their efforts.

"We can't hold Kufiah back for long!" Cried out Ven in despair. "Cera's control is too strong!" Haunting cries of pained anguish and hatred now echoed throughout Levia's Sanctum and its flowing waters suddenly fell still. The swirling mass of ashes upon Kufiah's seal disturbingly began to forge itself into his imposing figure; the Spirit's eyes burned like Hell-fire within their blackened pits and a putrid stench of death swiftly filtered through the air around.

"Quickly… stand over here!" Screamed Levia frantically, he and Ven then dragged the others onto Pahoe's seal away from the growing nightmare. A blinding red light burst from Pahoe's seal to permeate the friends with its a radiant glow, the seal's spiritual energy then steadily lifted to surround their bodies whilst Moah used this moment to break away from them.

"Moah!" Cried out Ven in disbelief. "What are you doing?" Moah was casually surrendering himself to Kufiah; he did appear defiant, though a panic was also evident in him, as he knelt beneath the Dark Spirit's corpse-like body.

"Come back… Moah!" Cried out Cara. "You can't fight it!" She shook her head in dismay to what was unfolding before her, it was almost too painful to watch.

"This… is my destiny, Cara." Replied Moah, his whole body trembled through fright. "You must free Alaskia…GO!" He commanded with tremoring lips.

"It does not need to be this way," pleaded Ven, himself doubtful of how Moah could survive such a conflict with the Spirit of Darkness. "You have turned from your dark path… join us!" Kufiah towered himself menacingly over Moah, raising his arms as if in a mock embrace to the former Dark Acolyte. Cara desperately begged again for Moah to flee; she wished to spare him from this apparent act of sacrifice. Moah, despite the compassion being shown to him from his friends, continued to focus on Kufiah's piercing eyes and terrifying presence.

"Leave me, let me suffer for the sins I have wrought upon Impartia!" Whimpered Moah remorsefully to his companions. Though held in a reluctant surrender to Kufiah's will, Moah managed to force himself to look upon his friends for one last time - for one last memory he could possibly share with them.

"Please, Moah." Sobbed Cara. "We must leave… we will need your help to beat Cera!" Kufiah released a horrifying laughter towards Cara in response, his gaze then firmly met with hers and a strange union seemed to meet with them both afterwards.

"The Sanctuaries of Impartia *will* burn!" Declared the Dark Spirit cruelly, his voice rose ever-greater within Levia's Sanctum. "None are safe… neither is your child… Nira's bane *will* be captured!" Cara screamed in terror against Kufiah; she sensed that the Dark Spirit's words were truth and then looked to Ven for any comfort he could possibly offer.

"Ven…" Stammered Cara sorrowfully. "We *must* save Sophilia!" The Guardian of Earth looked upon Cara's tearful expression then back towards Kufiah's malevolent presence; he yearned to end this tenacious suffering, though could not break his solemn vow to protect the Spirit of Balance.

"Moah… turn back!" Shouted Ven. "Your sins have *already* been forgiven… we need you!" He declared in sincerity.

"No!" Roared Moah in return. "Save yourselves…save Sophilia! Do not weep at my loss, for I am not worthy of it!" The Dark Acolyte then resolved himself to Kufiah's waiting absolution - an apparent act of willing repentance and deep-seated remorse. "Leave this place… and warn the others." The Elemental Guardians heeded Moah's plea without question; they hastily broke from Pahoe's seal to then place themselves separately upon two others that lay away from their companions. Levia stood himself within the Sanctuary of Air's seal whilst Ven knelt upon his own, neither lifted their gaze back towards Cara as she tried in vain to free herself from the restraining light.

"You would forsake us?" Cried out Cara. "… How could you?" The light of Pahoe's seal seemingly paralysed Cara within the now activated portal, she continued to scream frantically at the Guardian's in dismay - lost beyond any words as to why they would leave her and their friends in such a dire situation.

"I *will* save Sophilia!" Responded Ven to Cara, his body only just visible within the permeating jade light of his seal. "Trust me... I will not fail you! You will find us where the ocean meets with the air... seek aid from Impartia's Eternal Flame first... it is... the only way!" The Guardian's body slowly began to vanish amongst his seal's empowered beam, he looked once more to Cara though now with a glint of hope in his eyes. "*I bid thee enter thine sacred Sanctum!*" Levia too raised his hands towards Cara at this moment, his whole seemed to writhe as he struggled against the drawing power surrounding him.

"*I bid thee enter thine sacred sanctum...* have faith, Cara!" Said Levia passionately. "You are bonded to Cerebrante, the Spirit of Balance will guide your way!" Suddenly, the Seals beneath Levia and Ven burst in their vibrant colours, instantly teleporting them away from the beleaguered Sanctum chamber. Cara and her terrified friends helplessly looked on at Moah as he continued to linger beneath his master's foreboding presence.

"Please, Moah." Begged Firin this time. "This is your only chance to escape..." Moah silently raised a palm towards Pahoe's seal in response, as he lined his fingertips against it a powerful burst of scarlet light released – teleporting the group of friends away into safety and leaving him alone to suffer a fate, which was yet, unknown.

"Oh, Great Spirit." Mumbled Moah fearfully. "It is done." Time now felt as if it had stopped for the Dark Acolyte, his breathing laboured tremendously as he fought against the tormenting voices that now scattered themselves around Levia's Sanctum – all singing within a corrupt unison Kufiah's vile hymn.

"You *are* a traitor!" Cackled Kufiah as he paced his heavy footsteps closer towards Moah. "Rise, thine servant... you have done well to fulfil such a treacherous task!" The Dark Spirit then growled in his guttural voice, which itself almost seemed anguished, as he clenched onto Moah to stand him. "Impartia is now falling into chaos, and our Queen awaits your glorious return... Guardian of Darkness!" Kufiah formed a grimacing smile that even haunted Moah with its death-like appearance.

"All is revealed, my Master." Said Moah unnervingly. "Queen Cera, did she receive my messages about the Elemental passwords and their Guardians' plan to save Alaskia?" Moah then mirrored his stance to Kufiah's own they both then stood proudly together, basking in their muchly-desired occupation of Levia's Sanctuary – a feat which Cera had tried so long to achieve, though in vain.

"Yes, the obsidian tablets have served their purpose." Responded Kufiah coldly and with a menacing smirk. "Magmorrah's Queen now graciously wishes to speak with you... alone." Kufiah lowered his skeletal head slowly towards Moah, as he raised it again the Spirit's facial features morphed to resemble more closely that of a more feminine demeanour.

"Kufiah?" Questioned Moah in perplexment. "My Master... what is happening to you?" The harrowing face of Queen Cera now emerged upon the Dark Spirit, she channelled herself through Kufiah with an apparent ease that disturbed Moah initially - this unexpected transformation had never been achieved before.

"Moah!" Screamed Cera in delight. "My most-loyal ally! How it pleases me to be speaking with you once again." A growl abruptly left from Kufiah and Moah was unsure whether it was the Dark Spirit or Queen who had caused it – such a terrifying sound.

"I assume, that I am now speaking directly to you... Majesty?" Questioned Moah submissively. He spoke with a respectful tone to his Queen, though inside was growing anxious over Cera's apparent hold on Kufiah. "I believe, that your sister has escaped and is now making for the Sanctuary of Fire to meet with its Guardian – Pahoe. That Guardian is notoriously ferocious with her defences, your army would not last long against her. We must focus instead on Cara, as she is seeking all the elemental passwords in aim of freeing Alaskia at Skynah's mountain - the Spirit of Light's supposed Sanctum." Moah struggled greatly to swallow after speaking, his thoughts continued to draw back on the friends he had so easily betrayed. Kufiah laughed again, though the Spirit's voice resonated with Cera's own wicked tones.

"Perfect!" Declared Cera intently. "My sister has finally proven that she *is* a traitor to our nation!" The Queen then allowed for Moah to continue in unveiling his theory, as the Dark Guardian forced his remorseful eyes to meet against hers once more he felt an ominous joy which deeply unsettled him.

"The Guardian of Air will be our final obstacle before Cara can reach Alaskia." Replied Moah anxiously. "I propose that we allow for your sister to gain all the passwords then, when she has done so, the pathway to eradicate Alaskia and bring order to this world through your divine reign will be at hand!" Moah bowed himself reservedly before his two masters, though every negative emotion possible flowed through him as he did – they were a vicious cocktail of regret, anger and unseated melancholy.

"Guardian of the Dark..." Said Cera in a dismissive tone. "A far greater threat to my immortal existence has been identified and it lies safely, for now at least, within Viridia's Sanctuary; this very news came to me by your own giving - oh devoted servant." Cackled the Queen knowingly, Kufiah's voice now struggled to coping through her sickening possession over the Spirit.

"What new threat do you speak of?" Asked Moah gravely. "We must counter your sister's quest before any else... surely?" The Dark Guardian remained silent and held deeply in his troubled thoughts, in realising that he may have unwittingly revealed something to the Queen within their secret messages.

"When you spoke with me in Talam, I overheard Cara speaking of her daughter's mark..." Said Cera in a scornful voice. "I was unaware of this threat until that very moment...you have proven to be a most-valuable asset!" Moah wretched noticeably as an agonising regret hit him through Cera's words. He reasoned that Sophilia could surely not pose such a fatal threat to the Queen, though Cera's self-preservation now became ever-apparent to Moah as being nothing more than a selfish act of jealousy and revenge against her sister. "The mark of Cerebrante has borne itself strongly upon that child, and from what I have come to understand, Cara's own is now fading." Kufiah's torso tremored as the Queen's hatred filtered through it, Cera's rage had risen beyond any measure of relenting now. "Sophilia is the most likely chosen host for Cerebrante's expected re-birth which, as you must understand, be prevented at all costs!" The sporadic flames within Kufiah's eyes flared aggressively with each passing word spoken by Cera, the heat from them now painfully scorched at Moah's skin.

"The child is defenceless, she will be of no consequence to your plans." Responded Moah bravely. "I assure you..." Quivered the Dark Acolyte.

"That wretched child will come before me to be 'cleansed' within Kufiah's Sanctum, General Nira is seeing to it as we speak!" Snapped Cera. "My journey to rid Impartia of Alaskia's weakness *will* be done and my reign *will* last eternally!" The Queen's cruel laughter that followed also revealed to Moah a true lack of love and empathy in her; she had become delusional and as dangerous as her father Kanaan - whom Cera herself loathed more than any other.

"How will Nira penetrate the Guardian of Earth's protective Seal?" Asked Moah to Cera in a genuine search for answers. "We have barely *just* managed to enter this Sanctum, I am afraid, that this was only done through the misplaced trust of its Guardian Levia... in me." Moah tremored fearfully, he knew that Cera would have discovered a way though dared not to discover how. "We cannot break Viridia's defences the same way, focus on Skynah and ready your forces to invade!" The Smokey mass of Kufiah suddenly grew to dominate Levia's Sanctum and Moah further, filling them with an instant and judgemental hatred.

"General Nira has been gifted by your acolytes with a solution to this... problem." Replied Cera with a content grin. "Nothing can stand in my way... not even the power of Impartia's Elemental beings!" The seal from which Kufiah had risen spread its shadow heavily over Levia's Sanctum platform, thereafter releasing a beam of Hell-fire that emitted a pathway back to the Dark Spirit's own sanctuary. "Return now, my Guardian... your skills will be needed in dealing with this new threat... should she arrive here unharmed." Moah reluctantly stepped into the flames of Kufiah's portal; he tried with all his might not to reveal what true conflict was steadily emerging within himself, especially with the Spirit of Darkness watching over him.

"I will do what is asked of me..." Spoke Moah mournfully, his actions now too late to reverse.

Chapter Six: Through the Eyes of Innocence

The Acolytes of Earth had obeyed their Guardian's orders devoutly and without any question towards his selfless actions; in offering protection over the unknown stranger and her child from General Nira's ambush, Ven had proven to them all how mighty he truly was. Ven's senior acolyte – Jenayan – was the one who had reached out for Sophilia first, she swiftly carried the distressed child away from Nira's ensuing carnage into Viridia's ancient Sanctuary of Earth where she hoped they would be safe.

Jenayan looked back helplessly upon her mentor's capture, who himself seemed to show no reluctance in surrendering before the sadistic Magmorran General – Ven's actions could only have served a greater purpose, she felt. Through her tears, Sophilia looked upon Jenayan to find she had a perfectly pale complexion with luscious ginger hairlocks that the young girl took an instant liking to.

"What are they doing to my Mummy?" Cried Sophilia pitifully, as she rubbed at her sobbing eyes. "I want my Mummy!" Jenayan remained fearfully quiet as she forced herself against aiding Ven from his imminent fate, she instead ran hastily beneath the Sanctuary's three gargantuan trunks towards its entrance seal.

"Your mother will be okay," Replied Jenayan with a shaken voice. "I'm going to look after you." Jenayan then gently nursed Sophilia in her arms, as she lowered them both upon the entrance seal, far beneath Viridia's towering Sanctuary above. A blinding jade light suddenly emanated from the portal, and upon a further command given by Jenayan, it proceeded to transport the two into Ven's protective Sanctum – lain deep within the Sanctuary's very heart. "You are safe now… no one can get you in here." Said Jenayan in a reassuring tone as she placed the terrified girl upon her own feet. "I don't know why those Magmorran soldiers were after you, but they will never reach us in here… not while I'm looking after you!" Sophilia wiped away the tears in her eyes and soon gained enough courage to speak again with the strange-looking acolyte who was stood before her, despite an initial reluctance.

"Who are you… who are the others and what is this place?" Asked the child in a pained, whispering voice. "How do I know that you're not bad like those other people?"

"We are the 'Acolytes of Earth' and we have a duty to help our Guardian look after this *huge* tree… it is called the *Sanctuary of Earth*." Explained Jenayan, though in truth she felt this would be too much to take in for the innocent girl. "We help to look after the Sanctuary's magical secrets and, for now, we will serve to protect you as well whilst you're staying with us." Jenayan quickly sensed a reserved hesitation within the startled child; she ushered for her fellow acolytes, who themselves had now emerged from the entrance seal, to move away in granting Sophilia some room to breathe. "My name is Jenayan, I watch over the other acolytes for our master when he is not here…" Said the Acolyte calmly. "May I ask… what is your name?" Sophilia whimpered in her uncertainty, though was gradually feeling a slight trust now grow between herself and Jenayan – who, at present, seemed to show no apparent threat towards her.

"My name is Sophilia." Replied the girl cautiously. "Mummy likes to call me *Lia*, I like to be called Lia as well, so can I call you Jenny… please?" Jenayan smiled as she held out an open palm of trust towards the frightened child, triggering within Sophilia a loving memory of her mother's own similar gesture - when trying to bring calm between them during stressful situations. Sophilia slowly placed her own hands within Jenayan's and then faintly smiled back at her.

"Yes, you are more than welcome to call me Jenny." Said Jenayan gladly. "Your mother will be okay; she is with Ven - our Guardian - he is a powerful and magical Spirit… they will only be away from us for a little while." Jenayan then carefully tightened her grip upon Sophilia's hands, wishing for this to be conveyed as an assuring gesture in wake of such a dire promise. "Our sanctuary will be your new home for now and I promise that you will be safe and happy here with us, Lia. There are plenty of things for us to do together, that is, until your mummy comes back for you… which I know she will." Sophilia's reserve towards Jenayan diminished on hearing this, she was also happier now in the knowledge of being protected within Ven's beautiful Sanctum. The spiritual platform, which now lay beneath Jenayan and Sophilia, did not have an empty void below as did the Sanctuary of Darkness, nor a chasm of flowing waterfalls like in Hydrania: countless roots and vines swarmed throughout the aged structure, all moving themselves chaotically to form a solid earthly bed that flowed across the mystic platform and its seals.

"Your home is very pretty… I like it!" Rejoiced Sophilia to Jenayan, she greatly admired each delicate flower that spawned around her and found the air to be pleasantly clear – itself purified by the many delightful scents from the plant life that flourished within.

Jenayan laughed aloud in response which further excited Sophilia; she had been so accustomed to the formalities of her Sanctuary duties that Jenayan had forgotten what joy such a relaxed conversation could bring. Following soon in Sophilia's footsteps, Jenayan too admired the beauty that they were housed in, having taken for granted its splendour over the many years she had spent living there.

"It *is* pretty… isn't it, Lia?" Said Jenayan with a naïve expression. "I never realised just how lucky I am to live here… until you told me!" She laughed. "Our Guardian is to thank for this though; he looks after us all and our Sanctuary so well, your mummy is truly safe being with him." Jenayan then hung her head in reflection of Ven's current incarceration, though quickly displaced this with a smile as to not dishearten Sophilia more than she already felt. The child, despite Jenayan's obvious grief, skipped on playfully over a trail of roots and then selectively picked a handful of flowers to make a bracelet with.

"Ven is a brave and kind man, isn't he?" Countered Sophilia curiously. "He did help my mummy… I *know* that he will bring her back soon!" She exclaimed.

"Yes… he certainly is, Lia." Said Jenayan as she tried to fight back her rising tears. "Look, why don't we go and see my other friends, I bet that they'd love to meet you!"

"…Okay." Replied Sophilia awkwardly. "I hope that they are as kind as you." Jenayan reached out tenderly towards Sophilia; as their hands met they quickly began to dance with one another under the coursing rays of sunlight, each passing moment somehow removed their present suffering. One by one, the other acolytes returned into the Sanctum on hearing the welcome sounds of laughter coming from within it. They reported to Jenayan that the area outside of their Sanctuary was now clear from General Nira and her hostile soldiers all then took in a unified sigh of relief. Jenayan embraced Sophilia tightly on hearing this news and swung the child gleefully around her - much to both their delight.

"Did you here that Lia?" Gasped Jenayan in ecstasy. "We are all safe now… those evil soldiers have gone away!" Sophilia released herself from Jenayan's grip to clap her hands happily, it was a momentary freedom from the fear that had taken over her - being so far away from Cara's maternal presence.

"I'm *so* happy that they're not outside anymore!" Said Sophilia with a gasp of relief. "But," she briefly calmed her excitement to draw in a much-needed breath. The anxious child then slowly walked over to the edge of Ven's Sanctum platform to look out through its earthly windows. Sophilia soon noticed a distant smoke that came from the south and then thought to herself if it could be where her mother was now heading, these troubling thoughts instantly silenced her joy to be replaced by a renewed sense of dread.

"What's the matter?" Asked Jenayan with a concerning look to Sophilia. "You'll be alright now with us…"

"Mummy *will* be okay… won't she?" Whimpered Sophilia as she hugged herself tightly into Jenayan's silken robes, bringing to them both a much-needed sense of comfort.

"I promise," said Jenayan firmly, whilst trying not to show her own present grief. "Come now with us, we'll show you to your room…" Ven's acolytes then guided Sophilia to her personal chamber, making sure that they drew the child's attention away from her woes to all the magnificent flowers which spanned their Sanctuary's winding passageways. On entering, Sophilia gazed in astonishment at her new housing with an innocent smile - Jenayan had deliberately chosen to place the child in her own room, it was filled with countless flowers of varying colours and scents that entranced her unexpected guest instantly. "Do you… like it?" Questioned Jenayan hesitantly. "This is by far the prettiest room that we could have given to you. Late at night, you can sometimes hear the distant waterfalls from Hydrania coursing through the air outside… I find it helps me to sleep." Sophilia happily ran up to her bed and started to jump on it, this was a small pleasure she had never known before and soon the child found an admiration towards some blossoming white roses which grew nearby.

"I *love* it… I love it all, Jenny!" Screamed Sophilia in merriment. "I've never had my own bed or room before, this is so *amazing*!" The Acolytes smiled in relief to one another on seeing Sophilia's contentment, they did not expect for such an innocence to flourish within these dark times. Jenayan turned first to exit the chamber and was soon followed by her brethren, allowing for the overwhelmed child to play peacefully without any further distractions made by themselves. Jenayan herself had never understood the privilege of bearing a child, nor at least having to care for one. The honour of having to watch over Sophilia was now proving to be a much-needed form of solace that Jenayan needed greatly from alleviating the troubles which she alone now bore.

"Try and get some rest, Lia…" Whispered Jenayan in a commanding tone. "We'll come back for you when supper is ready, okay?"

"I don't want to rest!" Replied Sophilia firmly with a cheeky grin. "I want to smell all of the flowers and make some chains for you and your friends."

"Okay!" Replied Jenayan in a humoured submission. "But do try to get some sleep before supper, we will have a *very* busy evening ahead of us…" She then gently sealed the door to Sophilia's room by using some of Ven's own spiritual teachings, Jenayan meticulously manipulated the surrounding branches to form as a doorway and afterwards faced her fellow acolytes - who now all stared back to her in a unified silence. "What concerns you all, my brothers and sisters?" Said Jenayan in a sympathetic voice. "Speak… do not hold onto your troubles so." One of the acolytes anxiously stepped towards Jenayan in response, their head bowed lowly as not to look upon her and their hands trembled noticeably.

"Jen…" Stammered the acolyte fearfully. "Did you happen to notice the distinct birthmark on Sophilia's right hand?" Jenayan reluctantly nodded in agreement with them, though also frowned against this apparent prejudice.

"What of it?" Snapped the leading acolyte. "Sophilia is a vulnerable, little girl and our Guardian has ordered for us to protect her… would you defy Ven in such a way, and what concern does this mark truly bring to you?"

"I have seen that mark before," interjected a separate Acolyte bitterly in response. "It lies upon the centre of our Sanctum Platform… on Cerebrante's seal." Jenayan slowly closed her eyes and then opened them again though with a dismayed look; she did not want to create a tension between herself and the acolytes, though this dire fact would certainly warrant an explanation.

"Yes, Sophilia's birthmark *is* a connection with the Spirit of Balance, but remember this, she is only a child for goodness sake!" Said Jenayan exhaustively. "Sophilia obviously has no knowledge of the burden that she now carries and do not mistake her for Cerebrante's present host – King Kanaan – for no evil lingers in her as it does in that monster!" The acolytes bowed respectfully towards Jenayan, her clearer understanding of Cerebrante's purpose was something they had all failed to gain for themselves – despite Ven's numerous teachings on the matter. From one of the darkening passageways, came a lone Sanctuary guard who abruptly summoned the acolytes for their daily meeting together.

"Brothers and Sisters!" Spoke the guard in authority. "Today has brought with it ill-tidings, we must discuss what actions are now to be taken in retrieving our great Guardian!"

"Indeed…" Replied Jenayan solemnly. "Please, lead the way." As the acolytes and guard walked through their Sanctuary's maze-like catacombs, one of Ven's newest followers turned to face Jenayan – who herself was still held in doubt of how this horrific situation could be rectified.

"Can you honestly guarantee that Ven and the child's mother will return safely to us, Jen?" The acolyte had a child-like fear in their eyes as they met with Jenayan's, swiftly this turned into a harrowing look of torment. "If not, have we not been tasked to shelter the greatest threat against Queen Cera of Magmorrah - thus making us targets for her malice as well?"
Jenayan moved herself in closer to the scared acolyte, her resolve and faith remained firmly strong towards her mentor's eventual return.

"We *must* protect Sophilia at all costs; whether or not this brings the darkness of Queen Cera and Kufiah down upon us is… irrelevant." Said Jenayan as she began to shake through her rising anxiety. "It is not fitting for any of us to challenge Ven's authority, especially at this crucial moment in time. Our Guardian of Earth would not expect such discord to come from his beloved acolytes, not unless it were to serve a greater purpose…have faith in Ven's judgement and pray that he does return to us unharmed."

"I'm sorry, Jen." Responded the acolyte timidly. "We *do* have faith in Ven's judgement, it's just… without his powers, how can we possibly fight against the Spirit of Darkness?"

"Pray that such a conflict never comes to us," whispered Jenayan cautiously. "I have been gifted with some of Ven's spiritual might, though against Kufiah, I truthfully doubt that they would be of any use." Evening soon fell over Viridia's ancient Sanctuary of Earth, Ven's acolytes and guards had spent many hours discussing how they might, in some way, be able to free their incarcerated Guardian – though sadly to no avail. Still held secluded in her room, Sophilia by now had steadily become bored of her forced solitude. The impatient girl paced around in anticipation of meeting with her new friends again, the prospect of some decent food in her belly also became more prevalent on her eager mind.

"Where are they?" Mumbled Sophilia in frustration. "It must be supper-time!" Centred inside the Sanctum chamber, an oak table carved with etchings of the Sanctuary's past Guardians had been laid out perfectly. Various fruits and herbs from the surrounding forest were carefully placed along it by Ven's acolytes, who at this point had ended their unproductive meeting together. Sophilia was soon freed to her instant delight from Jenayan's chamber; she quickly ran past Ven's acolytes towards the Sanctum and gasped in joy at it's amazing banquet.

"Wow!" Screamed the child excitedly. "There's so much food!" Sophilia hastily sat herself before the long table and then rocked back and forth upon her chair – to the instant disapproval of her fellow, more reserved, diners. Jenayan purposefully placed herself beside Sophilia in a hope to increase their trust together, and ferment in the other acolytes that no actual threat came from Cerebrante's apparent replacement.

"Are you enjoying your stay with us so far?" Enquired one of the Acolytes coyly to Sophilia, in a forced show of interest towards her. The child giggled to herself in response as a form of escape, having been locked in her room for so many tedious hours.

"Yes, Thanks!" Spoke Sophilia, as she grabbed a handful of fresh fruit, which was then thrown greedily into her mouth without any care for necessary manners. "I like my room, but it got boring after a few minutes…"

"I'm… very glad to hear that, Lia." Chuckled Jenayan, it was reassuring to see the child eating, despite her present sadness. "We're very sorry that you had to wait so long for us, how *did* you pass the time?"

"I sang some songs that Mummy taught me!" Replied Sophilia with a vibrant smile. "Would you like to hear one?"

"Of course," Said Jenayan kindly, to the horrified looks of her fellow Acolytes in return. "We would *love* to hear you perform." She clapped her hands slowly in anticipation to encourage the excitable child.

"Okay," said Sophilia, as she kicked some fruit out of the way to proudly stand herself upon Ven's aged table. "Here it goes…"

'Is it true what you said in my dream… are you standing right here by me… can you see all the things I do… can you feel all the pain I'm going through?'

123

"Oh," gasped Jenayan with a shocked expression. "That's quite a sad song, Lia… do you know any happier ones?"

"Yes!" Snapped Sophilia defensively. "But, that was the song Mummy used to sing to herself when she thought I was asleep; it reminds me of her and I miss Mummy so much…"

"We know, sweetheart… we know." Replied one of the acolytes more sympathetically. "Your mother will come back soon… why don't you sing to us a song that makes you both feel better?" Sophilia gently brushed away some breadcrumbs from her woolen dress, then after also shifting some hair from her mouth, moved to perform once again.

'You are the Light in my Darkness… no tears shall come through… home is far away now… this land to us is new… we'll always have each other… even if time goes by… you are the light in my darkness… our love will never die…'

The Acolytes all fell into an instant silence, their hearts moved greatly by Sophilia's emotional performance. Jenayan herself now fathomed just how powerful the bond was between Sophilia and her mother, whose fate yet remained unknown.

"You have a lovely singing voice," said Jenayan tearfully to Sophilia. "You *are* in a new and strange world, here at our Sanctuary… I just hope that you feel safe with us?"

"I do and it's lovely here, but…" Stuttered Sophilia as she indulged herself with another mouthful of fruit. "We're really high up, it's *very* scary… are you not all scared?"

"Well, Sophilia… being so high up keeps us safe, doesn't it?" Interrupted another acolyte. "No one can reach us in this Sanctum, not unless we give them permission to do so."

"That's a very good point…" Said Jenayan enthusiastically. "Also, with being so high up, you can see so many places around the world… we can show you tomorrow if you like, Lia?"

"Really?" Responded Sophilia with an equal excitement. "Can you see the whole of Impartia?"

"Sort of…" Murmured Jenayan in response. "There is an observatory on top of this Sanctuary where our Guardian goes to meditate, you can see so much from there!" Sophilia bounced up and down on her chair in a display of pure happiness; she had observed so many foreign sights already just from being in her own room and was intrigued by the prospect of possibly finding more, with the help of her new friends.

"Yes please… can *you* show me, Jenny?" Said Sophilia in a demanding voice. "I would *really* like that!" The Acolytes each laughed at Jenayan's obvious new demotion in being a babysitter; they too were only used to nurturing the element of earth, not the curiosities of an energetic ten-year-old girl.

"I would love to show you, Lia!" Said Jenayan with a knowing smirk towards her fellow acolytes. "Maybe, you will see places up there that you never knew existed… how fun will that be?" Sophilia clumsily fell from her chair in excitement towards Jenayan's proposal. As she rose, Ven's acolytes bowed to one another again and then retired back to their individual chambers – each weary from sharing in such an eventful meal with the boisterous child. Jenayan assisted Sophilia into bed, she gently tucked her under some silken bedsheets and a haunting stare met between them both shortly afterwards - so many questions and emotions coursed through each of their minds.

"Jenny…" Whispered Sophilia as she toyed her petite fingertips over the bedsheets. "When I wake up, will I see my mummy?" She motioned pleadingly.

"I will stay awake all night just to keep an eye out for her," Assured Jenayan, a pleasant twinkle lifted in her eyes. "What is your mother's name, so that I can make sure we are letting the right person into our Sanctuary?"

"Mummy's real name is… Cara." Replied Sophilia with a perplexed look, she had rarely needed to use her mother's name before. "Mummy has long hair and yellow eyes, like me!"

"I'll look for her, but for now… get some sleep!" Jenayan wrapped the bedsheets even tighter around Sophilia's shoulders. "We have a big day ahead of us tomorrow! Goodnight… Lia." With a gentle brush of her fingers across Sophilia's brow, Jenayan slowly removed herself from the child's company to exit her room, praying quietly to herself that her would indeed bring some comfort.

"Goodnight, Jenny… don't fall asleep!" Sophilia shifted back and forth in her bed, despite her physical comfort it would be the first time she had ever spent an evening apart from her mother. Sophilia tried to think of happier memories that she had shared with Cara, which would hopefully help soothe her off to sleep, though the uncertainty of her mother's current whereabouts only continued to bring a terrible torment.

After an hour or so of failing to sleep, Sophilia leapt with a tired yawn from Jenayan's bed to look out from her window across the evening's dark horizon. She could make out some dwindling lights that lay within Hydrania; their flickering movements seemingly hypnotised the child, though had little effect in settling her. Jenayan herself could not find peace as she repeatedly checked on the entrance portal for any signs of infiltration, something that may have gone unnoticed by her fellow acolytes and guards.

"Where are you, Ven?" Thought Jenayan bitterly as she paced frantically. "You should have escaped by now…surely?" Jenayan held a dimly-lit candle as she walked through the winding paths of her Sanctuary's catacombs, it occasionally wavered back towards where Sophilia was being kept and this disturbed the acolyte greatly. Jenayan quietly passed by Sophilia's room then halted in her steps; she listened intently upon the child singing to herself once again, though this time they were far-more familiar verses being sung.

"Cast aside the fear and pain… sleep beneath the stars above..."

Jenayan's breathing grew heavy as she carefully broke her seal to enter the room. Sophilia was surprisingly asleep and was nurturing a handful of white roses - there was no inclination at all that the child had any awareness of her strange actions.

"Lia…" Whispered Jenayan gently. "Are you awake?" Sophilia awoke with a gasp and turned herself to stare blindly at the dark outline of Jenayan, her shock though soon turned to relief on recognising the acolyte's now familiar voice.

"I'm awake now, Jenny!" Responded Sophilia with a displeased grunt. "It took me ages to fall asleep… I was having such a lovely dream as well."

"You were singing in your sleep, Lia…" Said Jenayan in an apologetic tone. "That's why I came back to check on you. Can you remember the song from your dream?"

"Yes…" Murmured Sophilia thoughtfully. "A little boy in my dream taught me it and he was so sad at first, but when I learned the words he seemed a lot happier."

"Did this little boy tell you his name?" Asked Jenayan with an eager expression. "What did he look like?"

"No, he didn't tell me his name." Sophilia was now becoming impatient with Jenayan's questioning, all she wanted to do was fall back asleep. "He had hair like mine though, and the same eye colour…"

"That's very interesting," whispered the Acolyte in a concerned tone. "The Celestial Spirits take on an appearance of Cerebrante's physical host, this Sanctuary has been known to awaken such a connection…"

"What are you on about?" Quirked Sophilia as she jolted herself upright. "You're not making any sense, Jenny."

"Sorry… go back to sleep, sweetheart." Said Jenayan in a soothing voice, as she tucked the energetic child back into her bed. The song of which Sophilia had been singing was indeed the Hymn of Alaskia; its words had been mostly forgotten to many within Impartia – how such a naïve little girl could know their verses perplexed and excited Jenayan immensely. With a further grunt, at not being able to rest, Sophilia stormed herself away from Jenayan to gaze out of her window again across the many stars that lay above them. Jenayan slowly walked over to the child, on standing beside her she began to rub at Sophilia's hands in a hope of reforming their recent bond and then they both admired the heavenly cosmos together.

"There are so many stars, aren't they?" Pondered Sophilia affectionately. "Mummy and I draw pictures with them by using our fingers… we like to join them all together and make animals... have you ever done that?" Sophilia then flickered her hand sporadically across the stars in front of her, creating imaginary visions of creatures she had only ever seen in her dreams.

"Sadly not," Remarked Jenayan. "That's a very good idea though, Lia. Can I make some drawings with you now?" Sophilia nodded back enthusiastically, as doing this would remind her of happier memories which she had shared with her mother – whilst both were free. She sat herself cross-legged on the vines which formed the floor beneath her, and with Jenayan, drew outlines of various animals and other fantastical creatures which gradually helped to open themselves up emotionally with one another. "What are you drawing?" Said Jenayan as she studied Sophilia's graceful movements.

"It's a horse!" Replied Sophilia with a widened smile. "Mummy said, that she used to ride horses when she was a little girl." Sophilia continued to draw the crude outline of an animal she had never seen, and with enthusiasm.

"I've heard that Magmorran horses are the fastest…" Jenayan instantly regretted her words. "Never mind…"

"What's a Magmorran horse?" Questioned Sophilia back sternly, though persisted in drawing her favourite creature. "We live in Viridia!"

"Just ignore me," Jenayan remorsefully shook her face within the palms of her hands. "I'm very tired and when I'm sleepy, I don't make a lot of sense." Sophilia herself could slowly feel her eyes growing heavier now in their deprivation, the playful artistry which she and Jenayan had taken part in worked tremendously in tiring both. Jenayan debated for a moment whether to leave the child so that she could sleep upon the soft vines, or risk awakening her further by placing Sophilia back into bed.

"Let's get some rest now… tomorrow will be fun, I promise you." Jenayan finally decided to lie beside the vulnerable girl, hoping to keep both warm and bring some much-needed comfort. The two soon fell into a deep slumber within their calm surroundings, though only just as the sun began to rise in the east; its radiating heat penetrated the earthly walls of Ven's Sanctum – a vast difference in comparison to the present situation affecting Impartia's Earth Guardian. As Sophilia re-awoke, she initially mistook the sleeping acolyte beside her to be that of her own mother. Jenayan herself quickly stirred by the sudden movement from Sophilia's loving embrace, and then quickly rubbed away at the tears forming in her eyes as she realised that her mother had not yet returned.

"I thought that you were Mummy," Cried Sophilia in dismay. "She's *never* been away from me this long before…" Jenayan gave a compassionate sigh and then held tightly onto Sophilia, motioning her side-to-side in wanting for the child's fearful awareness to dissipate.

"Your mother will come back… do you remember the promise I made to you last night?" Said Jenayan tenderly. "I promised to show you all of the amazing sights around this Sanctuary, there are so many to look at, and I think you'll enjoy each one." Jenayan affirmed this by forcing a smile towards the young girl.

"Jenny… I almost forgot!" Gasped Sophilia. "You *must* show me everything, I want to see the whole world!" Sophilia wiped away the last remaining tears that had formed in her eyes, the child then made for her room's exit and playfully ushered Jenayan to follow. "Come on!" Demanded the child firmly. "Let's get some breakfast, then we can go to Ven's observatory… can't we?" The elated child laughed wildly as she clasped onto Jenayan's robes, she then proceeded to drag her through the doorway to make for the inner-Sanctum.

"Calm down, Lia!" Chuckled Jenayan, though soon took on a more serious tone. "The passageways leading to Ven's Sanctum were littered with flowing vines and branches, she and Sophilia would need to tread carefully. "Slow down…we have plenty of time!" At the breakfast table, which again had been so delicately laid out by Ven's acolytes, Jenayan and Sophilia greeted those who had also arrived early. They looked hungrily upon the vast selection of fruits and toasted breads now available, their mouths watered from each enticing smell. "How are we all this fine morning…" Asked Jenayan. "I trust that each of you slept well?" She cautiously examined the varying expressions from her still-conflicted acolytes, individually, they had hung their heads in a unified silence - only one of Jenayan's closer friends broke in their repose to speak with her.

"Some of us *did* manage to rest." Responded one of the Acolytes with a knowing wink towards Jenayan. "We rose as normal, with the morning sun… unlike yourself." An awkward hesitation followed from each of the acolytes, they looked to one another in eager anticipation of their senior's response to them. "We could hear you pacing outside our chambers in the early hours… it is no wonder that you look so tired now."

"I was keeping a watchful eye to see if Ven and Sophilia's mother had returned," Replied Jenayan calmly. "There are also many other troubles that burden me at this time. However, if there is anything that *any* of you would wish to say, then do so now and openly. I am the acting Guardian for this Sanctuary in Ven's absence… treat me as his equal and I shall honour your concerns." Ven's acolytes each lowered what food they had within their hands back upon the table, Sophilia herself could sense the intense atmosphere building up around her and looked to Jenayan for a reassuring smile – something that during this moment she could not muster.

"The sunrise this morning," stuttered Jenayan's closest friend - a male Acolyte who was around the same age as her. A terrified gaze then swiftly appeared on her face. "It rose with a crimson hue, Jen… it has not done so for such a long time." Jenayan nervously tapped her fingertips on the table as she waited for a further divulgence into this observation. The noise created by this unwittingly irritated Sophilia, who placed her hands protectively across her ears to shield them from the repetitive nuisance.

"Not since King Kanaan of Magmorrah wrought the desolation of his own nation… has there been a crimson sunrise!" Replied an older Acolyte sternly. "Surely, this is an omen that we should all take heed of? We *must* fortify our Sanctuary at once!"

"Lower your voice, Brother." Commanded Jenayan, she could clearly see the anxiety building in Sophilia. "Our Sanctuary already has a seal placed over it by Ven… none can enter without permission and any attacks would be futile. We must instead focus on protecting Sophilia, as Ven instructed, not dwell on a superstitious belief…"

"Pardon my ill-manner," responded the elder Acolyte, as he placed a palm over his heart to signify the regret now coursing through him. "We are the Acolytes of Earth and should behave in such a way to display this privilege." A peaceful silence resonated throughout the Sanctum, it drove an increasingly restless Sophilia mad; she had no idea of what dire implications were being discussed. Sophilia pushed her seat away sharply from the table and then jumped upon it again, centring herself within the shocked acolytes to gain their undivided attention.

"Will you all just stop being *so* moody!" Demanded Sophilia, with her hands clasped firmly onto her hips to attain an authority over the others. "Today, we are *all* taking part on an adventure! Jenny promised me, that we are going to the very top of this tree so that I can look at all the pretty sights around it…didn't you, Jenny?" She giggled ardently against the stunned looks in return from her hosts. The acolytes raised their eyebrows and then turned themselves to face Jenayan once more, each waiting for a confirmation.

"Well!" gulped Jenayan with an awkward jolt. "You've certainly put me in my place, Lia." She shifted her gaze towards back to the other acolytes. "I thought it would be nice for her to visit Ven's observatory, she has never seen the world outside of Viridia, and it's about time we all had some fun around here… don't you agree?" The Acolytes grinned back to Jenayan, though in a shared reluctance. They understood truthfully that their current leader's intentions were well meant, and that this distraction may in fact provide them with a relief from the stresses being imposed on them.

"A marvellous idea!" Rejoiced the eldest acolyte, he then looked directly at Sophilia. "Shall we finish our meal first, though? It is quite a trek up to Ven's observatory… we will need some sustenance!" Once her belly was at its fullest, Sophilia kindly ordered for the acolytes and Jenayan to lead her way up towards Ven's observatory. To reach it, Sophilia had to walk from the Sanctum up a steep and winding staircase – an arduous trek the eldest acolyte so rightly warned her of. As they reached the gargantuan tree's summit there was a single, small platform made from stone – a reflection of what Sophilia saw within the Sanctum chamber – it stood immersed within a trail of oversized leaves to serve as Ven's 'secret' observatory.

"Wow!" Sophilia's mouth opened wide in surprise, what she was seeing now was beyond any of her expectations. "Thank you, Jenny…" The air around Ven's observatory platform was pleasantly warm, which came as a great surprise to Sophilia. She had thought, quite rightly, that with being so high up it would have been freezing from the passing wind currents; they however moved by without even lifting a single strand of her hair.

"You have waited so patiently for this, Lia." Said Jenayan with a proud stance. "Before us now lies Impartia; for such a small world, there are so many different lands and cultures - each one unique to the other. I hope that today, you may find out more about them."

Sophilia circled around the small platform in her excitement, she attempted to take in as much as possible from what was unfolding around her and only stopped when one of the acolytes gently grabbed her by the shoulders.

"This is a privilege for some of us as well, little one." Said one of the more-aged acolytes. Sophilia found this peculiar; the naïve child presumed, with being so old, that the woman talking with her would have seen these sights before. "Where we are standing now is very sacred, only a handful of followers have been granted access to this platform! I have yearned for so many years to look upon my homeland once again..." The Acolyte pointed Sophilia westwards towards a golden stretch of land. "...Talam!"

"What is Talam like?" Enquired the Child innocently. "Mummy has never mentioned it before..." She hmphed.

"Talam is the largest nation within Impartia," continued the frail-looking Acolyte, as she pointed to the horizon with an arthritic hand. "In the south are deserts that stretch as far as the eye can see, then there is its capital city further north and beyond lies an ocean... of lava!" Sophilia gave back a confused glance to the acolyte, all she had known were the forests in Viridia where Cara had raised her.

"I don't like being under the sun for too long, it hurts my eyes." Said Sophilia in a dismissive tone, firmly assuring she had no further interest in learning about Talam. "I saw some twinkling lights come from over there last night..." Sophilia pointed out the vast green lands of Hydrania to west.

"Ah... Hydrania!" Interrupted another, though far younger, acolyte. "There are amazing waterfalls, deep lakes and huge mountains there..." Jenayan herself stepped forward to divulge further.

"I bet that you would love to see them one day, Lia... so would I." Jenayan held affectionately onto the fascinated child as she guided her vision over Hydrania's eastern shoreline, its lakes glimmered with a splendour in their ancient tranquillity. "A close friend of mine – Lenya, is an acolyte in the Sanctuary of Water, I would love more than anything to see her again in person."

"Maybe, we can go together... when Mummy and your friend come back?" Replied Sophilia with a pleading stare.

"What is that strange object over there in the ocean, Jen...I can't make out what it is?" Queried one of the acolytes, their reaction soon travelled through their counterparts as they each then looked to Jenayan's for an answer. She looked further north from Hydrania where her gaze was being directed to, it was the sacred mountain of Skynah which stood prominently within the clashing ocean waves. At its peak, encircled a dense layer of ethereal clouds that shrouded the mountain's summit away from mortal eyes. Jenayan took in a deep breath; Ven had requested that she would never reveal any knowledge of Skynah to even their own brethren.

"There lies Impartia's 'supposed' Sanctuary of Air - Skynah. I doubt though that any of us here will ever manage to visit it in person, it is impossible to reach by sea and is strictly prohibited to anyone other than the Elemental Guardians." Jenayan cut her words swiftly in attempt to distract from any further questions about the secretive site, she instead pointed out to her fellow acolytes and Sophilia a vision of blindingly-white sands that lay northwards of the great mountain. "Beyond! Skynah is the 'neutral' realm of Weissamorah." Said Jenayan hastily. "You will not find any sign of civilisation there, nor any mountainous plains, lakes or forests…all that exits are miles of flattened plains that are strewn with the purest sand. Apparently, Weissamorah is where the Sanctuary of Cerebrante - the Spirit of Balance is hidden. I hear that it is in the form of a crystal pyramid that shines in varying colours, though, this place has never been seen or proven to exist by any recent sources – only Ven truly knows… I guess." Sophilia could barely see the white speck over the horizon and soon lost interest in it, she turned the opposite way from where Jenayan and her acolytes still glared to find a harrowing sight which seemed to grow in the south.

"What is that… place?" Stammered Sophilia in fear, as she looked to darkened horizon with an innate sensation of dread. A dark and haunting mass spread out over the south, the acolytes themselves gasped in dismay on finding out what it was that Sophilia's attention had been drawn to.

"My dear," Said the elderly Acolyte to Sophilia softly, her crippled hands stroked at her hair in want of bringing some reassurance. "Do not look upon that forsaken realm… for it has long been tainted." The ominous clouds stretching over the distance looked so unnatural in their movements, they unnerved some of the acolytes greatly though Jenayan just stared at them with a vacant disdain. Impartia's crimson sunrise which was witnessed earlier began to filter again through the immediate thoughts of Ven's acolytes; they looked in turn to their current leader for her further wisdom and assured resolve.

"Why do they move in such a malignant manner, Jen?" Asked an acolyte, their whole body tremored. "Is it this a creation of Kufiah… or the Dark Spirit's puppet-master?"

"Not now, Silvran!" Ordered Jenayan, she nodded the acolyte discreetly towards Sophilia who was becoming ever-more anxious. "Lia, let's look back to Hydrania…"

"No!" Shouted the child with a desperate air in her voice. "I want to know… what is that place, and why is everyone so scared of those weird clouds?" Jenayan finally succumbed to her initial reluctance, despite not knowing truthfully what was happening, the leading acolyte felt that these ash clouds could only be a symbol of Queen Cera's growing malice. Jenayan then took Sophilia's hands into her own, together they looked over towards Magmorrah in uncertainty – its dominating darkness and evil seemed to reach even them despite being so far away.

"That is the forsaken land of ash - Magmorrah." Said Jenayan sombrely, her acolytes shuddered by the mere mention of this land's detested name. "A dark and malevolent ruler took over some time ago, ever since then, Impartia has suffered under her wicked reign."

"What is her name… this nasty Queen?" Mumbled Sophilia inquisitively. The Acolytes looked back to their leader reservedly.

"Her name is…" Jenayan was instantly met by a further set of furious stares from her Acolytes, their desperate expressions pleaded for her not to reveal any else regarding the Queen. "Sophilia has a right to know," she responded frankly to them, the Acolytes turned away as not to witness the proceeding scene. "Magmorrah's Queen is named Cera, she has taken control of a very powerful and evil Spirit called Kufiah… she is the one who, I believe, has taken your mother and Ven from us." Sophilia tore her hands sharply away from Jenayan's, this name was somehow familiar to the naïve child; despite having no recollection of her true homeland, Cara had made it certain that Sophilia knew of it – though only small fragments.

"My mummy said, that I have an Aunt Cera." Despaired the child, as small tears started to form in her eyes again to make them sore. "Does that mean that we are evil as well… how could you say such a horrible thing? Mummy always said that we'd go back to where she born one day, I don't want to if it is *that* scary!" Sophilia knelt herself away from the shocked acolytes, hiding her face into her hands as she wept into them.

"Please forgive me, Lia?" Begged Jenayan, she should have perhaps taken her acolytes' advice. "I only wanted to be honest with you, it is not right that such knowledge be kept away. You and Cara are not at all evil, in anyway, we all know this and that is all that should matter…" Sophilia whimpered and struggled to capture her breath; she had never felt so alone or alienated as she did right now, nor angered by such an obvious ignorance towards her bloodline.

"That 'wicked' Queen is *still* my Aunt Cera!" Sophilia struck at the ground with her fists in torment. "Mummy said that all my aunt wants to do is to live alone, that's why we had to leave and come here… please, don't say such horrible things about my family… Aunt Cera is all we have left." The daunting realisation of how great a burden it was to care for Sophilia now hit the acolytes hard, they all shook in fear against it and could not turn away from Magmorrah's menacing site. Each one felt that they had been led into a possible and fatal trap, without their Guardian to protect them, Cera's reach would undoubtedly reach them eventually.

"I'm so sorry…" Repeated Jenayan in remorse. "I'm… so sorry!" She held onto the child's hands, desperate to calm her anger.

"It's okay, Jenny…" Said Sophilia with a gentle nod of her head. "I know that you're not really such a nasty person, sometimes, people say things without thinking? I would very much like to see Hydrania's lakes one day… and with you." She wrapped her arms around Jenayan to ferment this renewed trust in them both. "I will make sure, that my mummy knows Magmorrah isn't a place we should go to, so don't worry."

"Hydrania is a beautiful place; it has a Sanctuary like we do, and a very special man is in charge of it called Levia." Jenayan regained her composure slightly. "He would love to meet you and your mummy, so we will have to bring Cara along with us as well!"

"What is Levia like... is he scary?" Asked Sophilia as she playfully began to skip between the distancing acolytes, who were moving themselves away to avoid any unnecessary accidents. Jenayan laughed tremendously at this unexpected remark.

"Levia is not scary at all, Lia." Said Jenayan bluntly. "He has magic powers, like Ven, and can play the most amazing musical instrument that you could ever see; it is a pipe organ that uses the power from all the massive waterfalls in Levia's Sanctum to make music... he can even control the very waves of the oceans with it!" Jenayan smiled knowingly to her brethren as few had ever met Levia in person themselves. "Levia is also Ven's best friend."

"I might like him then..." Quirked Sophilia with a jubilant grin. "We'll *definitely* have to go and see Levia now!" Sophilia and Ven's acolytes laughed together for a good length of time afterwards, until the sun gradually began to fade. An unveiling darkness grew as dusk covered the Sanctuary and lands of Impartia, radiating them all with a unified golden colour and serene beauty. The countless stars of the cosmos then appeared as if one by one, lingering high above the awestruck acolytes as they excused themselves away from Jenayan and Sophilia's company to prepare their evening meal.

"Thank you for today, Jenny." Said Sophilia abruptly, she started to draw pictures with the stars again and urged her new friend to play along. "I never knew just how big our world actually is!"

"You never know, Lia." Whispered Jenayan willingly. "One day, you and your mummy may have a chance to see all the other lands for yourselves... wouldn't that be great?"

"Yes..." Sophilia gave out a wide and loud yawn. "I'm not hungry, to be honest, and I hope that we sleep better tonight."

"Come on, let's go back now." Jenayan aided Sophilia to her feet, kindly brushing at the child's dirty dress as she did so. "It won't hurt us to miss supper for one night... will it?"

Another day passed without Ven's protection over his Sanctuary, this troubled the acolytes even more as a feeling of vulnerability now started to settle in. Jenayan entered the Sanctum alone for breakfast as Sophilia remained asleep. She was met by a harrowing silence from her fellow acolytes, something Jenayan wished to disperse immediately. "I can sense that something is worrying you all..." Said Jenayan with a sympathetic shrug. "Please, be open with me... what is the matter now?" One of the acolytes abruptly moved away from the table to circle their Sanctum platform in anxiety, looking back to Jenayan with an intent stare as to how she could effectively remove their pressing worries.

"The child, that we are all burdened with, is a *direct* descendant of King Kanaan!" Blared the Acolyte angrily. "We are protecting a princess of Magmorrah, albeit and exiled one, here in *our* Sanctuary walls; how does this not concern you as it does with us, Jen?" The acolyte's fury was met with similar grunts from Jenayan's other followers. "What if Ven does not return… what if we are left to face the wrath of that deplorable Queen and her General again… how can we stop such an evil?" Jenayan fought hard to stay collective, in having to deal with this show of insubordination from own brethren. She quickened her pace over to the lone acolyte who stood in challenging the authority of Ven's instructions and held out to them a single seed which was placed within one of her hands.

"This seed was given to me by Ven, he found it within our Sanctum and is incredibly rare to come by." Jenayan carefully lifted the seed above her head, allowing for the rays of sunlight to touch it and reveal a stream of emerald energy coursing through. "This tiny, insignificant thing could grow to become a tree just like our Sanctuary; it is granted by the Guardian of Earth, but to only those whom they would trust in protecting their Sanctum and knowledge." The Acolytes' previous frustration instantly fell, they understood what it was that Jenayan was conveying. "Ven threw this to me the other night, before General Nira took him. He obviously had no doubts in his mind of *my* loyalty to him, I would hope that you would see this gesture is also aimed at yourselves as well."

"Ven did not know when he was taken, that Sophilia is related to Queen Cera…" Snarled one of the Acolytes to another. "We accept you willingly as our leader in his absence, but your powers are nowhere as strong as Ven's."

"If Sophilia were your own child, would you not wish for a similar protection over her as what we are offering?" Said Jenayan in a gesture of disbelief. "We must pray for Ven's safe return though in the meantime, concentrate on making Sophilia's time here enjoyable… she has enough to worry about."

"Yes… but…" Mumbled the opposing Acolyte sporadically. "She will put us all at risk!"

"There is not 'but'… we are to protect the child, even if it costs us our lives!" Jenayan moved to leave the Sanctum in her risen frustration. Her departure was abruptly cut short however, as just beyond the doorway now stood Sophilia with a satisfied smile on her face.

"Where are you going, Jenny… have you already eaten your breakfast?" Asked Sophilia in a meek voice. "You should have woken me!"

"No, sweetheart." Jenayan quickly tried to calm her temperament. "Come in, we've just started." The Sanctum fell awkwardly silent as the acolytes dwelled in their shame, each succumbing to the spiritual and moral duty of caring for Sophilia. They each made their excuses again and returned to their own chambers, Jenayan's words struck hard and were soon absorbed.

"Anyway…Good Morning, Lia!" Rejoiced Jenayan in a boisterous tone, hoping to relinquish any previous tension made by the leaving acolytes. "I'm presuming, that you slept better last night… from rising so late?"

"Yes... I had a *lovely* sleep!" Sophilia clumsily sat herself beside Jenayan. "I dreamt that we visited Levia's Palace, and we were listening to the beautiful music he was playing!" Various pieces of fruit spewed from the child's mouth as she spoke, most landed on Jenayan to Sophilia's amusement. "I would like to see more today please, if that is okay with you?"
Jenayan clapped her hands joyfully at this request, causing Sophilia to jump from her seat in surprise in not expecting such a reaction.

"Today Lia, I will give you a grand tour of this Sanctuary... I may even show you some of its more secret places!" Continued Jenayan with an ecstatic tremor. Sophilia leapt towards Jenayan to wrap her arms tightly around her again, beaming her teeth with an exaggerated smile to display her needful excitement.

"Can you show me *just* the secret places, Jenny?" Sophilia looked around for any unwanted listeners. "You're more fun than the others are..."

"Sure... just me and you!" Jenayan gave an appreciative grin to Sophilia, she had longed for such a friendly bond and now wanted to make the most of it. "Where shall we go first?" Jenayan's smile grew wider on noticing how excited Sophilia was now becoming. "How about the mystical *Pool of Insight* which is hidden beneath the Sanctum chamber?" It was the most difficult place to find within Ven's Sanctuary, and Jenayan painfully hoped that Sophilia would comply with this suggestion.

"Yes... as long as I can swim in this pool?" Sophilia bared her teeth in joy. "It's been *ages* since I last had a swim!" She said in a begging gesture.

"The Pool of Insight is a divine place where you can reflect on memories which may lie hidden." Countered Jenayan in a more serious voice. "But I guess that, technically, you can swim there... I was hoping that it would reveal more happier memories to you – if being honest." There was no more needed to be said on Jenayan's part in convincing Sophilia, together they left from the Sanctum and hastily made towards a wall of Ivy nearby – a mere façade which led to the secret pool. "The pool is down here," explained Jenayan with a cautious voice, she was only doing this to increase Sophilia's anticipation. "Don't be put off with it being dark at first, the sunrays peak through a little further in..." The descent took far longer than Sophilia had hoped for, and fatigue soon took a hold over her waning mental strength. Half-way down, Jenayan realised that she would need to carry the weary girl, carefully they traversed over the ancient steps which had become slippery from falling moss – a result of being neglected over many years. "We're nearly there, Lia... hold on!" Cried out Jenayan, her legs were starting to give way under Sophilia's weight. "We haven't got much farther to go... it'll be worth it!" Sophilia gave a bored sigh then nestled her head into Jenayan's hair, she found that playing with the red curls helped pass the time – there wasn't much else to do at this point.

"I don't think I can swim now, Jenny…" Yawned Sophilia to the acolyte's dismay. "I'm far too tired, can we go back and play with the others?" Jenayan shifted Sophilia's body so that she was resting upon her back, there was only a few steps left to take in reaching the named pool and this drove both to lighten their spirits.

"This is a great honour, you know… visiting Ven's sacred pool?" Jenayan wished to enforce how risky this journey was to her in Sophilia. "I could get into a lot of trouble for showing you it!"

"I still want to go!" Pleaded Sophilia as she untangled one of her fingers from Jenayan's hair. "If you're getting tired… I can walk?" Jenayan smiled then laughed at this kind, though late, offer.

"Thank you, Lia. You'll be glad to know that we're pretty-much there now!" The air suddenly became denser in its floral scents and a strange presence seemed to linger around Sophilia. Jenayan halted for a moment, there was a feeling that they were no longer alone.

"Did you say something, Lia?" Questioned the acolyte with a nervous undertone.

"No!" Sophilia moved on ahead, she didn't appear to notice anything strange herself. "What did you hear?" Questioned the child with a naïve curiosity.

"I'm sure, I heard you say something?" Jenayan thought for a fleeting moment that bringing Sophilia to such a spiritually active place may have, in hindsight, been a bad idea. Ven had shown Jenayan the Pool of Insight many times before, yet when they visited there was an entirely different and more pleasant atmosphere. "We'll just stay for a little while, don't touch the water unless I say so…"

Chapter Seven: The Pool of Insight

The final steps which lead to Ven's sacred pool gradually submerged into a dark vat of motionless water, its depth could not be fully gauged - despite the filtering rays of sunlight that were feeding into it. Sophilia peered inquisitively at her faint reflection in the pool, she felt both scared and excited by its mysterious appearance and soon lowered herself to look closer.

"Is it warm?" Asked Sophilia eagerly. She raised a hand to place it into the pool, though was swiftly halted by Jenayan who still felt unnerved by the strange atmosphere building around them. "I just want to see!"

"Wait a moment please, Lia." Said Jenayan firmly. "The Pool of Insight can reveal memories from your past, as well as find some answers relating to your future. I know that your excited, but we must be cautious… and respectful."

"When will the magic happen?" Questioned Sophilia as she defiantly submerged her feet into the pool, despite Jenayan's strict orders not to. "Work, magic… Work!"

"You have to look at yourself within the water, Lia." Jenayan moved Sophilia's face with a gentle nudge to look directly into the pool. "If you are special, which you are, some images will start to appear. It doesn't always happen first-time; I needed a few visits before anything appeared… let's see." The flickering sunrays seeped upon the water around Sophilia's feet; they revealed within the pool a set of small jade lights that swiftly rose from the murky depths and appeared sentient in nature. Sophilia stared at the dancing lights that continued to float playfully beneath her feet, one by one they bound together, and images started to emerge from them that only the child could see.

"It's working, Jenny!" Gasped Sophilia as she twiddled her toes towards the shifting lights. "I must be special!" Tears of joy trickled from Jenayan's eyes; the pool would only ever respond to a person with unprecedented spiritual powers such as her own and Ven's, her suspicion that Sophilia was truly a gifted child had now been confirmed.

"That's brilliant, Lia…" Jenayan rubbed excitedly at Sophilia's shoulders. "Can you see any pictures yet?" Sophilia held a tremendous focus on the blurry images now forming in front of her, she did not want to disappoint Jenayan by losing her concentration. At first, Sophilia saw a vision of Viridia's ancient forests which she and her mother loved to explore together. The birds flying by seemed so real and somehow Sophilia could even smell the different scents from the surrounding fauna.

"I can see Mummy," Replied Sophilia, her stare still fixated on the shifting lights. "We're walking through the forests like we used to!"

"That's fantastic!" Said Jenayan, she desperately tried to see the images for herself but could not. "Keep looking…" This following vision showed to Sophilia Viridia's shoreline at night, upon its sands knelt a robed woman who was nurturing a small infant in her hands. Sophilia could hear the stranger crying and raised an arm towards her as if to offer some comfort.

"There's a lady and a little baby…" Whispered Sophilia, whilst trying not to cry from the moving scene. "She is sad, but I can't see why?" Jenayan placed a hand of comfort across Sophilia's to reassure her during this strange spiritual experience, the acolyte sensed who it was being shown and herself fought against a deepening sorrow.

"Sadness does not last forever," said Jenayan softly. "I believe… eventually, this lady and her baby would have found happiness together."
Suddenly, Sophilia's body shuddered as in fright. The lights that danced beneath her had become more erratic and aggressive in their movements, unleashing a darker and far-more sinister vision.

"Jenny… I'm scared, I don't like this anymore!" Cried out Sophilia. She tried hard to remove her feet from the pool, only to find that it dragged further in as she did. "Jenny!"
Jenayan grabbed onto the petrified child with all her strength, she desperately fought to draw both herself and Sophilia away from the pool though its water latched onto them when a greater ferocity. "Jenny… help me!" Sophilia screamed frantically. She was being dragged now further into the depths by a violent force and they soon submerged her with an oppressing hold – Sophilia just managed to keep her head over the surface. "I don't want to die!" The lights moved as if they were scarlet flames, bursting with a terrifying heat that met against Sophilia's delicate skin. Soon, an image formed that showed General Nira and her tanks as they entered the forests of Viridia, leaving a path of destruction in their wake.
"I don't want to see her… make it her go away, Jenny! Make it stop!" Sheer panic took over Sophilia and Jenayan as the pool became even more erratic in its movement. The vines that fed into it whipped together around Sophilia, only just missing her flailing movements as she tried in vain to free herself. "Help me!" The vines tightly wrapped themselves around Sophilia's legs, completely encompassing the child within their powerful grasp to drag her far below. Sophilia now found herself surrounded by a veil of pure darkness, she could no longer hear Jenayan and the dancing lights reacted suddenly on touching her birthmark. A blinding flash lifted from the pool and Jenayan swore that she could hear voices in it, though none were recognisable.

"Lia!" Shouted Jenayan, though it was only in vain. "…What have I done?" The image of a great metropolis emerged before Sophilia. It had countless towering structures that stood hundreds of feet high, some even seemed to reach the clouds above. Below, thousands of smartly-dressed citizens were gathered together, forming a sea of angered faces that marched in unison against a large obsidian palace that was centred within the city.

"Open your eyes, child... Breathe!" Said a terrifying voice that spoke directly into Sophilia's sub-conscious. *"You must see this... it is your destiny!"* Sophilia clenched her eyes away from the vision, but it persisted to play out within the child's mind regardless.

"I don't want to look..." Whimpered Sophilia to herself. "I don't know where I am!"

"You... are Home..."

Jenayan looked on helplessly at Sophilia's ordeal; she tried to reach in with her hands again for the child, only to have them snapped painfully away by a set of flouncing vines.

"What's going on?" Panicked Sophilia, she was now flying weightlessly and against her own will over the vast crowds below. Sophilia began to hear a resonating hatred come from the amassed populace, though yet could not decipher at whom this was aimed at.

"Who are they angry with?" Pondered Sophilia anxiously. "I can't see!" She screamed.

"...You will see..."

Without warning, Sophilia suddenly found herself above the city's grand palace. She could clearly make out the image of a tall man, who had had upon his head a golden crown embossed with many priceless gems. Sophilia jolted in fright as the figure waved his fists violently against the crowds who now stood before his gates, his words echoed with their sadistic tones to a tirade of abuse in return.

"His eyes..." Shuddered Sophilia, they were amber - just like hers. "Who *is* he?"

Beside the regal figure, silently emerged a dark and demonic mass of black smoke. It released from within a foreboding shadow to spread far across the city landscape and its picturesque landscape – the citizens cried out in terror.

"Jenny..." Sophilia's heartbeat raced in unison with the growing shadow.

"Help me!" Some of Ven's acolytes stationed near the Sanctum above had thankfully heard the agonising screams coming from beneath them. Quickly and without any hesitation, they proceeded to run down the exposed stairwell to find Jenayan weeping into her hands before the Pool of Insight. The horrific experience Sophilia was being forced to encounter felt as if it was happening over only a matter of seconds to her, yet for those helplessly trying to aid the child it seemed to stretch out far longer in duration.

"What is happening here, Jen?" Asked the eldest Acolyte with a judgemental look. "Where is the child?"

"Just…Help me!" Screamed Jenayan with pleading eyes. "I can't get Sophilia out, the vines are pulling her further in!" The spiritual connection Sophilia was now under proved too strong for the despairing acolytes to break. They each pulled hard at the vines and prayed that Sophilia could somehow be saved, though only found that the more they pulled, the more violent the pool's water and vines retaliated. The malignant mass forced Sophilia closer, against all the child's effort to break from its invisible grasp. Emerging from within this dark plume, a grotesque monster disturbingly began to form: the creature's eyes glowed as if aflame, it's transparent skin barely covered the Demon's supporting bones, a deathly stench rose from the corpse-like figure and to Sophilia's absolute horror she found herself now placed directly before it.

"I see you… Princess of Magmorrah…" Taunted the malevolent creature.

"Princess?" Sophilia shook her head dismissively. "I'm not a Princess…"

"No… you are more… your destiny has only just begun!" Cackled the Demon.

The terrified citizens chaotically forced themselves against a wall of soldiers which stood in defiance of their protest. The crowned figurehead defiled his subject's cries of anguish by viciously raising his fists higher into the air towards them.
"Traitors… Infidels!" Roared the regal figure. "How dare you defy my rule!" With an emotionless stare, the King suddenly reached for a golden amulet that was hidden within his black robes and lain upon his muscular chest. He gave a cruel towards a group of shadowy figures that had silently joined with him from behind, their responsive smiles instantly raised Sophilia's concern even greater. "You say, that I am monster?" Retorted the King with a mocking sense of shock towards his subjects. "I say… that you are all blind!" The sporadic flames within the Demon's eyes grew in their intensity, it then wrapped both arms around its torso as if in agony. The Dark Spirit lingered motionless thereafter in anticipation of its master's first command, it stared across the crowd momentarily in knowing what fate was about to meet with them.

"You must bear witness… Princess…"

"Why…what are you going to do?" Sophilia's lips trembled as she spoke. The petrified child then coarsely released a piercing scream from her small lungs, wishing to escape from this horrific nightmare and the evil being now glaring its wicked eyes upon her.

"You need not fear me, Kufiah, as other mortals do…." Whispered the Spirit of Darkness to Sophilia, as if in pain to her, also showing freely their own agonised state of existence. *"I am Impartia's Spirit of Darkness and Reaper of the Void! Where there is light, I shall forever exist with it… I am Kufiah and you cannot hide away from me forever!"* Sophilia gained enough courage to speak against the creature's tortured words; she wished to know more of what was being said to her by it, though failed to utter any reply as she now noticed the Demon's shadow spread even further over the city towards its distant horizon.

"I have seen you before… in my nightmares." Replied Sophilia reluctantly, she started to feel a strange form of pity towards the tortured Spirit and wept a single tear for them.

"Be my witness, Child… to the true resolve of mankind… nature's greatest folly!" The haunting vision suddenly became clearer and far more disturbing.

"You demand peace and freedom?" Shouted the king with a determined vigour, he raised his cursed amulet higher for all to see and grinned at the confused expressions it wrought. "I *will* grant you this liberty, though have I not already brought prosperity to our great nation?" The King's eyes flared in unison to Kufiah's own. "All of you will now *burn* for your heinous acts of insolence against me! You shall dwell for an eternity in the Void… of Kufiah!" The crowds erratically dispersed in their sudden realisation of what King Kanaan was implying; many had tried to seek shelter from this unknown threat, as the shadow that now fell over them suddenly resonated with an unearthly and guttural roar. Kufiah at this point, remained transfixed on Sophilia and tenderly wiped away the tears that ran down from her face.

"Look upon my forced servitude, girl… forgive, and learn from it as others in your bloodline should have… I am a necessary evil." Kufiah cried out in acute pain as he held his arms outwardly over the surrounding landscape of Magmorrah, still standing in this vision to Sophilia as it had once done within its ancient glory. The eerie shadow that had spread from Kufiah's mass suddenly drew itself back into his physical body.

"Render them!" Commanded the King with a desperation in his voice. "Render them all!"

Kufiah shook violently from the powerful energy that had accumulated within himself then, without any warning, the Spirit released it as a blast that created an unimaginable heat and wave of devastation which tore across Magmorrah's capital and surrounding landscapes.

"No!" Sophilia cried out in vain to Kufiah, the Spirit of Darkness no longer had any control over his own will. An immense pain tore itself through Sophilia, the surrounded her whole body and she could feel ever intense sensation. "Stop it… don't kill them!" The infliction that had been wrought upon Sophilia by Kufiah's raw power suddenly died away, releasing her from the relentless pain and in its aftermath also revealed the ruins of Magmorrah's once magnificent city and subjects – all now silenced and encased within their own ashes as a preserved display of Kanaan's evil will for all eternity.

"Remember what you have seen here, young mortal." The Spirit of Darkness appeared so weary now to Sophilia, she could not sense the same level of malice as was present moments before. *"You have shared in the pain of those people… my darkness is ever-lasting… so… is The Sacred Balance…"* Kufiah and the haunting vision of Magmorrah's decimation faded away from Sophilia, she momentarily regained consciousness to find herself in Jenayan's loving arms.

"Lia!" Shouted Jenayan repeatedly at the child to awaken her fully. "This wasn't meant to happen… please, forgive me!"

"What do you think has happened to her, Jen?" Questioned one of the acolytes, as they assisted two others in lifting Sophilia from their leader's arms. "Has anything like this occurred here before? You should not have brought such a vulnerable child to this volatile place…" They sighed bitterly.

"I *had* to bring Sophilia here!" Assured Jenayan with a firm stare. "I thought, that Cerebrante's mark may have revealed where her mother and Ven are now being kept…" The Acolytes present wallowed in empathy to their leader's resolve; they reasoned that Jenayan would not have taken such a risky move, if it were not for their desperate situation.

"The spiritual power of our Sanctum should help the child with her healing…" Spoke another Acolyte in hope. "We will place her within the central seal there, Cerebrante's influence may be the only thing now that will be able to save Sophilia."

"What are we waiting for?" Responded Jenayan as she frantically righted herself. "Take her there… now!" The Sanctum's platform and Seals radiated with the flowing rays of sun that seeped through its outer branches. Cerebrante's own seal emanated a golden light which the acolytes swiftly placed Sophilia within, hoping that it would heal the gravely weakened child from her catatonic state. "I will stay with Sophilia, until she recovers." Said Jenayan in remorse of her actions to the acolytes. "Keep an eye out for her mother – Cara, and Ven if he too returns. This… might take a while." Sophilia remained upon Cerebrante's seal for, what felt like, many days in a wakeful slumber. Her petite body shifted against Jenayan occasionally as the acolyte attempted to hold the child within her arms as a comforting presence.

"No…please…please, don't hurt them...Ku…Kuf…" Mumbled the child, almost indecipherably and in torment.

"Lia… are you awake?" Jenayan stroked at Sophilia's hair gently, she would have given her own life at this moment if it were to save the child's. "Please be okay…" The Acolytes returned on hearing Sophilia's strange screams and looked to Jenayan for any possible answers regarding these ramblings. They felt greatly saddened and pained in how helpless they were to end the child's infliction; yet with each passing second, she seemed to be regaining consciousness.

"Stop this… the Void…you're burning them all… Kufiah!" Sophilia suddenly gasped herself awake and then fell back into a deeper state of sleep. The spiritual connection which she had bonded with Kufiah was draining her of what youthful energy remained, it was like a poison coursing through the child's veins.

"I have never seen this kind of reaction before, not even Ven has encountered such a strong spiritual connection in the Pool of Insight." Said Jenayan in shock, as the eldest acolyte rubbed at her shoulders in sympathy. "I can't say for certain what it was that Sophilia saw in her vision… but, it was nothing like I had expected." Another Acolyte carefully stepped forward, they knelt silently beside Sophilia and placed the child's cold hands over her chest then removed their own robe place it over in creating some form of warmth.

"She spoke of Kufiah. Sophilia *clearly* named the Spirit of Darkness, Jen." Despaired the acolyte fearfully. "How could such a small, innocent girl with no knowledge of Impartia's Spirits know of this being… let alone have such a vivid encounter with it?"

"I *don't know*, Silvran!" Jenayan burst into tears, her hands shook through her flowing sorrow and deep regret entered the acolyte's thoughts. "I wish… I wish that Ven was here." The harsh reality of Jenayan's new responsibility as being their Sanctuary's leader, now dawned on the acolytes as they each embraced her one-by-one.

"We have faith in your guidance, Jen." Assured Silvran, the most vocal of Ven's acolytes. "You have proven to be a valiant leader and protector, I would entrust my own children's safety in your care… if the circumstance was different." He placed a hand solemnly over his heart, it's beat racing faster now.

"Thank you…" Jenayan suddenly jolted, a burning scent began to enter the Sanctum chamber from outside. Ven's acolytes quickly covered their mouths to repel its choking stench, then moved towards the exposed branches to see where this foreign smoke was coming from.

"It cannot be…" Despaired the elderly female Acolyte to her kin. "Jenayan!" A group of Sanctuary Guards ran into the Sanctum and swiftly fell to their knees before their current leader. They were exhausted by the consuming fumes looked to the acolytes desperately for their aid, a sight unheard of previously.

"Brothers… Sisters," Exhaled one of the guards, as she fought to catch her breath. "Viridia… has been set aflame!" She screamed in despair.

"Impossible," responded Jenayan with a perplexed glance. "How can this be?" The Sanctum suddenly took on a darker atmosphere, its once flourishing life appearing to diminish.

"Viridia's forests… are burning," Continued the guard in fatigue. "Even the mountains to the south have not evaded this plight, what are we going to do?"

"This Sanctuary is impenetrable…" Said Jenayan defiantly, though her body language spoke otherwise. "No mortal flame can pierce our Guardian's seal!"

"We also gained word from our allies this evening, Lady Jenayan." Interrupted a separate guard, their expression fearful. "Talam's capital has been *completely* destroyed and it is likely… that Hydrania will suffer the same fate. The true will of Magmorrah has been awoken, the Dark Spirit's reach… is spreading!"

"Impossible!" Repeated Jenayan to herself in a terrified voice. "Queen Cera is not that powerful, she can't have destroyed an entire city not without...."

"The full power of Kufiah…" Spoke another Guard forcefully to Jenayan. "The Queen of Magmorrah *has* done the impossible, this cannot be denied now. As heir to our Sanctuary in Ven's wake, we look to you for your orders – Lady Jenayan."

"Secure the Sanctum and the seal to our Sanctuary's entrance, no one leaves or enters it!" Ordered Jenayan firmly, she then quickly gathered her fellow acolytes together within the platform. "We *must* keep Sophilia safe, the connection she shared with the Spirit of Darkness would have alerted Queen Cera to her exact whereabouts - the child is our priority now."

Ven's guards swiftly made their exit towards the Sanctuary's entrance seal, a choking plume of smoke billowed throughout the passageways as they ran along them. Inside the Sanctum, the remaining Acolytes of Earth moved to form a protective circle against its entrance. Jenayan sat herself again beside Sophilia to stroke at the child's hair, she started to sing hymns which Ven had taught her in a vain hope that they may hasten the child's spiritual recovery. "Lia…you must be strong now." Whispered Jenayan tearfully. "I promised that you would see your mother again…don't give in… don't leave us here alone... we miss your laughter so much already." Jenayan pressed Sophilia tightly into her bosom, suddenly a sign of warmth came from the child's faint breaths – much to the acolyte's relief.

"You… are…" Sophilia strained her words painfully, then the child's voice took on a darker and far more sinister undertone. "…***Infidels***…"

"Sophilia?" Jenayan struggled to remain calm, the acolyte had only ever known of two figures who used this defiling term: one was seemingly dead and the other was still in Jenayan's anxious thoughts at this time. "Are you trying to warn me about *her*?" Sophilia stirred slightly and opened her eyes to meet with Jenayan's, she raised a sweet smile then fell back into a death-like sleep. "Cerebrante… I know you can hear me." Said Jenayan as she looked to the Spirit's seal beneath Sophilia. "Heal this child, she may be our only hope to save Impartia." As if by divine intervention, Sophilia immediately awoke and fully this time. She first stroked at Jenayan's hair to return the acolyte's kind gesture in staying with her, then formed an embrace which neither wanted to ever cease.

"Jenny!" Cried out the child with an endearing smile, though her body shook as if in agony from a coursing venom. "I knew that you'd look after me!"

"Are you hurt?" Jenayan pinched at Sophilia's skin, ensuring the warmth she had felt had not dwindled. "I didn't think the Pool of Insight would react in such a way; you should have never been put in danger like that."

"Jenny…" Sophilia was unsure about how to react; she only remembered fragments from the vision, though the horrifying image of Kufiah still clearly stood in her mind. "I saw *him*."

"I know…" Before Jenayan could delve any deeper into Sophilia's dread, a transient red light from outside suddenly took her attention away. "What was that?" Jenayan and Sophilia hastily sprinted towards the Sanctum's windows to discover what was causing this strange light. What met with them was a gigantic shadow that silently glided through the night air, its carcass masked the stars beyond and from the beast's belly came a reign of scarlet energy beams. "So, that is what has set our forest aflame?" Remarked Jenayan, the sight of this strange monster instantly wrought a new horror in her. "We cannot be harmed in here, Lia." The Acolyte's body language unwittingly showed a contradiction to her words. "Stay low away from these smoke fumes, we *will* make it through this… we must!" Beneath the Sanctuary tree and upon its entrance seal, six of Ven's guards stood bravely at their stations in preparation for any incoming attack – which they all feared was inevitable now.

"This is terrible," Despaired one of the Guards to another. "I doubt if any of the Forest-Dwellers will survive… let alone us."

"Silence…" Ordered any guard sternly. "Who knows what may be watching us?" A strange figure abruptly began to creep through the billows of smoke; Ven's guards dutifully noticed this and within moments they made their own cautious approach, each with their swords drawn ready in anticipation of what new evil may have arisen.

"Who goes there…?" Cried out one of the guards fiercely. "Show yourself!" A young female silently emerged from the choking fumes in response, she then calmly passed under a rain of falling tree embers without any sign of fear or discomfort towards Ven's guards - who themselves were shocked by this unnerving sight. The stranger's eyes noticeably glistened with a piercing flame-like stare that she held firmly against the raised weapons before her, of which none seemed to create any willed-fear.

"Halt!" Commanded the Guards in unison, with their weapons raised higher now. "None may enter this Sanctuary… by decree of its Guardian!" Their voices pitifully struggled to reach over the roaring flames; with each passing second, it seemed that Viridia's immolation grew even more violent.

"You *will* grant my entry!" Commanded the woman forcefully, her voice seemed to carry through the loud atmosphere with an unnatural ease. "How *dare* you abandon me to these flames; a poor, defenceless woman with no other to offer aid!" The Guards suffered an instant confliction; if they did permit this vulnerable stranger into their Sanctuary, then they would be disobeying direct orders given to them by Jenayan.

"I'm sorry," responded one of the Guards with a remorseful shrug. "Leave this area now… for there is no safety that we can offer you!"

"You would have me burn to death?" Said the woman in a more pleading tone. "I must find my daughter; she was taken from me and I cannot rest until she is found!"

"Look, we don't want any trouble!" The addressing guard, despite his stubborn obedience, shuddered momentarily as this story did seem very familiar. "Leave here immediately without any resistance, and you shall find that no harm will come to you… by us." The woman responded with some mocking laughter and then immediately reached for a sword that was sheathed to her side: it was pure-black and unlike any weapon which the guards had seen before, this furthered their individual reservations in aiding the enigmatic stranger.

"You are no threat to me!" Countered the woman passively and with a menacing smile. "I *know* that my daughter is here… stop being so cruel and stupid… let me in!" Ven's guards rushed to speak amongst themselves; they had indeed been waiting for the return of Sophilia's mother, though the woman standing before them now did not exactly fit the kindly description given to them by Jenayan.

"What is your name…" Questioned one of the guards anxiously, as a cocktail of emotions flowed through them. "Perhaps, if you share this with us, then we may permit access into our sacred Sanctuary?"

"My name…" The woman paused, a grimacing expression appeared instantly on her face. "My name is Cara. I am the first-born daughter of Kanaan – Magmorrah's fallen king – and sister to the rightful Queen… Cera. I know for certain that my daughter is being kept here and you *will* take me to her at once!"

"She is *definitely* the child's mother," Whispered one of the guards in frustration to the others. "There's no denying it; they have the same amber eyes and hair colour, even that mark on her face is like Sophilia's… there aren't many who bear it!" Time was quickly running out for Ven's guards to make their informed decision; the forest fire was spreading more rapidly, and their unexpected guest had become more hostile with each lingering second. "Cara, it is a great relief to see that you have returned here… unharmed." Spoke one of the guards duly, their eyes inspected Cara's peculiar robes – finding that, somehow, they were similar to those worn by Kufiah's Dark Acolytes. "There are few who have survived Queen Cera's wrath… we will take you to Sophilia immediately."

"Good," Replied with the woman smugly, and with a scornful leer she then sheathed her blade in unison to those raised by Ven's guards. "Trust me, you have made the right decision." The entrance portal spontaneously emitted a blinding, emerald light as Ven's guards summoned together for its immediate activation. Without further hesitation, they eagerly gestured for their guest to approach the empowered seal, and soon all were transported into the Sanctuary dwellings situated high above. The guards stationed inside understandably panicked on noticing the re-opened entranceway, in a dreaded confusion they approached with their weapons drawn and hearts ready for battle.

"Who goes there… what is the meaning of this?" Questioned an inner guard with a nervous cry. "None may enter this Sanctuary!"

"Lower your weapons!" Responded the outer-guards in unison, at this point they had also formed a protective circle around their secretive visitor. "We have good reason to forsake Jenayan's orders!"

"Who is that with you, and what good reason do you have to break your vows?" The inner guards keenly noticed the stranger's unfamiliar attire, their cold welcome was respective of this. "She looks like a Dark Acolyte…"

"I know, but she is Cara – Sophilia's mother!" Replied another guard excitedly "She has managed to break free from Queen Cera's imprisonment and has come back for the child."

"Well, it is a true honour to finally meet you… Cara." Said an inner guard as they continued to perform a judgemental stare. "It has been such a joy… caring for your daughter." A tension suddenly rose between the talking guard and their guest. "If you don't mind me asking: How *did* you manage to escape from Magmorrah's forces yet our Guardian, who has abilities beyond any of us here, could not?"

"A Mother's love is a powerful force…" Countered the woman bitterly, it seemed like this statement pained her somehow. "Queen Cera has proven what a merciful ruler she is… by pardoning me – an exile and traitor of Magmorrah's glorious nation."

"I apologise, Cara… if I was being discourteous." Replied the guard in shock. "But Queen Cera is not…"

"I am positive that Sophilia will be happy to see me." Interrupted the woman again forcefully, she grinded her teeth at the guard with an obvious detest. "Keep the portal open, I wish to leave this putrid place as soon as I have my child!" Her callous mannerisms were so unlike the loving ones mentioned by Jenayan, despite this, Ven's guards felt that they had no option but to obey.

"Surely, would you and your child not be safer in here with us?" Spoke an older guard. "The fires outside are intensifying, and there is no sign of them dying out. If only our Guardian was here; Ven could have transported us to a safer location with the use of his Sanctum seals…" With a sadistic smile, the woman shook her head and laughed on hearing this unfortunate confession.

"Yes, that does leave you vulnerable… doesn't it?" Her apparent pleasure at this disturbed the guards greatly.

"Nothing can penetrate this holy site… not even those wild flames outside!" Replied a younger guard in defiance. "How can you find this situation so amusing?"

"I have made arrangements to leave Viridia this very evening… the destruction of your forest does not move me in the slightest." The woman's eyes flared from her rising agitation, this forced the guards against their better judgement into an unwilling submission. "Take me to Sophilia… Now!"

"We will," Answered a guard lowly. "Please, follow us… the Sanctum is not far from here." With a desperate haste, the guards and their new burden traversed through the Sanctuary's winding catacombs - a usual journey that would feel far from normal to each of them now. The cloaked woman reeled in delight upon reaching Ven's sacred chamber, her child-like joy was vastly contrasted however by the looks of astonishment being given by Jenayan and her fellow acolytes.

"I ordered for the Sanctuary to be sealed… none were to enter or leave! Who *is* this that hides behind you all?" Snarled Jenayan furiously to the anxious guards. She immediately retracted her angered tone after observing the hooded woman closer, finding that there was an unmistakeable likeness in her to Sophilia. "Can it be… Cara…is that you?" Jenayan leaped forwards to embrace the stranger, though her show of compassion was quickly rejected.

"I *am* Cara…" The woman's face contorted once more, her fingers then discreetly moved to cloak the sword held at her side away from view. "I would appreciate not having to suffer from your sickening pleasantries for a moment longer… just bring me the child!" Little emotion, other than malice, showed as she gestured Jenayan away from her towards Sophilia.

"Okay…" Mumbled Jenayan thoughtfully, something different feel right about this. "I'll go and check on her." Jenayan reservedly approached Sophilia, who herself remained in a weakened state upon the central seal of Ven's Sanctum platform. The acolyte nestled in beside the sleeping child, she stroked tenderly at her hair then looked again towards Ven's acolytes with an expression of uncertainty.

"What is taking so long… wake her!" Commanded the woman viciously, her body trembled in hatred. "Bring her to me this instant!" Jenayan and her acolytes were uneased by the cold personality of this woman who, in comparison to the loving protector Sophilia had described, appeared to be so heartless. The acolytes, without any given instruction, silently barred themselves between Sophilia and her supposed mother, their protective reflex came as a relief to Jenayan but wrought a sudden scorn from their increasingly frustrated guest.

"I suggest, you give me back my daughter…" Responded the woman, her voice now sounded more like a beast's growl. "Do this the easy way or…"

"I think, for Sophilia's sake… that it should be *you* who wakes her." Said Jenayan calmly as she looked upon the child's angelic face. To the acolytes' shared surprise, they were then ordered to move aside in allowing a pathway towards their leader. "Seeing you will bring Sophilia so much comfort," Continued Jenayan in a whisper. "Especially, with what she has been through over the last few days."

"Get out of my way!" Ordered the woman coldly to Jenayan's acolytes, they freely obeyed but shook their heads in disagreement against this wrongful move. "She *belongs* to me…" She then swiftly knelt before the child and, after a momentary hesitation, proceeded to rock at her abruptly in hope of breaking Sophilia's peaceful slumber. "… Wake up!" She seethed. The Acolytes of Earth compulsively moved to cease this sickening act, their display of affection was abruptly halted however by Jenayan – who hinted to them all secretively that she had this horrid situation under control. Jenayan kept a raised a palm firmly against her acolytes, every impulse to stop this woman from shaking the child coursed through her and now rose into an unavoidable confrontation.

"Be gentle…" Enforced Jenayan with a caring glance to Sophilia. "She has suffered enough." Without warning, Cerebrante's seal radiated with a mighty beam of golden light. The acolytes and their dubious guest jolted in response, though Sophilia thankfully appeared unscathed by this surprise event. As the light dimmed Sophilia slowly adapted her eyes towards Jenayan and the dark figure knelt beside her – who at first seemed so menacing, yet recognisable.

"Mummy...?" Whispered the shaken child in disbelief, a set of blissful tears quickly formed within her tired eyes. "You came back for me… just like Jenny said you would!" Sophilia instinctively lunged towards her mother, she was however grasped by Jenayan who then held firmly onto the child's hands and resisting body. "What are you doing, Jenny? Let me go!" Jenayan bitterly moved Sophilia further back upon the Sanctum platform, their struggling actions only seemed to enrage the dark figure even more.

"GIVE… ME… THE… CHILD!" Screeched the demonic vision of Cara, she could barely contain her rage at this moment. Ven's acolytes suddenly gave a sigh of relief, they each noticed that the guards had now entered the Sanctum chamber – their swords drawn out high.

"Are you not going to speak with your daughter… or at least, show some love for her?" Jenayan forced a tighter grip upon Sophilia as she spoke. The malevolent woman standing before them began to noticeably breath more erratic, her eyes flared even more in a show of aggression and a wicked evil radiated from the very depths of her being.

"Come, Sophilia." Responded the figure coldly. "We are leaving this forsaken tree…you've spent enough time already in the company of these *freaks*!" The child's smile, which had been raised by so many hopeful and doting thoughts, now turned to a saddened frown. Sophilia pushed herself against Jenayan's torso, wishing to partially hide under the acolyte's lengthy robes so that she could look upon her 'mother' from a far safer place.

"Sophilia, I am your mother… come to me…" Said the woman in a callous tone, gesturing the child towards her in an equally ruthless manner. She urged for the child to leave Jenayan's side but, in doing this, had unwittingly revealed a shiny coat of armour from beneath her flowing robes. "Come now and do this the easy way!"

"Why are you calling me… Sophilia?" Mumbled the child to her mother with a confused stare, her lips wavered heavily as she spoke.

"…So that these fools know that *I am* your mother, that is why." Countered the woman viciously, her mouth foaming slightly from the rising anger.

"You have a sword… I can see it under your robes. Why do you have a sword for, Mummy?"

"I stole it from my captors… I am lucky to be alive; if it were not for Queen Cera's mercy, her soldiers would have killed me!" The woman's hands shook angrily against their master's forced restriction.

"You're wearing a necklace now…" Sophilia's whole demeanour fell into a state of utter sorrow, her voice faltered with each passing word and from this adornment she could sense something truly terrifying. "I don't like it… and *you* don't like to wear jewellery – unless I make it."

"So many questions from such a young, naive mind…" Quivered the woman as she forged a dismissive smile towards Ven's acolytes and guards. They sternly ignored her pleading looks and instead shifted to surround the Sanctum platform, a move they each felt could soon be regretted.

"You always said, that you would *never* use any kind of weapon… no matter what. You *never* wear gold jewellery - only the daisy chains I make. You've *never* called Aunt Cera… a Queen!" A painful desperation lifted in Sophilia's voice, her face was strewn by countless tears as she addressed the increasingly-angered figure. "What's going on with you, Mummy? I can hear whispers coming from that horrible necklace around your neck, they sound like… Him!"

"You wretched little… come to me… now!" Seethed the figure, a clenched hand now nestled against her revealed sword. "You will regret it… all of you… if she doesn't comply!"

"You are not what you seem…are you?" Snapped Jenayan on behalf of Sophilia. She observed the small, golden pendant closer and a dreadful reality suddenly hit the wise acolyte. "There *are* whispers… I can hear them now as well."

"You Acolytes have been told far too many faerie tales, it seems." Sneered the woman with a mocking grin. "What concern does this *pendant* actually bring to you… is it really that scary?"

"Tell me, *Cara*…" Jenayan's tone lowered to meet with the woman's own scornful approach. "Why would an exile of Magmorrah, like yourself, wear jewellery and weapons from this nation?"

"Wouldn't you like to know…?" The dark figure wrapped her fingertips over the sword's hilt, she caressed it with a sickening lust as if wanting to find an excuse to unsheathe the sordid blade.

"He's talking to me… from that necklace!" Cried out Sophilia suddenly. Jenayan placed herself in front of the child with her arms spread out wide, acting as a spiritual protection. "Kufiah… he's saying something about… Nira?"

"Enough of this charade!" The scornful woman abruptly tore away the necklace with her free hand, then with a fierce throw she hurled it over towards Sophilia. "You should have just done this... the easy way... Infidels!" Instantly, her disturbing features began to morph. They soon revealed a muscular and scarred body that was shielded heavily by obsidian, Magmorran armour. The flowing locks of golden hair that had previously sat upon the woman's head now shrivelled back, revealing a shaven scalp which adorned a face that was hideously reptilian in appearance.

"General Nira..." Gasped the Acolytes between themselves. "... No! Never has our Sanctuary been breached!"

"...Yes!" Rejoiced Nira with a violent laugh as she finally unsheathed her precious blade. In response, Ven's acolytes linked their arms to form a protecting line in front of Jenayan and Sophilia, the guards then huddled together in anticipation of their enemy's next move.

"Leave this Sanctuary at once!" Demanded one of the guards nervously. "You are no longer welcome here!"

"Like I care what *you* say?" Cackled Nira maliciously. "I am Queen Cera's General... her greatest warrior, you are no match for me!" The Sanctuary Guards released an emotional war-cry and then, without any reluctance, lunged themselves selflessly against Nira's taunting blade. Their first-strike was easily parried by the skilful General who, without any sign of exertion, sliced her blade cruelly through half of Ven's guards to render them each lifeless.

"Pathetic..." Mocked the heartless General in excitement. "I could kill you all with my eyes closed!" The remaining guards clustered themselves to attempt one last strike against Nira, they circled her with their swords raised and gave Ven's acolytes an endearing nod to signal a lasting reassurance in them.

"You will not harm Sophilia!" Screamed a guard in torment. "Not as long as we still hold breath!"

"THAT can be remedied...as can you all!" Laughed the General, Nira knew that her goal was now soon to be had. "Come... play with me!" One-by-one, Ven's remaining guards fell under the General's ferocious and precise blows, Nira had even closed her eyes to prove the point she had made to them moments before. "This is *too* easy!" Screeched Nira lustfully, whilst she observed the pool of blood now forming around her. "I hope, that you Acolytes will give me some more pleasurable sport?" Jenayan dragged Sophilia further back so that they rested against the Sanctum's wall. Together they prayed for a peaceful outcome, though in their hearts a dreadful understanding coursed that Nira would not stop until her mission was complete.

"Stop it... stop hurting them, please!" Screamed Sophilia whilst hiding her eyes away from the horrific sight of General Nira, and the massacre she had so joyfully committed. "Please, go away!"

"You are *my* prisoner now, child." Scorned Nira. "Come freely, or these fools shall meet the same ill-fate!"

"Never!" Responded Jenayan in defiance, her acolytes nodded in agreement to her and then tightened their held line. "Our Guardian will return soon… he will stop you!"

"Ahh!" Nira pointed her sword in jest towards the Sanctum seal of Levia's Sanctuary. "He will have some difficulty; the Sanctuary of Water and its platform Seals are now under Queen Cera's control!"

"You are lying, Monster!" Spoke the eldest Acolyte bravely. "That has never been achieved, and never will!"

"I will make you suffer for this show of insubordination." Teased Nira in response. "Impartia needs her Elemental Guardians and their followers… no more!" The General lifted her arms in mockery of Jenayan's own stance. Ven's acolytes looked to her in beleaguerment, they could not understand what gesture was now being seemingly offered. "Go freely, Acolytes of Earth! Leave the child with me and you shall come to no harm…" Nira appeared genuine in her offer. She casually allowed for her sword to fall into a root that lay beneath, which instilled a sense of urgency in Ven's acolytes to act swiftly. "This will be your only chance to escape… it's now or never!" Some of the younger acolytes turned to face Jenayan, their expressions were similar to that of Sophilia's dread, as they gave her a pleading look.

"Move now… or you *will* suffer!" Nira was becoming more impatient with each passing second, a few of Ven's acolytes saw this and then reluctantly broke away from their line.

"I'm sorry, Jen…" Whimpered Silvran, her most loyal friend. "My children, I must leave for their sake!"

"Go to them," pleaded Jenayan with an empathetic smile. "Send my love to Rosira and Silvra… they will need their father, and your wife will need her husband."

"Thank you… Thank you so much for understanding, Jen." Silvran led the younger acolytes past General Nira, who was continuing to stare intently upon Sophilia and Jenayan. They could sense Nira's malignant presence, even after passing by her, as the General emitted a darkness despite not even being an Acolyte or Spirit Guardian herself.

"Thank you, General… for showing us mercy." Said Silvran hesitantly to Nira as he approached the Sanctum's entranceway.

"Yes, I *am* merciful…" Replied Nira in a distant voice. "But, would it not be more kind to spare you of what Queen Cera has in store?" The sadistic General then revealed a set of small, obsidian daggers which had been kept hidden within her Dark Acolyte robes. She clasped onto them with both hands and without looking, aimed them each at the fleeing Acolytes of Earth.

"No!" Screamed Jenayan in an excruciating grief. "You Beast!" Silvran felt a sudden, sharp pain enter between his shoulder blades. He turned to a young boy who was stood beside him and found that he too had a trail of blood flowing down his light-green robes. Within seconds, the inflicted acolytes turned into ashes from where the cursed daggers had stuck them – no trace of their bodies was left there-after.

"I am out of daggers now…" Sighed Nira with a whimsical grin. "This will be the only opportunity for the rest of you to escape… RUN!" The remaining acolytes were instantly struck by panic. They ran in separate directions to evade Nira's blade as she retrieved it from the root beneath her, though each soon came to a brutal end by it. Only one Acolyte of Earth stayed in defence of Sophilia and Jenayan; she was the elderly lady who had spoken of Talam, only a few days before. "Aren't you a brave one?" Questioned Nira to the elderly acolyte with a dismissing wink. "What makes *you* so special, no one stands before me and lives to tell of their ordeal!" The elderly Acolyte silently looked past Nira towards Levia's seal behind, its blue light was flickering with an irregular hint of jade - something of which Jenayan also noticed. The leading acolyte placed her palms calmly upon a flowing stream of vines beneath, while her dutiful follower moved herself closer towards Magmorrah's imposing General.

"You know little of this world," lectured the elderly acolyte in a patronising tone. "For a General of Queen Cera, you have not been instructed on the ways of Spirits very well."

"Keep talking… old fool." Grimaced Nira hatefully as she lifted her sword horizontal towards the defiant acolyte. "I know that my Queen will become a God and I, her devoted servant, will rule Impartia alongside…"

"I *pity* you, Nira." The acolyte's voice trembled with age, though no fear came through it. "An Elemental Guardian is now on their way here… your sword skills cannot match such a power."

"You assume, that I would wish for such a glorious death?" Nira cackled strangely as she flipped her sword so that its hilt met against the acolyte's chest. "I am offering you my blade, it was my father's and is never given away so freely. Kill me. I *dare* you!"

"No, I will not accept…" Nira gave no time for a response; she clasped onto the acolyte's frail hands and then willingly forced her weapon into them. The elderly woman screamed in pain and fought hard to tear away her crippled fingers from Nira's cold blade, an agonising fire ran through them but the wicked General only persisted in tightening her cruel grip to raise the sword higher.

"Does it hurt?" Jeered Nira with a perverse laugh, she then strengthened her grip to fracture the acolyte's fragile hands. "I hope it does. Go on, kill me… while you still can!"

"Leave her alone!" Begged Sophilia desperately, she could barely see what was going on through her tears but could sense every horrific act. "I will go with you… just stop it!"

"A wise move," cackled the General passively. "It's just a shame… you hadn't made that choice earlier." Nira suddenly raised the frail acolyte's arms into the air, making sure that she tore them from their sockets as she did. With a smooth swipe, the evil General then forced her sword's tip into the throat of Jenayan's last acolyte – a harrowing image which Sophilia unfortunately bore witness to.

"Mauden never harmed a single soul! For eighty-four years, she has done nothing but show love and compassion to others…" Seethed Jenayan to Nira, as she looked upon the lifeless remains of her frail acolyte. "This dark path which you have chosen, General, only leads to the Void – Kufiah's realm of torture - is that what you honestly long for?" Nira calmly wiped the coursing blood from her blade on the robes of Ven's fallen acolytes. For a fleeting moment the General considered her own mortality, though this soon passed; it was swiftly replaced by a fierce determination to see out Cera's will and end this decade-long struggle to obtain the Queen's greatest nemesis.

"I *will* spare you, though only if the child comes with me now… I promise." Said the General through gritted teeth, she then slowly lowered her sword as she moved closer towards Sophilia. In response, Jenayan clasped onto the shifting vines beneath even tighter and gave Nira one more look of detest – a fitting expression to one so vile and hateful.

"We both know that you won't keep that promise, Nira." Muttered Jenayan as she cautiously repositioned Sophilia directly behind herself. The child obeyed with a willing heart, though greatly feared what was about to follow. "You have failed your Queen, and you will not take Sophilia from this Sanctum… return to Magmorrah now and live out the rest of your days as Cera's slave!"

"Infidel!" Screamed Nira, instantly she raised her blade again with a dire accuracy towards Jenayan. "You are weaker than I first thought. I am no slave… *you* are… to a world filled with fantasy, where Spirits reign and mortals perish!"

"So… deluded and cold-hearted." Jenayan contemplated as she locked her eyes shut, shielding them from Nira's scene of slaughter. In a trance-like state, she then gently caressed the streaming vines beneath and, to Nira's shock, gradually emitted a jade light from within them. "You *will* learn to respect the Spirits of this world."

"Ha! You are no Guardian…" Stammered Nira in perplexment towards the motioning vines. "This is mere sorcery and prayers will not help you now! Ven has forsaken his Sanctuary, his powers are useless to save the child from her fate… at my hands!" Jenayan stayed focused in her meditation, despite Nira's cruel taunting and Sophilia's anguished cries, she locked herself into an empowering trance. The mighty acolyte initially struggled to block out the painful vision of her brethren dying; she resolved however, that their deaths would not be in vain and could sense each of their transcending souls now leave for Eternamorrah.

"Pathetic…absolutely pathetic!" Cackled Nira again, she had never understood the apparent obsession acolytes showed with meditating to enhance their powers. "I'm coming for you, little princess… you will be a threat to my Queen - no more!"

"I don't think so…" A surge of emerald light released from Jenayan's fingertips into the vines that spread throughout Ven's Sanctum, unveiling their sentient life and purpose. Nira staggered away Sophilia as she felt the very ground from beneath them rise into life.

"Impossible!" Magmorrah's hardest warrior was left speechless, at first, by this unprecedented show of power from Jenayan - then came a limitless rage. "I will cut through these... then you!" Jenayan formed a wall of whips from her vines that flailed mercilessly against Nira. The General screamed out with a pure hatred towards her enemies as she sliced through the whips one-by-one, slowly progressing towards her most sought-after prize. To Sophilia and Jenayan's dismay, the possessed vines fell easily under Nira's ferocious swipes and soon they felt her evil essence standing over them.

"Jenny, I think... she is standing in front of us now." Whimpered Sophilia. The child cautiously attempted to look around Jenayan for a peek at Nira, though was swiftly held back. "I'm really scared...."

"Don't look, Lia..." Replied Jenayan sombrely, her trembling hands stayed fixed upon the flow of vines despite their destruction. "Whatever happens... don't *ever* let her frighten you."

Nira roared in delight at the massacre that lay around her, and at Jenayan's futile attempt to reassure Sophilia. The cruel General's bloodlust was almost satisfied now; if it were not for the last Acolyte of Earth who continued to exist before her.

"A new and glorious era has begun!" Declared Nira boldly, as she raised her arms over Jenayan to bask in a perverse sense of victory. "My Queen... my Cera... *will* rule as master now over this broken world, and the Elemental Guardians shall soon be forgotten!" Jenayan felt a cold wisp of air suddenly pass by, she knew it was the General's blade, though it did not deter her calm acceptance to what dire fate lay ahead. "Do you have any last words... puny Acolyte?" Jenayan showed no anger or remorse in wake of Nira's dominance over her beloved Sanctuary. Ven's dearest Acolyte was instead lost within a serene sensation of peace, at what she had achieved over her short life and in protecting Sophilia as best as she could from Cera's wrath.

"Lia..." Whispered Jenayan tenderly to the sorrowful child. "It was a true honour to spend time with you... your journey in life has only just started and long may you live."

"Jenny..." Sophilia could barely hold a response as she held into the acolyte tighter. "Don't leave me."

"Sorrow is a fleeting emotion, child... as is love." Said Nira with a malicious grin. "The Sanctuary of Darkness awaits you, Princess Sophilia... however, your friend here cannot come with us!"

"No!" Screamed Sophilia harrowingly. The child nestled her head into Jenayan's warming presence and longed for a lengthier time to be spent between them. "I don't want to see... Kufiah."

"Oh well," uttered Nira in dismissal towards the child's obvious fear. "I have waited a long time for this... moment." As Sophilia unleashed a terrified cry, General Nira forced her sword slowly into Jenayan's pacing heart. The crude obsidian blade pierced her flesh with a scorching heat, a dark and malignant energy then fed fast from it to instantly render Ven's greatest Acolyte of Earth lifeless – to Sophilia's immediate heartache.

"No…Jenny… No!" Sophilia tearfully curled herself into Jenayan's body and then rocked at her in a vain hope that eventually she would awaken. The emerald light that had arisen in Jenayan's eyes gradually faded, only to be replaced by a glazed look of death that Nira keenly rejoiced over. "You killed her… you've killed them all!" Sophilia suddenly gasped on seeing the horrific sight of blood that flowed over Ven's Sanctum platform, the once luscious plant-life upon it eerily ran crimson and lingered within an atmospheric evil.

"… Should I…?" Whispered Nira to herself with a callous hatred, she contemplated lifting her sabre against Sophilia's own heart like Jenayan's, though a far-worse judgement swiftly changed the General's twisted mind. *Dead or alive… that is what Cera ordered. I believe however, that it will prove to be far more rewarding, for myself at least, to let you live your life with the scarring memories made here today… wouldn't you agree… little Princess?"

"Leave me alone!" Screamed Sophilia in a blind dread. She kicked at Nira's armoured legs to gain her freedom and, despite the pain they wrought her, eventually managed to crawl away. "My Mummy is coming for me…" Sophilia's escape was abruptly halted as the spilled blood from Ven's Acolytes seeped under her hands - forcing the child to move back against Jenayan's corpse. "Go away, I don't want to be with you!"

"You are coming with me, whether you want to… or not!" Growled Nira as she tore at the child's arms, forcing Sophilia to her feet. The ever-prepared General was still wary of the flickering Sanctum seal which linked to Levia's Sanctuary; it caused a certain level of anxiety in her, as she pondered who may be trying to break through. "Do you really not wish to meet your true family - your Aunt Cera?" Nira swallowed heavily, she hated the fact that Sophilia had this privileged connection to the tyrannical ruler. "My Queen has long-awaited your return, and so has Magmorrah; you *are* a member of the Royal family… after-all." Sophilia suddenly lowered her defence against General Nira; the child had secretly dreamed of being reunited with the aunt she had never come to know.

"Mummy never said that Aunt Cera was a bad person to me…" Pondered Sophilia aloud. "I guess, it would be nice to finally meet her?"

"Good girl," applauded Nira with a mocking smile, she stroked her grotesque fingertips through Sophilia's hair then grasped her again with an iron-grip. "That is a wise choice for both your sake and your mother's… Come!" Nira proceeded to drag Sophilia by her hair through the Sanctuary catacombs, back to its entrance portal which remained open – as she had instructed. The General cruelly ignored Sophilia's repeating pleas to release the painful grip she had on her scalp, it soon became apparent that Nira enjoyed every resisting squirm the child was making.

"You're hurting me!" Screeched Sophilia. She slapped at Nira's hands, but they only continued to tighten further on her. "Let go!"

"SILENCE!" Commanded Nira with an impatient shriek. "We will reach Magmorrah in no time, during our journey there you *will* remain… silent!" On entering the empowered portal, Sophilia tearfully thought back over all the joyous memories she had made in the few days spent with Jenayan and her acolytes. She could still see every detail of their faces, before and after death, and struggled greatly to understand why they had to die the horrific way in which Nira had constructed. "Actually, I don't think I like you being quiet…" Scorned Nira. "It makes me feel like you're plotting something!"

"Where are you taking me now?" Responded the startled child, whilst still pulling at Nira's fingers to release them away from her burning scalp.

"I TOLD you!" Roared the General. "We are returning to your homeland, you will be kept safe there with your Aunt Cera!" Nira laughed again cruelly, she was fully aware of the horrid fate which would meet against Sophilia - once they reached the Sanctuary of Darkness. "Are you stupid… like your mother?"

"No, my Mummy's not stupid!" Snapped Sophilia with a powerful glare. "I meant, how are we going to reach that dark place… isn't it far away?"

"By tank, maybe?" Sniggered the General with a knowing glance. "Our gracious Queen has made a ship that can fly; that is how we are going to reach Magmorrah so swiftly now – on *Divinity*!" The relentless heat from Viridia's forest fire scorched at Nira and Sophilia as they left from their portal's protective beam. Nira hastily quickened her pace as she pulled Sophilia towards a group of Magmorran tanks which were now stationed nearby, each one awaited their General's triumphant return and the elite-soldiers stood in front of them all rapturously applauded at their General's approach.

"Take this wretch to the Queen Cera's airship at once!" Commanded the General as she looked back to the entrance portal, her voice also seemed desperate and out of character to the soldiers. "Our destination will be the Sanctuary of Darkness, where Her Majesty is waiting for this most-prized possession of hers! You are dismissed!" Nira cackled sadistically, as she threw Sophilia into the open arms of her obedient soldiers, who then held firmly onto the resistive child without question. Cera's General then stepped away momentarily from her warriors to admire over her evil doings; Ven's Sanctuary shone eerily from the dark flames and smoke that now surrounded it, its effervescent emerald glow that had once emanated now dimmed horrendously under the evil energy which proceeded to penetrate it. "It has taken us ten years, but we have finally done it… my Cera…" Nira fell under a sickened trance as she stared upon the dying remains of Viridia, it's crackling trees seemed like a thunderous applause to her. "Nothing can stop us now!" Nira then started to make her way towards her personal tank in a demented state of self-righteousness. The General laughed wickedly to herself with each step taken and was held in ecstasy of how Queen Cera may now reward her – particularly over the success of this blood-soaked mission.

"…Only the mountain realm of Skynah is left for us to destroy now!" As Nira mounted the obsidian frame of her tank, a bellowing voice suddenly travelled through the roaring flames – demanding an immediate attention. Within the Sanctuary's gateway stood a tall, robed figure who appeared to be trembling as they looked upon the Magmorran General.

"So, you've come back?" Gasped Nira ecstatically towards the familiar assailant. "It seems, the Dark Acolytes were wrong when they said that 'no-one could escape' from their Sanctuary…"

Chapter Eight: The Trial of Eternal Flames

Ven collapsed upon his Sanctum seal in exhaustion. As the light empowering it slowly died away he saw nothing, at first, but a crimson blur which surrounded him. An immense level of spiritual power had been drained from Ven at this point; under normal circumstances he should have been transported from Levia's Sanctuary within seconds, yet, to the Guardian's dismay it took far longer - for some unknown reason.

"Kufiah…" Ven gradually adjusted his weary eyes to the rising sun, its rays dwindled within Viridia's Earth Sanctum and they too appeared to shine with a scarlet light. In hindsight, The Guardian of Earth soon wished that his eyes had remained beyond use, as before him now was scene more harrowing than any other he had yet encountered in his life.

"No…my brothers and sisters… No!" Scattered around Ven were the mutilated remains of his beloved acolytes and Sanctuary guards, their blood still flowed from them across the many vines of which formed his sacred Sanctum's floor. The doting Guardian could find no words for what bare emotions now coursed through him, he hastily ran to each of his followers to desperately check for any sign of life in them, though he reluctantly knew that this would be done in vain.

"…Why?" Ven quickly noticed, to his instant despair, that against the Sanctum's farthest wall lay his closest friend – Jenayan. She was still seated as if in her meditated state: her hands still clasping the vines beneath her, her robes noticeably soaked by a trail of fresh blood and beside her was the seed of Viridia's Sanctuary which was now split clearly in half. The Guardian cried out in grief as he ran over to Jenayan, on grabbing hold of her lifeless body Ven suddenly let go in the realisation of what devastation had befallen his most-dearest companions. "Who could have done this to you and our brethren, Jen?" Wept Ven gently as he stroked at Jenayan's auburn locks. "Why would anyone wish to harm such… innocent souls? This heinous attack *will not* go unpunished!" Ven keenly observed the precise slash marks upon the bodies of his fallen acolytes; noticing on each a faint scorch mark, that ran parallel along the grievous wounds. "Only a Magmorran blade could have done this," Ven shook his head in disbelief as a daunting thought entered him. "No… only the cursed blade of Magmorrah's General would leave such wounds!" A shimmer of gold suddenly caught Ven's eye which lay beside Jenayan. He recoiled sharply as he further inspected this strange pendant, it lay in fragments within a pool of blood though shone clearly in the wavering sunrays.

"Cera… only she and her Dark Acolytes could have fashioned such an accursed item!" Ven defensively covered the broken necklace with some vines that lay beside it; he was disgusted by its grotesque sight and at its purpose in aiding with the deaths of his forsaken followers.

The stench from Viridia's burning forest soon began to painfully enter Ven's senses; he recoiled from their nauseating fumes and leapt from Jenayan's side to approach his Sanctum's windows, hoping for a closer look outside. The ancient trees moaned within the consuming flames that had spread throughout them, Viridia's entire landscape to the Guardian was now totally unrecognisable. "Cera, how could you do... this?" Ven fell to his knees in an overwhelming sorrow, though his thoughts soon turned back to Sophilia whom he had come to rescue on Cara's behalf. The child, to Ven's further concern, was nowhere in sight and he no could not sense Sophilia's presence within his Sanctuary walls – only a residual fragment of her Spirit remained within the disturbed atmosphere.

"I'm so sorry, Cara... I didn't reach her in time." Through the increasing sound of flames outside, loud engine noises abruptly rose into creation. Ven bolted towards the Sanctum's windows and found, to an unwanted surprise, some distinct shadows of several Magmorran tanks with a handful of obsidian-clad warriors stood before them. "Perhaps, it is not too late, Cara!" Rejoiced the Guardian in hope. "I may yet still have time to save your Sophilia!" Ven lost all sense of exhaustion and with a renewed desire that coursed within him, he fled from the Sanctum towards the Sanctuary's entrance portal – itself still activated through Nira's trickery. "I am coming, little Sophilia!" Screamed Ven frantically. "I will not fail you!"

As the Guardian left from his portal's light, he was met with a thick wave of smoke that instantly scorched at his struggling lungs. Ven used his robes to shield himself from the falling embers, then as he walked blindly towards where he believed the Magmorran tanks were stationed a distinct figure eerily began to arise before him.

"Nira!" Roared Ven with a hatred in his voice that even surprised the unsuspecting General. Nira slowly turned with a sadistic smile towards the grief-stricken Guardian, realising now who it was that demanded her attention.

"Guardian of Earth, do you like what I've done with the place?" Cackled Nira cruelly, her monstrous laugh proved far more menacing to Ven than the spreading flames around them. "How does it feel, lesser Spirit... to lose your only loved ones and to see the nation you call home - decimated?"

"...Why?" Ven's initial rage dwindled and was swiftly replaced by an overpowering sense of loss, Nira's malicious words to him only fuelled this. "They were defenceless, Nira! Why did you feel the need to slaughter them all like animals? Each of my followers had families; their devotion to this Sanctuary was to protect *them*... you have torn apart so many lives!" Nira merely shrugged in dismissal.

"It wouldn't have been as fun to keep them alive though and besides, your Sanctuary Guards attacked me first... I had little choice but to defend myself." Taunted Nira, as she moved closer towards the Guardian's held position.

"My Acolytes... they had no weapons!" Cried out Ven with a trembling voice, his anger now reignited against the malevolent General. "You will pay for your selfish actions!"

"I can end your suffering too, if you so wish?" Nira tilted her head as if in sympathy to Ven's pain, however her grimacing smirk spoke otherwise. "It must hurt so bad knowing that you are all that remains of this Sanctuary's legacy... do you wish to die as a coward, like your *friends* did, or face me to achieve a more honourable death?" Nira slowly unsheathed her sword, it was still seeped in the blood from Ven's followers and glistened with a haunting scarlet stream that ran down its lengthy blade.

"You are nothing but a ruthless murderer," scorned Ven with a look of detest in his eyes. "There is no honour in what you have done here... you are nothing more than a pawn in Queen Cera's game, Nira!" The Guardian struggled to carry his words over to Nira, as she hissed back louder at him through clenching teeth. "Don't deny this truth!"

"How *dare* you challenge my place in such a way, vermin!" Nira slashed her sword violently through the air to catch a few embers upon it, then with a rageful stare aimed them back against Ven. "How *dare* you even mention my Queen; she is the greatest ruler Impartia has ever known and will forever dominate all life within it!" Declared the General whilst she aggressively quickened her pace forwards. Nira joyfully swayed her sword with more ferocity back and forth, hoping to taunt Ven with the unpredictable actions as she neared him though he only remained defiant.

"I will *speak* to you how I like, Puppet!" The emerald light in Ven's eyes began to grow mightily as he spoke. "When Cera has gained what she wants, you will merely be cast aside as nothing more than a distant relic of her rise into madness and power! You are a disposable tool, Nira... just like any other mortal in your Queen's life!"

"INFIDEL!" Howled Nira in response, the level of malice she felt against Ven now had no signs of diminishing. "Cera and I have a mutual understanding, she worships me as I do her and you *will* regret such foolish words... I shall make certain of that!" Magmorrah's General raised her blade high into the air, its shadow cast a hideous-looking serpent before Ven - who himself sensed it as a vision of Nira's own twisted soul.

"You are only lying to yourself!" A series of tremors suddenly shook the ground beneath Ven, they soon passed throughout Viridia's Sanctuary to make it groan - as if it were alive. "Queen Cera has never known love and will never care for you as what your darkened heart truly desires; the sooner you realise this fact, the sooner you may seek redemption!" Ven positioned himself in a defensive stance and then hovered his arms above a set of small roots that flowed beneath, feeling their shifting energy draw ever-nearer to him.

"Lies...you know *nothing*, Spirit!" Nira appeared to cry as she confronted Ven, a noticeable weakness the General quickly rectified with a furious swipe of her sword. "Your precious Sanctuary and Acolytes are all dead... soon, you will be too!" Nira released a harrowing war cry against the Guardian, it was fuelled by her sheer rage and echoed through the flames of Viridia's forsaken forest around them.

"It is time… that you were taught a lesson." Muttered Ven calmly as he motioned his fingertips into the ash-laden earth beneath. A single root leapt straight into the Guardian's hands which he hastily fashioned a new staff from by using his spiritual connection. "I am your mentor now… your physical skills shall be no match against the Elemental powers which bend to my will alone!"

"You think that your *magic* can save you… from me?" Cackled Nira viciously. She forced her blade hard into the roots below, as both a show of mockery towards Ven and to relieve some of her rising blood-lust. "I have the power of Kufiah behind me, you Elemental Guardians are so *weak*, I will enjoy turning you all into ashes for your lacking show of respect towards my divine Queen!" A hesitant pause momentarily centred around the duelling pair. Nira and Ven glared intently at one another in anticipation of their rival's first move, both held onto their raised weapons with a fierce determination and neither backed down as the forest fires rose greater to surround them.

"Perhaps…" Ven willingly broke the daunting silence to give Nira a final warning. "You will learn the truth about adoration when I am done here… General of Magmorrah. Kufiah's accursed power can only protect you for so long, like Cera's supposed love, it won't last forever." Ven nervously ran his fingers over the staff held within his grasp, it brought little comfort to free him of his grief and conflicting emotions. "As an Elemental Guardian, I am forbidden to take another's life… though there are ways around this. Leave now in that wretched tank of yours, Nira… or suffer a fate worse than death!" Cera's devout General unleashed a blood-curling cry in response and then, without further word, she unnaturally threw herself towards Ven's position. Nira slashed her obsidian blade through the smoke-ridden air to create a deadly first-strike, it ferociously descended and then clashed against Ven's crude staff, forging many sparks as the two spiritually-charged weapons finally met with one another.

"Die… INFIDEL… Die!" Hissed Nira, as she slid her blade cautiously away from Ven's staff, only to make a second hate-filled strike against it that was met by a precise parry from the more focused Guardian. "I am Magmorrah's greatest warrior!" Ven serenely countered each blow from Nira's sword with a seeming level of ease, revealing a side to him that had lain dormant for countless years.

"I was once a warrior of Viridia," laughed Ven in a fleeting moment of reminiscence. "Your skills are going to be put to the test!" He boasted assuredly.

"You'll grow tired soon enough, Spirit." Taunted Nira, whilst her cursed blade locked upon Ven's staff again. "Using your powers has such a draining effect… I've been told! Try to keep up with me!"

"You will find, we Spirits don't tire so easily… mortal General!" Responded Ven, as he managed to make an unsuspecting strike from his staff against Nira's forehead. "I could do this sordid dance for an eternity… if it would mean stopping you from committing any further acts of evil!" Ven suddenly spun his staff against Nira, almost catching her off guard as she reluctantly began to admit to herself that this adversary was far stronger than expected.

"You're not too bad, old man!" Ridiculed Nira as she regained her offensive stance. A line of blood trickled down from the General's forehead which she quickly wiped away in disgust; it was a sight never seen before and one that Nira did not want to witness again. "I'm… actually impressed. It's a pity your pathetic Acolytes didn't fight in the same way."

"You abhorrent…" Ven paused suddenly in defence, a choking billow of ashes swept between himself and Nira to cause a momentary truce. "…No!" The resourceful General used this brief opportunity to make for her tank and, more precisely, its formidable energy cannon. Nira was undeterred by the wave of falling embers and Ven's increasing might as she sprinted towards her powerful war machine.

"You shall not escape my retribution…" Ven's entire body immediately radiated with an emerald light from the depths of his spiritual aura. "… This time!" A terrifying bellow followed from within the Sanctuary of Earth in unison to its Guardian's intensified connection, also creating a shockwave that gave rise to several large roots of which landed upon Nira's tank to crush it beyond any use.

"That's cheating!" Cackled Nira with an arrogant smirk. "No matter, I do not fear you nor your puny powers… filthy Spirit!" A further wave of dense smoke quickly re-entered the space between Nira and Ven. The General's dark armour and blade now became harder for Ven to distinguish as the thick fumes shielded them perfectly from sight; Ven knew that his tactics would need to change quickly - if he were to survive this current battle.

"You're mine!" Declared Nira ecstatically. She then blindly slashed her obsidian blade through the smouldering ashes against Ven, catching at his flesh at least twice to the Guardian's instant dismay. "You cannot hide from me!" As Ven frantically swung his staff in a vain effort to deflect Nira's strikes, he suddenly remembered a special move that had been taught to him many years ago.

The Guardian held his staff firmly behind, as if lowering his defences, then strangely leant forward in allowing for a clearer target to meet with Nira's next strike. "Yes!" Nira swiftly acted against Ven's peculiar move and aimed to stab the Guardian directly in his heart. "Now... you die!" Ven abruptly swung his staff from behind, then surprisingly around, to catch Nira from under her chin. Its powerful force sent the General far into the air, she then landed helplessly upon the exposed roots below – a blow to her both physically and mentally. "There is no point in fighting against me!" Nira struggled to speak from the pain inflicted by Ven's staff, she could also sense that Kufiah's protection was now fading away from her. "Do not underestimate my skills as others have before you!" Ven now clearly understood that there was no possibility of Nira ever redeeming herself, instead he calmed his own thoughts further into an empowering trance. The Guardian's aura glared intensely with an illuminating jade radiance from which the strength of his spiritual connection now fully manifested.

"For a mortal, there is a malice that lingers in you which only the Spirit of Darkness could outmatch!" A series of emerald flames erupted from Ven's body, his voice deepened, and his stature grew to horrify Nira - despite her best efforts not to show this. "You are too dangerous to be kept alive in this form... I see now, that I must act!" Nira, whilst still shaking in her rage and fear, lifted her sword again to make a killing blow against the ancient Guardian of Earth; who to her now seemed at his most vulnerable in this transient state.

"You don't scare me at all..." Stammered the General with a defiant glare. "My blade has been cursed with Kufiah's power, that Spirit holds a greater strength over your weak abilities!" With a gentle twitch of Ven's fingertips, the entire ground beneath Nira suddenly shook then tore apart into fragments. A storm of tree roots followed that rose with a sentient aggression, they whipped violently towards Nira, forcing the hapless General to her knees in a reluctant submission. "Coward!" Screeched out the despairing General in frustration. "I will destroy you and desecrate your Sanctuary!"

"My Sanctuary is ever-lasting!" Boasted the proud Guardian of Earth with a thunderous voice. "My valiant Acolytes and Sanctum Guards will live on forever in Eternamorrah, their needless deaths... shall be avenged!" Nira swiped viciously at the attacking roots as Ven spoke, she soon found that they were empowered far beyond the ones which Jenayan had used against her. "You will learn to respect the Spirits of Impartia, mortal... or fall into the void of Kufiah - along with your repugnant Queen!" Nira rose herself with a renewed and lustful anger against Ven; she lunged at the mighty Spirit with her fearsome blade, defiantly ignoring the shifting ground beneath and flailing tree roots that continued to thrash in offense. Ven used his spiritual foresight to feed more energy into the towering whips, they quickly shielded their master from Nira's deathly blow and some even forced themselves back into the earth from whence they came - in attempt to crush Cera's malignant General.

"Why won't you... just DIE?" Despaired Nira in contempt. "Why can't you just understand, that my Queen is the benevolent ruler Impartia needs, that your powers are no longer required for this world to survive?"

"It is not I… that lacks understanding!" Countered Ven sternly. "You still have much to learn!" Nira only just managed to evade Ven's proceeding attacks; she fled from them across a passing Sanctuary root to near upon the Guardian's current position, with her sword still lifted in readiness to strike at him again. Ven had anticipated these predictable moves by Nira, in response he fiercely punctured the ground beneath with his staff to raise its earth and himself high into the air. A shower of rocks and scorching embers then fell heavily upon the unsuspecting General, she halted in her advance for only a few seconds, gaining enough time for Ven to elevate safely away from Nira's venomous grasp.

"Keep running… flee from me… my blade *will* still reach you!" Declared Nira in a demonic tone. In truth, the intense spiritual energy that was needed by Ven to continue with this onslaught now gravely weakened him. The Guardian lowered himself slowly back to the ground in a heightened level of exhaustion, his attacking roots became limp and the fear they had inflicted upon Nira soon diminished alongside. "Are you giving up so easily, Spirit?" Taunted Nira as she rested herself briefly against her blade, this now felt like an opportune moment for the cruel General to impose a greater pain over Ven. "They begged for their lives, you know… your pitiful Acolytes? I tore apart their innocence and slashed at their unclean bodies in an act of merciful response." Ven's body writhed in anguish on hearing this, his only comfort now came from the radiant energy from the Sanctuary situated behind. "The oldest one, her death brought me so much joy… you could hear the brittle bones break as I ripped that wretched woman's arms away from their sockets…"

"ENOUGH!" Commanded Ven, he could no longer bear to learn anymore of the torture his beloved Acolytes had endured under Nira. "I will silence your vile tongue…" The Guardian shook his head in restraint at first, then without further hesitation, Ven placed his free hand upon the smouldering earth below – the other tightened itself around his empowered staff.

"Do your worst, Guardian of Filth!" Mockingly Pleaded Nira with a hideous cackle, she noticed the Guardian's changing mood and longed to witness a greater show of his supposed power. "Go on… make me suffer!" The ground beneath Nira shook violently in unison with Ven's harsh resolve, she desperately clung onto her blade that was stabbed deep into the coursing roots below and looked upon it with an uncertainty - as to what fate was now unfolding. "I am destined to rule with Cera," Whimpered Nira with a terrified expression. "Impartia is ours... we were meant to reign eternal over it!"

"No… Nira." Ven seemed to display a sense of pity in his voice towards the General, this quickly passed however. "You will both linger in penance for your tyranny, for what your evil campaign against the innocents of this world has wrought, then maybe someday… you will appreciate the true value of life?"

"I doubt it…" Nira spat towards the Guardian hatefully, she then struggled again to free her sword from Ven's rampaging roots. "I'll get you eventually!" An intense wave of spiritual energy left from Ven's staff that swiftly rippled through the tremendous Sanctuary roots; forcing them back to the surface in a powerful eruption, for them to then wrap around Nira's helpless body. The besieged General now found herself trapped within a vice-like grip, Ven's sentient roots crushed at Nira with a brutal force and slowly fed their way around each of her limbs – mimicking the diseased veins that flowed throughout them. "No… I can't die… I won't… not this way!" Cried out Nira passionately as she stabbed at the tightening roots with her sharpened fingernails, to her persisting sorrow, this effort for freedom came to no avail. "I deserve a greater death than this!"

"Why do you despair?" Laughed Ven, whilst allowing for a stream of emerald light to flow from him into the roots restraining Nira. "I am granting the immortality which you so desire, now you will live on forever… and suffer for what you have done along with it!" Nira riled in the imposing torment Ven's dire judgement brought to her; his invasive roots burned from the General's own flames as they encased her body slowly, an irony even she could not accept willingly.

"What are you doing to me?" Stammered Nira anxiously as she continued to writhe at the constricting roots. "Stop this… stop this at once!" The earthly fibres from Ven's roots began to adapt themselves with Nira on a cellular level; they quickly transformed her body into the harrowing vision of a deformed tree, itself bare of any leaves and still smouldering with the embers that she had so freely created in them.

"My humble Sanctuary, which you alone have defiled, will now be the place of your much-needed repentance." Explained Ven tearfully. He gave a vacant stare towards Nira as her body continued to deform and felt no remorse in any way against his extreme actions. "Those searing embers shall forever burn within you, Nira…as you will remain alive in this form until the end of days!"

"CURSE YOU!" Screamed the General in dismay. Nira then wailed heavily at her solemn fate, though a twisted smile soon formed as the engines from Cera's airship now carried through the passing breeze. "My work here is done, Queen Cera is going to destroy Alaskia and Cerebrante… nothing can stop her now." Nira let out a final scream at the horrifying sight of her blistered skin, it was taking on an appearance of ashen bark and her limbs suddenly stiffened beyond any movement - at last, the General's malice came to a disturbing end.

"Forgive me, Natara." Whispered Ven remorsefully, whilst looking back to his Sanctuary. He would often think of his loving wife during such sorrowful times; this moment especially was poignant; it was Nira's grandfather – General Viran, who had murdered Ven's entire family. "I had no choice... it was not revenge for your death, I swear... I miss you so much..." The flames surrounding Ven thankfully started to dwindle as the Guardian collapsed into a needful sleep. While the Guardian of Earth rested, Impartia's sunrise gradually penetrated through the dispersing smoke clouds above, their gleaming rays shone down on him though on touching Nira's cursed body faded – no light could ever reach her ever again.

"Cara!" Ven lifted himself from the scorched earth in a panic. The Guardian had no idea how long it had been since he fought against Nira; in this confusion Ven's thoughts quickly turned back to his friends, who he hoped had reached Pahoe's Sanctuary unharmed. "Stay safe, Cara... we have little time left to prevent Cera's plan from succeeding." The Guardian collected his staff from under a thin layer of ashes that had fallen upon it. After brushing away the pungent dirt, Ven leant against his staff wearily and then used it as an aid to reach the Sanctuary's entrance portal. The seal struggled to ignite under Ven's drained energy, however after many attempts, eventually it teleported him back into his Sanctuary dwellings where a haunting silence now lingered in place of the laughter that did previously exist.

"My home..." Ven absorbed his ominous surroundings tearfully, even the vibrant flowers that trailed beside seemed lifeless to him - as if they were also aware of what awful events had taken place. "... My family." On entering the Sanctum chamber, Ven found that it still ran with the blood of his massacred Acolytes and Sanctuary Guards. He knelt beside each and offered them a parting kiss upon their brows, leaving Jenayan until last so that he could lament over her loss for longer. "You protected our Sanctuary with honour, my beloved Jen." Ven wiped at his tears, then forced a hopeful smile to emerge. "Cara is with Pahoe now... your deaths were not in vain."

Far in the north of Talam: Cara, Firin and Spero now found themselves within a landscape equalled only to a Hellish scene from their worst nightmares. Large rivers of molten lava spewed endlessly from towering volcanoes at their source; each flowed into several vast lakes that stretched as far as the eye could see and the sky radiated with a scarlet hue – adding a greater sense of dread to this perilous environment.

"Whereabouts in Impartia have the Guardians brought us to now?" Snapped Spero angrily at his companions. "I can't see any sign of a Sanctuary... something is wrong."

"There's a lot of fire, but no Guardian!" Responded Firin with a nervous hint of laugher. "This platform we're standing on... it looks different to other ones, doesn't it?" This observation proved to be true; Cara herself noticed that the platform appeared more modern to those seen at Levia's Sanctuary, she knelt for a closer look then turned back towards Spero with a confused expression.

"We won't have been sent here without a reason," pondered Cara aloud. "Ven did say to me, that Pahoe doesn't appreciate visitors… we'll just have to find her Sanctuary on foot."

A violent eruption suddenly shook the friends from a nearby volcano. Cara huddled herself fearfully into Spero and was soon joined by Firin, they then each cowered into the centre of their Sanctum platform praying that no further threat could come to them.

"What are we going to do?" said Spero in disillusionment. "How about we go that way… there's not as much lava over there?" He quickly pointed southwards across a rugged range of mountains that, to him at least, appeared far more inviting despite their steep altitude.

"Please tell me your joking?" Replied Firin with a shocked expression. "If we even made it over those mountains, the great canyon of Mandalaur spans out for hundreds of miles beyond them…I'd honestly prefer to risk drowning in a lake of lava - than going in that direction!"

"Spero…" Cara gave a firm glare then raised her eyebrows in disappointment to him. "How did you not know about this canyon?" She shook her head in dismissal, then after wiping her eyes looked back against the fiery plains. "Besides, I doubt Pahoe's Sanctuary lies that way."

"Are you sure, Firin?" Said Spero in a condescending tone. "I've never heard of such a canyon, and I've been all over the world with Hydrania's Navy!"

"Mandalaur Canyon is infamous throughout the people of these desert lands, it is steeped in legend!" Responded Firin in an equal manner to Spero.

"Ah, so it's *only* a legend then?" Spero rolled his eyes against Firin, then looked back to the inviting mountains further south. "Your fairy tales don't scare me… we go *that* way!"

"What does the legend say, Firin?" Asked Cara reservedly, though with a hint of hope in her eyes. "I could do with something to take my mind off this awful place."

"Well…" Firin clapped his hands together excitedly, giving a sly wink to Spero as he did so. "Legend has it: that many years ago the Guardian of Fire and a Prince of Talam fell in love with one another though this union, however, was not permitted by either the Sanctuary's Acolytes nor the King himself. This situation escalated, eventually resulting in the Prince and Guardian having to end their relationship." Cara gasped in amazement, she wondered if the Guardian being mentioned by Firin was the very same on they were now trying to contact.

"Supposedly, The Guardian of Fire felt betrayed by this Prince for giving up on her so easily, and in an act of revenge, she used her spiritual powers to divide the north of Talam from the south!" Continued Firin with an exaggerated look of astonishment.

"How did she do that?" Questioned Cara. Spero also wished to know, though discreetly and in a reluctance.

"The Guardian created a huge earthquake by controlling the fiery magma beneath Impartia's surface. The result: A gargantuan canyon that she hoped would deter the Prince from ever returning, not to mention an impassable mountain range and lakes of lava to go with it."

"You can't deny it, Spero…" Whispered Cara carefully, as to not embarrass her friend further. "We're in the middle of those lava lakes now, what are you betting that this canyon does exist after-all?"

"Fine." Sighed Spero wearily. "We'll just stay here and sweat to death while waiting for this Guardian to appear!" He grunted in frustration. "I must admit, I'm a bit anxious about meeting this Guardian… she doesn't sound too friendly."

"You'll be fine!" Firin gave Spero a hard slap on his back in reassurance. "As long as you don't try to hit on her, we'll be okay!" Without warning, several volcanoes coincidently erupted with a burst of deafening explosions that echoed against the three friends. As the shockwaves passed, it seemed to Cara and her companions that a woman's shrieking voice could also be hear in them. "Do you think, the Guardian heard what I said about her?" Said Firin apprehensively, as he scoured over the ruptured mountains. "Great… she's pissed off already and we haven't even met her yet!"

"No matter the risk, we *must* find the Sanctuary of Fire and gain its Guardian's password!" Interrupted Cara with a forceful voice, feeling that she now needed to be more assertive over her immature companions. "My little girl's life depends on us finishing this stupid quest… there has to be a way of reaching Pahoe!"

"Sorry…" Replied Firin with an awkward shrug. "We're going to save your Sophilia…even if it means having to cross over this apocalyptic sea of death!" He then reached an arm out to offer Cara some reassurance, though unwittingly knocked Spero away from the platform at the same time.

"Thanks, Firin!" Spero groaned as he pulled his legs from the sinking ash beneath, he then stepped away further from the platform on noticing some strange markings etched upon it. The small symbols turned out to be written in Talam's native tongue, something which Spero immediately pointed out to his companions.

"I don't think that we were deliberately sent here by Levia and Ven…" Commented Spero in assurance, he then hastily ushered for his friends to look upon the markings for themselves. "Look, maybe this platform is a bypass to Pahoe's Sanctuary… can you read them, Firin?"

"Yeah, no problem." Firin proudly leaned in to inspect the etchings closer. "The writing is in old Talamite… but I should be able to make out most of it."

'Trespassers. Only those worthy enough may be enchanted by my presence. A trial awaits you. Cross these plains. if you dare.'

"I might have read a few words wrong, hopefully… are you sure that you want to meet this Guardian, Cara?" Firin had a grave look of concern on his face as he looked to both his friends, the over-powering heat flowing from Pahoe's lava was already enough to deter him from venturing any further into these treacherous plains. "We're going to die here, aren't we?" Cara gasped suddenly as an immediate thought of realisation struck her. She momentarily focused on the meaning behind Pahoe's warning then turned to her companions with a gleeful smile, a gesture that was understandably not returned.

"Sanctum seals react under the influence of their Guardians…" Cara started to pace around the platform, inspecting ever fine detail upon it. "Perhaps by mentioning their names, it may be enough to activate the powers within them. I have an idea!" It was a long-shot, but Firin and Spero had little else to go off in finding a solution to their current predicament.

"It's worth a try, Cara. I can't see any other way of us getting over these plains without bringing a more risk to our lives" Said Spero as he recoiled from the falling embers scattering around them. "Try it, say the Guardian's name when you stand back on the seal and then see what happens… this might be our only hope of getting to her?" Spero offered Cara a hand of support as she stood herself back upon the mystical platform. "Good luck…" Cara closed her eyes and thought of what wisdom Ven may have granted in such a strange situation. However, on thinking about Ven, Cara inadvertently focused her thoughts back to Sophilia who the Guardian had gone to rescue in Viridia. The torment of her child's uncertain fate proved to be enough for Cara, she placed herself slowly back upon Pahoe's seal then silently prayed that her plan would work.

"Pahoe - ancient Guardian of Fire - *we* are worthy of your presence!" Cried out Cara bravely, despite her trembling limbs. "Please, allow us into your Sanctum!" An ethereal, scarlet glow rapidly lifted from around the seal in response to Cara, illuminating her body with a transient light and display a piercing flare that quickly reached into the sky above.

"How dare you refer to me as ancient, mortal!" Spoke a thunderous voice from within the Seal. *"Prove to me your worth, then you and the other trespassers may enter my Sanctum!'*

"I'm assuming that was Pahoe?" stuttered Firin as he stared in fascination towards the phantom light. "What does she want us to do?

"You heard her, we have to pass a trial so that we can reach the Sanctuary of Fire…" Explained Cara plainly. "It can't be any worse than what we've been through already?"

"Don't say that!" Countered Spero in disbelief. He clasped frantically onto Firin's shoulders to motion them both upon the activated seal and then, after saying a silent prayer, looked back again to Cara. "Pahoe won't have made this trial of hers easy to pass…" A tremendous shockwave abruptly spread across the lava plains before Cara and her companions. Immediately afterwards, a series of obsidian platforms rose with narrowed bridges in-between them from the depths of Pahoe's fiery lake, their eerie emergence soon gave rise to a greater sense of impending doom in Firin.

"You've only gone and jinxed us, Cara." Muttered Firin under his breath. "What did you say about this trial… it *can't be any worse*?"

"I don't care how bad this looks…" Said Cara with a mournful glint in her eyes. "I have to save my Sophilia." Pahoe's last shockwave had cleared away most of the dense ash clouds that lay before Cara and her companions. As the plumes slowly dispersed, a gigantic black tower came into sight which brought a feeling of hope in Cara but dread in Firin and Spero – each reasoned it to be the elusive Sanctuary of Fire.

"Doesn't it look inviting?" Sniggered Firin sarcastically. "I can't wait to see what the Sanctum looks like." The Sanctuary of Fire was an obsidian monolith which stood alone within a surrounding lake of molten magma. Its imposing structure rose hundreds of feet into the air and at its centre was a single balcony that looked out towards the mountain range further south. At its summit sat a large, triangular chasm with a crimson wall of light held within it – a feature Cara looked intently upon in awe. None of the three dared to move at first, fearful of what hidden traps or other trickery could now await them along this dangerous trail. Cara jokingly dismissed Firin and Spero's initial cowardice, she then bravely made a few steps onto the first narrow bridge that connected with another obsidian platform nearby – each one gradually leading towards Pahoe's Sanctuary in the near distance.

"Come on, you two!" Pleaded Cara to Firin and Spero, who themselves were lagging far behind at this point. "You're not going to let me do this alone… are you?" So far, nothing seemed to pose any apparent threat to Cara, other than what she and her friends were already faced with, under the resounding volcanoes and flowing streams of lava. Firin nudged at Spero in anticipation for him to follow along Cara's footsteps; she had already made a good progress over the first walkway and was currently making him feel emasculated.

"I have a bad feeling about this trial, this seems *way* too easy." Commented Firin as he slowly followed in the rear of Spero's company. "I've been in some tight spots over the years, when I was a sniper, but never *anything* this serious!" He unwittingly peered over the bridge's side then recoiled, Firin had noticed how the flames seemed to be flaring now with more aggression and this uneased him even more.

"Stop worrying, Firin… just keep your eyes on the Sanctuary ahead and take each step slowly." Said Cara in a strangely calm manner. "The sooner we get this next password… the sooner we can halt Cera's plans and get back to our own lives." She discreetly held onto Spero who now stood as a comforting presence alongside, repeating the Hymn of Alaskia to him as a distraction away from their threatening ordeal. The trio had managed to cross over the first platform and luckily without any injuries, though six more lay ahead and each one descended closer towards a billowing pool of searing lava below.

"The platforms are getting smaller, why would Pahoe feel the need to defend her Sanctuary like this?" Questioned Spero as he motioned for Firin to catch up with himself and Cara. "Do you think she will even help us; if we do reach the Sanctuary in one piece?" A blast of viscous lava suddenly rose from beside the companions, forcing them onto their hands and knees in a shared feeling of fright. Carefully they righted themselves from this unexpected attack, then within a staunch determination made their way onto the second obsidian platform.

"Should we take that as a no, then?" Bleated Firin angrily. He stood himself directly against the Sanctuary ahead, then raised a shaking fist towards it. "Is that all you've got... some little fireworks? Some Guardian of Fire you are, Pahoe!"

"You idiot!" Cara briskly shunted Spero aside to scold Firin for his begotten taunts. As her firm stare met against his, another series of explosive flames released from the molten lake below. "Are you trying to get us killed?"

"I don't know who *she* thinks she is?" Countered Firin with a roll of his eyes. "Does Pahoe not realise that we're trying to save the world?" Another wave of scorching lava lifted into the air from beside Cara and her friends. The companions ran for their survival as the enveloping flames swept across their bridge, it flowed across where only moments before they each stood. Cara and Spero leaped onto the second platform and were swiftly followed by Firin, who himself landed heavily on top of them as he evaded the chasing lava – though only by a few yards.

"Right, no more insults against the Guardian and no more playing around." Commanded Cara in authority, she spoke to Firin and Spero as she would have with Sophilia when the child misbehaved. "We make a break for it, run as fast as you can over these last few platforms and we *should* get to the Sanctuary in no time!" Cara ignored her friends' immediate plea to reconsider this proposal, she instead sprinted over the next bridge with her eyes firmly held against Pahoe's Sanctuary.

"Wait... Cara!" Cried out Spero, he had a great concern for her safety as the waves of lava beneath clashed now with even more ferocity. "We don't know what Pahoe will throw at us next, we need to think about this... Wait!" Cara continued to display her surprising stamina, she easily avoided the targeting flames as with each passing second her resolve to save Sophilia grew even stronger. An explosion, which sounded larger than the rest, echoed nearby that left a strange whistling sound to linger within the smoke-filled air. Firin keenly observed the difference in this terrifying sound and looked south to where it seemed to come from.

"Magmorran missiles leave that kind of noise…" To Firin's reluctant discovery, he found that a legion of Magmorran tanks were moving forth from the mountain range behind. Several of the formidable war-machines had already reached Pahoe's fake seal and were aiming their cannons upwards against the Guardian's tower. "Why am I always right? Spero… Cara… wait, I need to show you something!" Firin quickly gained ground on Spero to alert him first of this new threat, then after a nervous moment of inspecting Cera's tanks, they then cried out to Cara who herself had now reached the third platform.

"Cara!" Yelled Firin in desperation but to no avail, she was still too far away for him to be heard.

"…Cara!" Spero screamed at the top of his lungs then, after contemplating what he and Firin were inadvertently asking, changed his mind. "Don't stop, keep running!" Amongst the ceaseless eruptions and explosions, Cara could hear a faint voice travelling through them and so halted in her sprint to see where they were coming from.

"Spero?" Cara cautiously turned back to her friends. "No!" She couldn't believe what horrid sight met with her.

"Keep running!" Despaired Spero, he waved his arms frantically to will Cara back into a sprint. "Cera's forces are here!"

"I don't understand, how could she have known that we came here?" Cara shook her head at her sister's tanks and an awful feeling of sickness soon entered. "Cera couldn't have known…"

"Kufiah saw us leave on Pahoe's seal, maybe that's how?" Replied Spero, whilst struggling to catch his breath. "But you're right, there's no way her tanks could have made it here in such a short time… Cera must have worked out our plan - to reach Alaskia before her?"

"Calm down," chuckled Firin calmly, to the immediate surprise of his friends. "There is *no way* that those heavy tanks can cross over these narrow bridges…they'll fall in!" To his smug relief, as Cera's tanks made their way up to the molten lake's shoreline, they halted against its first causeway - seemingly stumped by this perilous terrain. "See, they can't reach us… we'll be safe enough here!" Firin joyfully made a few vulgar gestures against his new enemy, then turned to casually walk upon the next bridge without any doubt that it was okay to do so.

"I wouldn't be so sure, Firin…" Stammered Cara anxiously. "They're not retreating."

A unified roar came from the tanks, their external armour then suddenly began to transform, as they somehow narrowed in their width. One by one, Cera's adaptable war-machines slowly started to traverse over the first bridge, whilst the three companions looked on in horror and disbelief.

"That's not fair!" Cried out Firin angrily. "What else is Cera going to throw at us?" He swiped a fist through the air to vent his growing frustration.

"It's obvious, Cera *did* plan ahead for this attack…" Remarked Cara mournfully, she then wrapped her arms tightly around Spero, who also began to tremor at this unprecedented sight. "Ven was right… we need to reach Pahoe!" The trio hastily ran onto the next obsidian platform and realised, to a shared confoundment, that no further onslaught from Pahoe's flames now attacked them as they did. Beneath them, the waves of lava grew and now seemed to aim southwards against Cera's tanks – who were steadily moving close in their pursuit.

"You have no power here!"

Pahoe's molten waves cascaded tremendously over the first few platforms, engulfing a great many of Cera's tanks in their wake. The surging attack also forced several other war-machines from their present course, resulting in each to land helplessly back upon the shoreline of Talam's mainland.

"Pahoe… she is helping us!" Rejoiced Cara ecstatically. A second tsunami of lava soon lifted from the lake against Cera's tanks, a few had returned to the first bridge in attempt to complete their mission though were again driven back by this formidable show of power.

"Ha! They're retreating!" Shouted Firin after a burst of nervous laughter, he then began another tirade of vulgar gestures against the beleaguered tanks. "We have a Guardian on our side… time to go back home!" The relief of the companions, however, was soon to be proven short-lived. A new roaring sound came from the south; it was a group of strange, metallic lizards that surfaced over the near-horizon – evidently making their way towards the first bridge. These peculiar vehicles looked similar in design to the other Magmorran tanks, though these had four reptilian arms that spread out diagonally across their thin torsos, with vice grips at their ends. The reptilian monstrosities plunged their limbs powerfully into the ashen earth, within their mouths sat large and intimidating cannons which were precisely aimed towards the Pahoe's Sanctuary.

"What evil has Queen Cera created now?" Asked Spero sorrowfully to himself as he grabbed onto his companions, forwarding them each into a sprint over the last volcanic bridge. "Come on Pahoe… do something!" Cera's reptilian tanks instantaneously fired a barrage from their cannons across the lake, sending fountains of lava high into the air as they struggled to aim against the fleeing company. Some of the missiles stuck against Pahoe's Sanctuary to release an immense amount of energy upon it, though with no obvious signs of damage left afterwards. Cara and her friends fought hard against the rising fatigue now inflicting them. As they neared the entrance way of Pahoe's Sanctuary, another tsunami of lava was unleashed towards the enemy vehicles with an increased might. The fiery wave consumed many of the obsidian platforms and their bridges, in attempt to knock the lizard tanks into the lake below.

"That should do it!" Boasted Spero in hope. "They just can't take a hint, can they?"

Some of Cera's tanks succumbed to the forceful waves and coursed thereafter helplessly into the scorching pit of lava below. Only five had managed to skilfully evade Pahoe's attack by clinging onto the undersides of her bridges, then traversing themselves along by using the flexibility of their adaptable arms, resurfaced unharmed and with even more determination in fulfilling their abhorrent purpose.

"Cera has really thought ahead this time…" Said Spero with a look of melancholy to his friends. "This is our last chance…run… don't look back!" The companions finally entered Pahoe's Sanctuary, after passing through a vast open doorway, they then made towards its entrance portals - where one seal had already been activated. The scarlet light from Pahoe's entrance seal burst then instantly transported Cara and her friends into the Guardian's Sanctum situated far above. As their seal's light diminished, the companions then found themselves surrounded by several Acolytes of Fire who were each dressed in crimson robes and standing before them in observation.

"Where is Pahoe?" Questioned Cara desperately. "Where is your Guardian?" An immediate look of unease met back with her from the anxious followers.

"Over there…" Replied one of the acolytes nervously, they then pointed towards an opening where the Sanctuary's central balcony was situated. "She is waiting for you." Cara silently gestured for Firin and Spero to wait for her upon the Sanctum platform; she felt that, after having Pahoe's displeasure towards men made clear, it would be unwise for them to approach the Guardian at this time.

"…Pahoe?" Whispered Cara cautiously. As she made her way onto the balcony, it soon became apparent that the Guardian's attention was still drawn against Cera's invading forces outside. "Thank you for helping us escape." The Guardian of Fire was greatly more imposing than Levia and Ven: She wore blood-red armour that was scale-like in appearance, acting as a strong protection over her entire body. Pahoe's hair flowed hauntingly like a fiery sunset right down to her waist, each of its strands blazed like a roaring flame and her eyes glimmered equally in comparison. The Guardian looked no older than Cara, though there was an ancient wisdom that emanated from Pahoe's mighty aura - which encapsulated all who dared to look upon her.

"Under normal circumstances… I would bid you welcome, *worthy* mortal." Sighed Pahoe, as she turned to face Cara. "However, I see that you have brought with you an unwelcome party of Magmorran soldiers, who are currently canvasing my Sanctuary with their cannon-fire."

"I don't know how they found us," Replied Cara in a tremoring voice. "Cera…" She was swiftly halted from speaking further by the acutely paranoid Guardian.

"You bear the mark of Cerebrante…" Interrupted Pahoe, her piercing eyes radiated more intensely with a knowing stare. "May I ask, could this have something to do with that Queen invading my sacred plains?" A sudden, blinding flash burst out closely to where Cara and Pahoe now stood. The Guardian's acolytes cowered alongside Firin and Spero, in return Pahoe looked back over the tumultuous lake with her arms raised high against it – her dominating presence rose also. "To attack my Sanctuary, is to also declare war upon the divine powers themselves!" Declared Pahoe hatefully towards Cera's remaining lizard tanks, who were no almost at the final platform. "You *will* regret these blasphemous actions; your Queen and forsaken lands will burn with my flames… for this show of impudence!" A responding barrage of cannon-fire met against Pahoe's position. She immediately summoned another wave of lave to strike against Cera's tanks, though they were too close now to take any effective damage.

"Where are your Sanctuary Guards?" Asked Cara in a pleading tone, the Acolytes of Fire appeared to be holding no weapons. "We'll need them…"

"I have no need for such guards," Snapped Pahoe in response, her glare still fixed against the lake of lava ahead. "Ven only has them for when he is not at his Sanctuary, and if you have met Lenya in Hydrania… then you will see why Levia has no need for any either." One of the Sanctum seals sporadically came into life; it radiated with a mighty, jade beam which instantly filled the chamber with its blinding light. The worn figure of Ven gradually emerged from his seal, his hands were covered in blood and only his staff seemed to be keeping him upright. Ven reached out tearfully to Pahoe, as she herself held a hand out to him, then together they looked towards the withdrawing Magmorran tanks in shared feeling of dread.

"I'm so glad you're here, Ven." Muttered Pahoe in relief. "I can't stop them… they're evading every attack which I've made so far." Ven moved quickly away from Pahoe to look down from her balcony upon the incoming lizard tanks. The Guardian of Earth tightened the grip he had upon his crude staff, a rage then grew in Ven's eyes as he turned back fully towards the Sanctum platform.

"…Cara." Ven stammered as he looked to her. "I will deal with this." An air of confusion swiftly rose within the Sanctum, its Acolytes suffered the most – it seemed.

"Ven, what has happened to you?" Cara moved with haste towards the Guardian of Earth then, to her immediate horror, Ven backed away to throw himself willingly over the balcony. "…No!"

"Have faith in Ven!" Said Pahoe in a commanding voice. "It was he that helped me to construct those bridges…" The Guardian of Earth heavily descended from Pahoe's tower; he fell for what seemed like minutes towards Cera's lizards-tanks below, though only a few seconds in truth had passed. Ven's body rapidly burst into emerald flames as he neared the ash-laden earth, whilst also avoiding a series of cannon-fire that aimed hard against him. On impact, the empowered Guardian forced his staff destructively into the ground, creating from it an all-powerful shockwave that ran across Pahoe's lake of lava, obliterating all its structures and Cera's remaining tanks with casc.

"I knew you could it, Ven." Whispered Pahoe in endearment. "You may not be the oldest Guardian, but you *are* the strongest…" Those held within Pahoe's Sanctum breathed with a sigh of gratitude, as Ven once again appeared from the entrance seal, they knew that Cera's threat had been successfully halted. Ven's face noticeably bore many cuts and bruises, he collapsed as if in agony against his staff whilst Pahoe ran over to offer him some support.

"Brother!" Pahoe ran her fingertips across Ven's brow slowly, hoping that her spiritual power could somehow heal him from his present physical wounds. "I will be forever grateful for how you have saved my Sanctuary this day…."

"Don't mention it…" Humoured Ven wearily. "You would do the same for me." Pahoe nurtured her friend's reassuring smile and then, on realising that he was quickly recovering, leant in to seek some much-needed answers from him.

"Ven, how did you know to come here?" Pahoe fleeted her glance back towards Cara and her companions. "Are they perhaps the reason?" Ven sat himself upright after a brief struggle, he then looked beyond Pahoe towards Cara and could barely find the courage needed to speak with her.

"I am…" The Guardian of Earth mumbled almost indecipherably, it was apparent that he had a terrible burden to share. "I am so sorry, Cara." She shook her head silently in response. Cara was both perplexed and disturbed by Ven's unnerving reaction, which Pahoe herself also felt uneased by as she moved in closer.

"What are you apologising for, Ven?" Cara's hands started to shake. "You just saved us, we are all thankful that you are here." In truth, she dreaded the answer that may be given. Firin and Spero sensed Cara's anxiety, they walked over to join in with the awkward atmosphere but continued to keep a careful distance away from Pahoe.

"My Sanctuary, it was breached before I could get there." Ven ashamedly lowered his glance away from Cara, focusing instead on the more familiar face of Pahoe beside him. "Cera used Kufiah's sorcery to allow for General Nira…" The Guardian froze, then after a few deep breaths continued. "Nira managed to reach the Sanctum…she killed my Acolytes… all of them."

"Impossible," Pahoe didn't know what to say, this horrifying feat had not been achieved before. "The Queen's connection with Kufiah must be at its strongest now… for such a power to exist." Cara felt a sudden wave of nausea take hold over her; all she could now envision was the terrifying ordeal Sophilia must have suffered, with being captured or killed by General Nira. Ven sorrowfully held out his hands in remorse, he looked to Cara like a sinner begging for forgiveness.

"You promised me…" Stuttered Cara painfully, as she fought against a rising anger and helplessness. "You said: No one can breach the Sanctum."

"I was wrong." Ven rubbed at his scorched face in disbelief. "Nira's soldiers have taken your Sophilia, but to where… remains unclear. I have failed to protect your child, Cara." Tears started to run down the Guardian's face, the memories of what Ven had seen continued to haunt him. "I have failed those who spent their entire lives serving me and my Sanctuary…"

"You did your best, Ven." Cara wrapped her arms lovingly around Ven's body, in sympathy with his agonising loss. "Sophilia will be okay, we've almost completed our quest… I only need two more passwords." Pahoe stood herself to tower over the others, it was becoming clear to her now as to why these strange visitors had come to her Sanctuary - so unexpected. The Guardian of fire tactfully looked again to Cerebrante's mark upon Cara, then gestured for her acolytes to leave without further word to them.

"I am sorry to hear of your loss…Cara." Pahoe gave a judgemental stare towards her fearful guests, paying particular attention to the young woman who was continuing to comfort Ven. "… Daughter of King Kanaan… Sister to Queen Cera… am I correct?" Cara instinctively shifted her eyes away from Pahoe, the Guardian of Fire was frightening enough to look upon without these intrusive comments being made. "Interesting… the first thing you did there, was to hide your amber eyes from me." Pahoe leant menacingly in towards Cara, her pacing breaths quickly met against the young princess's skin. "The amber eyes of Magmorrah's Royal bloodline… they are far too obvious not to notice, especially for those who have seen them countless times before – like myself. I presume, that Ven here believes it is you that shall bring our world back into balance?"

"We are all on quest," responded Cara in frustration, she did not agree with Pahoe's intimidating tactics. "I need the Elemental Passwords, so that Alaskia can be freed… the Spirit of Light will stop Cera."

"*The Sacred Balance* is beyond saving, Cerebrante's connection with yourself is evidently weak…" Pahoe gently raised Ven to look at her by tilting his chin upwards. "You knew of this mortal's relevance, Brother?"

"Yes!" Ven nodded vigorously in agreement to Pahoe, he then slowly stood himself up to stand against her in addressing all still held within the Sanctum. "Queen Cera's malicious intent is worse than what we first feared, Pahoe. You have no idea."

"How?" Pahoe gave a dismissive smirk. "The protective seal which we Elemental Guardians have placed over Alaskia is… impenetrable."

"Like Levia and Ven's Sanctuaries?" Interrupted Spero bravely. "Cera had no issue gaining access to them!"

"You would be wise to stay silent, young man." Responded Pahoe in a condescending tone. "Besides, none of us know the true location of where Alaskia has been imprisoned... what hope does Cera have?" Pahoe laughed faintly, she then turned back to Cara with a forced smile. "Unless, King Kanaan revealed to his eldest daughter the whereabouts?"

"No!" Cara snapped, her frustration with Pahoe was now at its breaking-point. "Father *hated* me... and I still *hate* him! You don't know anything about me or my past!"

"You remind me so much of your grandmother... Karolheid." Sniggered Pahoe with a satisfied grin. "She had the same stubborn attitude!"

"Please, Friends..." Ven calmly wavered his palms to cease the building tension. "Queen Cera means to eradicate all Spirits from Impartia - not just Alaskia." Cara and Pahoe knelt themselves submissively, neither openly admitted the shame they now felt. "Cara is our greatest hope to stop this fate from happening, despite her mark being so faded... If I could take this burden from you, I would without any hesitation." Said Ven as bowed himself before her in respect. At this moment, the Guardian of Earth realised just how enormous Cara's burden truly was.

"You believe that Cerebrante will choose... *her*?" Pahoe shook her head firmly in disagreement to Ven. "I am sorry if this upsets you, but I can sense a conflict in you... with regards to your sister, Cara."

"I thought that the Elemental Guardians were supposed to be mighty and wise beings!" Spero barged himself between Cara and Pahoe, desperately holding back his anger whilst doing so. "Cara has been through enough without you knocking her down further; she has been exiled from her own nation, raised her daughter in Viridia's wild forests without any aid and is now burdened with saving this world from her own family's reign!"

"Your words are not helping, Sister." Muttered Ven cautiously under his breath to Pahoe. "We must be constructive... time is against us."

"Cerebrante's mark has been tainted, it is nothing more than a lie." Pahoe stepped away from her Sanctum platform back towards the Sanctuary's balcony. "Its bearers are not always worthy of bonding with that Celestial Spirit." The Guardian swiftly turned to face Cara again. "King Kanaan, Queen Cera and Princess Cara all bear the sacred mark... such a corruption has never been known of before!" Pahoe lowered her eyes, she knew what was to be said next would hurt Cara greatly. "I also assume that this child, which General Nira has apprehended, bears Cerebrante's mark also?" Cara tremored despairingly; Pahoe had never met Sophilia before, yet she knew of this intimate detail about her.

"It's on her right hand," Replied Cara in a saddened whisper. "I can't let Cera harm her... we must find Alaskia!" Ven glared at Pahoe, he had hoped that she would have cast aside her own solitary beliefs to aid them on this quest, not render their morale further into misery and defeat.

"Grant Cara your password, Pahoe… as myself and Levia have done so already." Ven's voice seemed tired as he spoke, this irregular change in his personality thankfully managed to persuade Pahoe's greater involvement. "I believe now, that Alaskia is incarcerated within Skynah's mountain… not at the Celestial Spirit's original Sanctuary in Weissamorrah. We will gain more advice from Aira before travelling there, maybe then we can end this cycle of devastation?" Pahoe hesitated for a moment, she was deeply uncertain of how successful this quest Ven had undertaken would be - in vanquishing Cera's threat. She then held out her palms willingly upon Cara's temples, stroking at them with her fingertips to allow for a strong spiritual connection.

"I Pahoe, Guardian of the Eternal Flames, grant thee pass into thine divine Sanctum." Cara felt a surge of energy flow through her entire body, it created a burning sensation that soon entered deep into her soul, though no lasting harm came by it. Cara bowed in gratitude before the Guardian of Fire, who herself felt a mutual respect now grow between them both.

"Know this, Cara." Said Pahoe in a politer manner. "The conflict I spoke of… is your desire to end Cera's decimation upon Impartia, though you are also clouded by the thoughts of redeeming your sister and preserving Sophilia's current wellbeing." The Guardian gently lifted Cara's hands into her own. "You can only choose one of these paths to pursue, if they are to be rightly accomplished…the choice is yours and only for you to make freely." Cara staggered herself back against Ven's torso to allow for a moment of respite, from these daunting truths. She looked across to Firin and Spero, who themselves shared in Cara's torment – neither wanted to make this awful decision for her.

"You are wrong, Pahoe…I'm sorry, but you're wrong." Cara postured herself defiantly against the formidable Guardian. "I *will* save my daughter and sister, with the help of Alaskia, have no doubt in that!" Cara carefully removed a single white flower that had been hidden within her clothing, a flower that was gifted to her by Sophilia just before their capture in Viridia. "My Sophilia's life means more to me than any spiritual war, which we all have now found ourselves embroiled in." Cara forcefully placed the delicate flower into Pahoe's palms. "I am going to the Sanctuary of Air… whether you think this is in vain or not!" Ven moved himself quickly towards Cara and Pahoe with a raised arm, as the Guardian met with them, he ran his hands slowly over the brittle flower to lift its wilted petals back into their true appearance – much to Cara's appreciation and heart-felt joy. "Such a small gesture, but it means a lot to me." Said Cara, a genuine smile lifted from her towards Ven. "This flower is all that I have to remind me of my little girl… of her innocence and how vulnerable she is."

"I scarcely managed to defeat Nira at my Sanctuary, though thankfully that wicked creature can no longer hinder our efforts now." Said Ven, his expression remained mournful despite the glad-tidings he had announced. "Viridia has been decimated, its forests burned, and this was not a single act of random malice. The attack was a calculated and desperate move to capture Sophilia... there is no other reason." Ven held onto Cara's arms endearingly, she welcomed them without refrain. "If your child has been taken to Kufiah's Sanctuary, then our only hope of truly saving her is to free Alaskia and reform Cerebrante." Spero stood himself directly before the two Guardians, he was disgusted though regrettably held in agreement with what they were saying. The longing faces of Cara and Firin ate away at Spero, who himself wished to hasten this frustrating saga to end.

"If this is the reality of Cara's situation, then take us to see this *Aira* at once!" Spero shrugged off Firin's attempt to draw him away from Pahoe, he had no fear of her scorn at all. "We can't afford to jeopardise Sophilia's safety... nor lose any more time than we already have done!"

"Patience, Mortal." Replied Pahoe sternly. The Guardian of Fire then noticed Firin, who had so far managed to evade her unwanted attention. "You... look very familiar!"

"No, I don't!" Firin anxiously fleeted his eyes towards Spero. "Help me..." he slowly backed away from the increasingly agitated Guardian.

"But...you do!" Pahoe clenched Firin's jaw to inspect him more meticulously. "Same eyes, same hair... you're a Prince of Talam and spawn of that wretched traitor!"

"No, I'm not!" Firin ripped his jaw away from the Guardian, thankfully Ven came over at this point to intervene. "You're crazy!"

"Firin is no Prince, he is a scavenger we found in the southern deserts!" Blared Ven disapprovingly to Pahoe. "Focus on our quest, please... my Sister. This is not the time to make new enemies!"

"Fine. I'll summon for Aira's Seal to activate... I can't stand a minute longer in this filth's company." Pahoe began to sing the Hymn of Alaskia, surprisingly in a serene voice, and its words empowered a seal upon her platform that radiated gradually with a silver light. The spiritual energy flowed warmly into Cara and her companions as they stood upon it, their worn bodies also eased instantly, and their disheartened spirits soon lifted. "You have made a wise decision, Cara." Shouted Pahoe in assurance. "I have faith in you to fulfil this sacred duty...release Alaskia... and put an end to your sister's venomous reign!"

"Like I had a choice in the first place?" Despaired Cara as she held onto Firin and Spero's hands. Aira's seal encased their bodies within its powerful light and then, within a mere matter of seconds, transported them to their next mystical destination. The Elemental Guardians observed the seal's diminishing light with a renewing sense of hope, it was a feeling they had each long forgotten. Pahoe and Ven then began to contemplate their next move, of how to aid Cara by holding back Cera's forces.

"Can we really trust this exiled princess to complete such an enormous task, Ven?" Muttered Pahoe in uncertainty. "Even if Cara and her friends do reach the Celestial Spirit, who knows what will await them - when trying to free Alaskia from his prison?"

"Do not lose hope," Ven slammed his staff into the platform to rid any lingering feelings of grief. "Come, let us speak together in private… it has been so long." Pahoe obeyed this request and led Ven through her Sanctuary's winding catacombs, eventually reaching its peak where they could look out across the northern nations of Impartia. Ven closely inspected the near horizon to focus his gaze upon the gargantuan mountain of Skynah nearby. He breathed out a deep and heavy sigh and then turned back towards his fellow Guardian, wishing to divulge further into this current affair that troubled them both greatly.

"Us Guardians must hold onto our faith, more-so during these challenging times." Said Ven with a determined glance to Pahoe. "Cerebrante's powers are unfathomable with their effect upon this world, our own kin cannot truly understand them… not even Levia." Pahoe rolled her eyes, she was not as close to Levia in comparison with Ven. "Our destinies now lie in a young woman, who only days ago lived as a peasant with her young daughter in Viridia. Speaking of Levia, have you heard from him recently?" Pahoe nodded gently to confirm this with Ven, she proceeded to reach into her armour where a small parchment had been secretly hidden away. On it were a set of peculiar lines, at the bottom was a mountain which Ven reasoned to be Skynah and within its centre there were several etched crosses, each marked in different locations. "This is Weissamorrah…" Ven looked upon the document in confusion, its purpose still unclear to him. "Why do you have this and what is Levia's involvement?"

Pahoe smiled reassuringly to her perplexed counterpart, she eagerly pointed out the number of small crosses which were dotted over her map and then looked to Ven with a gleeful expression.

"Levia was given this map by Aira, he sent it to me only minutes before Cara arrived at my Sanctum." Pahoe lifted the parchement to place it into Ven's hands for an easier inspection. "Those crosses mark where the last pocket of resistance is made up, they are from varying naval fleets that have managed to escape Cera's invasion forces. From what I have briefly gathered, they are hidden upon Weissamorrah's southern shoreline and Levia plans to travel there… he is hoping to unite them all against Magmorrah's Armada - which will in no doubt be pressing against Skynah as we speak."

"We are *not* alone in our fight, then." Ven gave a fleeting smile to Pahoe, it was however soon replaced by an apprehension. "One of my companions, who sadly did not make it this far, was an Acolyte of Kufiah - before turning away from the corruption of Queen Cera." Pahoe moved her head side-to-side, she did not like where this conversation was now going. "He spoke of other Celestial Guardians... ones that are separate from Cerebrante. When we placed our seal of protection over Alaskia, I felt no presence of any other kindred Spirit; I do not understand how a Dark Acolyte could no such a thing and yet we Elemental Guardians appear blind to it?" Pahoe recoiled her steps cautiously away from Ven as a sickening shock suddenly took a hold over her.

"Brother... perhaps you wrongly placed your trust in this, so-called, friend of yours?" A tense atmosphere immediately rose between Pahoe and Ven. "The true and *only* Celestial Guardian is Cerebrante, if others now exist, it can only mean that Kanaan's defilement has seeped farther within *The Sacred balance* than we had first dreaded!"

Chapter Nine: Through Forsaken Eyes

Queen Cera rested herself upon Kufiah's throne in utter contentment; the Spirit of Darkness no longer being Master of his own Sanctuary now, as she scoured his Sanctum platform with a yearning glare. She toyed playfully with Kanaan's accursed amulet to pass the time, which, as always, remained firmly placed upon her chest. The mark of Cerebrante hidden beneath Cera's precious adornment had grown fainter recently; a sordid result of her delving further into Kufiah's malignant spirit, which she admired more than any other living presence – even herself.

"What is taking so long?" Cera's patience was depleting swiftly. "They should be here by now!" She seethed, with an embittered stare aimed solely towards Kufiah's Seal. "Where are you?" The Sanctum chamber suddenly filled with a haunting amber light as Kufiah's seal re-ignited, bringing to Cera a perverse joy which took hold over her gaunt features instantly. Two dark figures emerged from the blaring flames: One towered over the other and was beastly in appearance, the lowly man knelt beside looked lost in his expression as he turned to face Queen Cera. "Finally, you have returned… my begotten Guardian of Darkness!" Cera screamed in delight as she removed herself from Kufiah's throne. "Kneel before me your Queen, whom you have served so well."

"Your Majesty." Stammered Moah. He was fighting against his conflicted emotions, in fear of what dire reprimand Cera may grant to him. "These past few days have been a prolonged suffering… being so far away from your divine presence." Moah held his head down heavily, as the burden from his previous actions continued to drain him, he dared not meet his eyes against the imposing Queen. "It is good news that I bring you." Cera approached Moah with her arms held out, as if to offer him a longing embrace, a kindly gesture so unfamiliar to her scornful nature.

"Arise, Moah… I too have good-tidings to share." The Queen lifted a sadistic smile to meet with her reluctant servant. "Hydrania and Talam have now fallen, Viridia will burn from our flames and my enemies shall linger in defeat! The people of Impartia will learn to adore me or suffer the consequences - when we have fulfilled our plan's final act!" Cera invited for Moah to stand closer to her, he submissively obeyed, though the Queen's words disturbed him from mentioning Viridia's apparent destruction.

"Yes, my Queen." Moah righted his shaking voice as he forced himself to look upon her. "The Elemental Guardians are unworthy of their gifted powers... unlike those of which you have gained so rightfully." Moah bowed in subservience, as not wishing to raise any suspicion of his current feelings. On rising, the Dark Guardian noticed that his fellow Acolytes had now entered Kufiah's Sanctum from behind, his breaths passed painfully as he turned to greet the new arrivals. "Brothers... Sisters... it is good to see you again." Declared Moah in a powerful voice. "Bow before your Queen and Master Spirit!" The Acolytes of Darkness lowered themselves willingly towards Cera and Kufiah, none had yet noticed the nervous tremors which Moah was displaying - to his understandable relief.

"Talam, under my blessed rule, will be reborn from its current desolation... into a land filled with prosperity and order!" Cera gleamed with pride as her Dark Acolytes rejoiced at this declaration. "My new weapon proved too powerful against its peoples' dissent. Finally, Magmorrah will reap from Talam's resources which my father so pitifully failed to gain during his time as our ruler, this nation shall again bask in glory!" Cera laughed wickedly, echoing the disturbing sounds of her voice around the Sanctum to haunt Moah, her Guardian of Darkness had no knowledge of such a weapon.

"Your Majesty, please bid my pardon for asking such an invasive question to yourself but, what is this mighty arsenal of which you speak?" Moah shivered as he knowingly thought back to the blinding light he and Cara had witnessed when in Hydrania. "Is the power of Kufiah not strong enough to spread your further control over Impartia?" Cera's laughter dwindled as she rested her skeletal palms upon Moah's shoulders, an intimate connection which he quickly sought release from, then gave to him a frank look of dismay.

"This Weapon of Mass Destruction was created by Kufiah and myself alone... I am surprised, you could not sense its spiritual power – being so close to the darkness?" Cera tutted in disappointment to Moah and then, to his hidden pleasure, moved away back towards Kufiah. "The Spirit of Darkness and I found a way to concentrate his destructive influence; it is contained within a cursed gem that I have aptly named – a *Kufian Shard.* Upon my wilful command, the shard releases its immense power with a blinding array of light upon those who would oppose me... ultimately reducing any object held within its path into ashes within mere seconds!" Cera stroked at Kufiah's ashen robes, the Spirit remained silent as if oblivious to this acknowledgment. "The forsaken lands of Impartia will suffer as we in Magmorrah did, under the foolish actions of my father, they will soon yield in their treachery to me - or suffer an eternal damnation!" Moah felt a sudden and paining realisation enter him.

"I saw it... the blast in Talam." Cera's weapon and its apparent capabilities terrified Moah now more anything else. He bowed respectively to Cera again though, in truth, wished to tear the amulet away from her in want of ending this terrifying capability. "This weapon..."

"It is not just for offense, my naïve servant." Cackled Cera in satisfaction. "A second shard was created that powers my revived airship – Divinity. General Nira has been privileged with using it to reach Viridia's Sanctuary… her return is expected at any time now."

"Magmorrah has military strength beyond any of the other nations," Moah struggled to remain calm as he spoke. "Is there really a need for such a device?" Cera sharply turned to face her Dark Guardian, unsure of where his mindset was leading. "This world and its people are now *mine*… we no longer need concern ourselves with such material obstructions as armies to face us!" The Queen caressed her amulet, then lifted it before Moah. "As for yourself, I have a far greater and pressing task to be carried out now."

"I will do as you bid…without question." Responded Moah with an anxious nod of endearment. "What is this task?" A group of Elite Magmorran soldiers suddenly entered Kufiah's Sanctum, their facial expressions displayed a fear towards their Queen's reprimand and of what news they needed to share with her.

"How *dare* you enter this Sanctum without prior consent!" Roared Cera ferociously. "What is the meaning of this?"

"My Queen…" Replied a soldier nervously, as the others along with him knelt before Cera. "… the General."

"What of Nira and where *is* my valiant defender?" Questioned Cera in excitement. "Was your mission successful?" The soldiers looked to one another in apprehension, it did not help that Kufiah's towering presence continued to linger ominously before them, their Queen's anticipation was also noticeably turning to anger.

"General Nira, she did not make it back to Divinity as planned." The soldier instantly froze in awaiting Cera's expected scorn, she however shrugged her shoulders dismissively and instead looked back upon Kanaan's amulet. "The Guardian of Earth… we believe that he returned to his Sanctuary after we were dismissed. He has either taken General Nira hostage or worse…"

"The Elemental Guardians will not be a threat to us for much longer," Replied Cera smugly, there was no sign of grief in her from Nira's loss. "Did you retrieve the child?" The Queen's eyes swiftly met with her soldiers under a piercing stare. "If not, I will ensure that Kufiah deals with you all… personally!"

"Yes, we have Princess Sophilia." Spoke another soldier in haste, they instantly regretted addressing the child in this way. "I mean…"

"*She* is no Princess of Magmorrah!" Screamed Cera hatefully, her malignant voice echoed around the Sanctum many times before vanishing into its chasm below. "That bastard child and her mother are nothing but exiled rats and should be addressed in such a way! Bring her before me this instant!"

"At once, my Queen." The soldiers made for a quick exit, under Cera's watchful gaze and her Acolytes scornful stares. "We shall bring her before you now."

"Wait!" Ordered the Queen abruptly, a great conflict now showed in her expression. "I would rather not have to see her... yet. Throw the child into one of our vaults here, she will be dealt with soon."

"As you wish, Your Majesty." Cera's soldiers sprinted from the Sanctum now, each were thankful to leave Kufiah and their Queen far behind. "Long live the Queen!" They nervously cried on leaving the foreboding chamber. The Acolytes of Darkness bowed in respect to their Guardian and then in silence, left their master's Sanctum without further word. Moah, to his further condemnation, was now left alone with Queen Cera and Kufiah; their company would usually bring no concern to him, but times had changed and so had Moah's allegiance.

"Your insight so far has been proven invaluable to me, Moah." Spoke Cera with a hint of disgust in her voice, she deeply despised showing any kind of acknowledgment to those other than herself. "Through you, we now know how to reach the hidden Sanctum of Alaskia and thus vanquish that interfering Spirit from this plain forever. You have already brought such a great honour upon your master's Sanctuary, and for this, you shall be greatly rewarded!" Cera cackled again as stood over Moah's cowering figure, whilst still clasping at her cursed amulet that itself now appeared to glow crimson within its golden centre. "Kufiah..." Cera turned her head slowly to address the malignant Spirit of Darkness. "He will grant you this reward, but only once your next task is complete!" Kufiah's ashen robes released a wave of choking smoke against Moah, the Spirit growled like a rabid beast in torment and a deathly cold entered the air as he turned back towards his submissive servant.

"Master, I beseech your immortal wisdom and power!" Stuttered Moah in reverence and fear. "I am eternally your humble Guardian and will serve thee with all thine mortal being..."
Kufiah's entrancing, flame-like pupils met harshly against Moah in response; as if the Dark Spirit was looking deep into his Guardian's own corrupted soul, sensing somehow the risen conflict within it.

"Cera..." Kufiah's voice growled as he unexpectedly spoke to address the Queen instead of Moah. "My Guardian is worthy, I will grant his reward now... should you permit me so?"

"By all means... Oh, Mightiest of Spirits!" Cera willingly moved aside in allowing for Kufiah's intrusive presence to move closer before their tremoring Guardian. The thick smoke that flowed from Kufiah's mass continued to fill Moah's lungs painfully and reignited each negative memory held within him. "But first, I shall explain Moah's task fully to him... before such a privilege is bestowed." Interrupted Cera as she moved herself in-between Kufiah and Moah.

"What is your bidding, my Queen?" Asked Moah in reluctance, he could barely speak from the choking fumes surrounding him.

"Nira has sacrificed herself, so that my sister's child could be brought here." Cera continued to show no remorse over her General's lacking presence, despite Moah's shock. "I entrust in you alone to avenge my General's demise; eradicate the threat that Sophilia imposes on me with her persisting existence… that, is your task now!" Cera glared coldly into Moah's eyes, ensuring that he firmly understood that he would have no choice in otherwise fulfilling this cruel command. Moah struggled immensely to restrain his growing despair, he forced an obedient expression towards Cera in return and his heart begged for the child's forgiveness.

"What fatal threat does this child *truly* hold over you… to justify such an extreme reaction?" Moah had little time to consider the consequences of such an unwitting defiance made against Cera, though initially she seemed unmoved by it. "Shall we not just keep her as prisoner within our Sanctuary walls, there is no chance of the child escaping?" Cera flared her stance to tower above Moah's smaller stature.

"Sophilia has upon her body the mark of Cerebrante, as does Cara." The Queen's face writhed on saying her sister's name. "If I am to stamp out the light of Alaskia and render Cerebrante worthless, then no remnants of their power can survive… especially while I do so!" Cera suddenly revealed from under her amulet Cerebrante's faded mark to Moah. "I trust that you will find a way to resolve this pressing threat against me and my rule, Guardian… or shall I make certain that you will suffer under Kufiah's sacred immolation as an act of repentance?" Moah tremored as he forced himself to bow before the demented Queen.

"I beg for pardon, Your Majesty. I will enact your will and solve this current issue, so that no further inconvenience comes by this child…" Cera laughed in a cruel satisfaction over Moah's submission to her. The Queen then released from her tightened grip Kanaan's accursed amulet, immediately awakening a brief freedom in Kufiah's ability to act on his own free-will.

"You are indeed worthy of such a gift, my Guardian." Approved Cera disturbingly. "Now feel the flow of Kufiah's divine rage enter your very soul! You will be as equal in power to the Spirit of Darkness as I am now! Use this might to aid in my destiny as Impartia's rightful ruler… its Eternal Empress!" Moah felt a surge of intense dark energy suddenly flow into him from Cera, she was creating a stronger connection to his spiritual master - a gift that the Guardian of Darkness truly welcomed without resistance. "End Sophilia's life now and you shall become eternally honoured through my divine grace!" Declared Cera enthusiastically as she actioned to Moah for his immediate dismissal. "Do not disappoint me!" As he left Kufiah's Sanctum and his two oppressors, Moah found several of his fellow Acolytes waiting for him outside and with some heavily-armoured Magmorran soldiers there also to protect them. The Guardian of Darkness took in a deep breath, which was still painful from Kufiah's lingering smoke within them, then walked towards his awaiting escorts.

"Take me to the child…" Commanded Moah in a weakened voice. The Dark Acolytes each bowed then led him through a winding set of catacombs to where Sophilia was now being held. The short journey proved torturous to Moah, in how slow his progress was in reaching the hidden chamber where Sophilia had been stored, each step felt as if he were being made to walk many miles within a sorrowful condemnation.

"We're nearly there," said one of the acolytes in a snarling tone. "One more passage to go…" Soon the Guardian found himself before a solitary chamber within the Sanctuary's lower halls.

"Was there really a need to keep her this far down?" Groaned Moah angrily to himself. "It's time to finally meet you… little Sophilia." He peered carefully into the chamber to discover that there was a small distressing figure of a young girl within it, she had huddled herself upon the farthest corner and whimpered sadly for her mother's comfort.

"Vile, little thing… isn't she?" Seethed one of Moah's acolytes. "The child is yours now, my Guardian."

"So…" Moah just restrained himself from slamming the scornful acolyte's face into the heavy obsidian door. "This frightened child is the greatest threat to our Queen and nation, is she?" A unified silence met against the Guardian from his acolytes, one of them then cautiously proceeded to unlock Sophilia's chamber. "Leave us!" He commanded. Moah slowly approached the vulnerable child, initially not uttering a word, from still being held within his own remorseful guilt over Sophilia's capture. The young princess stared anxiously towards the dark-cloven stranger as he entered, whilst trying to focus again on the thoughts of her loving mother - whom she still believed would be coming at any given moment to rescue her.

"Go away…" Cried Sophilia meekly. "Leave me alone…" Moah knelt himself before the petrified child and swiftly removed his hood, that had until this moment shielded him from recognition.

"I believe, that your name is Sophilia?" Asked Moah to an instant, silent response from the child. The Guardian had expected nothing less, given that he was dressed similarly to those who had already treated Sophilia with such unnecessary scorn. "Or should I say… Lia?"

"Yes, it is. But… how do *you* know my name?" Sophilia looked upon Moah in both a fear and hope, several tears then gradually emerged from her eyes. "Only my Mummy calls me 'Lia'… where is she?" Moah attempted to form a reassuring smile, though it had little effect on Sophilia.

"I am a friend of your mother – Cara." Said Moah, as he smiled sincerely. "She has sent me here to rescue you!" The Guardian discreetly tilted his head to listen for any unwanted listeners outside, thankfully he could sense none. "Please, Lia…you must try to trust me. I wish no harm upon you *or* your mother, just do as I say, and everything will be alright… I promise!" Sophilia breathed a sigh of relief then wrapped her arms tenderly around Moah's torso, now feeling that a bonding trust had formed quickly between them. Moah initially felt as if he would recoil, from the unfamiliarity of sharing in such a pleasant gesture, though the innocence of Sophilia's reaction warmed a part of his soul that the Guardian had previously neglected. "I am going to take you to a place now in here called the *Sanctum*," Explained Moah gently. "It may be a little imposing, but you will be safe there…" He held out a hand towards Sophilia, hoping to mirror Cara's own sign of trust with the child - whenever she was scared. "We don't have much time so please, Lia… trust me."

"I *do* trust you!" Replied Sophilia as she firmly placed her hands upon Moah's shoulders. "What is your name though… are you not going to tell me? What are you doing here?" Her question caused Moah to chuckle to himself; he was woefully unprepared to care for such an energetic child.

"My name is Moah and it is a pleasure to meet you in person, Lia." The Guardian checked once again for any foreign threat outside. "Come now, we must be quick, before the bad guys realise that you are missing!"

"Okay! Okay!" Repeated Sophilia many times, before affirming that Moah had already accepted her participation. "Let's go!" Moah became increasingly perplexed by the lacking challenge he and Sophilia had faced on their journey back through the Sanctuary catacombs. As the fleeing pair neared Kufiah's Sanctum, a harrowing sound of numerous footsteps evidently began to surround their current position – Forcing the Guardian of Darkness to take on a drastic action.

"Quickly, Lia!" Moah grasped the child's body into his arms. "Get inside!" Moah hastily placed Sophilia into the nearest chamber that he could find, wishing to hide her away from whoever it was that now approached them. He frantically searched for the source of these phantom footsteps, they sounded so close to Moah, yet there were no signs of any nearing assailants.

"What are you doing… why are you putting me in here?" Asked Sophilia tearfully. Moah gently nudged her into the small chamber within his own pained reservations, mostly as to how safe she would be whilst kept in there. "I don't like the dark!"

"Please, Lia!" Begged Moah, in a strained whisper. "Stay in here for now and no harm will come to you… I swear it!" The footsteps grew louder and seemed only metres away. "I promised your mother, that I would never let anyone hurt you my dear child. Stay in here and be silent until I return for you… can you do that for me?" Moah swiftly replaced his hood, in a hope that he could also hide himself away from this nightmare situation.

"Fine, don't be long though." Sophilia obediently complied with Moah's request, she stepped herself further into the pitch-black chamber while Moah turned away in concern.

"We'll be free soon..." Replied Moah eagerly. However, in front of him now stood a few of his acolytes and Cera's Elite Guards, who all strangely bowed together on seeing Moah – despite the suspicious circumstance.

"Oh, Mighty Guardian of Darkness," said one of the Dark Acolytes drearily. "Queen Cera is still waiting within our Sanctum, she is displeased at how long you are taking with fulfilling your honourable task." Moah fleeted his eyes back upon the chamber where he had stowed Sophilia away. "You are to go there without further delay."

"So be it!" Responded Moah in frustration. "I shall meet with Queen Cera, though my task is not yet complete!"

"You're going to be in so much trouble," taunted one of the Acolytes under their breath.

"Remember your place, Brother!" Moah clenched his fingers tightly around the offending acolyte's throat.

"I am the Guardian of Darkness... not a mere remnant like yourself!" Scorned Moah, whilst tightening his hold around his brethren's throat more fiercely. "Know your place!"

"Queen Cera is still waiting..." Interjected a separate Acolyte, but with more caution in his manner than his counterpart. "It would be wise, not to leave her Majesty for much longer...her patience has already grown thin of late." Moah glumly made his way back into his Sanctum, a succumbing sensation overpowered the Guardian as he entered, with his thoughts still held on Sophilia's present well-being. The world around Moah now seemed to blur, he quickly noticed that Queen Cera had once again placed herself upon Kufiah's throne in her predictable aura of pure malice.

"Moah!" Roared Cera in contempt. "Explain to me, why you have removed the child from her present holding chamber... be swift in your response!" She bared her razor-like teeth to Moah hatefully and a thin line of foam began to draw away from the Queen's mouth, as evidence of her seething rage. "Answer me!"

"I was taking her to the Vault of Loss," Moah spoke without thinking, his judgement clouded be a sea of fearing nerves. "That is where I was planning to leave the child... as punishment for her sins against you." The Guardian shuddered, as he noticed Cera's Elite Guards were now placing their hands readily upon the weapons sheathed to their sides.

"Why the Vault of Loss?" Questioned Cera in beleaguerment. "I commanded that her life be extinguished!" The Queen tapped her fingers vigorously upon the arms of Kufiah's throne, barely containing her wild aggression. Moah bowed in an apparent subservience to Cera.

"Your Majesty... does not such a dismal prison for the child bring you peace of mind?" Implored Moah. The Elite Guards suddenly raised their weapons higher as Cera stood herself.

"You appear… nervous, Moah?" Cera keenly observed the apparent discomfort being displayed by the Guardian in his tremoring body language, she then slowly approached him with her arms folded tightly behind her back. "The Vault of Loss robs those within it of their memories, does it not?" Cera's question was obviously rhetorical, though Moah replied to her honestly as he would have always done.

"Yes," said Moah frankly. "It is the perfect place within this Sanctuary, to harbour such a great threat as Sophilia."

"I beg to differ!" Cera's voice rose menacingly. "How could it affect a child, whose life is too short to lose such treasured memories, and thus render them harmless?" A sickening tension quickly lifted between Moah and his Queen. "She is ten years old, a little *too* young for the Vault of Loss to have a desired impact… don't you think?"

"You are correct as always, Your Majesty." Spoke Moah in response bitterly. "I should not have disobeyed such a strict order." The Guardian of Darkness bowed his head lowly in submission, though at this point he had lost all allegiance towards Cera.

"I think a far more appropriate sentence is required, if you are not willing to kill the child!" Cera started to slowly cackle, her eyes beamed as a disturbing thought suddenly entered. "She has not suffered enough, with the memories that this world may yet offer…" The Queen's abhorrent laughter rose as she noticed her Dark Acolytes enter the Sanctum. "Yes, we shall grant her such *terrible* memories! I will rob Sophilia's childhood in the very same way her Mother's was!"

"How?" Moah swallowed heavily as he motioned this question. "Surely, you don't…"
Cera viciously lifted her palms against Moah to silence him, then turned towards the Dark Acolytes in haste with a perverse smile.

"Take my sister's offspring to our deepest vault… the one where Father resides." Grimaced Cera perversely. "Kanaan will teach Sophilia things that she will *never* forget!" A noticeable tear now seeped itself away from Moah, though it surprisingly remained unseen by Cera who herself remained entranced within her blinding hatred. "Go with your acolytes… take the child to Kanaan and prove your loyalty!" Commanded the Queen sternly. "I have little time to waste, my forces are already moving!" The Dark Acolytes waited for their Guardian's direction and, after regaining his composure, Moah reluctantly led the way to where he had sheltered Sophilia. Moah stood outside the small chamber hesitantly, despairing and sickened beyond any measure by what he was now being forced to do. The Guardian dutifully called out for Sophilia, demanding that she return to him, though he honestly desired the opposite.

"Lia, come to my voice…" Whispered Moah through a small window in the chamber's door. "I am here, I came back for you… just as promised!" Sophilia nervously emerged from the darkness. "Why are *they* with you?" The child was instantly disturbed by the noticeable presence of Moah's other acolytes, who remained stood silently behind their Guardian. "Why did leave me in such a horrible place for so long?" Moah clenched his eyes tightly, to hide the tears building up within them, and then he held out a hand of trust again to Sophilia - with each moment passing now proving harder to cope with.

"Forgive me, Lia. I was wrong in doing that to you." Moah forged a fake smile of hope to the child. "We are going to take you to a place that's even safer than the Sanctum." Sophilia remained sorrowful in her expression towards her supposed protector. "Come with me and my friends here…you are going to meet another member from your family!"

"Really?" Rejoiced Sophilia innocently. An instant calm took over her current sadness on hearing this as she ran over to Moah, embracing him again to the obvious disgust of his more-reserved followers. "Will I meet Aunt Cera, or is it someone else?"

"You will see…" Said Moah solemnly. "It is quite far, to where your relative resides, so if you become tired just let me know and I shall carry you." Sophilia nodded silently in agreement to Moah; there was still a trust held in her with him, but the same could not be said for the Guardian's malicious Acolytes. A haunting presence seemed to linger over Moah, as he guided Sophilia and his acolytes further into the foundations of their Sanctuary. They had to first pass through a maze of hideous catacombs, the narrow passageways each littered with grotesque statues of demons and sinful-mortals – decorations that Cera herself adored heartily.

"We're almost there." Stammered Moah, a nauseous sensation was swiftly growing in him now. "Are you alright, Lia?"

"I think so?" Sophilia too felt sickened by the foreboding surroundings, with each step taken, they only seemed to worsen. "I'm scared… but happy too." The child's face squirmed awkwardly from her conflicting emotions. "I've always wanted to meet my Mummy's family…"

"Don't be scared… I will look after you." Moah scuffed at Sophilia's hair playfully, to an instant look of perplexment from his acolytes. "This journey will be over soon." All signs of permeating light began to fade and the cold air around Moah's travelling party painfully swept through their lungs - on reaching Kanaan's prison chamber. It was situated at the Sanctuary's lowest level; a spherical vault that hung perilously above a vast, open chasm that itself seemed to have an endless descent. No sound nor sight could reach Kanaan's chamber from outside and only a narrow, obsidian bridge connected it to the main supporting structure. "This is it." Moah's heart paced with dread; in knowing what true horror would await the poor child, inside of Kanaan's imposing abode. "Sophilia…I…" An intensely-strong desire to flee now with her grew even more desperate inside of Moah, though he knew that his acolytes would only hinder any attempt to escape.

"I don't like this place, Moah!" Whimpered Sophilia. "I'm scared of the dark… I want to leave… right now!" She firmly leant herself into the Guardian's side, hoping to convince him otherwise from his decision to bring her to this horrifying place. Moah tenderly wrapped an arm around Sophilia, in sympathy towards her obvious concern, and then turned to face his next-senior acolyte with a pure look of scorn.

"Have you lost sight of your duty to our Queen and Master?" Seethed the Acolyte in response, as they removed their deformed mask to look upon Moah more clearly. "What is this vile display which you are forcing us, your own kin, to witness?" The other Acolytes shook their heads equally in disapproval towards their Guardian.

"Remember your place, Brother." Whispered Moah to his subordinate angrily. "Remember who it is, that you truly serve!"

"The child *cannot* remain a threat to our Queen for any longer!" Responded the dismaying Acolyte in a similar tone of fury. "Be done with this, bury her alongside the senile fool and prove your loyalty… to both ourselves and Kufiah!" Moah gently released Sophilia away from their reassuring embrace to stand closer before his mutinous followers. The Guardian defiantly met against Cera's Dark Acolytes with a mocking laughter, as he prepared to lecture them of their wrong-doings.

"Loyalty?" Spoke Moah in an empowered voice. "You speak of loyalty… as if you know where your own rightfully sits!" The Guardian's malice towards his brethren rose swiftly with each passing word. "You are traitors!" Cera's Acolytes moved awkwardly into a defensive stance, Moah's apparent treachery was a shock to each of them, they could not willingly permit for any existing threat to their Queen – not even him.

"Our Guardian has forsaken us!" Cried out the Senior-Acolyte in a fake display of despair. "Take no heed from him now, listen only to me!"

"Those who serve the Eternal Darkness should only bow before Kufiah…." Implored Moah more calmly, praying that his rationale would seep into his kin. "They are not slaves for some power-mad Queen to enact her delusional beliefs! We have lost our sacred purpose over time to Cera's will. The Acolytes of Darkness are meant to serve both Kufiah and Cerebrante's Sacred Balance…" Moah tremored nervously against his acolytes' vacant expressions. "How can you all not see this?"

"Enough of this blasphemy!" Cried out the Senior Acolyte, they then suddenly unsheathed a small, obsidian dagger from within their robes against Moah. "I will silence that venomous tongue of yours, Moah… without hesitation! You are not worthy to be our Guardian. We *true* Acolytes of Darkness shall ensure our Queen's reign continues over Impartia…just as *you* should have done!" Moah peacefully closed his eyes, ignoring the Senior Acolyte's blade that had now started to puncture at his flesh, to enter a spiritual trance – deepening his connection with Kufiah unfathomably. On opening them, to the utter disbelief of his forsaken brethren, Moah now revealed that the whites of his eyes had sunk into a darkened abyss as he fully bonded to Impartia's most-evil presence.

"You are not worthy!" Repeated the Senior Acolyte in beleaguerment to himself. "How is this possible?" A sudden wave of thick smoke left from Moah's torso, which then violently forced itself against his Acolytes. They all fell helplessly upon the bridge, under Moah's sheer display of dominance, some of whom had lost their grip upon it to plunge reluctantly into the infinite chasm below. "Murderer!" Roared the Senior Acolyte as he reached again for his dagger. "You will pay for this outrage!" Moah's new enemy swung his dagger aggressively through the choking smoke with a vicious intent, wishing to end his former Guardian's life without mercy. The plume of smoke gradually diminished and Moah in turn threw himself against his so-called ally, almost sending them both perilously through the air towards their premature deaths.

"Stop it… Stop it, all of you!" Screamed Sophilia as she backed against the sealed door behind, attempting to draw herself away from this most-disturbing scene. "Moah, I don't want you to die as well!"

"Don't move, Lia… hold your position!" Commanded Moah frantically. "I'll be alright, just stay away from me and the others!" The Guardian could scarcely contain Kufiah's transient presence within him; it was fuelling Moah's rage and strength, though also clouded his judgement and dwindling restraint.

"You would freely cast aside your divine privilege as Kufiah's Guardian of Darkness, for the sake of protecting an exiled runt? Despaired the Senior Acolyte. He callously drew his cursed dagger across Moah's face, only to find that the Guardian could suddenly heal this wound by using Kufiah's coursing power within him.

"Yes!" Moah's responding attack was swift and ferocious against the assailant. Kufiah's Guardian clenched at his enemy's throat, compressing it agonisingly as his passion to save Sophilia from her Aunt's malice rose. "Kanaan's *Guardian of Darkness*… should never have existed!" Moah suddenly kicked the Senior Acolyte away with ease, casting the wicked creature's body painfully upon the bridge once more. The other Dark Acolytes, who had now recovered from Moah's initial strike, looked upon him in awe and confusion; his words had created much doubt in their minds, though this too soon passed. "There *will* be balance again within Impartia!" Cried out Moah in a demonic voice. "Queen Cera shall not succeed in fulfilling her misguided destiny… Cerebrante will rise once more against her!" The Guardian of Darkness vigorously held out a stretched hand towards his Acolytes, willing from it a flowing stream of malignant fumes to form into mighty, black scourge; at its length were several threaded-tails that had obsidian shards upon each of them, that he swung hatefully towards his fearful followers.

"You will reap what you sow, Heathen!" Countered the Senior Acolyte in defiance. "Your betrayal to our Sanctuary and Queen… will haunt you for an eternity!" Moah cracked his scourge menacingly in the air above him to echo its piercing sounds.

"You will not harm the child, Cerebrante has chosen her and it shall be yourselves who will need to repent in Kufiah's Void!" The Guardian then latched his scourge around his nemesis' torso, tearing through the Senior Acolyte's robes and shredding the flesh bore beneath them ruthlessly. "This pain is momentary, your damnation however... has been sealed!" Seethed Moah's counterpart in torment, the remaining Dark Acolytes fled at this harrowing sight – in fear of suffering a similar fate.

"Traitor!" The Senior Acolyte knelt pitifully before Moah now. The indescribable pain which the multiple shards had reeked over his body had become overwhelming at this point. Moah twisted his scourge slowly and then, with a sudden action, lifted the tortured Acolyte's body high into the air. The Guardian finally moved to discard his enemy in an act of mercy, far into the vast chasm below them - all that was left now was for Moah to free Sophilia from her present incarceration.

"It's okay, Lia...I won't hurt you." Moah's voice seemed somehow weaker to the child, his spiritual exertion evidently had exhausted him as he crawled back towards her. "I said, that I would protect and reunite you with Cara... this promise shall not be broken!"

"Moah..." Sophilia struggled to speak through her increasing anxiety. "I want my Mummy, I want you to take me to her." Frantic echoes of voices and footsteps could now be heard coming from the Sanctuary's catacombs behind. Moah forced himself, against his pressing fatigue, to stand and reach out once again for Sophilia's company.

"Hurry, Lia!" Screamed Moah wearily to her. "I cannot take you to the Sanctum for it is too risky now. There is, however, a hidden cavern with many ships there... we can leave this evil place once and for all!" The Guardian clenched onto Sophilia's hands desperately. "I will guide our way, though sadly I may not be able to leave here with you. Run ahead of me, Lia and don't look back... just listen for my instructions!" Sophilia found trust again in Moah from his selfless actions and without hesitation obeyed the Guardian's command fully. She sprinted towards the dimly-lit entranceway as fast as her small legs could, with thoughts of seeing Cara again being the only driving force - in spite of Kufiah's imposing surroundings.

"Run Sophilia!" Ordered Moah in desperation. "I will not be far behind you!" In truth, the Guardian struggled through his exhaustion to keep up with Sophilia's youthful agility. Moah limped into the dark catacombs, though strong in his determination to save Sophilia - even if it would cost him his own life. "Turn right!" Instructed the Guardian passionately. "Follow the passageway by running your hands along its walls!" Within the catacomb's maze-like structure, Moah sporadically directed Sophilia to which way they next needed to head, firm in the belief that their salvation was within reach. "Left... then turn right at the next clearing!"

"I can't see, Moah!" Despaired Sophilia with a harrowing cry. "It's too dark!" The marching footsteps appeared to be growing in their number and were close to where Sophilia now ran. Moah prayed to himself that the soldiers had not yet had enough foresight to barricade Kufiah's hidden cavern; it had saved him once before, yet there still lingered a possibility that Cera could have destroyed his only means of exit.

"Right again, Lia… you're doing so well! Don't give up!" Stressed Moah as a sickening sensation suddenly took hold over his body. As if in restraint of the Guardian, this phantom force fed itself deeper into Moah's soul and conscious thought. "…Master?"

'Guardian of Darkness…do you wish to betray Queen Cera?'

Kufiah's dreadful voice quickly invaded Moah's inner thoughts and ability to control his own body, the Spirit of Darkness then proceeded to use their unique spiritual connection as a way in overcoming his weakened Guardian's state - uniting both against Moah's firm reluctance.

'Only in the void… can we remain'

"Get out of my head!" Cried out Moah in anguish. "Keep going, Lia… just keep going!" The Guardian further despaired as Kufiah now took on an even greater possession over him, his voice was no longer his own, and the following commands came instead from a far darker power.

"Left…Left, my child!"

Moah shook his head as he cleared from his eyes the painful tears that flowed in them. The Dark Guardian attempted to take back possession over his own voice, to correct Sophilia's misdirection, but could not as Kufiah's ancient strength rose in its full intensity over him.

"Where are you leading her, Master Spirit?" Moah pleaded in his questioning to Kufiah, a mutual respect strangely survived between both. "I only serve you…"

'The answer you seek, my Guardian… lies within thy Sanctum."

Moah collapsed into unconsciousness, as Kufiah finally released his possession away from the sorrowful Guardian. As he slowly awoke, still dazed and weakened by the Dark Spirit's hold, Moah scanned in confusion around a familiar-looking Sanctum chamber - where he somehow now found himself situated. Still fleeting in and out of his waking consciousness, Moah slowly began to regain enough strength so that he could scour over the remaining Dark Acolytes, who were each stood around him in a unified judgement and firmer hatred.

"Brothers," Moah's voice crackled as he spoke, still drained from his recent ordeal. "Find it in yourselves to see sense... the child, she is no threat to Queen Cera at all."

"Tell her that yourself, Moah!" Responded a Dark Acolyte sharply, they gradually shifted their eyes from the Guardian of Darkness to look just behind him. "Go on... tell her!" Moah reluctantly turned to face the Sanctum's inner seals; to his immediate shock, he discovered that Cera was indeed there. The Queen approached from a shadowy mass that lingered behind her, still clasping at Kanaan's prized amulet as she stared back to Moah with an increased disdain and malicious intent.

"How could you?" Said Cera to Moah, almost tearfully. "After all we've been through and accomplished together..." The Queen's Elite Guards abruptly entered Kufiah's Sanctum at this moment and at their centre was a small, cowering child - her head hung low in despair and wrists bound by hardened obsidian shackles. Sophilia fleeted her glance upwards against Moah, she however instantly removed them to wallow again in self pity and grief.

"Please forgive me, Lia..." Moah stammered as he fought through his flowing tears. "I tried...I tried so hard to unite you with your mother... I'm so sorry."

"Do not address the prisoner!" Commanded one of Cera's Guards sternly, as they struck a hand across the Guardian's face. "Speak only, if Her Majesty bids you to!" He then forcibly dragged Sophilia past the encircling Dark Acolytes and Moah towards Queen Cera - who herself shifted into an awkward stance as she looked upon her sister's child for the first time.

"So, *you* are my greatest nemesis?" Roared the Queen, she then instinctively looked to Cerebrante's mark upon Sophilia. "That symbol on your right hand proves it, little girl!" Cera nervously burst into laughter as she clasped her cold hands upon the child's own. "People say that I'm foolish, to believe in destiny and fate, but I *will* prove them all wrong."

Sophilia carefully inspected every inch of the Queen's body: her similar blond hair, her entrancing amber eyes and, most-notably, the mark of Cerebrante upon Cera's emaciated chest.

"You look like Mummy!" Exclaimed Sophilia innocently, the entire Sanctum fell fearfully silent. "You're my Aunt Cera... I've waited such a long time to meet you!" Cera recoiled from Sophilia in disgust; being reminded of their relationship instantly sent an overwhelming repulsion through the twisted Queen's body. In defence of her regal position, Cera placed herself intimidatingly over Sophilia to cruelly shake her head in dismissal before the naïve child.

"You will soon discover, that no similar joy lies within me on seeing you... child!" Seethed the Queen with a heartless glance. "Only a just-retribution awaits you now... for what your wrongful existence has put me through." Cera stroked at her father's amulet, whilst staring upon its golden metal with a demented smile. "I don't know what lies your mother has told you about me, it doesn't matter anyway... for your life is about to become much shorter!"

"Don't listen to her, Lia!" Cried out Moah in want of ending the child's emotional torture. "Cera will never know, or deserve, your love…pity, but do not fear her!"

"Silence your tongue, Moah." Spoke Cera in a gravelled voice. "You have done enough damage already…"

"Mummy did tell me stories about you." Spoke Sophilia quietly to the Queen. "She said that you were such a beautiful baby and she'll *always* love you." She moved closer against Cera, despite the tension building between them. "We're family… we should be together!"

Cera immediately silenced Sophilia with a sudden, hate-filled cry; in all the years she had spent plotting to reign over Impartia, she had not planned so meticulously for this painful meeting. The Queen shook from her rising malice as she looked back to her Dark Acolytes and Guards, she swiftly gestured for them to remove Sophilia - but not before granting one last sadistic message.

"You desire to know your family better do you, Cretin?" Cera placed her forehead against Sophilia's aggressively, hoping to cause some level of discomfort in the child. "Acolytes… Guards… take this wretch back to the lowest chamber in our Sanctuary at once, my father could do with such youthful company to occupy his needs!" The Queen cackled wickedly as she revelled in watching Sophilia being led away, a harrowing cry of anguish echoed throughout the Sanctum there-after from Moah.

"How could you do such a thing, Cera?" Said Moah pleadingly as he writhed his weakened body towards the Queen. "You are more-than aware of what your father did to Cara, when she was younger, is that *truly* what you wish upon Sophilia – your own niece?"

"Why the change of heart, Guardian?" Countered Cera in a condescending tone. "You are so pathetic now, where has Kufiah's ultimate warrior vanished to?" She perversely began to caress the cursed amulet again and its emanant evil soon radiated deep within the Queen's broken soul. Cera knelt herself gradually before Moah and then clasped onto his bloodied face with her hands, piercing the Guardian's skin purposefully with her long, neglected nails. "The child is no longer your concern… nor is Cara…nor is your duty towards this Sanctuary. It is only fitting, that your Master Spirit should be the power to deal with you now!"

"No!" Screamed Moah in terror. "I beg you, Cera!" Within the central seal of Kufiah's Sanctum, now came forth a billowing smoke that rose menacingly against Moah. The towering figure of Kufiah's physical body emerged from upon his activated seal, haunting the Sanctum chamber instantly with an ethereal and evil presence. "Master…" Moah looked to the Dark Spirit in defiance, whilst ignoring Cera's further words of hatred to him. "Great Spirit, I am your humble servant!"

"You are hereby relieved of your Guardianship, Moah!" Declared Cera with an apparent hint of hesitation. "As I speak, my entire naval force is moving against the sacred mountain of Skynah and its hidden Sanctuary. Soon, the Spirit of Light's power within this world shall die... along with Cerebrante, the Elemental Guardians, my sister *and* her child! Impartia *will* be reborn and hail its rightful Empress - me!" Moah reacted to this abhorrent declaration by spitting across Cera's face, understandably surprising the Queen, she angrily recoiled and struck him with a sweeping slash of her fingers - causing further scars to form upon the beaten Guardian. "Infidel..." Said Cera to Moah in disappointment. "Now, you will feel the true wrath of Kufiah's vengeance!" The Queen struck Moah hard across his face again, forcing him to reel in agony from the unnecessary attack. "It did not have to end like this!" After marvelling in the torment of which she had created, Queen Cera motioned herself to exit Kufiah's Sanctum but was suddenly halted in her stride by a group of Elite Guards.

"Your Majesty," stuttered one of the Guards, their comrades were equally as apprehensive. "The airship is suffering with some... malfunctions, we will need to use your Royal Flagship - if you are to reach Skynah in the time specified."

"Malfunctions?" Seethed the Queen. "No matter, it's not like I'm in a rush or anything!" She slammed a fist against the Sanctum door in dismay, echoing her anger throughout.

"Your ship is ready and fuelled to its full capacity, Majesty." Continued the Guard in a frank manner. "We shall catch up to the main fleet and reach Skynah within a matter of hours..."

"Kufiah!" Cera turned again to face the monstrous Spirit and Moah. "Make it quick..." The Sanctum's heavy doors slowly sealed themselves after Cera's departure, leaving Moah alone with Kufiah, the Guardian looked to his Master Spirit now though with an expression of adoration – not dread. Moah bowed himself willingly before the Spirit of Darkness, Kufiah in return granted a disturbing smile and gestured for his Guardian to finally be at ease.

"It is done..." Moah's voice returned to him powerfully. "Cera's journey to Skynah is going ahead, just as we anticipated, our plan to right the Sacred Balance will work – it has to!" Kufiah bowed his head in agreement to Moah on hearing these reassuring words come from him.

"Darkness can only endure within the Light..." Kufiah's demonic voice echoed hauntingly throughout the Sanctum chamber. "Long have I waited for this moment." The Dark Spirit then raised a single arm towards his loyal Guardian, releasing Moah's tightened restraints and empowering his spirit even more.

"Thank you, Master..." Said Moah, as he waved his arms freely, despite the deep wounds which had been by inflicted upon them by Cera's chains. Kufiah lingered his corpse-like hands over the Guardian's physical wounds, healing them without any apparent exertion as his mighty spiritual powers denied any further damage or suffering. "Soon, you will be free of Kanaan's curse... the Celestial Spirits shall govern Impartia once more." Kufiah silently seated himself upon his throne and then invited for Moah to stand before him.

"Rejoice, my loyal servant. Queen Cera is blinded by her own lust for power to see our true purpose here." Kufiah evidently strained to breath, Cera's control continued to hinder the Spirit's full strength. "Are you certain that Kanaan's amulet can be destroyed, thus releasing me of the hold that his daughter has over my will?" Moah initially hesitated in his response to the intimidating Spirit; his theory was merely based on ancient texts that he had found hidden deep within the Sanctuary Vaults, the aim of liberating Alaskia and Kufiah could also come at such a terrible price to Impartia - if their plan were to go wrong.

"It is our only hope," stuttered Moah apprehensively. "The girl I travelled with - Cara, also bears the mark of Cerebrante like her sister and father. If Cara so gains the power needed from Alaskia, then she should be able to free you from Cera's possession... otherwise, I fear you may need to intervene yourself to secure this much-needed outcome."

"Princess Cara Til-Magmorros... is but a mortal," Replied Kufiah reservedly. "The quest which she and her companions have undertaken, may cost them their own lives." The Spirit of Darkness rose himself to tower again over Moah. "Impartia is falling into chaos, should this plan of yours fail... a greater threat will return that even Cera cannot stop!"

"That doom will not come to pass, Master." Said Moah firmly in resolve. "We must aid Cara and her companions somehow, Kanaan is not as foolish as Cera would declare... a power the King placed within Skynah still remains that could halt our plan's success."

"Defeat her...do not forsake me!" Kufiah motioned towards the centre of his Sanctum platform, where he ignited a seal of which Moah had not yet seen used before. The Guardian stepped into the blinding-white light and then looked back obediently to his Master, soon all around them seemed to vanish into a surreal version of reality. "You have served me well!"

Deep within the Sanctuary's foundations, Sophilia kicked and punched against her captors desperately as they dragged the child back towards Kanaan's chamber. Kufiah's Dark Acolytes hastily released their seal of protection from the solitary vault, as its doors opened a sickening fog rose from within that filled Sophilia with an even stronger sense of dread.

"This is your home now…get in!" Ordered one of the Acolytes, as he cruelly ripped Sophilia's grip away from him to throw her inside. "You will never see the light of day again!" Sophilia whimpered at the callous treatment she had endured and placed her hands over her ears, as the huge doors sealed loudly behind to shroud Kanaan's vault in a thick layer of darkness. The chamber she now found herself in was only lit by a dim, solitary candle that hung within the vault's centre; it swayed ever-so slightly and the thin, surrounding air was nowhere near strong enough to extinguish the candle's puny flame.

"*You are the light in my darkness…*" Sophilia quietly sang to herself, hoping to ease the anguish she now felt in this new and discomforting environment. "Mummy…" No other sounds seemed to exist in this evil place, only the pacing breaths that echoed in Sophilia's head resonated.

"Silence… silence I say!" Commanded a presence hidden within the vault's shadows. "What form of torture do I have to contend with now?" The phantom voice seemed so aged and frail to Sophilia, though still incredibly intimidating. Its source came from a man concealed within a darkened corner of the vault: he wore ancient black robes that covered his skeletal body, his face covered by long strands of knotted greyed hair, his breathing laboured as an obvious side-effect from the vault's thin air and his eyes blared with an amber radiance.

"I'm sorry if I scared you…" Sophilia gasped whilst searching for where the unexpected voice came from. A foreign, rustling sound reverberated around the frightened child, she seated herself defensively within the vault's centre, in its only source of light, against this uncertain threat. Rising from his shadowy enclave, the haggard-looking man slowly made an approach towards Sophilia as he whined in agony with each step taken.

"What do we have here?" Questioned the stranger eagerly. "Not often do I have the luxury of receiving visitors; save my daughter, who only comes here to gloat of her sordid schemes and to ridicule me of this imprisonment - which *she* has so wrongfully enforced! Come into the light, my child… so that I may see you more clearly with these failing eyes of mine."

"My name is…" Sophilia barely uttered a word before being silenced again by the imposing stranger. He beckoned for her to move in closer towards the candle that hung between them, his eyes obviously struggled to adapt against the light – having shunned it away for so long.

"I have no interest in your name!" Snapped the man aggressively. "I only wish to see your innocent beauty… your perfect little features… something which I have been robbed of for many *tedious* years in this pit!" Sophilia carefully shuffled herself closer, though only by a few steps, as she restrained herself against who the creepy figure could really be and why he too was imprisoned. She sat herself awkwardly beneath the candle and attempted to make out any possible features of the stranger, who himself still dwelled within the darkness that shrouded them. "Do not fear me," implored the man disparagingly. "I am well beyond holding that sort of control over you now; my ageing body has become but an empty shell and my soul is broken." Sophilia greatly wanted to feel pity for the pathetic figure, but there was something dark about him that continued to grow a reluctance in her. "If you so wish to engage in pleasantries with me, to ease your mind perhaps, I will happily oblige." The stranger leant forwards to draw himself nearer to Sophilia.

"Sure…." Uttered Sophilia in uncertainty. Her eyes stared firmly into the darkness ahead, but she could still not make out any features of the mysterious man. "Who… are you?"

"My name is Kanaan. I am, or once was, the rightful King of Impartia's mightiest nation - before my throne was forcefully taken from me." Kanaan's voice faltered as he spoke. The fallen king was proud of his regal position and having lost it, brought him an immense feeling of pain still. "Now it's your turn, little girl. Who are you and where are you from… might I ask?" Kanaan focused his blurred vision upon the faint image of Sophilia, slowly he found a familiarity in her that wrought a swift excitement in him.

"My name is Sophilia," stammered the child. "I come from a big forest, which is very far away from here… and I live with just my Mummy." A wonderous expression of hope rose in her suddenly. "Mummy will be coming back for me soon… I won't be here with you for long." Kanaan cruelly laughed in response; displaying to Sophilia an innate, though small, glint of cruelty in his tone which had not yet diminished in him - despite serving a decade in solitary confinement at Cera's pleasure.

"I presume, you are talking about the lands of Viridia… such a vast and remote place for a small child like yourself to live in safely - is it not?" He sighed mockingly. "A mighty power from Magmorrah destroyed Viridia's civilisation…which obviously means, you and your mother are scavengers?" Kanaan's wavering eyes now started to focus on Sophilia more clearly, his interest in the child also rose in equal measure. "What would drive a Mother to raise her vulnerable daughter, in a realm that has no present civilisation or luxuries... something or someone *terrible* must have driven her there?" Sophilia laughed slightly as she shook her head in disagreement to Kanaan. It pleased her immeasurably to think again of her and Cara's 'homeland', doing so brought a much-needed comfort to meet against this evil dwelling which she was now housed within.

"Viridia's not *that* big and empty!" Countered Sophilia with a defiant shrug of her shoulders. "Mummy and I have walked through every forest... they're beautiful and not scary at all." Kanaan fought against himself to hide his risen curiosity.

"Have you both travelled to the Sanctuary in North Viridia, I hear, it is such a magnificent spectacle?" Kanaan's fingers twitched in anticipation towards the increasingly anxious child. "A powerful Guardian Spirit protects the ancient Sanctuary Tree, he was a friend of my royal bloodline once... believe it or not." Sophilia twisted her face in discomfort, while pondering why the man was asking these peculiar questions.

"Yes, I have been there... I only saw the Guardian for a few seconds though." The horrific killings of Ven's Acolytes suddenly entered Sophilia's thoughts once more. She turned away from Kanaan briefly to compose herself, then as Sophilia looked back a truly grotesque sight met with her. "You have gold eyes... like me." Kanaan's face contorted, and a sadistic grin soon stretched upon it against Sophilia. The King had gradually pieced together a very intricate puzzle, from what had just been revealed, and its connotations were truly unfathomable to him.

"Yes, these blessed eyes are the symbol of Magmorrah's Royalty... her *true* patriarch!" Declared Kanaan in a swift burst of rage, however he soon calmed himself to learn more of Sophilia's existence. "Why were you and your mother taken away from Viridia? Seldom are Magmorrah's Elite Guards used for such a purpose!" Kanaan frail expression noticeably changed to one of desperation as he persisted in staring towards Sophilia for an answer. "Tell me, child!"

"An evil woman called Nira took me..." Sophilia swallowed heavily. "She said, me and my Mummy were the biggest threat to their Queen...we were taken for no reason!" She met against Kanaan's angered glare equally in measure with her own. "We've done nothing wrong!" Kanaan cackled pathetically with his fragile voice, then placed his hands upon his straggling hair - as if to serve in a later purpose. "Did Mirtziah's daughter not explain why you are a threat?" The King laughed wickedly again, he could scarcely contain his amusement. "Cera is scared of a small child!" He cackled in utter delight. Sophilia bravely stood herself before the tyrannical King, in defiance of his cruelty towards her. She lunged into the darkness to clasp her hands around Kanaan's, proceeding to drag him back within the candlelight's reach in want of divulging further into his desired explanation.

"This is why!" Sophilia showed Kanaan clearly the mark of Cerebrante borne upon her right hand, the King in turn fell instantly silent. "Aunt Cera said that both Mummy and I have this special symbol... she said that it makes us traitors... I *hate* her!" Kanaan could innately sense the spiritual connection from Cerebrante's mark on Sophilia. His own began to burn in an apparent response, which he keenly displayed by parting the strands of thin hair covering it.

"You *are* Cara's child!" Kanaan rubbed at his weary eyes in astonishment. "I am complete!" He desperately reached out a tremoring hand to Sophilia, hoping for her to do the same. "Your mark is as strong as my own… there is no doubt in that. My time upon this plain is coming to an end and I accept this now… willingly. Come to me, my child… for I have a mighty gift to bestow upon you!" A perverse smile emerged upon Kanaan, as Sophilia freely accepted his kindly invitation by drawing herself closer towards him for a fateful embrace.

"I relinquish my sacred bond… I relinquish you… Cerebrante!"

Chapter Ten: Above Clouds and Beneath the Stars

Floating in mid-air, as if locked within an enchanted dream, Cara now felt her weightless body rise into a wave of golden clouds. She considered for a daunting moment if, somehow, the ordeal with Kufiah at Levia's Sanctuary had killed her and that this strange reality was in fact Impartia's after-life… Eternamorrah. Firin, in great contrast to Cara, felt immensely uneased by his own helpless ascent into the darkness of Impartia's stratosphere. The warming sunrays which surrounded Firin's body brought him no real comfort either, he instead continued in a vain attempt to escape from this disturbing nightmare by flouncing his limbs frantically. Spero held out his arms in a willing acceptance of the beauty and freedom that this unearthly experience wrought him. He calmly closed his eyes and thought of all the friends and loved ones that he had lost, through the pointless battles which they had fought in together, feeling that this too was his own final pathway to enlightenment and that his transcendence was gracefully closing in on him.

"Welcome…worthy mortals."

The three companions finally met in their ascendance and together they observed Impartia's magnificent scene growing beneath them, each in an initial awe-struck silence. Cara turned to face Firin and Spero, feeling a tranquillity come to her from their presences, relieved that she was not alone in this mysterious venture.

"It's beautiful, can you believe *that* is our world?" Said Cara as she allowed for her arms to fall freely above her. "There's Viridia… and Hydrania… the nations look so small!"

Spero turned towards Cara and then reached out for one of her hands, himself feeling torn between the reality and fantasy that they were now sharing in, he too admittedly savoured in the peace created by this divine moment.

"What's happening to us, Cara?" Remarked Firin, as he continued to fight against the restraining force that drew him up higher. "This can't be the Sanctuary of Air!"

"Firin's right, Cara." Responded Spero fearfully. "Where is the Sanctum portal that we should have been sent to… where is the Guardian of Air?" Cara laughed back unexpectedly to her terrified friends, she herself felt no immediate threat from the power of which now had this controlling hold over them. Instead, Cara waved her arms as if flying and smiled in excitement towards Firin and Spero.

"Do you not think this is amazing, Firin?" Screamed Cara in delight. "We are like birds… free to do anything and free to go anywhere!"

"That's easy for you to say, Cara!" Countered Firin with a beleaguered expression. "We don't even know where we are being taken… do *you* know what's making us float like this?" He closed his eyes tensely, wishing beyond any measure for this unnatural journey to end.

"You worry *way* too much… just enjoy the ride!" Responded Cara with a casual flick of her hands, she then looked across to Spero, who himself smiled back to her nervously in response. "See, Firin… Spero's having a good time!" The golden clouds gradually dispersed away; releasing their warm haze from around Cara and her fellow companions as a beaming light from above directly immersed them instead, drawing each towards an empowered and welcoming spiritual force.

"Is *this* the Sanctuary of Air, do you think?" Questioned Cara as she basked contently in the serene light. "I've never felt so… relaxed."

"Maybe, if it isn't though… who cares?" Laughed Spero as he too started to unwind. "I'd quite happily stay up in these clouds, at least Queen Cera can't get to us here!"

"How did I end up being stuck with you two!" Humoured Firin, hoping to ease his own tensions. "Mortals aren't meant to fly!" The intense light fiercely increased with a sudden burst of energy; its blinding flare that followed forced Cara and her friends to protectively shield their eyes - though it bore no apparent pain to them. A tall, feminine figure gracefully emerged from the transient light: She had silver hair that shone radiantly in the light of Impartia's sun, which also fell to land upon her exposed ankles and bare feet. Her robes were almost transparent, to Firin's indiscreet awareness, flowing freely behind the figure's body as if they were waves upon a tranquil ocean. Her eye's emanated with an ancient, silver light that instantly caught the attention of Cara – a clear and desired indicator of whom now spoke to them.

"Beneath the stars and above the clouds, I bid you enter… my worthy guests."

The haunting words echoed then faded softly, as did the light that imbued Cara and her companions now. They quickly found themselves situated within a large, crystal sphere that observed over Impartia's lands below from an unimaginable height. Beneath their feet was the familiar sight of a Sanctum platform, though uniformly decorated with several seals that appeared far older in comparison to the other Elemental Sanctuaries'. Cara, Firin and Spero knelt respectfully before the benevolent figure that stood calmly in greeting them, who herself seemed to rejoice over their sudden arrival.

"It is my honour to welcome you here." Spoke the woman in a soothing voice. "I am Aira, my eternal duty is to serve as Impartia's Guardian of Air... though I believe that you know this already?" Aira barely moved, say for the gentile smile upon her face, the Guardian's entire presence was both entrancing and strangely intimidating at the same time. "Seldom are mortals allowed to visit this Sanctum... however, my kin would not have sent you here without a dire reason – a purpose - which I am fully aware of." Cara bowed again before Aira in enthusiasm; she was hastily followed by Firin, who himself winced nervously on looking down upon the distant land masses below, then an awe-struck Spero.

"Thank you, Aira... for accepting us." Said Cara as she looked over the Guardian's angelic features endearingly. "It was Levia and Ven that brought us here, they did so, because Queen Cera of Magmorrah is planning to kill Alaskia. We need your password to save the Spirit of Light." Aira continued to smile back then waved her hands dismissively against Cara's formal response.

"Please, you need not feel so diminutive in my presence. The Sanctum of Air exists as a beacon of liberty, so you do not need to follow such earthly rituals here... Princess Cara." Laughed the Guardian, to a surprised response from her guests. "Simply call me - Aira, I understand that you have all acquainted yourselves with my kin... so please forgive me as I already know each of your names."

"Excuse me, Aira..." Spero shuffled himself reservedly towards the curious Guardian. "It burdens me to tell you this, but the other Guardians are in grave danger now - as we are." Aira removed her smile, replacing it swiftly with an expression of concern. "The Spirit of Darkness infiltrated Levia's Sanctum... nowhere is safe anymore."

"Do not be so disheartened, son of Hydrania." A glint of hope seemed to appear in Aira's eyes as she spoke. "What is occuring within the lands beneath us, has already been foretold. The Sacred Balance of Cerebrante is yet to reveal itself... we should be joyful, not melancholy." Cara was noticeably disturbed by the Guardian's response, she could not herself feel such optimism. "I believe, as do my kin, that you three are key to Alaskia's salvation and Cerebrante's rebirth. Fate has chosen you to render the corruption that poisons Impartia, not us Elemental Spirits...we have had quite enough time to intervene yet, regrettably, have failed." Cara nestled herself into Spero's side for his comforting warmth then looked to Aira, shaking her head in dismissal of the kindred Spirit's resolve and in conflict with her seemingly misplaced beliefs. Aira in response, tilted her head in sympathy towards the sorrowful mortals and was genuinely impressed by their obvious perseverance.

"I don't know if we can do it, Aira." Sighed Cara woefully. "I don't know if we're strong enough to take on both Cera and Kufiah."

"But you are stronger, Cara… stronger than you could ever know. I saw it for myself when you were fleeing from those dreadful Tracking-Hounds" Aira's entire body suddenly released a silver flame from within it, a sign of her empowered spiritual connection. "Why should you not hold such importance, is it because you're an exile or lack the powers of us Elemental Guardians? You have proven your worth… you will save Impartia, its Sacred Balance *and* Princess Sophilia!" Cara gasped in astonishment against the Guardian's apparent insight, whilst still kneeling in an adamant denial of receiving such praise from her. Aira gestured for guests to rise and invited for Firin and Spero to come in closer, feeling a faint pity towards them as their silence echoed the fears which ultimately resonated throughout Impartia's mortal citizens. "Thank you for helping us in Viridia." Smiled Cara awkwardly. "I want to save my little girl more than anything!" Cried out Cara, she clasped onto Aira's flowing robes in a desperate release of her emotions. "I can't let Cera hurt her!"

"It is time for mortals, such as yourselves, to take back control over this broken world." Aira's voice rose into a mighty bellow. "The age of Spirits will one day come to a necessary end. This you must understand: Alaskia and Kufiah reign eternal in their constant struggle, to seek a balance between one another, and they must continue doing this for a lasting existence of harmony to endure. This gift that I shall now bestow upon you – Cara, is to aid these Celestial Spirits in finding their rightful peace…"

"I, Aira, Guardian of Air grant thee passage into thine Sanctum of Light!"

Aira gently rested an open palm across Cara's mark; feeding a powerful spiritual energy into both her soul and physical being through it, willingly empowering Impartia's last hope with the final password now required to reach Alaskia at their secret prison.

"There are others who will aid you in this fight, Cara." Aira's voice returned to calmer and more natural tone. "I have given Levia the whereabouts of a resistance force, who are hidden at this time upon Weissamorrah's shores. They will help you, as shall we Elemental Guardians, none shall need to face this final battle against Queen Cera alone… please, do not lose faith!" Cara remained shaken by her spiritual connection to Aira, even after the Guardian had released their bond, as so much now rested upon the success of Alaskia's freedom. Firin and Spero each leant into Cara wishing to support her, both amazed by the resistance shown to the immense energy that had coursed through her

"You'll be alright, Cara." Reassured Spero with a forced grin to her, he was not as content with Aira's words of assurance. "We have all the passwords needed; Alaskia can freed now, then after the Spirit stops Cera's plan… you and Sophilia won't need to be scared ever again."

"None of us will." Replied Cara, joyful tears lifted in her eyes as she looked back to Spero. "I just pray, that Cera doesn't come to any harm… she is still my little sister."

"Your quest ends at Skynah…" Declared Aira, as she gestured for Cara and her friends to stand upon the Sanctum's central seal. "At that sacred mountain, you will be faced with demons that surpass even the darkness of Queen Cera's blackened heart. Beware, for it *does* serve as a reluctant prison to Alaskia, though Skynah's sanctity has long been corrupted by those with less-purer intentions. Do not allow for selfish revenge to overcome you…" The Sanctum seal resonated with a peculiar array of varying colours, streaming out around Cara and her friends as Aira continued to speak. "In that forsaken place you may easily fall into the Void, in which you will find neither life nor death can ever again flourish. Have faith in each other and you will survive this task, the Spirit of Balance too *must* be reborn or Impartia… will fall."

"We won't fail." Whispered Cara, as closed her eyes against the permeating light. "Take us to Skynah…" The activated seal burst to instantly teleport Cara and her companions away, leaving Aira to dwell in solitude as she had done for many, lonesome years. The Guardian looked down upon Skynah's encircling clouds with her hands lain solemnly across her heart, praying for Cara to fulfil this unwanted destiny and to end Cera's rule without having to take the Queen's own life.

"If you can hear me, my Brothers and Sisters…" Aira peacefully locked herself into a trance, focusing her thoughts upon the other Elemental Spirits. "The time has come, where we Guardians must join in battle with mortals to protect Impartia and the cosmos. Kufiah's darkness grows with every malignant thought the Queen of Magmorrah creates, this must be stopped at all costs… our duty… must be served."

The peace which they had felt in the Sanctum of Air now seemed so distant to Cara, Firin and Spero. In place of tranquillity, echoed a deafening roar from the ocean waves as they crashed against the vast, steep mountainside of Skynah beneath. The companions now found themselves upon, what seemed to be, a ruined Sanctum platform that was situated against Skynah's face within an ancient balcony, covered by dense foliage and noticeably neglected in appearance. Beyond the platform were several marble pillars that led to a set of temple housings, each similar to what Cara and her companions had seen within Hydrania's capital city though grander in scale. Uncomforted by the exposed high winds that struck against her; Cara quickly huddled herself into Firin and Spero for their warmth, though found they too shook uncontrollably from the bitter air current. Cara then edged her way gradually from her friends to peer over the decaying balcony's edge, she soon recoiled on realising the distance from where they stood to the thrashing waves below and of how remote their current position truly was.

"Look at this place!" Gasped Cara in a cocktail of excitement and fear. "Skynah is even bigger than I thought it would be, from Hydrania the mountain seemed huge but this..." She excitedly pointed out to her friends the circling clouds above, in awe of their magnificence and eerie movements. "Skynah is like something from a dream." Firin blinked his eyes and tried to hide the feeling of nausea, on seeing this formidable spectacle. He carefully lowered himself upon the platform and despaired at how his circumstances led to this unforeseeable situation.

"I think I'm done with the sightseeing now, Cara." Stuttered Firin, whilst forcing a mouthful of vomit back into his stomach. "I get the feeling that we're not by ourselves, should we see if anyone else is here?" He lifted himself clumsily to look upon the temple housings. "Maybe over there, that'd be a good start... wouldn't it?"

"Don't talk stupid," replied Spero with a dismissive nod. "There can't be anyone else here... look at the state of this place!" The small houses were, without doubt, totally ruined and beyond habitation. Spero inspected each one, while trying not to make this obvious to Firin, soon finding to his relief that there was no evidence of any dwellers.

"Suit yourself, Spero... I'm going for a look." Firin hurriedly made his way up a series of worn steps towards the dilapidated buildings, taking in mind to be cautious of the unlevel ground beneath. Spero begrudgingly followed, though unlike Firin, was held in an uncertain restraint before inviting Cara to join them. "The closer we are to the mountainside, the better!" Shouted Firin in a pleading manner. "Come on, we need to find this Alaskia don't we... what are you betting that the Spirit is being kept inside this mountain?" As Cara placed her first step away from the Sanctum platform, she began to hear faint voices speak that had no familiarity or definitive tone. A strong, spiritual connection to the mountain suddenly entered Cara's being; she felt that somehow Skynah was communicating with her, to convey a message or warning - perhaps.

"There's something so *different* about this place," whispered Cara to Spero, as she met with him upon the ancient steps. "It doesn't feel like the other Sanctuaries, a powerful presence is surrounding us..." Spero looked around cautiously, searching for any signs of life or further threats in response to Cara's concerns.

"I can't feel anything strange, Cara." Whispered Spero, he continued to look upon the housings just in case anything moved. "It *is* creepy, but we're definitely alone." He glanced over to Firin nearby with a grimacing expression. "I hate to say it, but Firin is right... we need to press on and find Alaskia... it won't take long for Cera to find us."

"I can't believe how things have turned out," despaired Cara, she then looked back across the ocean's horizon with a mournful stare. "For the last ten years I wanted nothing more than to see my sister again, to rebuild our relationship, now I have to fight against her... destiny will always tear us apart." She leant herself into Spero, his calm exterior was welcome though did little to comfort Cara at this moment.

"Come on you two!" Shouted Firin in dismay. "There's nothing but freezing winds out here and I'm already sick of them, let's see what's inside these temples..." He looked nervously upon the crumbling structures ahead. "We might at least find out why Aira sent us to this ghost town in them?" On closer inspection, the temple houses were greatly varied in their design and age: some appeared mighty and were adorned with accurate statues of unknown figures, others were minute in scale and were barely able to house a single person within them – if that – their purpose was left truly perplexing. Footsteps gradually filtered around the companions and in defence of them they hastily huddled back in to one another again, circling their steps in a frantic search for the cause of these phantom sounds. "I feel worse being here than I did back in Kufiah's Sanctuary!" Bleated Firin yet trying not to come across as terrified. "There, we knew what we were dealing with... I didn't sign up for this!" The torturous playing of footsteps moved in closer and seemed to surround him.

"Show yourselves, we're not afraid of you... we know that you're there!" Commanded Spero as he placed himself in front of Cara protectively. "If anything happens to us... the Elemental Guardians will seek revenge!"

"Guardians are not permitted to seek revenge... for they are pure Spirits."

Skynah's pummelling air, that hit against Cara and her friends, began to die down and the phantom footsteps slowly came to a halt. The distant voice, which had just spoken in response to Spero, had seemingly vanished to leave only a tense atmosphere – as if it wasn't daunting enough already.

"Where are you?" Muttered Firin in frustration as he waved his fists erratically. "We haven't come here to fight or be captured by anyone... we've come here to free the Spirit of Light!" Without warning, a sudden silence now took hold of where the companions stood; no gust of wind nor crashing waves fell into their space as a new calm seemed to flow over them.

"Please!" Cara strained her voice to be heard throughout the housings. "Don't hide, show yourselves to us... if you mean now harm." In a gradual response to her, several figures emerged from inside the small temples who were each cloven in grey, their arms held out to display their lack of ill-intent, their expressions curious towards Cara and the other trespassers.

"We were not expecting visitors, in fact, we haven't had any for nearly a decade." Responded one of the hooded figures pleasantly. "We are the Acolytes of Air and this is our current Sanctuary... or what is left of it." Aira's acolytes collected themselves together in haste, forming a militaristic line to stand proudly before the startled trio of friends. Cara was the first to make her approach, now sensing no threat and curious as to why these figures were originally so reluctant in revealing their presences.

"This is the Sanctuary of Air... I don't understand?" Pondered Cara towards the Acolytes in beleaguerment. "We have *just* been sent here by Aira herself, why would she send us to her Sanctuary and not Alaskia's prison?" Her perplexed look was greatly outmatched by the acolytes in their own response.

"You have met our Guardian in person?" Replied an acolyte in obvious shock. "That is *such* a great privilege, most of us here have not even seen Aira... yet we are still devoted to her - nevertheless." The Acolytes nodded together simultaneously in a solemn agreement. "Our Sanctum lies high above the clouds of this world, under the cosmic stars, only a Guardian may permit a soul to enter... and only if in urgent need of Aira's guidance. It makes sense now, as to how you came by our forgotten Sanctuary, few are worthy of being in our Guardian's presence... you have been chosen!" Aira's leading Acolyte bowed herself before Cara and her friends in a show of sincere respect to them, swiftly followed by the others who each smiled adoringly.

"Seriously, *what* happened here?" Interrupted Firin, who himself was growing tired with all the formalities involved when dealing with Spirits and Acolytes. "For a place that's meant to be holy... it's falling apart!" He eagerly brushed his fingers across a temple housing to remove some segments of its wall away. "You haven't cared for your Sanctuary very well, have you?" The leading Acolyte tutted at Firin then gently replaced the crumbling masonry.

"With respect Sir, the Sanctuary of Air lies all around us... these ruins are just to remind people of a Celestial power that has long been forgotten to Impartia." The Acolyte glanced back upon Skynah's towering mountain with a sorrowful expression. "We are using this lost city to prepare for the battle ahead... against Queen Cera of Magmorrah. Ill-tidings have reached our Guardian and as such, Aira has instructed for us to wait here in support of this world's final resistance against the risen darkness. Kufiah... is coming." Cara immediately surprised Aira's Acolytes by not flinching at the mention of Kufiah's name, a Spirit each of them dreaded with all their hearts, she instead remained defiant and headstrong with the impassioned desire to see her daughter again taking control over everything else.

"The Spirit of Darkness is under Cera's spell, they are one and both *can* be stopped." Muttered Cara frankly. "Alaskia will do this... Alaskia, will save my Sophilia – they have to." She repeated frantically.

"This *Resistance;* they will be a fraction in size, compared to Magmorrah's amassed army… won't they?" Questioned Spero in authority, his military training apparently reignited. "How could such a small force possibly stand against Queen Cera's might *and* a Celestial Spirit… is this not just an act of suicide on their part?" The leading Acolyte shook her head sternly to Spero, she was evidently assured of victory from Aira's given wisdom.

"They have a strong faith, as should you, in our Elemental Guardians and especially your fellow mortals." She turned to Cara endearingly. "To lose hope so easily… is to accept defeat without even standing against it."

"It's hard to see a light at the end, when everything around is falling apart." Responded Cara bitterly. She reached a hand out gently to Spero again, sensing his increasing anger. "…Spero?"

"We've witnessed first-hand what the Queen can do; Cera has infiltrated two Sanctuaries, without even barely lifting a finger!" Spero tremored in frustration as he spoke. "The only way to defeat this evil, is to free Alaskia… that is what Ven told us anyway." Aira's Acolytes lowered their heads as if in grief towards Cara's party; they were aware of these travesties, though could not bear to admit it.

"The resisting forces have united in Weissamorrah as a single fleet," replied the leading acolyte boldly, in trying to calm Spero and strengthen Cara's will. "There is nothing there that could prove of any interest, or gain, to Queen Cera… for those lands are barren and have few resources to plunder." She breathed in a deep sigh and then focused again on Cara as an emotional support. "As we speak, the Guardian of Water himself is guiding this last force, as to how they should deal with Cera's impending attack on Skynah. It will not be long before Magmorrah's army and their Queen arrive here."

"I think… the wait might be over?" Commented Firin as he nervously pointed southwards across the ocean strait. "Those are *certainly* not friendly ships!" Numerous dark shapes grew hauntingly upon the horizon, silently they moved like leaves upon the breeze with no showing signs of mercy. It became suddenly apparent to all witnessing that Cera had summoned her entire fleet of warships, all gathered in assault against Skynah's sacred mountain and all were approaching with a dreadful haste.

"We're too late!" Consumed by panic, Cara held onto Spero and shook against him through her renewed fear. She had felt somehow safe upon the great mountain, until this moment at least, as Skynah's sheer size wrought with it a divine repose. The Acolytes of Air showed little emotion, they merely began to encircle the three companions and bowed once again to each of them.

"How long will it be before Weissamorrah's fleet arrive?" Asked Spero in terror, as he stared across the imposing display of Cera's armada. "We have no way of defending ourselves, I can't see this ending well." He felt so helpless and vulnerable, an impulse so foreign to Spero; with his hope of survival now laying upon an army of strangers whose protection felt so far away. "I'm sorry, Cara…" He breathed sadly.

"Weissamorrah's fleet is made up of ships from the different nations; each will have varying capabilities, it is difficult to say which battalion shall arrive first and when." Replied the leading Acolyte, still held within their subservient hope. "Our part in this battle is over… yours has just begun" She signalled to her fellow acolytes to move in close around Cara.

"Take us to Alaskia's Sanctum now!" Cried out Cara in desperation. "We can't wait around for Levia's army!" She exclaimed in a breaking voice. "Please take us to the Spirit, I don't know what we'll be faced with but Cera cannot win!"

"Destiny chose well with you, Cara." Said one of the Acolytes with an earnest smile. "It is time, but first…" The Acolytes removed themselves from Cara's company and without word stood upon the neglected Sanctum platform. They rose their arms in unison towards the hidden summit of Skynah; its swirling clouds appeared to respond by calming in their ferocity, the golden light within them also increased. The Elemental seals beneath Aira's acolytes illuminated with their corresponding Sanctuary colours, a powerful surge of energy quickly flowed from them to send beams of light high into the atmosphere above.

"We summon thee, oh mighty Guardians of Impartia!" Spoke the Acolytes in one voice, tears ran down each face as they unleashed their impassioned emotions. *"Come before us and protect this holy site from the evil that now approaches!"* The activated beams enflamed into their greatest display of intensity, a wave of spiritual power then lingered around them there-after. *"Join your strengths and weaknesses… defy the Spirit of Darkness and Queen Cera!"*

Firstly, entered Pahoe upon her Sanctuary seal. The Guardian of Fire appeared furious and immediately focused her gaze upon the Magmorran ships across Skynah's ocean strait. Ven emerged secondly upon his own seal, still held in fatigue and scarred by the previous battle he had fought in against General Nira. Aira gracefully entered the ruined platform last, savouring her long-lost earthly connection to Impartia which only intensified as she turned towards her Acolytes - for whom the Guardian had not seen in person for many years.

"Praise be… you have heard our prayers!" Rejoiced the Leading-Acolyte in relief. "We are faced with the greatest darkness our world has ever seen!" They cried in dread. "Through your powers though… may our fears be vanquished and with your blessings… may the Sacred Balance be finally restored!" Aira bowed to her devoted followers and then inspected the worn temples beyond where they stood.

"Evil comes in different forms; Impartia has witnessed so many come and go, as this place has also..." Said Ven, as he glanced towards Cara, then Firin and Spero with a great sigh of joy. The Guardian could see their determination clearly displayed without having to sense it, this rose his own spirit and desire to end Cera's reign. "Do not be troubled, my friends. You know what must be done now; our destiny lies in defending this sacred mountain, as is yours in freeing the Spirit of Light and ultimately... Cerebrante!" Ven clenched his fists in anticipation, gradually forcing himself into a spiritual trance. "Go to Alaskia and have no doubt in yourselves, drown out the chaos that seeks to surround you and find the light within the darkness...only *you* can truly save us!"

"The powers we Spirits have, is nothing compared to what now courses through each of you... a will to survive!" Declared Pahoe, in a strangely polite tone for her. "Mortals hold a strength and freedom that we Guardians shall never again harness. Have faith, Cara. You will succeed in bringing an end to this burden of yours...I know you will!" Pahoe entered her own spiritual trance and, as she did, the seals rose in their connections to empower the shared might between Impartia's Elemental Guardians.

"I have met thousands of souls during my time upon this plain, though none who were as resilient as you... Cara." Spoke Aira as she fell into her own meditated state. "You're not doing this for us, nor your friends, nor the rest of Impartia... free Alaskia and do so for Sophilia." Cara slowly stepped back towards Skynah's face, lost in her racing thoughts as she contemplated the wisdom given by Ven and the other Guardians. Firin and Spero both placed a hand of support upon Cara's shoulders to help her, then together they watched as the sun now began to set, displaying with it a crimson haze that cast itself forebodingly over Cera's warships.

"You'll be okay, Cara... we'll get through this." Said Spero whilst he rested his brow upon Cara's, so that both share in a tender moment of peace amongst the chaos. "Firin and I won't let anything happen to you."

"We have the passwords... let's just get this over with." Interrupted Firin, he couldn't bear a second longer spent in the cold winds upon Skynah's platform. "What are waiting for?" Cara embraced her friends dearly with a heartfelt display of love, something she had wished to share with them for some time now and it also served to prevent her from looking upon the impending threat of Cera's fleet nearby.

"Thank you, thank you both so much." Smiled Cara endearingly. The leading-Acolyte of Air briskly placed herself before Cara, Firin and Spero. She proceeded to lead them through Skynah's ancient housings, eventually directing the way towards a small, cavernous opening that was hidden behind a façade of one decimated temple.

"From this moment forth, you will be venturing into Skynah's forgotten Sanctuary." Explained the Acolyte with an auspicious grin. "Within the mountain lies a gateway to both Eternamorrah and the Void, realms of which mortals have never seen before... are you all ready?" She stared upon Cara in particular, knowing that it would be her most-likely effected by what revelations may lie in store. "They are the realms of eternal life... and death."

"We are ready…aren't we?" Trembled Cara in response, Firin and Spero's affirmative nods finally persuaded her to enter the secretive entrance way in despite of any foretold risks. "We'll free Alaskia in no time!"

"We won't leave you, Cara." Assured Spero in excitement.

"Yes, no matter what horrors might be in there…we started this quest together, so we'll finish it just the same!" Exclaimed Firin as he laughed to himself nervously, in ease of his own anxiety. "I'm not afraid!" Cara and her companions said their farewells to Aira's leading Acolyte, then cautiously they stepped into the unknown of Skynah's hidden passageways. Sounds from the outside world faded instantly as they walked further in, a peculiar air lingered in their lungs and a sensation haunted them - that all was not as it seemed. Aira removed herself temporarily from the platform to allow for her Acolytes' safe exit.

"You have carried out your duties with honour, now leave this mountain." Said the Guardian of Air in reluctance, being that most faces passing by her were so painfully unfamiliar. "Go to my Sanctum and await my further orders… have faith and when this is over I shall enjoy getting to know you all better."

"Bless you, Lady Aira." Replied the leading Acolyte tearfully. "Please, stay safe…" Now left as Skynah's only defenders the Elemental Guardians remained stood within their own air of uncertainty, as they toiled over the possible imminent sacrifice that could be made in protecting its sacred mountain. Occasionally, each would glance to their counterpart with a saddened smile in being fully aware of the dire fate which could soon meet with them. Queen Cera's Armada relentlessly pressed on towards the Elemental Guardians, there was no inclination that they would be halting in their advance and beyond them Magmorrah's ash clouds seemed to rise - as if in pursuit.

"Is there something that you can do about this crimson sunset, Aira?" Questioned Pahoe sternly. "It is hardly helping our morale and if anything, such a morbid omen will only boost Queen Cera's…" Aira tutted humorously and then looked up towards the blood-red sky, focusing her spiritual aura above where Cera's fleet now approached.

"I'll do my best, Sister." The Guardian's eyes illuminated through her kindred powers, thus creating monstrous clouds to forge into a thunderous vortex that encircled Cera's ships. "Is that better?" Pahoe equally empowered her own spiritual connection to fuel a sea of immense fire within the darkening clouds. "It'll have to do!" The Guardian magnified her tenacious flames whilst Ven stared upon Levia's seal beside them - from where he patiently awaited his dearest friend's expected arrival.

"So, this is it my Sisters; our greatest test of faith… we *must* protect Cara and this mountain at all costs!" Commanded Ven, his eyes still fixed upon Levia's seal. "If our lifeforce is drained, then so be it! We must not let the Usurper of Magmorrah enter this most-sacred of Sanctuaries… you hear?" Without warning, Levia emerged from the ocean depths beneath Skynah's mountain to land upon his respective seal beside Ven.

"Sorry I'm late; it wasn't easy getting back here from Weissamorrah!" Panted Levia, as he gleamed within the faint light of his seal. "I see that the Queen's forces have arrived sooner than we all expected… has Cara entered Skynah's Sanctuary?" He swallowed heavily upon looking over the nearing warships. "I hope she has, or else we're doomed…the Weissamorran ships are few in number."

"Yes, Cara and her companions have entered the mountain and she has all our passwords." Responded Ven in a shared relief with Levia. "Is the Resistance Fleet ready for battle yet, my dear Brother?"

"Trust me… they are ready, and the Queen won't know what hit her!" Levia grinned ecstatically at the thought of Cera's undoing, rubbing his hands together to emphasise this. "The united armies in Weissamorrah will soon be here and with a renewed show of force that Cera could never dream of imagining!" Ven was not as hopeful in comparison to Levia.

"I pray that you are correct, Brother." Said Ven anxiously. "Cara may have discovered some of her strength, but if she fails to free the Spirit of Light… then Kufiah's decimation *will* be wrought upon Impartia without fail." Ven fleetingly looked back to where Cara was last seen and breathed a sigh of remorse, knowing of the dangers he had now placed his new friends in. The Guardians bowed in a sombre respect to one another; they did so in knowing that their forthcoming actions could determine Impartia's fate, or merely allow for its destruction.

"It's my turn to strike!" Declared Levia, as he lifted his arms towards Cera's Armada to summon the very waves beneath them. "Do you think that Obsidian Armour can withstand one of my Tsunamis?" He humoured to Ven apprehensively. "Let's find out…" The empowered Guardian clasped his hands together forcefully; a series of ensuing waves then roared from their tremendous clashes against Cera's fleet., sending them momentarily off course, though they soon righted again on their determined path. "Apparently… they can."

"Nice try!" Cackled Cera in jubilation. "I have anticipated every move that these fools can throw against me!" Magmorrah's Queen stood proudly upon her Royal vessel which followed the attacking fleet at its rear. Without General Nira leading at her side, Cera now had full command over Magmorrah's army and she relished in ecstasy with the greater control this brought to her. Showing no hesitation, Cera signalled for her many pawns to tighten in their movements against Skynah, undisturbed by the spiritual display of might now casting itself violently above them through Pahoe and Aira's fiery hurricane clouds. "Those pathetic Guardians believe that their magic will deter me?" Cera began to laugh contently, as she turned to face her vessel's commanding officer. "Send forth the first battalion! We will *destroy* those wretched Spirits with one, swift barrage!"

"As you wish, Your Majesty." Cera's commanding officer obeyed his Queen's orders without any show of confliction, despite the formidable enemy which they were up against. "Signal for the Alpha-Division to attack!" A separate officer hastily raised a single flag upon the ship's deck and within seconds Cera's first wave increased their speed towards Skynah.

"Cera moves against us..." Commented Aira sorrowfully. "There will be many lives lost this day and so needlessly."

"Not if Cara succeeds in fulfilling her quest!" Responded Ven with compassion. "Do not lose faith!" The Guardians each breathed in deeply to enhance their individual forms of meditation, intensifying the spiritual powers within them. Levia then nodded confidently to Ven, as Cera's Alpha-Division neared with their cannons raised and speed hastening.

"How dare they defy my Eternal reign!" Seethed Cera, whilst she glared over the Guardians stood together in their defiance. A sickened anger was coursing through the Queen's prominent veins, as all the hatred that Cera had come to contain over her short life now took its horrific form in this new act of dominance. "Enshroud that accursed mountain with our flames and reduce it to ashes!" She screamed. "Send those Spirit Guardians a message that they will forever dwell upon... that I... do *not* fear them!" Magmorrah's Alpha-Division fell silent and then fired a unified wave of incendiaries against the mountainside - unleashing Cera's merciless cruelty upon it. Levia quickly retaliated by raising his arms, lifting with them from Skynah's ocean a towering wall of water to halt the incoming missiles and enemy vessels progress. A burst of water vapour lingered in the air afterwards, shrouding both parties with an eerie haze though this did not discourage Queen Cera's resolve to Levia's dismay. "Fire again... Fire more!" Ordered Cera frantically to her officers. "I *will not* stand for any show of cowardice; teach those traitors who is the true, defining power in this world, or I shall have every retreating vessel decimated for insubordination!"

"Yes… Your Majesty." The Commanding Officer trembled this time as he spoke. Never had he, nor any of Cera's army, witnessed such a power as what the Guardians were creating. "Signal for Alpha-Division to fire-at-will… Now!" A rampaging volley of incendiaries followed, shooting through the air again towards Skynah and its ancient outer-platform.

"Rest, my Brother." Implored Aira calmly to Levia, who himself was noticeably weakened. "I will deal with this attack…" With a slight flick of her wrist, Aira sent a powerful flow of air from the Sanctum platform against Cera's incoming missiles, igniting their fury over Skynah's ocean strait with little exertion required. "Perhaps now, Cera will take the hint that her invasion if futile?"

"Useless… *absolutely* useless!" Cera's frustration now dramatically escalated from her battalion failing to succeed in their mission so far. "Line up the entire fleet to fire against Skynah and bring me my Dark Acolytes, *they* will turn the tide in this battle!"

"As you wish, my Queen." The Commanding Officer slowly gazed to his fellow crew members in fear; they knew little of Kufiah's Acolytes, but what was known was that the power that dwelled within them proved to be unnatural. "Summon the Acolytes of Darkness from their quarters… Her Majesty insists."

"Order our ships into full-speed whilst firing, it will be our only chance to make it through the Guardian's counter-attacks!" Commanded Cera in frustration, her disappointment growing stronger with every passing second. "Their Hurricanes and Tsunamis must not stop our advance!" Queen Cera's Armada unleashed their full capacity of destructive force against Skynah and the Elemental Guardians protecting it. Levia, regardless of his weary spiritual connection, focused again on the flowing waves, raising once more a formidable Tsunami to send most of Cera's warships into the murky fathoms below.

"I have broken our most-solemn vow… not to take a life," Despaired Levia in remorse for his actions. "I pray that the Queen will soon surrender; would Cera willingly allow for her entire naval force to be decimated… to further her own selfish pride?" Ven sternly shook his head in response.

"Do not be so hopeful with such a thought, my old friend." Sighed Ven. "Queen Cera will not give in so easily, she has planned for this attack over many years and each move that is made has been calculated… do *not* let your guard down!" He commanded.

"You summoned us, Queen Cera?" Asked one of Kufiah's Acolytes in anticipation, as they eagerly entered the bridge. "Has the time come for our master's revelation to be known?"

"Yes…" Cera's expression suddenly changed from being scornful to ecstatic. "Impartia will *burn* in the immolation of Kufiah… help me now to bring forth my Divine Darkness!" The Queen clenched onto Kanaan's amulet with a perverse joy, whilst her subservient Acolytes began to sing in chorus to Kufiah's abhorrent Hymn. "Prove your worth!"

"Your Majesty!" Cried out her ship's Captain, whilst glancing excitedly at his radar screen. "The Submersibles… they have arrived."

"Good…" Cera responded callously, she no longer favoured her army's physical strength to win over the tide in his battle. "They better do some damage!"

"I can sense something," Cried out Levia, as if in acute pain. "Large objects are moving beneath the ocean waves… they are not natural!"

"I know what faces us," replied Ven with a despondent expression. "let *me* deal with them!" Cera's submarines coursed through the ocean with an immense level of speed, armed and ready to unleash their strength against Skynah. Ven fused his earthly connection to Levia's own spiritual power, so that both could aid in discovering where Magmorrah's hidden warships lay. "I can see them now," whispered Ven, as he focused his concentration. The connection that he and Levia had created with one another unwittingly shared their inner-thoughts, they were a cocktail of fear, anger, determination and remorse. "We *must* forsake our vows if Impartia is to survive, Brother!"

"But… we swore never to kill, Ven!" Despaired Levia. "We will become monsters, just like Cera and Kanaan, to take so many lives!" The spiritual connection began to falter under Levia's grief, forcing Ven to take drastic action before it was lost completely.

"Cera's underdogs know what they are doing, and they have had every chance to dethrone the Queen… their fate is sealed." Ven then summoned an immense earthquake upon the ocean bed, forcing spear-like fractures to lift from it against Cera's submersibles and without any mercy shown. One by one, Magmorrah's hidden force were impaled by Ven's earthly shards to render them beyond any usage or recovery.

"What a sad fate they chose… I pray, they find freedom and peace in Eternamorrah." Levia grimly sensed what Ven had done, they dwelled in a momentary silence there-after before looking back towards Cera's remaining fleet.

"Where…are…my…Submarines?" Seethed the Queen, disappointment was clearly displayed in her flaring eyes. "Ten years I spent planning for this attack, and for what… to be humiliated!" Cera looked to her Captain with a greater disdain. "If only I had my airship… 'Divinity' would have put an end to this battle already!"

"Your Majesty, we still have a number of ships left that are able to fight." Responded the Captain apprehensively, not wanting to infuriate Cera further. "Magmorrah's soldiers would not forsake you, not without making a last stand…" His eyes suddenly opened wide in shock as now manoeuvring around Skynah's vast mountain, in what light remained from Impartia's sun, came a fleet of varying warships that aimed towards Queen Cera's Armada.

"Filthy scum!" Cera viciously tore her nails into the Captain's shoulders, using them to drag him upon the ship's deck for a closer inspection. "My Orders were clear to you: 'Invade the other nations and destroy every warship they have'… so why can I see some before me now?"

"My Queen…" The Captain strained his voice in agony. "They are no match for our weapons!"

"You'd better be correct, Captain." Cera slowly released her grip from him to signal for her Dark Acolytes immediate company. "Give them everything that we have, I'm not here to take prisoners… FIRE AT WILL!" She screamed with all her malice. "KILL THEM ALL!" The remaining warships from Hydrania led Weissamorrah's United Fleet, followed cautiously by Talam's and then a smaller number of Viridian Sailboats. Each vessel harboured unique capabilities, which they hoped could overpower Queen Cera's advanced weaponry. Levia's previous Tsunami had left the ocean waves turbulent, making the United Fleet's approach even more dangerous and difficult to navigate over.

"Captain Jardiah!" Shouted a crew member from upon the deck Hydrania's leading vessel. "What are our Orders?"

"We will keep our present course," Responded the Captain with a proud smile, showing no fear or uncertainty. "Today, we will avenge our homeland's invasion… we will avenge all who have fallen under Magmorrah's wrath!"

"Yes, Captain!" Replied the crew member and few others joyously. "We'll make Magmorrah's Queen pay for what she has done to Impartia!" Cera struck her talon-like nails into the Captain's throat, and then proceeded to drag him back to their ship's steering wheel.

"Move us forward… NOW!" She then frantically wrapped her fingers around Kanaan's amulet, using it to transcend her voice across the waves and many warships gathered. "This *fleet* who now oppose us, they are nothing more than a last strand of hopeless fools and all are doomed to die! End their pathetic mark upon this world… my *honourable* warriors!" Cera kept her fingers tightened around the accursed amulet; drawing from its power a strength needed at this defining moment, whilst she looked back across to Kufiah's servants with a look of desperation. "Acolytes of Darkness hasten your efforts, for I need your Master to be at his full potential… if this battle is to be won!" The Elemental Guardians themselves stared down upon Weissamorrah's United Fleet. It was a poignant moment for each of them, knowing what awful fate could be met with the defending ships and their crews.

"Let the mortals battle against Cera alone; Impartia belongs to them now, so it is they who should defend it." Said Pahoe wearily, as she signalled to her kin for a much-needed rest in their intervention. "There is no point in us fighting, if we are depleted of power."

"I agree with you, Sister." Replied Levia, much to Ven and Aira's astonishment. "Is it not their lands that Queen Cera has defiled… who are we to rob them of vengeance?" The Guardian then knelt himself sorrowfully upon his seal, allowing for its strong energy to replenish him. "I am almost drained, never have we needed to use our powers like this before." Ven contemplated heavily on his brethren's words; they were difficult for him to accept, being that he had fought tirelessly alongside Impartia's mortals in their struggle for freedom.

"I can understand both your feelings," Said Ven plainly, as he addressed Levia and Pahoe. "But, should the mortals show any sign of distress… we *must* intervene. Kufiah is yet to make his presence known." He turned his gaze directly south, to where Kufiah's Sanctuary dwelled.

"Our brother speaks wisely." Aira responded with a knowing glance to her kin, she had watched over the Queen's reign closer than any other. "I can't understand why Cera has not yet summoned for the Spirit of Darkness, something isn't right… some newer evil is at work here." Hydrania's warships sliced through the turbulent ocean with ease, and all were aiming directly against Cera's fleet now. Showing no mercy themselves, they ignited their sonic-beams against Magmorrah's Armada in a blinding display that even startled the Elemental Guardians. Queen Cera's ships soon proved to be inferior; many shattered under the powerful energy rays, sending them down into the dark depths below.

"INFIDELS!" Screamed Cera in disbelief, she directed her hatred once again towards the Dark Acolytes. "My amulet's power is growing… I can feel it… your Master is nearly at his full-strength… FOCUS!" Magmorrah's remaining vessels countered with a vicious barrage against the Hydranian ships; some missed their mark, whilst others struck with a surprisingly-cold accuracy. "Magmorrah was and *should* be the greatest nation in Impartia," thought Cera sombrely to herself. "I will not suffer the same legacy as Father… I will not be forgotten." The Elemental Guardians winced in discomfort, as more and more opposing ships fell under each other's artillery before them. Both Aira and Pahoe shed a tear as they looked to Ven for his further wisdom, Levia too appeared to suffer from witnessing this horrific spectacle.

"How long should we allow for these mortals to endure such needless slaughter?" Pleaded Aira softly, though inside she wanted to scream. "So much death will be wrought by this futile conflict… and for what?" Aira's frustration increased and her eyes flared intensely with their silver light. "Please, as Guardians we must do something to aid these poor souls before there are none left to save!"

"Sister," Pahoe's voice trembled from her own conflicting thoughts. "This is a fight that we *must* allow, despite any of our reservations… if this world is to be righted. What are your thoughts, Brother Levia?" Levia pounded at the seal beneath him with his fists, he too struggled to reason with Ven's Order.

"Our place is here, in ensuring the safety of this divine Sanctuary from the Queen and Kufiah." Levia pounded the seal once more in anger. "*That* is our duty, is it not… Ven?"

"I never imagined it to be this bad," Stammered Ven, as he kept his gaze firmly set upon the countless explosions, however something else now caught his eye. "Look! The warships from Talam and Viridia have made it... hope is not lost!" Talam's warships fired into the air several, large metallic boulders from specialised cannons on their decks. The peculiar missiles sped over Hydrania's ships towards Cera's; a sudden burst of molten ore proceeded to cascade down as their spheres opened, melting the Magmorran soldiers who were unlucky enough to be stood within their path, though no major damage was dealt to the obsidian vessels.

"Fools!" Cackled Cera sadistically, she then turned to her fearful crew members. "Be assured, no flame can pierce these vessels... RETURN FIRE!" A rapid array of Magmorran incendiaries immediately littered the dusk sky. They showered down upon Talam's warships in a cruel strike, their explosive destruction only magnified by Aira's lightening which crackled above them in her Hurricane. "Talam's ships are made from iron," Cackled Cera again. "Watch as they buckle!" Talam's fleet seemed to groan and cry, as their hulls tore apart from the intense heat searing through them. The Elemental Guardians looked on helplessly as they watched Talam's remaining ships sink into darkness, their hearts and resolve ached more so now.

"Aira!" Cried out Ven desperately. "Use the power from your hurricane to hasten Viridia's entrance into this battle!" Aira nodded back affirmatively to him.

"As you wish, Brother." Aira clenched her eyes shut, focusing hard upon the formidable hurricane that had been strategically placed above Cera's Armada. Aira concentrated her air currents to draw in Viridia's Fleet, so that they were situated just behind Hydrania's in support of them. "Stay strong... free mortals!" What the Elemental Guardians had not yet realised, much to their folly, was that Cera could see the precise locations of her enemy each time a lightning bolt struck from Aira's hurricane above. Magmorrah's Queen swiftly noticed Viridia's incoming Fleet, thought they bore no fear in her.

"Let them savour in their false-hope, for it will not last much longer." The Queen scoured over her Acolytes though with a perverse smile this time, now brandishing Kanaan's amulet before them which glowed eerily with a crimson hue. "It is time to summon Kufiah! It is time for the Spirit of Darkness to reveal his *true* power!" Cera scratched her fingernails across each of the Acolytes ferociously, making sure that she drew blood from them in order to complete Kufiah's demonic ritual. "Bring forth Impartia's Reaper!"

"Why have the Magmorran ships stopped firing?" Questioned Levia reservedly, despite being relieved by this apparent truce. "Has Queen Cera finally given up?"

"No... can you sense it?" Replied Ven with a mournful expression. "Sense what, Ven?" Responded Levia sharply. "I dare not wish to know..."

"It is death and despair." Aira ensured that her words carried fully to the other Guardians. "Cera is preparing to summon Kufiah, we have to act...now!" She commanded.

"I for one can't watch this sordid display for a moment longer!" Shouted Pahoe in protest, her scarlet eyes reignited. "Aira's right, we must intervene and if none of you will… then I will make a start!" The Guardian of Fire instantly entered back into a spiritual trance, focusing the flames within Aira's hurricane to create a greater tenacity in them.

"I agree, enough blood has been spilled this day!" Said Ven as his own eyes reignited.

"Levia… Pahoe, forge your powers with mine to create an indestructible wall which neither army will be able to penetrate!" A mighty green flame lifted from Ven's entire aura as he spoke, empowered by his will to end this battle swiftly.

"So be it!" Responded Levia and Pahoe with a thankful smile. "Let's finish this!"

"Aira, cover our actions by drawing Cera's ships away from Skynah by using your hurricane!" Commanded Ven, as the intense spiritual connection between the Guardians grew beyond anything achieved before. "Cara needs all the time that we can spare her, it is she that will end this war… not us!"

"Both air and lightening shall strike against the dark forces!" Aira roared in unison with her lightning bolts, they streamed across the night's sky to illuminate it as a deliberate warning to Cera below. "We should have done this years ago!" Whilst Aira concentrated on empowering her hurricane above, Levia and Ven both focused their powers upon the ocean floor beneath. Together, they shifted its earthly plain to create an unprecedented earthquake that tore for miles across Impartia. Ven shook painfully as he held out his arms toward the separate fleets, gradually raising between them from the volatile depths numerous towers of rock to serve as a barrier.

"Pahoe, ignite these mountains which I have mustered with your fury… make it so none can ever pass!" Ordered Ven coarsely, despite succumbing slowly to the pain wrought by his spiritual endeavour. "Do it now!" Pahoe grinned endearingly in response. "You certainly know how to leave a lasting impression, Brother! You want volcanoes… I shall gladly make some for you!" The ocean waves clashed as Pahoe raised her arms against Ven's towering monoliths within them. Great vents of steam suddenly arose from inside the earthly structures to shatter their summits under immense flowing lava that followed shortly afterwards. The opposing fleets looked on at this terrifying sight with an equal panic, unsure of what unnatural occurrence was now taking place between them as the intense heat from Pahoe's volcanic display coursed over all their vessels.

"I hope this new plan of yours works, Ven." Said Aira jadedly. We've spent enough of our powers already deterring these armies. If Cera manages to conjure Kufiah before this battle is through, I have doubts for our own survival - let alone Impartia's mortals."

"Trust me, Sister. We have no other choice." Said Ven defiantly, though through many pants of fatigue. "Cara will free Alaskia… keep saying that to yourselves… Cara will free Alaskia and all of us!"

"Cara will free us!" Screamed out Levia passionately. "She is not alone!" Queen Cera's patience had now dwindled beyond any recovery. She violently unsheathed a dagger clung to her side and then held it intently against the senior Dark Acolyte's throat, pressing the blade into their flesh in want of wreaking an agony across their entire body.

"Help me to summon your Master Spirit now, you *weak* and *pathetic* slaves!" Cera forced her blade deeper into the Acolyte's muscle tissue. "Summon the Beast of Darkness with *all* of your devotion, sacrifice yourselves for me by Kufiah's immolation to grant the divine power I truly need - in destroying these Lesser Spirits!" The Acolytes of Darkness trembled subserviently before Queen Cera; in summoning Kufiah, and having to possibly suffer his wrath, now brought to them no grief in comparison with the cruelty they would face at the hands of their demented Queen. The Dark Acolytes completed their demonic hymn and then held onto each another, uniting their flesh to become one as their robes and bodies set ablaze within a sudden burst of rising flames where they now knelt. "It is a pity that Moah betrayed us," said the Queen bitterly. "He would have made Kufiah so much more powerful with the connection they had…" Cera stared curiously upon the swirling flicker of flames, whilst ignoring the cries of her burning servants as from their eventual ashes emerged Kufiah. Cera's crew members fled to hide themselves away from Kufiah's haunting presence, for none had ever seen the Spirit before this moment. Queen Cera moved herself proudly before the Spirit of Darkness and relished in the sense of death that flowed from him through in her own twisted form of ecstasy. "My accursed protector," whispered Cera, as she slowly embraced Kanaan's amulet. "Father failed to see your full potential… though I do not." The Queen seeped her corrupted will through Kanaan's amulet into Kufiah, causing him to breath heavily as each passing emotion gradually took hold.

"My Queen," spoke the Dark Spirit in a menacing tone. "What is thy bidding?"

"You know what to do…" Cera's eyes flared in delight. "Destroy the Elemental Guardians and Impartia's Spirit of Light, so that I alone can reign eternal!" Cera shook from her lustful longing of this moment, believing now that no force upon Impartia could now stop her performing such an unforgivable deed. "You are my slave… enact my will." Kufiah bowed in a reluctant obedience to Cera; together they then walked upon the vessel's deck outside, sending each of her soldiers fleeing from fright on witnessing the demonic vision that now passed by. "Cowards!" Quirked Cera to Kufiah. "They could never understand what ultimate power looks like, but they will soon learn." Kufiah gazed over each soldier that ran from him, sensing their innocent souls and what dire fate lay in store for them.

"Yes… My Queen." Roared Kufiah aggressively. Thunderous bursts of lava continued to erupt from the many towering volcanoes which Impartia's Elemental Guardians had created. Molten rocks fell and scattered around the damaged Magmorran vessels as they neared toward the flowing rivers of magma, their crew members all now felt an uncertainty against what their Queen was truly planning to do with them - considering this dire situation.

"Do not let Queen Cera enter these sacred waters, focus your powers even greater now my brothers and sisters… we *must* remain strong for Cara!" Cried out Ven on noticing Cera's vessel pierce itself through her fellow warships to centre against Skynah. "Use all your energy if you have to, this is our last chance to save Impartia from chaos!"

"Chaos is *not* what we are dealing with here," said Aira frankly, and with a knowing glance to Ven. "This is merely pure evil, awakened by our lack of insight… see this stand as an atonement for our sins and nothing less!" The line of volcanoes burst simultaneously at their full capacity to reign a further wave of lava over the ocean waves beneath; separating Cera's fleet from Weissamorrah's, as a greater molten wall formed itself now between them - which neither dared to cross. The united fleet of Weissamorrah swiftly retreated from the falling flames back around Skynah's foundations, keeping their distance from this hypnotising spectacle as well as preparing for their next attack. The Magmorran warships also drew to a standstill; being unsure of how to deal with such a formidable defence as Cera, now joined with Kufiah, overlooked the carnage taking place in acuity.

"The Elemental Guardians upon Skynah, are only defending it so that my sister can free Alaskia and then destroy us both!" Scorned Cera to Kufiah. "Turn their own powers against them, do what must be done Kufiah… my Dark Avenger!"

"Yes… My Queen." Responded Kufiah coldly. "Impartia's Darkness shall reign!" Kufiah looked above to Aira's swirling vortex of clouds, sensing the vast spiritual power that controlled them and what capabilities they had - should he take possession. With a mighty roar, Kufiah raised himself through the air into the heart of Aira's hurricane, his demonic cries could be heard far across Impartia's other nations. The Elemental Guardians merely looked on in despair at Kufiah's presence, as they had little fight left to counter such a foreboding force. From the Dark Spirit's robes then fell countless streams of dense smoke that ensnared Cera's own warships, lifting each of them effortlessly from the ocean up towards him.

"Your Majesty," stuttered Cera's Captain nervously. "What are you doing?"

"For Impartia to survive… sacrifices have to be made." Replied Magmorrah's Queen callously. "Starting with its lesser beings… such as you." The Magmorran ships cried out 'Mayday' to one another though in vain; they continued to rise into the fiery vortex above, only to be met by the welcoming Dark Spirit as he held out his arms towards them. Kufiah had also managed to synchronise himself spiritually with Aira at this point; possessing her unique powers and weakening the Guardian of Air grievously in the process.

"Aira… what's going on?" Shouted Levia, as he too now felt himself succumb to Kufiah's draining hold. "My powers… I can't control them!" Unbeknown to the Guardians, Kufiah had taken possession over all of them and now used their abilities to his and Queen Cera's advantage. The soldiers of Magmorrah threw themselves overboard in desperation, only to be torn apart into ashes as they fell through the air, their ships disintegrated into nothing as all were pulled closer into Kufiah's maelstrom.

"Teach them with your immolation!" Cried out Cera maliciously, the deaths of her own soldiers brought no apparent sadness or remorse. "Bask in your limitless power, Kufiah!"

The sea of ashes flowing through the air began to encircle Kufiah, eventually forging into his physical mass to increase the Spirit of Darkness' powers dramatically – a strength only achieved once before under King Kanaan's will.

"We cannot fight *this*, Brother!" Levia strained to speak with Ven and his brethren, as each fought tirelessly against the possession which now seemed to be growing even greater over them. "It's all my fault, I should never have severed my connection to Cerebrante!"

"No, Levia!" Replied Ven in sincerity. "You served as Cerebrante's host well, what is happening now is beyond any of our foresight… keep your faith strong in Cara and her companions!" The Elemental Guardians then each collapsed upon their seals, drained of their will as the light began to fade away from them. "Cerebrante will be reborn…"

"Kufiah!" Screamed Cera hatefully. "Do not allow for those Viridian vessels to escape!" The Spirit of Darkness immediately turned his gaze towards Viridia's fleeing sailboats, who were far slower than Hydrania's advanced fleet. With an instant thought, Kufiah rained down a flurry of lightning bolts to strike at each of them and then, after a series of intense explosions, they sank far into a begotten darkness below. "Good… very good!" Applauded Cera wickedly. "All nations are doomed to die in the same way, should they not bow willingly before me."

"Those poor souls," Muttered Ven in grief. "They didn't stand a chance."
"None of them did." Replied Aira remorsefully. "It is I, that should have halted Cera and Kanaan…when the opportunity was there." The Dark Spirit's enhanced hurricane suddenly started to disperse, its built-up energy then imploded within Kufiah's mass to immerse him into an even greater state of empowerment. Kufiah cried out hauntingly and revealed from his robes a set of ashen wings that allowed for him to fly unnaturally above the calmed waters of Skynah's ocean – taking aim towards the sacred mountain.

"None can withstand the power of a Celestial Spirit such as Kufiah!"
Rejoiced Cera to herself. "This will be too easy a victory!" Kufiah lingered in
his new-found might over Queen Cera as her personal Angel of Retribution,
the protection and destructive force the Spirit of Darkness now harboured was
enough to compensate for the loss of Magmorrah's entire fleet – in Cera's eye
at least. "Ten years I have waited for this!" Cackled Cera, her emaciated body
writhed in a sickened joy. "If only Nira was here to share in this momentous
event… such a pity and waste of a good General." Upon Skynah's outer
platform, the Elemental Guardians reluctantly accepted their defeat. They
turned to one another with a sorrowful glance, then activated their seals as a
last form of protection against Kufiah's growing attack.

"It has been a privilege to serve the Sacred Balance alongside you all, my
friends." Said Ven tenderly, as he looked upon each of his fellow Guardians.
"If this is our last day upon Impartia, then let it be long remembered, as a day
when both Spirits and mortals stood united against the most-evil of foes. The
peaceful realm of Eternamorrah now awaits us; may we all enter it with
honour, in having performed our duties as the cosmos would have wanted."
The returning smiles and tears from his brethren echoed through Ven's own
restrained emotions, whilst he himself succumbed to the harsh reality that they
were now faced with.

"Cara *will* finish her quest, Ven. If you have faith that she will succeed, then
so… do we." Responded Pahoe with a tearful wink.

"We have done all that was possible in holding back Queen Cera and
Kufiah," responded Ven sorrowfully. "Return to your Sanctuaries, rest, and
wait for my next command. If Cera reaches Alaskia… then it will be us alone
who will have to deal with the consequences."

"Cera won't reach Skynah's inner-Sanctum so easily!" Cried out Aira. Then,
to the surprise of her fellow Guardians, she unleashed several lightning bolts
against Kufiah's flying mass as the Spirit flew closer. "This is not the first time
I have fought Kufiah; he did not defer me then… and will not now!" Kufiah
shot through the air towards Skynah, missing Aira's lightning bolts only by
mere inches and none deterred the Spirit from meeting with his present course.
As the Guardians activated their seals to take them away from Skynah, Aira
summoned a gigantic lightning bolt to decimate the platform where they had
previously stood. Undeterred, Cera marvelled over Kufiah's capability and
then, with a satisfied smirk, granted him his final Order – one that would
change Impartia forever.

Chapter Eleven: The Asylum of Eternal Light

Cara ventured first into the narrow passage of Skynah's hidden entranceway, closely followed by Firin and Spero, who were keeping an ever-watchful eye over her. Skynah's inner-walls were vastly differently from the mountain's overgrown and neglected exterior: Crystal shimmers flowed across the reflective walls, as if they were stars held eternally within the night's sky and all shone in varying colours, only to fade back occasionally into a pitched darkness. The ground beneath, though quite earthly in its touch, felt so artificial as if forged by mortal hands instead of nature. Despite the heavenly lights, it was a claustrophobic environment that Cara and her companions took no pleasure in travelling through.

"This isn't like any of the other Sanctuaries we've been to." Whispered Firin, whilst gradually edging himself into Cara and Spero's personal space for their reassurance. "It feels so false, do you not feel like we're walking into some sort of trap?" Spero quickly turned around to Firin.

"We need to be careful… we don't know if we're alone in here." Spero then flicked a hand over Firin's mouth to force a silence in him, not wishing to cause any further concern to Cara who herself merely walked on ahead. "Cara has enough on her mind at the moment, the last thing she needs are comments like that."

"Okay!" Muffled Firin, with his eyes rolling and voice still restrained by Spero's firm hand. "I'll try not to be realistic for now on… should I start singing some happy songs to help?"

"Give it a rest..." Spero rolled his own eyes to Firin in frustration. "We need to be serious." The passageway began to meander into, what felt like, an endless maze. A serene ambience soon surrounded Cara and her friends which had a clouding effect on their judgement, a side-effect willed by the Sanctuary's sentient catacombs.

"Watch your step," implored Cara to her companions further behind. "The ground is more un-even here, it feels alive… it's moving!" The horrifying sounds of war coming from outside faintly diminished, as Cara, Firin and Spero delved deeper into the bowels of Skynah's gargantuan Sanctuary. They had heard many explosions; Spero recognised the Hydranian Sonic-Beams instantly, though grimaced at Magmorrah's returning incendiaries.

"Do you think that we'll be ever make it back out?" Questioned Cara anxiously, she held even tighter onto Spero's hand beside her. "Where *is* Alaskia's Sanctum?" Spero clasped Cara's hand into his chest gently.

"We'll make it, Cara." Assured Spero. "Remember what Ven said: Don't lose faith… and I know that you've been through worse than this." Their faces almost touched, until Firin awkwardly bumped into the pair during this tender moment.

"Save it for another time, you two!" Laughed Firin, his expression pleasantly surprised. "I'd rather we find this Alaskia that everyone's been talking about and get the Hell out of this weird place... sooner rather than later!" He patted at Cara and Spero on their shoulders, easing any tension between them. Firin then forced himself to take the lead by walking ahead.

"Sorry Firin, we forgot how sensitive you are when it comes to showing feelings around others... we promise, not to embarrass you again!" Joked Spero as he nudged his anxious companion in the back; shocking Firin initially, as the darkness enveloped them once more before emanating back into a varying stream of colours.

"I'm done with this whole, *spiritual* quest-thing now... I'm not used to all this action anymore!" Remarked Firin in a similar show of humour. The friends then turned into a passageway that seemed thankfully new to them; a pure-white light intensified upon the walls as they walked by, it warmed their hearts and bodies unlike the cold confusion suffered previously.

"We must be getting closer to Alaskia now?" Observed Cara, in awe of the lights as they individually danced around each other as if through song. "It isn't so bad here."

"Good, then that means we're not far from defeating Queen Cera." Said Spero as he breathed a sigh of relief. "Come on, judging by the explosions outside we don't have long to reach Alaskia!" The passage seemed to stretch out relentlessly; at its apparent end grew a blinding ray of golden light, which cast itself towards Cara and her companions. Despite the many steps taken, they found themselves no closer towards it. The tiring companions knelt themselves in defeat, reasoning that their quest had come to a forced conclusion without being able to rescue Alaskia. Spero suddenly felt an urge to address Cara with something which had been burdening his mind, since their first meeting. "Cara, there is something I need to ask you... I've been wishing to ask it for a while now." Stammered Spero, he twirled his fingers nervously through one another whilst looking upon her. "I know that now may not be the right time, but it's important to me..." Firin abruptly barged past the doting pair to dismiss their conversation.

"Come on Spero!" Exasperated Firin. "Whatever you're wanting to ask Cara can wait until this mission is over, I'm sure that we'll have plenty of time to listen to your ramblings then."

Cara smiled reassuringly back to Spero, also granting him a subtle wink to show her adoration and then followed Firin further into the unknown radiating light. Spero shook his head in contempt, then paced himself faster to meet with the other; a mixture of uncertainty and resolute excitement slowly started to filter through each of them.

"What do you think Alaskia will be like?" Asked Cara to Spero, hoping to distract herself from the nearing union. "Do you think, the Spirit will be terrifying... like Kufiah is?"

"Alaskia can't be any worse, can he?" Chuckle Spero in response. "I doubt though, that a Spirit of Light would want to turn us all into ashes or cast our souls into an endless void - as Kufiah would." Firin countered in disenchantment.

"I don't think we'll get much of a chance to know what Alaskia is truly like; once free, the Spirit's main concern will be to deal with Queen Cera and Kufiah." He then murmured softly. "I never believed that Impartia's Spirits and their Guardians held such a power over it. I was wrong. Now that I have seen it with my own eyes, there is no doubt that we 'mortals' must learn our place – if we are all to survive." He sighed woefully.

"What's made you so serious all of a sudden?" Gasped Spero in shock. "It doesn't matter now, let's just keep walking and hopefully we'll come across Alaskia at some point." The anxious companions individually reflected over what they had been through, over the past few days or so. As they each fell silent, deeply lost in their thoughts, a drawing presence seemed to stand now before them within the golden light. The three immediately began to run towards it with a renewed sense of hope, building itself inside of them to counter any previous dread which they had all been feeling. Whilst sprinting, Cara turned to Firin and Spero.

"Please, both of you, promise me that you won't forget our friendship when this war is over…" Pleaded Cara. "I can't wait for my Lia to meet the pair of you!" She held out her hands towards the welcoming, heavenly light. "Promise me!" Firin and Spero struggled to equal Cara's pace and through their own excitement, they now felt all sense of fear leave them behind; a sudden sense greater meaning encapsulated them both instead.

"We can't wait to meet Sophilia either, Cara!" Rejoiced Spero heartily.

"It will be an honour to meet her, now run… run as fast as you can!" Cried out Firin in determination to reach the light's source. "Go!" The great light burst with a sudden, searing heat over Cara and her friends; it seeped through their flesh, though painlessly, and entered their own spiritual auras. The ethereal energy that now coursed through them seemed to wash away any previous torment, gradually forcing each friend into a subconscious state of calm. The companions floating within an ocean of pulsing waves, no longer aware of time nor any other surroundings. They willingly allowed for its permeance to filter deeper into them, afterwards all their forgotten thoughts and emotions slowly began to reveal themselves. All of sudden, Firin felt as if he was falling from high in the sky and he looked down in sheer panic upon the vast desert landscape beneath, that now appeared through the hazy clouds. As Firin neared the ground, expecting his own imminent death, the rapid descent halted abruptly to leave him standing mid-air above the familiar setting of his hometown - Chiltam.

"What the Hell is going on?" Pondered Firin to himself. Without any warning, the long-lost vision of Firin's grandfather appeared solidly before him; his features and humoured smile looked just the same as they always had. "It cannot be, this cannot... be?" Whispered Firin in disbelief, whilst looking upon the father-figure he had lost so cruelly many years ago during his youth. "Are you real, are you really alive... or am I just dreaming?" Firin's grandfather walked with his hands held firmly behind his back towards him; acknowledging the understandably shocked reaction jubilantly, by displaying an ever-familiar smile in response.

"Yes, my dear boy!" Declared Firin's grandfather in ecstasy. "I am real and always will be, I have never left you...and *you* know that!" Firin began to weep softly, as he strained his longing arms towards the beloved grandfather who had been taken from him. Though as Firin edged himself closer to the image it began to fade, much to his immediate grief.

"You *did* leave me though, Grandpa! I was only a boy and you were *all* I had!" Firin trembled through his sorrow. "I struggled so much by myself afterwards, I thought that the pain would never end!" Firin's tears faintly streamed upon the parched desert sands below, his grandfather stepped cautiously over each them to move in closer.

"It was my *time*, Firin!" Moaned his grandfather wearily. "You must let go of your grief from my passing. I no longer suffer with the physical pain I had during life; my death had to come eventually, move on my dear boy... as I have." The vision of Firin's grandfather faded away more, despite both wishing for this reunion never to end.

"Grandpa, please don't leave me again." Pleaded Firin with a solemn expression. "I am sick of loneliness; being with you now, reminds me so much of all the great times we had."

"What are you on about, Firin?" Laughed his grandfather dismissively. "You're not alone, my dear boy. What about Cara and Spero... have you forgotten about them already?"

"No... of course not." Shrugged Firin ashamedly. "I'd never..."

"Cherish the bonds which you have been gifted with, Firin." Spoke his grandfather coarsely. "Leave the past where it belongs... with me." The vision dwindled further, leaving only a blurry trace of his image. "I will never leave you" He shook his head sternly. "...never." Firin suddenly fell once more into an unwelcomed darkness, the raw emotions from seeing his deceased guardian continued to flow through him with an ever-increasing pain. He also struggled to understand how this vision came into his consciousness and why it left him with more questions than answers.

"See you around, Grandpa…" The darkness ensnaring Firin gradually began to disperse into a new vision, which played out swiftly before his eyes. Fleeting images from the life he had known now flew relentlessly before Firin, showing him as he left the comfort of his hometown to the start in Talam's military academy, then as lead sniper in its secret military force. Firin looked on in perplexment, as he watched both happier and sad times appear, with the feeling of both joy and sadness overcoming him throughout them.

"What is the point in showing me these memories?" Asked Firin with resentment to the unknown source of this ordeal. "Why must I be reminded of times that I'd rather forget?"

"Where there is light, there is darkness… where there is darkness, there is light."

"What?" Snapped Firin bitterly, the phantom voice sounded so child-like and haunting. "I wish that Spirits wouldn't talk in riddles…" Another blinding flash of light pierced Firin's eyes; he raised his arms to protect them, but in dismay found that they could not from the powerful rays. The vision laid out before Firin now, showed him lying in a prone-position upon a barren, desert landscape. He was overlooking an encampment of travellers, their tribal village situated just before the great walls of Talam's capital city. A daunting realisation instantly hit Firin to the very core of his being. "No…" He begged. "Not this, show me anything… but this!" Pleaded Firin more desperately. "I beg you, whoever you are, don't make me relive this moment!" He attempted to shield his eyes again though to no avail, as the image only continued to intensify in its clarity.

"Where there is darkness…"

"Don't start with that again!" Screamed Firin. "Whatever you're trying to prove… stop it!"

"…There IS light…"

Firin watched himself perform the regular checks he would make with his beloved rifle; ensuring that it was clean and fit for its true, deadly purpose. Beside Firin was a small, make-shift transmitter that his commanding officers had given to him prior to this current assignment. Firin's past-self wiped the dusty sweat away from his brow, as the midday sun above rose higher with its scorching heat. He then lay patiently, holding tight onto his weapon with its trigger primed ready in anticipation for any incoming orders given by Talam's lead-command.

"…You copy?" Firin's transmitter crackled into use suddenly. "SNFN, do you copy…Over."

"I copy… Over." Responded Firin in a cautious whisper. "Scanning for Alpha-Target… Over." Through his Sniper-scope, Firin gradually focused on the towering figure of a man whose features were shrouded within a set of desert cloths, protecting him from the intense sunlight and possible identification. The man's only noticeable feature was a strange tattoo bore upon one of his hands; it looked like a bursting star and was a symbol which Firin had been ordered to look out for. "I've got you now…Scum!"

"Where balance exists… so does chaos…"

"Chaos?" Questioned Firin sternly. "That's an understatement, after this there was a civil war that lasted for five years!" Massed around the dominant figure were numerous members from his tribe, all going about their daily lives. Men and women traded various items with one another in the village's marketplace, as their children played freely amongst them, each apparently celebrating some sort of festival known only to this secluded culture. Firin lay in fixation, his sight never leaving the target-male who stood proud within the heart of this small community. A rippling of noise came through Firin's transmitter again; he quickly reached to activate it in response, not wishing to give away his prime position to any unwanted listeners nearby.

"SNFN, do you have target in sight? Over…" Asked a stringent voice through the transmitter.

"Yes…Over." Firin's heartbeat paced as he responded. "Alpha-Target confirmed."

"Your Orders have changed SNFN…" The transmitter crackled louder, making it hard for Firin to decipher its message. "Eliminate… threat… our King…"

"Repeat…" Firin raised his voice carefully so that it carried through. "You're breaking up."

"The Scavengers are harbouring a high-risk terrorist…they are sympathisers… you have authorisation to engage… Over!" Firin momentarily left his weapon's sight, he was greatly confused and disturbed by the change in Order made from the Command post. He looked again through his scope over the innocent faces before him, all looked so happy in their lives and none looked to be a threat.

"I read, though please clarify…" Commanded Firin hesitantly. "I have the Alpha-Target in sight…is *he* to be eliminated… Over?" Firin's breathing became rapid whilst an anxiety steadily rose in him. He loosened his grip slightly from the rifle's trigger and started to tremble, something which had yet felt so foreign to him during previous missions.

"You are to engage *all*, SNFN!" Screamed a Commander's voice, it broke easily through the crackles of Firin's transmitter. "All threats must be terminated... men, women and children! They are terrorist sympathisers and you have authorisation from the highest level to action this Order... complete your mission now, SNFN!" This cold confirmation gave rise to a swift conflict in Firin, anguish swiftly took hold over him, as his worst fears were now realised. Firin clasped the transmitter tightly in his hands again and this time yelled into it, enraged by such a calculated and evil judgement.

"I will eliminate the Alpha-Target! I didn't sign up to commit genocide!" Firin shook in dread; he had always been so patriotic and this act of defiance, he knew, would cost him dearly. "That was my Order and I'm taking it... OVER!" A steady stream of white-noise fed through Firin's transmitter in response. He waited impatiently for a few minutes, hoping that the commanding officers had reconsidered their unwise tactics. Firin soon gave up in waiting, he placed his rifle slowly upon the sands beneath and, with trembling fingers, proceeded to remove his weighted body armour away from him. In a pure display of anger, Firin then threw his transmitter across the sand dunes. Up until this moment, the experienced sniper had killed many times before, though only to save himself or fellow soldiers, not to wipe out an entire tribe of innocent people in cold blood. Crackling eventually resonated again from the transmitter, despite being partially buried within a dense heap of sand.

"So, SNFN... you have chosen exile... OPEN FIRE!" Crackled the transmitter.

"I don't want to watch this..." Said Firin to the disembodied presence, praying for them to heed his request. "This was the worst day in my life." Firin's transmitter fell eerily silent as he leant himself down to collect his beloved rifle, at this point he was totally lost within his own dire thoughts. Firin slowly began an arduous trek back over the southern desert plains and as he walked over the dunes higher summit, a horrific and familiar sound entered the sky above. In an instant moment of panic, Firin threw himself upon the sands beneath, placing his hands firmly over his ears to protect them from what he knew was about to occur. Several metallic arrows flew from the west where Firin's Commanders were posted, each shimmering in a brilliant reflection from the midday sun as they descended before the Talam's city walls. The tribespeople below observed in wonder as the strange objects approached them and then, in a moment of sudden despair, they fell under the missile explosions which tore cruelly across the small encampment - engulfing it instantly within a sea of flames.

"Bastards!" Cried out Firin in torment. "They were innocent, how could you slaughter them all like that?" He clasped onto his rifle tenderly, being an only element of comfort now. A thick wave of smoke rose from the attack zone that burned painfully at Firin's eyes, the stench from cooking flesh scorched within his lungs and the lasting silence continued to haunt him for many years after. Firin hastened himself over the desert plains, away from the horrific image of slaughter and adamant that he would now leave the life of servitude behind him. "Never again, will I spill innocent blood..."

"You have witnessed much death and grief, Firin - Son of Talam. Feel no guilt, for your redemption is now at hand. Face the Eternal Darkness… I will aid you as I can."

Spero himself had surrendered his body into a nightmarish scenario, only after an array of blinding light enraptured him to enforce a spiritual awakening - unlike anything he had encountered before. Spero soon found himself standing upon a narrow, wooden jetty that spanned out far into the great lake of Tinomar. The surroundings looked no different to how they had been during Spero's childhood. He quickly closed his eyes, savouring the treasured sounds and scents now lingering around him.

"Is this death?" Thought Spero. "If it is… this isn't too bad." Heavy footsteps began to approach Spero from behind; each one reverberated across the aged, wooden structure, though no fear came by them and soon they passed by. Spero observed within a silent joy as his beloved brother raced past him to throw himself into the emerald waters of Tinomar's majestic lake, performing their favourite past-time without showing any sign of acknowledgment – at first. Spero's brother strangely landed upon the lake's surface and started to dance gleefully upon it, on seeing his brother the boy smiled back and waved back frivolously. "Stevian?" Stuttered Spero in disbelief. "Is that… really you?"

The sun suddenly started to set, radiating with it a golden ray of light that shone upon the lake making its waters appear as if they were aflame. Spero shed a solemn tear on seeing his younger brother acting so carefree again and, in an instant, he ran across the jetty to meet with him. "Stevian, I am here… come to me little brother!" Shouted Spero frantically through his hands, praying that the words would carry over Tinomar's vast lake. "I'm here for you…please come to me, Stevian! It'll be dark soon… we need to go home!" Stevian rolled his eyes in objection to his brother's demand and continued to carry on dancing. After showing some reluctance, the child then walked back towards Spero, slowly stepping before him whilst both looked to one another with a powerful, loving stare.

"Come on Stevian, let's go home…" Pleaded Spero as he held out a longing hand for his little brother to grasp onto. "You know how dangerous it can be out here when it gets dark, let's go home where we'll be safe…okay?"

"Home… is safe?" Questioned the young boy naively. "Home… is… safe?" Spero felt a sudden sickness overpower him; there was something dark held in the atmosphere of this scene that felt all too familiar to him and in a severely concerning way. He looked cautiously beyond where Stevian stood towards the darkening landscape, searching for any threats that could be hiding themselves from them, though none appeared yet.

"Don't let go of my hand, Stevian." Said Spero firmly. "There are bad people who would want to hurt you around."

"Home... is safe." Replied the child with a vacant expression. "...Safe..."
Finally, the two brothers entered the small village where their family's cottage
was situated. Spero noticed how the streets were surprisingly barren, their
lamps all extinguished, bringing to him a foreboding sense of dread that grew
with each passing second. "You look scared, Spero... why?" Questioned
Stevian innocently. Spero remained silent as they both approached their home,
finding that its small gate was already ajar, and their front door was left wide
open – evidently forced away from its hinges.

"Stay close, Stevian." Spero clenched onto his brother protectively. "I don't
want for you to get hurt..." He then slowly entered through the broken
doorway, unsure of what dreadful scene may meet with him. A dim flicker of
candlelight shone from within the dining room, nothing seemed unordinary yet,
though Spero quickly felt an urge to call out for his parents in need of their
reassurance. "Mother, Father... where are you and what is going on in here?"
"Home... is safe." Mumbled Stevian again, his voice now sounded so weak
and frail. "Our home... our Sanctuary." Without warning, a masked intruder
appeared from behind and grabbed at Stevian by his hair, dragging the resisting
child away from Spero into a truly dismal setting. "Don't hurt him!" Cried out
Spero in desperation. He tried frantically to aid his little brother, but had
somehow become paralysed now, an invisible barrier seemingly stood between
him and his little brother. "Take it easy and let go of him." Begged Spero. "Let
go of my little brother now, or I swear that I'll kill you!" The intruder abruptly
dragged Stevian further into the dining room; where its furniture had been
upturned and walls desecrated with., what appeared to be, bloodstains.
"Coward! Leave my brother alone!" Screamed Spero. "I'll make you regret
this!"

The invisible barrier subsided and as he ventured into the dining room
himself, Spero came across a scene that would haunt him for the rest of his life.
He looked down on his parents' bodies which were strewn lifelessly upon the
floor, their hands and legs bound with crude ropes, their blood pooling around
them. The masked stranger now shook at Stevian, forcing the hysterical child
onto his knees to bathe in the congealed blood of his murdered parents.

"Please, don't hurt my little brother." Spero stammered as he pleaded with
the stranger, who in turn gave him no acknowledgment. "What threat is he to
you... what threat would he be to anyone?" The wicked intruder persisted in
blatantly ignoring Spero; whilst reaching for a small, rusted blade that lay
hidden inside their tattered waistcoat. A violent, anguished scream then left
from Spero's lungs, as he reluctantly watched Stevian's throat being slit before
him - the blunt blade magnifying his torture. "Barbarian!" Seethed Spero, he
frantically reached down to comfort his brother. "You killed them, and for
what... a few silver coins hidden on the mantelpiece." He gasped. "That's all
my family were worth to you... *five silver coins*!" Spero collapsed onto the
blood-soaked floor beside Stevian, emotionally drained and scarred by the
bitter memories that still saturated themselves within his guilt-ridden
conscience. "Our home *was* our Sanctuary." Whimpered Spero tearfully. "It
should have been safe!"

"It was not your only Sanctuary though was it, Spero?"

Spero jolted in shock as the phantom child spoke once again to him.
"No, it wasn't." Responded Spero vacantly. "I ran away after this… the Acolytes of Water took me in."

"You ran from them too… but why?"

"Are you… a Spirit?" Snapped Spero nervously. "I'm guessing that you are?" A blinding flash then filled the room in its entirety. Spero adjusted his eyes slowly to find amongst the hazy scene a hooded child, who had knelt themselves lowly before him.

"You only stayed at the Sanctuary of Water for a few weeks… home to you is not safe, is it?"

"I joined the Hydranian naval force as soon as I could." Replied Spero in honesty, fearing that the Spirit would sense a lie otherwise. "That way, I had no one to protect… no one to provide for… I only had myself to worry about."

"But you did worry. You cared for those whom you served alongside – your Sisters and Brothers at arms. Had you not lost your sense of time, upon the lake that night, your family's fate would have also been your own to suffer and this you know… to be true."

"I've survived when others should have, what makes me so worthy?" Dwelled Spero resentfully. "It's not fair…"

"Have you too forgotten… like Cara has?"

The child's cloak emanated with a golden light that sharply cast itself against Spero's vision, he could sense the spiritual might within it and greatly dreaded what vision may surface afterwards. As the heavenly light diminished, Spero found himself looking upon the vast ocean which lay just before Hydrania; he was stood aboard a military vessel, which the naval officer had come to know and love so well over many years in serving on it.

"What darkened memory are you going to force on me now?" Questioned Spero despairingly, as he stared across the transient ocean waves in reminiscence. "What did you mean, when you said had I *forgotten like Cara has*? I haven't forgotten anything, I just didn't want to…" A resounding alarm blared over Spero's vessel, it warned of an imminent attack and was a noise that he still fearfully reacted to. Spero felt totally helpless now; he was being dragged by an unknown force across the ship's deck, eventually placing him before the image of his own, younger self. It was a harrowing experience, one that Spero recognised in an instant.

"What's going on?" Shouted the ship's crew members to one another, whilst preparing themselves for this unexpected attack. "Who's attacking us?"

"General Nira…" Uttered Spero in dread to himself, his younger presence had no knowledge of this revelation at the time however. "That's who it was." The Hydranian vessel's megaphone suddenly sparked into life; it was Spero's Captain, who then began to explain the reasons behind these anticipatory manoeuvres.

"Attention! Attention! Magmorran warship sighted! Attention!"

Spero recounted this memory well, every fine detail of it, even down to how his fellow crew members each reacted. In fact, Spero watched on in contentment as he replayed the moments leading up to a truly fateful encounter. He stood by the younger image of himself and both looked out towards Magmorrah's northern shoreline; observing just before it a single, battered vessel which seemed to be fleeing from a far more advanced version of itself towards them.

"Disengage! Possible civilian-vessel sighted! Hold fire!"

Spero wrapped his fingers around the deck-railings in anticipation; yearning for a closer look across the turbulent ocean waves, longing for this surreal vision to replay a pivotal moment in his life that he had reminisced over repeatedly now for so long.

"Come to me, let me see you as I did back then." Whispered Spero to himself in a desperate voice. The civilian boat was struggling against a relentless onslaught of cannon fire, which continued to cruelly reign down from the pursuing Magmorran warship behind. Leading the attack was General Nira, she relished in the carnage being created and cackled maliciously after each given command. "You may have forgotten, Cara… but I haven't."

"Hold Fire! Let them pass! Only attack if they enter our waters!"

Spero greatly despaired at his Captain's Order; the smaller boat had no chance in escaping from its monstrous predator and here he was, being told to do absolutely nothing about it. The young naval officer acted on his own instinct despite any possible consequence, he quickly severed a lever that was connected to one of the many intercepting speedboats - each attached to his warship's starboard side. Spero then threw himself into the boat as it lowered, ignoring several pleas from his fellow crew members and Captain who all begged against his present actions.

"Man over-board! Man over-board! Do NOT engage Magmorran Warship!"

Spero clumsily ignited his speedboat's engine and adrenaline proceeded to course through him, as he accelerated towards the strange scene playing out ahead. The agile speedboat proved to be far more advanced with its speed, for Spero soon caught up parallel alongside the fleeing vessel. Aboard it, Spero could just make out the figure of a young woman, she was clad in silken, black robes that flowed freely around her from the surrounding high-winds.

"Come about!" Screamed Spero, in attempt to reach the cowering woman. "Get in *my* boat... it's faster and the Magmorran ship is close now!" He happened to also notice, that as the woman was clasping onto her ship's steering wheel with one hand, in the other was something hidden that she held tightly against her chest - as if protecting it from the bitter air currents. "Jump aboard mine... NOW!" The woman suddenly noticed Spero and looked to him with a puzzled expression, she had never known kindness and was concerned as to what his true intentions were. After another cautious glance, she revealed from under her silken robes a small infant who appeared blissfully unaware of the chaos going on around them.

"Please, get in my boat!" Cried out Spero, though more firmly this time on seeing the vulnerable child. "It's your only chance to escape that ship... please!"

"Okay! Okay!" Responded the woman anxiously, she looked back again towards the Magmorran warship. "Come closer, sir... you are too far away!"

"Keep your speed as it is... *I'll* move in!" Commanded Spero, he then carefully navigated for the two vessels to join alongside each other. The woman, now holding onto her young child even tighter, threw herself precariously aboard Spero's boat. "Praise be... I thought you'd never jump!"

"Hold fire! Civilian in sight! Hold fire!"

Spero shuddered on hearing his Captain's voice again; he knew that it was too late to turn back, he knew that a deserter's welcome would only meet with him now. The woman had nestled her child protectively against herself and again shielded them both with her long robes, uttering no word at all to Spero as she did.

"My name is Spero," He stuttered to the shrouded figure. "I'm a naval officer from Hydrania's Royal Fleet… please, don't be scared of me." Spero glanced back nervously, finding to his dismay that the Hydranian warship had now barred their enemy's path. "I will take you now to wherever it was you were going…" He frowned. "Where *were* you going to?" The woman slowly removed her robes away to speak with Spero.

"Thank you… for saving me and my daughter!" Replied the woman in a strained voice, and then she bowed herself respectfully towards Spero. "My name is Cara and, if I'm being honest, I really don't know where I was going to. All I wanted, was to escape from… her!" Cara pointed frantically at the Magmorran warship, which was now aiming itself against the Hydranian vessel.

"Her?" Asked Spero with a puzzled expression. "Who are you on about… who *is* chasing you?"

"General Nira!" Cried out Cara in agony, her entire body trembled. "I've been branded a traitor of Magmorrah, Queen Cera sentenced me and my little girl to death." She looked intently to Spero with pleading eyes. "Please, just take us anywhere they won't think to look for us!"

"Viridia is your safest bet… there are miles of forests where you could both hide in those lands." Replied Spero vacantly. Cara's innate beauty truly astounded him, her unusual amber eyes seemed to radiate with a haunting presence of which he had never seen before. "I just hope, you know what you're doing?"

"I had to leave, for Sophilia's sake," Explained Cara, as stroked at her child's brow tenderly. "I couldn't let them hurt her." The infant and her mother looked so alike through their shared angelic features, they served as a calming presence to Spero at this moment which he greatly needed. "Please, hurry! Take us anywhere!"

"Alert! Alert! Enemy vessel approaching! To your Battle stations! Alert! Alert!"

The Hydranian warship raised its alarms for an offensive attack to be made against Magmorrah's opposing force, though sadly there was little time to avert the current threat. General Nira screamed in torment on her ship, as she watched Queen Cera's nemesis escape from view. Nira then directed her scorn at the Hydranian warship, which she immediately ordered to be fired upon. A volley of Magmorran incendiaries flew into the air and they landed precisely on the Hydranian warship, tearing apart its structure and leaving its crew members aboard to die like slaughtered animals.

"What have I done?" Gasped Spero mournfully, as he looked back across the sea towards Nira's decimation. "Cara, I will take you to Viridia and then I must return to Hydrania. Are you sure that you and your child will be okay there?"

"We'll be fine," replied Cara with a defiant smile. "I have studied Viridia's landscape and the way of life its people have… we'll be safe there. I know we will." She kissed Sophilia gently on her cheek, as not to disturb the sleeping child. "What will happen to you though, won't they ask about your ship, when you return to Hydrania?"

"I'll… just lie to my Commanding Officers." Reasoned Spero hesitantly. "I'll just say, that there was a malfunction… that the ship sunk, and it was an accident. I can't imagine General Nira being honest with her Queen about what has happened today… maybe I'll get away with it?"

"You sacrificed so much for a person you had never met before…"

Spero's boat finally made it ashore upon the earthly banks of Viridia. He carefully aided Cara and Sophilia from the small vessel, comforting both as best he could - in face of the trial which they had all only just managed to survive together.

"Are you okay, Cara… how is your baby doing?" Asked Spero with sincerity, as he slowly pulled away the robes shielding Sophilia's face to look upon her. "Beautiful, she's just like her mother." Cara blushed awkwardly in response.

"Yes, we're fine now… Thanks." She said bashfully. "I appreciate you helping me and my little girl escape, though I'm so sorry that you have lost your ship and friends in doing so." She then began to weep softly. "I didn't want anyone to get hurt by running away… this is awful." Spero shook his head at Cara dismissively.

"It wasn't you that attacked my ship; it was General Nira and her soldiers," assured Spero. "And *they* will pay for what has happened to my comrades." He quickly removed his Officer's waistcoat to wrap it around Cara's shaking body. "Get that thought out of your head right now, you've done nothing wrong! Nothing! You and your baby are safe here and that's all that matters."

"Such selfless actions, for a man who wishes to love no one…"

"Maybe, Viridia will give us the new life which I have always dreamed of?" pondered Cara timidly, a pleasant smile formed on her face as she stared back upon Sophilia. "This will be our home now, my darling Lia. You will never have to suffer like I did, back in Magmorrah… Never."

"Might I suggest, that you head north from here?" Suggested Spero in a more serious tone. "You need to get away from the southern shoreline, just in case General Nira returns." He stood himself away from Cara to look upon the ash clouds that lingered over Magmorrah. "Queen Cera is after-all… famously stubborn."

"I will and thank you again." Muttered Cara tearfully, she herself could not look back upon Magmorrah's haunting shadow. "It was so hard at first to leave, but to find that there are people like you out here, who are willing to help total strangers… you have rekindled a hope in me that I thought was lost."

"Where there is light, there is darkness… Where there is darkness there is light. Face the Eternal Darkness, Spero… I will aid you as I can."

In her own spiritual vision, Cara found herself falling into a pool of rising flames and a relentless pain tore itself instantly through her flesh. She screamed out in desperation for mercy, whilst the flames sank deeper into her being, eventually forming into an endless pit of darkness that then seemed to surround Cara entirely.

"Your past… it causes you this much pain, Cara?"

The malicious agony that had surged through Cara's body gradually began to fade. As she slowly opened her eyes, Cara now discovered that she had been taken to the familiarity of her childhood dwellings - Magmorrah's Royal Palace.
"Who are you… Why have you brought me here?" Muttered Cara in confusion. The voice speaking to her sounded so innocent, she reasoned that it couldn't possibly have been the source of all the pain she had just endured. "What do you want from me?"

"Where there is darkness, there is light… there… is… light…"

Cara watched reservedly over the fleeting images of her secluded youth that now flashed before her eyes, each seemed so pointless in their depressive replay – she felt. The mother whom Cara would never come to know, glanced by within a swift second and she tried in vain to hold onto the image, wishing to observe and savour her features.
"Mother?" Sighed Cara dismally. "I never even met her once… she didn't look at all like me anyway." The dogmatic years of tutorage from Cara's various nannies and teachers morphed through their countless incarnations - none of which held any true endearment to her. She breathed gladly, as the unwanted memories passed by in an apparent merciful swiftness, though despair soon set in again. The random flashing images began to form into one, gradually displaying a horrific image of Cara's tyrannical father, despite her attempts to turn away from his sickening sight. "I do not wish to see that vile beast!" Seethed Cara hatefully. "Whoever's spell I am under, please…I beg you with all my heart and soul… do not force me to look upon this monster for a moment longer!"

"You have his regal eyes… Daughter of Kanaan."

"That is the only likeness which we share, that I am forever burdened with!" Cara tremored immensely as the imposing figure of Kanaan moved from her sight, though an equally dismal image quickly replaced him. Cara saw a new vision of herself during childhood, she was trying to escape from her stately bedroom to look upon her new-born sister – a meeting King Kanaan had strictly forbade.

"Cera! I want to see my little sister!" Demanded the young Cara in frustration to the unsympathetic Guards placed outside her room, who themselves had never uttered a single word of comfort to the lonely princess. "I *love* Baby Cera! Why won't you let me see her… Why won't Daddy let me see her?" The harrowing vision only revealed to Cara the malicious extent of solitude that she had needed to endure throughout her childhood, her younger reflection now morphed through the many years spent in this forced isolation - within her own royal household.

"Where there is darkness, there is light…"

Cara continued to silently watch her younger self study within the Palace's library; where she came to learn of Impartia's other lands and cultures, a world cruelly hidden away from her by Kanaan. The king's ignorance, towards his daughter's own free-will and longed-for desires, had controlled Cara's life more than she had ever come to realise – until now.

"Such heartache caused by my own father's doing…" Whispered Cara bitterly. "I wish to forget these memories, why are you forcing me to witness them all again?" She asked to the unknown force possessing her. A gentle and loving warmth suddenly responded to Cara.

"You have suffered a great deal, Princess Cara. You were born into a life of great wealth, yet you were so poor in its true beauty and essence. This suffering, of which you have valiantly fought against, will aid countless others like yourself in coping with their own daily plights – one day."
A surge of heavenly clouds then surrounded Cara and, as they eventually dispersed, they revealed the much-awaited first encounter with her younger sister – Cera. Cara's breathing became laboured and she clenched her fists tightly in preparation for the scene ahead, knowing with dread how it sadly played out that day.

"Cera, I mean… Your Majesty." Stammered Cara nervously, as she knelt herself before the newly-anointed monarch. "I am *so* glad to see you after such a long wait… you can't imagine how often I have dreamed of this moment, where I would finally get to meet you!" She held out her arms, willing for Cera's embrace, though the Queen remained emotionless in her own response.

"How *dare* you display such false adoration to me, *Sister!*" Scorned Cera, whilst tenderly rubbing her fingertips over Kanaan's accursed amulet. "Love is a reverent weakness, something which this world already accepts far too easily!" Cera then looked upon Cara in further detest, Kanaan's teachings had indefinitely corrupted her. "Father *was* right about you! Cara, you are so weak and feeble... a disgrace to this crown and our righteous bloodline! You have served your one and only true purpose, wretch..." The Queen looked down upon Cara's swollen stomach, her sister had only given birth a matter of days ago. "You are hereby released of your Royal privileges and are to await judgement for the treacherous actions that have been made against me!"

"Cera... Why are you being like this?" Despaired Cara. "How have I committed treason?" She screamed fearfully.

"The mark upon your face... that is how!" Screamed Cera violently, as she nestled her fingertips around Kanaan's amulet. "You would usurp me of my throne, wouldn't you?"

"No! Never!" Screamed Cara back in sincerity. "You are Magmorrah's Queen... not I."

Cera formed a malicious grin, on seeing her Dark Acolytes enter the throne room and they too looked upon Cara with a nauseating expression.

"Take Cara back to her chambers!" Ordered Cera coldly. "Tomorrow she is to be removed from this Palace and held at the Sanctuary of Darkness... Kufiah can deal with her then."

"I will always love you, Cera." Declared Cara in defiance. "Even if you do not feel the same way about me..."

"Do you still hold a place in your heart for Cera? Surely, Cara... you must know by now, that your sister is beyond any means of redemption? Her fate has been decided by the Celestial bodies, who watch over you mortals from on high in Eternamorrah..."

"Must we all be doomed by our past actions in such a way?" Replied Cara, as she violently shook her head in dismissal against the Spirit's revelations. "Cera is only the way she is, because of our father's hatred and ill-guidance. My sister knows no different, and I don't see why she alone should be condemned for Kanaan's corrupt teachings!" Implored Cara, whilst the emanating light intensified to penetrate itself deeper within her spiritual being.

"You have been chosen to renew Impartia's Sacred Balance, Cara. This world needs you so desperately now, why do you not value your own resilience and vital importance in changing the unfortunate acts - which your family have cursed us with? Your despairing words will amount to futile nothingness when faced against the Eternal Darkness, it is growing stronger over these lands and soon it will await you here... at my Sanctum."

"I am ready to face Cera *and* Kufiah!" Screamed Cara boldly. "I am ready to end the evil misery which has befallen Impartia under their reign! I know, though it burdens me, that I must free your spirit so that together we can then end this vicious cycle of death." She closed her eyes to sense the risen spiritual presence within. "I am ready to meet you… Alaskia."

"Are you? Are you honestly prepared to look upon me?"

"Yes!" shouted Cara firmly. "I have all the Elemental Passwords… I can free you now!"

"It will not be that simple, my child. Cerebrante's host, though blinded by rage, was careful in concealing me from ever returning to the physical plain…"

Cara pondered heavily on Alaskia's words; in them she sensed a dire warning but did not yet have the courage to confront the Celestial Spirit about this. Instead, Cara focused again on Sophilia, on being reunited with her.

"I will do whatever it takes to protect my daughter, she means everything to me." Whimpered Cara sorrowfully. "I still don't understand, how we have both been dragged into this war… it's not fair on either of us."

"Yes, it is unfair… but you are the key to my freedom and Cerebrante's resurgence. It is time that accepted your role within this world, Cara. You are a pivotal in it… after-all. You will face the Eternal Darkness and I will aid you as I can. Now…open your eyes…"

Chapter Twelve: Between the Darkness and Light

Cara opened her eyes as Alaskia had instructed and now found herself kneeling upon a familiar-looking, though seemingly grander, Sanctum platform. It was held inside the mountain's inner-core; a vast chamber made of numerous crystals that had streams of light flowing through them, though they sadly cast their beauty into an endless pit of darkness below. Within the Sanctum platform, stood two prominent pinnacles that appeared to be fashioned from Obsidian, and seemed so out of place in this sacred dwelling.

"Is that the 'Void' which Ven spoke of?" Contemplated Cara, as she peered into the endless abyss. "Is *this*... Alaskia's prison?"

"Hey, Cara!" Shouted Spero from behind with a beaming smile. "I'm so glad you're okay, how did we get here?"

"I feel sick," responded Firin with a nauseous groan, tears were still present on his face from Alaskia's vision. "None of this is natural..."

"It's like we're in totally different world." Responded Cara in awe of her surroundings. "I think this is it... Alaskia's Sanctum." Cara, Firin and Spero looked on in astonishment to one another, as within their hands they somehow each held a silver shield and sword - seemingly granted to them freely by the Celestial spirit of Alaskia after their ruminations with him.

"Alaskia said that he would help me..." Said Cara, unlike her companions she threw her gifted weapons to the ground in disgust. "Why would we need these?

"We must have been given them for a reason, Cara... it's obvious that Alaskia knows something which we don't yet." Commented Spero apprehensively, whilst admiring his new sword. "It's so light yet strong," He swung the sword around in a child-like joy. "Even if we don't need to use our weapons... I'm keeping mine."

"Did you both see and feel things, just now... from your past?" Stammered Firin fearfully, hoping that his friends suffered a similar and disturbing hallucination as he himself had. "I saw my grandfather... and other less pleasant memories."

"Yes, I did Firin." Replied Spero, as he gave a longing glance towards Cara. "It was like living inside a dream, but it felt so real. I saw times gone by which I never wished to see again, though some could have gone on a little longer than they did..." He smiled awkwardly to Cara, who in turn reflected his loving stare back to him, with the feeling of a forgotten familiarity now re-emerging between them.

"I would rather not talk about what I saw... it's too painful." Muttered Cara, as she walked closer towards the Sanctum's central seal. "I just want to free Alaskia, then find a way out of this place... Sophilia must be so scared. I dread to think what Cera has done with her."

"Where *is* Alaskia anyway?" Despaired Spero. "This platform is floating over an abyss and there aren't any passageways... I don't understand!" He kicked at his feet in frustration, a feeling now shared between each of the companions. "Why were we brought here?" Something abruptly drew Cara's attention upwards; situated above was a gigantic mystical spectacle, a cosmic display that lingered high above within the mountain's very summit.

"What is that?" Gasped Cara, the sea of stars and many galaxies above entranced her immediately. "It's amazing!"

"Do you think that it might be a portal?" Asked Spero, as he lowered his weapons in shock. "We are in a Sanctuary, aren't we?" He bemused.

"I'm not looking at that for a moment longer," enforced Firin with a displeased expression, he chose to instead look upon his own reflection in the shield gifted by Alaskia. "I'm creeped out enough as it is!"

"I don't think it's creepy at all," Countered Cara with a faint chuckle. "there's an ancient feeling in here... I kind of like it." The Celestial bodies spread out infinitely above, as if they were in a dance between the ever-lasting darkness and Light which bonded them together. Cara reluctantly tore her sights away from the captivating lights to look back across Firin and Spero, seeing that they had both already removed their interest from the peculiar spectacle above. "I think there is more to this mountain, than it just being Alaskia's prison." Remarked Cara, she placed herself before Spero. "Do you think so?" Spero shifted his eyes away from Cara nervously.

"What do you mean, Cara?" Questioned Spero apprehensively. "The Elemental Guardians told us that this is Alaskia's Sanctum of Light... why would it be anything else?" He quickly looked across to Firin for his support. "What do you think, Firin?"

"I *really* don't care!" Snapped Firin with a sudden shrug. He moved towards the platforms edge, then instantly recoiled in fear. "Can we find Alaskia now?"

"There is no way of getting in here physically, we were only permitted to enter by a Celestial Spirit. "Pondered Cara openly, she then paced around the platform in attempt of clarifying her thoughts. "Below us is the 'Void' of Kufiah and above is 'Eternamorrah' – Alaskia's realm." Cara looked up once more towards the cosmic vision. "It's all starting to make sense!"

"Impressive... very impressive!"

"That voice, it didn't sound like Alaskia did when he spoke with me." Stuttered Spero anxiously, as he raised his sword against the phantom threat. "Say the Elemental Passwords, Cara... get us out of here!" He said with an enforcing gesture.

"I don't know what to do, Spero!" Cried out Cara in anguish. "The Guardians, they did not tell me what to say!" She despaired.

"Just repeat what they said to you," suggested Firin frantically. "Try anything...just be quick!"

"Okay!" Breathed Cara, as she closed her eyes and focused on the four Elemental Guardians, their wisdom and spiritual presences. "Bid me, Cara, to enter thine Divine Sanctum!" Upon the central seal, an explosive burst of flames erupted that transcended between each of the elemental colours - blue, silver, green and red. However, the flames died out as soon as they came, leaving only an empty space between the obsidian pinnacles where Cara had hoped for Alaskia's emergence.

"I don't get it... shouldn't we be seeing Alaskia now?" Remarked Spero, with an expression of dismay and anger. "What are the Guardians playing at?"

"Moah said something strange to Ven and myself in Hydrania," said Cara anxiously. "He mentioned something about there being Guardians of Light and Darkness... what if I needed their passwords too?"

"You *are* joking?" Firin could not hide his angst for a moment longer. "This is getting ridiculous; how many Guardians are there in this world?"

"There are many others, foolish mortal... though you are not worthy of their powers!"

Cara, Firin and Spero jolted and quickly huddled themselves together in protection against the disembodied menace. The entire mountain seemed to shudder, and a series of flashing lights then ensued inside of its Sanctum. Without any further warning, came the sound of slow clapping which reverberated around the crystal walls in aim towards Cara and her cowering friends.

"I – Illuminecia, Guardian of Light – do NOT bid your welcome into to my Master Spirit's Sanctum... in the name of King Kanaan... In the name of Cerebrante's true host!"

After a lengthier flash of blinding light, the figure of an unnaturally-tall woman revealed herself before Cara and her companions – Illuminecia. She wore a long-flowing, ivory dress which was majestically adorned with golden leaves that spanned out across her entire breadth. Illuminecia's eyes shone with a permeating white light, each deathly pale in colour like her translucent skin, they were notably piercing and radiated far across the Sanctum platform. Illuminecia's silver hair slithered down her arms and back like a serpent, preparing to pounce on its prey at any given moment. On the Guardian of Light's left wrist was a golden bracelet, it looked to be crudely fashioned and burned into her flesh – something which Cara noticed almost immediately.

"You were very close with your assumptions there, puny mortal." Cackled Illuminecia maliciously. "Though, I'm afraid to say that you are gravely mistaken, and in so many ways!" The supposed Guardian then hovered herself somehow in mid-air to study Cara's features from a safer distance, she then instantly recoiled on seeing Cerebrante's distinctive mark. "A False-Prophet! How *dare* you defile this Sanctuary!"

"Be careful, Cara!" Shouted Spero. He tried to reach out for her, but an invisible force seemingly barred his way. "I can't move!"

"If I am a False-Prophet... then tell me how, Illuminecia?" Countered Cara defiantly, in ignorance towards her friend's objections. "For a Spirit Guardian... you are not very pleasant, are you?" Illuminecia continued to cackle and snarl, sounding so strangely alike to Queen Cera's own voice.

"The Void that lies beneath us, is the realm where chaos lies and in there all soulless creatures are bound to an eternity of damnation." Illuminecia rose her arms towards the colourful portal overhead. "The cosmic display above, is a sacred gateway into the everlasting realm of Eternamorrah; a dimension where all blessed life travels to, once it is extinguished upon this earthly plain." She continued to stare at Cara with a hateful expression. "Cerebrante – The Guardian of Impartia's Sacred Balance – has only one true host... my King... *your* father... Kanaan!" The king's name echoed hauntingly throughout the Sanctum, resonating Illuminecia's rage and disturbed mindset along with it.

"Kanaan is DEAD!" Cried out Cara in a jubilant manner. "I have come here to free Alaskia... to end the suffering which my father and sister have forced on this world!"

Illuminecia tilted her head gently to one side, as if in a show of sympathy towards Cara. Her attention then turned back against the Sanctum's central seal, where up to now nothing had yet appeared.

"Young fool, I am Alaskia's Guardian... I alone protect Impartia against the Eternal Darkness and calamity of Kufiah!" Declared Illuminecia in a gravelled voice. "King Kanaan granted me this sacred duty, to him and Cerebrante I hold my allegiance, now... and forever."

"No offense, but... you don't come across as someone who is meant to represent the light in this world?" Stated Firin as he moved himself into a proud stance, despite his obvious fear. "Are you not aware, Guardian of Light, that the Queen of Magmorrah wants Alaskia dead and has the Spirit of Darkness under her control now?" He licked at his lips anxiously. "Cera is making her way here, *right now*, to destroy the Spirit of Light – your own Master Spirit! You of all people should be doing something to stop her!" Firin turned to Cara and smiled reassuringly. "If you really are Alaskia's Guardian... then help Cara to free the Spirit!"

"Firin is right!" Agreed Spero passionately. "You don't seem at all concerned, Illuminecia. I don't think you are the true Guardian of Light... I think, that it is *you* who is the imposter here!"

"INFIDELS! HEATHENS" Screeched the Guardian with all her might. "You are wrong... Magmorrah's Royal bloodline *is* divine... I am divine... my King and Queen Cera are both blessed souls!" Illuminecia hissed again in detest against Cara. "You would usurp them, *traitor*! You would will chaos upon Impartia!"

"She's lost the plot!" Gasped Firin amusingly to Cara and Spero, as he lifted his sword towards Illuminecia. "Listen to me, crazy bitch... give Cara your password, free Alaskia and then we can all part ways, okay?"

"Blasphemer!" Screamed Illuminecia in response. "I will grant you no password... only your deaths!"

"Please, Illuminecia…" Implored Cara, in a more polite and gentile tone to Firin, whilst kneeling herself lowly before the deranged Guardian. "Cera will stop at nothing to kill Alaskia, which means that she will destroy you too. If you are the Guardian of Light, then it is your duty to protect them… to protect the Sacred Balance. Grant me your password… I beg of you!"

"Yet again, you are mistaken… Princess!" Cackled Illuminecia, with a mocking swipe of her hands. "King Kanaan is the rightful ruler over Impartia, he has chosen Queen Cera to be the one that releases me and Alaskia from this incarceration… *not you!*" Suddenly a golden stream of energy flowed from Illuminecia's heart, up through her arms to form into a golden spear and shield, which she then aimed intently against the three companions.

"You are lost in corruption!" Cried out Spero, as he placed himself in front of Cara to protect her. "Queen Cera is pure evil, if you wish to fight us… then go ahead!"

"Look at her wrist, Spero!" Gasped Cara in desperation, as she pointed it out to him. "That bracelet looks just like the amulet Cera wears… Illuminecia is under a curse!"

"Cursed or not, she's going DOWN!" Roared Firin, as he swung his blade under where Illuminecia's floated. "You'll give Cara your password soon enough!" Illuminecia laughed wickedly, basking in the delight of her aggressor's ignorance. She landed upon the Sanctum platform heavily. Cara and her friends stared at their new enemy in uncertainty; none of them knew how to defeat a Spirit Guardian, let alone one who obviously far more powerful than they were.

"Look above and below you now, Mortals!" Commanded Illuminecia, as she swung her spear in rage against the three companions. "I shall free you all from the physical burden of life to graciously allow you into Eternamorrah *or* the Void, for it is time… to repent for your sins." Firin and Spero eagerly nodded to one another and placed themselves into an offensive stance. Illuminecia echoed her laughter once more across the Sanctum chamber, as she too moved into an attack position, focusing her sights solely on Cara who reluctantly cowered behind her two devoted friends.

"We're going nowhere, you're the one that needs to beg forgiveness… Guardian!" Cried out Spero bravely. "You will not harm Cara… and you will not help Cera fulfil her sordid plan!"

"Why oppose me?" Countered Illuminecia with a perplexed grin. "Your death's will be swift… I can assure you of that!" She then lunged her spear fiercely at Firin who was stood the closest, still enraged by his earlier comments and intent on killing him with a single blow. Illuminecia unwittingly missed her mark, though only just, the Guardian's spear had swiped beside Firin's face to draw some blood slightly away from his flesh.

"Firin!" Screamed Spero frantically. He used this precious moment to mount his own attack against the corrupted Spirit, as he reached out to clasp her spear's hilt. "Attack her… NOW!" A burning sensation swiftly flowed through Spero; it surged across his body like electricity from the Guardian's godly weapon, willed by her own hatred. "No!" Spero then fell helplessly beneath Illuminecia, writhing in his insufferable agony whilst she cruelly snatched the spear away from his grip.

"You CANNOT defeat me!" The Guardian continued to glare upon Cara and then closed in on her to make a finishing move. "You have failed your father, Princess… you must pay for your lack of vision!" Firin swung his sword aggressively at Illuminecia, though she evaded each move with ease. The two continued to duel and with each parry made, the Guardian moved herself nearer to Cara's held position. Spero was powerless to intervene, the intense shockwaves persisted in tormenting his body from Illuminecia's spear, he tried to get up but fell back upon the platform each time.

"Firin, you can't fight her alone!" Screamed Cara. She raised her own sword against Illuminecia, though only for it to be blocked by the mighty Guardian. "Cera can't win… I must save my Sophilia!"

"I can sense so much pain in your memories!" Taunted Illuminecia. "My powers allow for me to delve into them… let me show you." She released a wave of spiritual energy into the three companions from her body; it focused on images from their pasts, both happier and sad times. "I can take them away… I can free you all!" She cackled cruelly.

"No!" Screamed the companions in unison.

"Don't rob of us of our memories!" Begged Cara, her body trembling with fear. "Please, Illuminecia… have mercy!"

"You have the darkest of memories, Princess." Muttered the Guardian callously. "I would have thought, that you of all would wish for their removal?" Suddenly, as if by a divine intervention, the Sanctum platform became shrouded within a dense plume of black smoke. All that was visible was a single, red light that flared intensely through the darkness.

"Sister…"

The disembodied voice was strangely recognisable to Cara and her friends, though it seemed more menacing and darker somehow. It was Moah, who now revealed himself as the smoke faded. He was stood prominently upon Kufiah's seal and was eagerly awaiting Illuminecia's own response to his arrival.

"You!" Screamed the Guardian of Light, in shock to Moah. "You would *dare* to enter my Sanctuary… the very Sanctum of Light itself?" Moah gleefully ignored Illuminecia's disgust in him. Instead, he chose to compassionately look over the familiar faces of his new companions, whom he had reluctantly betrayed back in Hydrania.

"My friends…" Sighed Moah tenderly. "It is time…for all of this to end."

"Moah, you're alive?" Gasped Cara in relief, as she strained to speak through her joyous tears. "How can this be… how did you ever manage to survive Kufiah's attack?" Illuminecia raised her brows inquisitively and then released some mocking laughter again. The Guardian then raised her spear towards Moah, moving her head side-to-side in acknowledgment of his obvious deceit.

"*He*… survive an attack from Kufiah?" Derided Illuminecia, as she glared towards Moah. "This wretch is the Guardian of Darkness, and no doubt a traitor… like yourselves!" She revelled in the passing moments of confusion and torment shared by each of the companions, as they each looked to Moah in anguish. "Explain yourself to them, I will enjoy this!"

"She's lying," said Spero hesitantly, as he shook his head in dismissal. "He would have told us, wouldn't you… Moah?" Cara wiped at her face wearily.

"Is she telling the truth; are you really a Guardian, Moah?" Stammered Cara in torment. She was wholly doubtful of Illuminecia's honesty, though this revelation still troubled Cara. "If you are Kufiah's Guardian, then why would you have helped us escape from Cera… why would you have betrayed your own Master Spirit?"

"Don't listen to her, Cara!" Blared Firin. He quickly repositioned himself back into an offensive pose; trying to judge between Illuminecia and Moah, as to who he should be really defending against. "She is trying to turn us against one another… don't let her!"

"Please… calm yourself, my friend." Implored Moah nervously to Firin. "Illuminecia is telling you the truth, as I should have done with you all from the very beginning." He gave a remorseful glance to Cara, Moah felt the greatest shame towards her by his actions. "I *am* the Guardian of Darkness, and Kufiah *is* my Master. I never wanted to betray any of you… but I had little choice." He could not dare witness the reactions of his friends, as they each turned to him in a painful astonishment.

"Betrayal is in your nature, is it not… Brother?" Sneered Illuminecia coldly to him. "Moah has committed many terrible atrocities during his life; allowing for Cera to become Queen of Magmorrah, is only one of them!"

"No, that can't be true!" Cried out Cara sorrowfully. "Moah is our friend, he helped us escape from The Sanctuary of Darkness and Kufiah!"

"Moah is no friend to any mortal, don't be so naïve." Taunted Illuminecia, whilst raising her spear again towards Cara. "He is nothing more than a slave to Queen Cera, a forsaken remnant of King Kanaan's benevolent rule." She then stabbed her spear hard into the solid stone beneath. "His life will soon come to its needful ending… as will yours."

"Please understand, Cara…you have been fed lies by the Elemental Guardians!" Gasped Moah hysterically. "You have been led to believe, that Alaskia can stop Queen Cera… but this cannot be done – not at this moment." He quickly stared upon Illuminecia with a knowing glance. "As long as Kanaan remains alive… Cerebrante cannot be reborn. Only the Spirit of Balance can truly restore Impartia, and for Alaskia to be released from their incarceration it must be done by the very power that placed him within it – Kufiah."

"What?" Breathed Cara in agony. "That would explain why nothing happened, after I broke the Elemental Seal."

"All lies!" Screeched Illuminecia scornfully. "Alaskia was imprisoned, so that the Magmorran bloodline could restore balance in this world. None of you have the right to defy King Kanaan, not even you... Moah!" She swiped her spear aggressively through the air again. "I will not allow it!"

"Our very existence, Illuminecia... is abhorrent." Said Moah in a pleading voice. "Cerebrante is the *true* Guardian over the Celestial Spirts – not us!" His voice strained painfully, as he looked back upon Cara and her friends again. "Forgive me, my friends... I had to find a way to free my master, for only Kufiah can release Alaskia from their accursed prison."

"I forgive you, Moah." Replied Cara tearfully. "But if Kufiah is under Cera's control, has our quest not already failed?"

"We forgive you, too." Responded Spero, as he and Firin both gave to Moah an affirmative nod. "Please tell us that Cara is wrong though... that we didn't suffer over the last few days for nothing."

"You will see..." Whispered Moah with a forced smile. He returned his stare back against Illuminecia, who herself was evidently disturbed by what the Guardian of Darkness had shared "All will be revealed soon. The prophecies of Alaskia and Kufiah shall come into being... there is no turning back now."

"Silence! I have had it with your nonsense, vile betrayer! King Kanaan is righteous, his reign... eternal!" Screamed Illuminecia. The corrupted Guardian's words resounded throughout the Sanctum chamber once more, as she threw her spear violently into its air. Illuminecia's blade swiftly pierced Firin through his side, he had only turned away from her for a split moment to concentrate on Moah. Firin looked to his wound, then fell heavily into a seeping pool of blood.

"No! FIRIN!" Cried out Cara in disbelief. She lay herself over him protectively, as he continued to writhe in distress from the invasive wound. Illuminecia's spear gradually vanished within Firin, and whilst its light faded, the weapon then suddenly re-forged within her cold hands. "No!"

"Kanaan's destiny must be fulfilled! None of you can leave this place... not with the knowledge you now have!" Illuminecia hastily reached out her free hand across the vulnerable companions again She filtered her spiritual powers back into them, yearning to find their happiest memories, desperate to obliterate each one. "Let me free you of your burdens!" The three friends instantly succumbed to the invisible force which now penetrated their skulls, each were helpless in their fight against losing some of their most-treasured memories. Firin tried desperately to keep his mind empty from Illuminecia's invasion, but his thoughts repeatedly turned to those of his grandfather; longing for his welcome, should he pass away during this horrific moment. The image of Firin's father-figure gradually began to fade through Illuminecia's powerful hold, however, it was soon broken by Moah who cast a wave of dark smoke around the companions to shield them all.

"Kanaan's poison has truly taken its toll on you, Sister." Spoke Moah bitterly to Illuminecia, as he slowly drew in the plumes of smoke towards his body. "Our time on Impartia has finally come to its end, I pray that you are ready for death... as I am." Illuminecia laughed sadistically in disapproval. "We cannot die... we are immortal, Brother!"

"That is a wrong, that I shall now right...." Said Moah proudly. He breathed in a deep breath to focus himself, his eyes suddenly sank within a shroud of darkness and his robes flowed like black flames upon him. Moah then turned to his shocked friends, revealing only to them a long scourge that he had clasped in one his hands.

"Moah?" Stammered Cara meekly. "What are going to do?"

"I will grant you the passwords needed to free Alaskia, Cara." Assured Moah with a fervent grin. "Whether Illuminecia allows me to or not, for I *am* the Guardian of Darkness... I *am* Kufiah's reaper!" Without any further word, Moah swung his armed hand across Illuminecia's position. A following trail of obsidian shards, that adorned the hideous scourge, then tore mercilessly across her torso.

"Traitor!" Illuminecia reeled in agony on the Sanctum platform, whilst looking to her countless slash wounds with a horrified expression. She cursed Moah maliciously under her breath, the golden bracelet upon Illuminecia's wrist now burned fiercer too - her hatred intensified. "You will suffer for this impertinence, Moah!"

"Grant Cara your password and I will take mercy on you, Sister." Said Moah with reluctance, as he discreetly prepared his scourge for another attack. "There is no need for you to protect Kanaan any longer... his fate has been sealed."

"NEVER!" Declared Illuminecia stubbornly. She then countered against many more slashes made from Moah's scourge, as the two continued to battle. Blinding flashes of light left from Illuminecia's spear across the Sanctum with each mounting strike, in turn Moah responded with waves of dark energy that struck hard against his counterpart. "You will die!" The two Guardians fought tirelessly against one another, both suffering many grievous wounds from their present ordeal. Cara and Spero shielded Firin's ever-weakening body with their own, they prayed for an absolution and could do little to stop what was happening now.

"Why would you protect these worthless mortals?" Cried out Illuminecia, as she fought against Moah's increasing tirade of blows. "Why forsake your own kin?"

"*The Sacred Balance…* must be reborn!" Cried out Moah in fatigue. The Guardian of Darkness then motioned for his final move against Illuminecia. He flounced his whip to encase its shards around her entire body, tearing them deep into the Guardian of Light's flesh with a tightened hold. "*We* must die, Sister!" The penetrating shards paralysed Illuminecia where she now lay. Her unimaginable and restraining pain became so evident to the companions who watched on, as the Guardian's arrogant demeanour quickly ceased. All that remained, was the pitiful sight of a creature; one desperate to be released from their despair.

"There is no more need to fight," Whispered Moah in a firm voice. He then used his scourge to reel in Illuminecia's body, moving it closer towards him upon Kufiah's seal. "Now… we must become one, Sister." The Guardian of Darkness leaned himself over Illuminecia to place his hands upon her brow, while she screeched back in recoil to him. "Our bodies will now be bound!" A powerful shockwave suddenly erupted from the central seal. "The darkness and light shall be reunited – in us!" Moah transfused his darkened energy with Illuminecia's own, fusing them both into becoming one spiritual mass - almost killing the pair in doing so.

"Moah." Breathed Firin heavily, he could barely muster enough strength to move his lips. "The passwords…" In response, the Guardians of Darkness and Light turned their heads together in one gradual movement, then both spoke with a single haunting voice.

"Cara… there is not much time!" The Guardians' radiating auras of white and black fluctuated greatly around them like surging flames. "I cannot hold her for much longer, so listen carefully!" Begged Moah. "You must speak the names of the Celestial spirits, so that Alaskia can be revealed! Don't waste time in pitying me!" Moah trembled in exhaustion, his faced grimacing in torment. "Kufiah is coming and *you will* see Sophilia again… I am not afraid to die!"

"No, Moah! Is there not another way?" Simpered Cara remorsefully. "We don't want to lose you again!" Her words were mirrored by Firin and Spero's own melancholy, they shook their heads against this awful fate.

"Farewell… my friends." Moah held his glance firmly upon the companions, smiling to each of them as if in relief. The rising smoke and sudden flashes emitted more erratically from within the two Guardians, their very bodies began to rip apart from the immense power building up inside of them. "Have faith… you *must* finish your quest!" Cara reached out a hand towards Moah, wishing to save him from whatever dire action he was planning. However, she quickly realised that any efforts to intervene would now be vain, for the two Guardians' spiritual powers had reached a point of no return. Cara held onto Spero tenderly for his usual comforting touch, then together they started to mourn for their new losses.

"We Guardians of Darkness and light… permit thee to enter thine sacred Sanctum!"

A dazzling burst of crimson light filled the entirety of Skynah's inner-chamber, followed shortly afterwards by an immense shockwave that almost threw the three friends off its Sanctum platform. Once the light faded, it left no sign of Moah or Illuminecia in its wake; all that remained were shards from the Guardian of Light's cursed bracelet, which rested in several pieces upon Kufiah's seal.

"They're gone…" Sighed Cara mournfully. She then looked around the Sanctum platform for any hint that Moah had survived, though only found an empty space instead. "He sacrificed himself for us, and to think that we didn't trust him at first." Her tears ran into the central seal, where a faint white light had now started to radiate. "…Alaskia?"

"Cara… move back!" Cried out Spero frantically, as he reached out to grab her. "The seal is activating!" Skynah's central seal suddenly fired out a massive beam of golden light, reaching far up into the summit portal where Eternamorrah's realm lay. Cara brushed aside Spero's restraining hands to bravely fight her way towards the monstrous ray of light, reasoning that this would be the last step needed in freeing Alaskia.

"I can hear his voice," whispered Cara in curiosity. "Alaskia is in there… I know he is!" As Cara approached the pulsating beam she felt as if its energy reached out towards her; filling her thoughts with so many varying images of past events, and some of which had not yet come to pass.

"Come back… Cara." Pleaded Firin wearily, his desperation echoed in Spero's own apparent anguish. "Please!"

"I can't," Responded Cara in a determined voice. "I have to save Sophilia!" She closed her eyes and then raised her arms slowly into the column of coursing light. A welcoming sensation swiftly flowed through Cara, that fed itself into her very soul and outer-aura – empowering every cell of the princess' body and mindset like no other mortal had ever felt.

"ALASKIA… KUFIAH!"

The entire mountain of Skynah shook violently after Cara's given command and its tremors were felt in every corner of Impartia. Cara's granted energy suddenly imploded within itself, back into the central seal, where the radiant beam suddenly dwindled to leave a mystical haze in its place. Now centred within the Sanctum platform, knelt the small figure of a hooded child who was noticeably clad in the purest of white robes, their head bowed down as if in prayer and their arms bound by obsidian chains connected to the parallel pinnacles at either side.

"You have done well, Cara." Said the child angelically, his voice evidently that of a young boy. "However, despite all you have been through, I cannot be made free…yet." Gradually he raised his head to look upon Cara and her companions, revealing to them the disturbing image of a youthful-looking Kanaan.

"Oh!" Quirked Cara awkwardly, as she quickly turned her gaze away from the child. "You look just like my father... Alaskia?"

"Does he?" Remarked Spero with an astonished expression. "How can that be?" Alaskia then chuckled innocently in response, feeling no disrespect by this.

"I *am* Alaskia – the Celestial Spirit of Light. I appear in this child-like form, because it was during Kanaan's youth that he lost any trace of light within him, before he was corrupted by his own demonic desires - to dominate all life in Impartia. Celestial Spirits, like myself, take on the appearance of their physical hosts... I hope this answers your confusion?"

"Yes, it does... Thank You." Uttered Cara reservedly. She still could not face looking upon the daunting features of her father, even if Alaskia did appear so innocent. "We have come to release you of your imprisonment, but I'm afraid... we don't really know how to." She scratched at her head awkwardly. "Is there any way that you can help us, like you said that you would?"

"Were my swords and shields not good enough for you?" Humoured Alaskia with a pleasant grin, though he quickly took on a more serious expression again. "I understand that this may dishearten you all, but what Moah said about my incarceration is, regrettably, the truth. Only Kufiah can release me, for it was my brother that forced this imprisoned on myself – under Kanaan's influence."

"There must be another way!" Exclaimed Cara, as she moved to caress Alaskia's face in sympathy. After a moment of silence, Cara then attempted to break Alaskia's bonds with her sword, though the strong blade shattered immediately upon impact. "No! This isn't fair!"

"I have *told* you, Cara... only Kufiah can grant my freedom." Sighed Alaskia. "Have faith and do not despair, my brother will be here soon... it has been foretold." He forged a smile once more. However, in it Cara could sense the anxiousness lingering that spoke louder than any words could have.

"Alaskia, you know that the Spirit of Darkness will kill us all on first sight!" Shouted Cara in frustration. "Kufiah is under the full control of my sister - Cera, she will not grant us any mercy... there has to be another way of breaking these chains!"

"Cara!" Cried out Spero, hoping to grab her attention with an immediate effect. He had hold of Firin's body tightly in his arms; it was now growing limper with each passing second. "We're losing him..."

"Relinquish your sorrow, Son of Hydrania. There is still a hope that Impartia, and your friend, will survive this conflict." Reassured Alaskia with a passive smile, as a darkening sense began to circulate throughout the Sanctum. "My Brother... is coming."

Kufiah lingered ominously outside, within his powerful maelstrom, still hovering above Cera's lead-warship as her beloved Angel of Death with a truly sadistic purpose. The Dark Spirit was now fuelling his will into Aira's hurricane; surging it far over Skynah's sacred mountain and the Elemental Guardians, who themselves continued to protect it valiantly. The Guardians at this point, had grown spiritually fatigued and were preparing to journey back to their individual Sanctuaries – no longer able to fend off the immense evil that now stood against them.

"Their powers are all but spent!" Revelled Cera cruelly, on witnessing the activated portals upon Skynah's outer-platform "The Elemental Guardians will meet their doom this day... long has it been foretold!" The Queen felt a sudden wave of orgasmic joy overcome her, as she clasped tightly onto Kanaan's accursed amulet again to strengthen Kufiah's bond. Cera then turned to her cowering crewmembers, who had each hidden away in fright from the imposing demon flying above them. Magmorrah's Queen hissed in disgust at the apparent lack of patriotic celebration in her subordinates, she then quickly moved to scold them each for their evident weakness. "You have all lived to bear witness to our nation's greatest moment, yet, you choose to hide away like filthy vermin?" Seethed the enraged Queen. "You're all pathetic! All of you are unworthy to serve under my divine reign!" Cera grimaced bitterly, as she watched her ship's Captain stand himself in defiance against her - along with the support of his fellow officers.

"WE are not weak, Your Highness!" Declared Cera's Captain boldly, though he spoke with a prominent and fearful stammer. "WE are mourning the loss of our fellow soldiers... those whom you have only just murdered - to empower your Demon!" Cera merely responded to her crew's mutiny by glaring coldly away from them; Magmorrah's Queen felt no remorse at all for her heinous actions. Instead, she chose to lovingly observe Kufiah, as he rose even higher above to cast out his foreboding shadow. Cera had fully succumbed in her obsession to the Spirit of Darkness, any humanity that had remained now faded from the ruthless Queen's soul. Kufiah, in response to Cera's devotion, roared proudly with his new-found power, forming from his abhorrent mass six hideous wings that snapped through the air aggressively against Skynah's mountain.

"Kufiah!" Roared Cera, with her arms raised in adoration towards the malignant creature. "Thine mighty Spirit of Death! Show us what is hate!" The surviving Magmorran crew members looked to one another in despair; never had they seen their Queen act so deranged before, despite her infamous acts of cruelty. Cera's Captain stepped cautiously towards her. His heart had reached its lowest point, his resolve however had reached its strongest.

"My Queen, there is no possible way we can make it to Skynah safely now…" The Captain halted his steps abruptly, sensing Cera's emanating anger. "Our ship *cannot* cross this plateau of volcanoes and their flowing lava. To make such a move would be an act of suicide!" Cera responded by calmly flickering away a thin layer of hair from where it had landed across her eyes and then, in a very disturbing manner, turned to speak with the subservient crew members. Magmorrah's tyrannical ruler had lost all sense of empathy towards others, her only goal now was to fulfil the sordid destiny that she had spent over a decade planning.

"So lost and hopeless you all are; with your disillusionment. Despite serving in Magmorrah's greatest Armada, you have chosen to take the side of Impartia's lesser-beings… FOOLS!" Cera appeared almost tearful whilst speaking, a sure side-effect to her growing derangement. "Kufiah will create our pathway to Skynah. The Elemental Guardians and their toy army, that you all seem to fear so wrongly, are no match for the power I now have!"

"Your Majesty…" Stuttered the Captain, within his eyes rose an evident dread. "Your recent actions have proven to us all, that you are not fit to be our Queen any longer… we are taking control of Magmorrah back from you!"

"A coup?" Cackled Cera in surprise, as she tilted her head slowly with a judgemental stare. "You… YOU… would wish to usurp my throne from me?" The crew members each quickly lifted their small pistols towards Cera in a show of determination.

"We are not making this choice lightly, Cera!" Wheezed the Captain anxiously, whilst taking aim with his pistol. "This ship is our last, we are all that remains of Magmorrah's greatest Armada! Can you see how mad you have become?"

"Oh, I *am* mad…" Scorned Cera, as she lifted Kanaan's amulet menacingly towards her treacherous subordinates. "I am mad at you, at all of you TRAITORS!" She looked again to Kufiah in endearment. "Kufiah! Teach them with your immolation!" Kufiah roared in obedience to his master's plea. A wave of dark energy then fell from the Spirit of Darkness upon Cera's ship, immediately striking against her crew members to turn them all into ashes. Magmorrah's Queen quietly sighed in relief, whilst her crew's dwindling embers floated off across the ocean waves. "Take us to Skynah!" Commanded Cera to Kufiah. "Soon, I shall take vengeance on the Spirits of this world!"

The Elemental Guardians looked on helplessly at Kufiah's rising terror. Every attempt they had made so far to defy Cera had failed, their ancient powers seemingly robbed from them by the Spirit of Darkness himself.

"What are we going to do, Ven? We're no match against a Celestial Spirit… even with our combined strengths!" Despaired Levia. "Kufiah's power exceeds our own! Have we truly failed in our duty to protect Impartia, to protect the Sacred Balance?" He lowered his head solemnly in a saddened acceptance of this apparent defeat.

"Have faith in Cara, my Brother." Replied Ven in an impassioned voice, as he struck a hand firmly upon his chest to signify this command. "We must distract Cera's attention for as long as possible! Cara *will* free Alaskia... I know she will. Never have I seen such determination in a mortal before."

"Speaking of mortals," interrupted Pahoe, whilst she looked to Ven wearily and with a stern glare. "They have all fled from this battle... and we cannot keep fighting like this! My spiritual powers have almost drained completely!"

"We have served our purpose, Ven." Concurred Aira. She stood herself upright upon her seal, despite suffering from an overwhelming exhaustion to match Ven's stature. "However, let us display our defiance once more against the Spirit of Darkness... let us show Queen Cera that we will not bow down to her - willingly!" Ven shook his head in dismay. "We must return to our Sanctuaries and replenish our spiritual connections to them. If Cera succeeds, then we Elemental Guardians will be all that can stand against her there-after!" Kufiah suddenly shot through the air towards Skynah, towards the now-vulnerable Elemental Guardians.

"GO!" Cried out Ven. "Go to your Sanctuaries and await my further command!" One-by-one, the Guardians vanished within their activated seals. Only Aira and Ven remained, where the two gazed upon one another in uncertainty. "Aira," whispered Ven sorrowfully. "Go to your Sanctuary..."

"Not without one, last strike against that Demon!" Replied the Guardian of Air, as her eyes radiated intensely through their risen spiritual connection. "I have defied the Dark Spirit before... and I shall do again!" Kufiah aimed himself precisely against Skynah's outer-platform, greatly desiring to vanquish the remaining Elemental Guardians left on it. Without warning, Aira summoned a tirade of searing lightning bolts to strike down against the Spirit of Darkness. Kufiah evaded each, though only just, as he sped towards the sacred mountain with an intensified roar of hatred.

"Go to your Sanctuary, Aira!" Cried out Ven again, desperation lifted through his tremoring voice now. "Please, Sister! You need not die this day!"

"I grant your pardon, Brother." Said Aira vacantly, on gesturing to Ven for his own departure. "I have a parting gift for Queen Cera!" Ven activated his seal in reluctance, leaving only Aira left to withstand Kufiah's malice. The Guardian of Air then focused her powers upon the very platform where she stood, whilst intensifying Kufiah's lightening above to summon it into a single, cataclysmic beam. Aira swiftly activated her seal, only moments before the mightiest of lightning bolts struck down upon Skynah's entire outer-platform and temple housings around it – decimating all within seconds.

"NO!!!" Cera fell to her knees in anguish. Aira's move was unexpected, especially as she was considered the meekest of Impartia's Elemental Guardians. "The Sanctum's entrance has been sealed from us, Kufiah!" She roared to the Demon, who himself was deeply shocked. "Return to me... at once!" The Spirit of Darkness flew back to Cera's ship as instructed, showing no sign of contempt in forsaking his master's wishes to desolate the troublesome Elemental Guardians. "My Dark Angel, your duty to me now... is to destroy Alaskia." Uttered Cera pleadingly to the Spirit, as he lingered on above her. "Your prophecy is almost complete, you need only decimate Skynah's sacred dwelling now." Kufiah growled and then sharply released his arms towards Skynah in response, spreading the Queen's sentient malice against it to her immediate delight. Cera clapped her hands excitedly like an ecstatic child and proceeded to dance across the ship's deck, overjoyed by seeing such a display of power being willed by her very own hands - yet still she hungered for more. "Kufiah! Show me your truest show of desolation!" Ordered Cera passionately, her father's amulet burned greater with each breath taken. "You alone turned an entire civilisation into ashes, so destroying this mountain should be easy... in comparison. Unleash your mass destruction upon Skynah, Slave! Fulfil your prophecy and grant to me my divine right to rule Impartia as its destined Empress!" She then abruptly fell into an uncharacteristic silence, focusing all intent upon Kanaan's amulet to strengthen hers and Kufiah's connection immensely. "*Render* this mountain to the seas!"

Kufiah thoughtlessly obeyed Queen Cera, his freedom to act otherwise still robbed of him. The Spirit of Darkness gradually condensed his attained energy, compressing it into the farthest reaches of his very own soul to magnify it. Kufiah then winced and howled, as he curled himself into a foetal position, within a protective sphere of surging dark energy and all the time staring upon Skynah's ancient monolith in detest.

"Destroy it!" Commanded Cera frantically. "Destroy all life upon that accursed mountain!"

Kufiah thrashed his head painfully against his skeletal hands; the formidable energy accumulating inside almost tore apart the Dark Spirit's physical being, as he continued to write in agony from each tormenting moment. Slowly, the waves beneath Skynah fell still and the air surrounding its mountain grew hauntingly quiet. All the while, Queen Cera watched on in anticipation, knowing that her fateful destiny was about to come into realisation.

Within the depths of Skynah's hidden Sanctum, Cara threw herself against Spero fearfully and together they closed their eyes in an anxious dread. Many random and deafening tremors had violently begun to shake their surroundings; Skynah's core itself bellowed like a wounded beast from them. Firin continued to lay lifeless, oblivious to the new threat arising and showed no signs of recovery, as with every passing second the wound that had inflicted him only seemed to worsen.

"Alaskia, *please*… do something to help us!" Begged Cara desperately, she then screamed in horror on seeing several cracks suddenly emerge along the Sanctum's walls. "Has Kufiah made it to Skynah… has my sister?" She slowly stroked at Firin's knotted hair to bring some form of comfort to him, as the light within his eyes slowly began to fade before her. "Is there nothing you can do to save our friend? Why should Firin be the one to suffer; all he did was help us?" Alaskia stared back at Cara vacantly.

"Where there is darkness there is light, where there is light there is darkness." Mumbled Alaskia catatonically. "This is Impartia's *Eternal Cycle*. Bad things happen to those who do not deserve it… and so do good things." Without further word, the Spirit of Light breathed in deeply to fall into an eventual meditation, relinquishing any earthly woes or concerns from himself.

"…Brother…" To Cara and Spero's immediate horror, Alaskia then strangely began to sing the *Hymn of Kufiah*, its demonic verses resonated and wrought a swift despair in the observing companions.

"What are you DOING?" Cried out Cara to Alaskia. "Why are you singing Kufiah's Hymn?" She despaired.

"He's been tainted by Kanaan too!" Remarked Spero angrily, as he leaned himself in protection over Cara and Firin. "Ven was wrong! Our quest has failed!" Alaskia abruptly lifted an open palm against Spero in response.

"Silence…Son of Hydrania." Commanded the Spirit of Light in a soft tone. "Kufiah will soon release me, and I shall release my brother in return. Hope is not lost." The tearing cracks spread further around Skynah's inner-wall now. From their wake, crystal boulders sheared away that clashed down fiercely upon the Sanctum platform - some into the endless Void below, where no light could ever reach them. "I said, that I will help you as I can… Cara. Join me within my seal, so that I may protect you and your friends from the evil that now threatens us."

"I can't die… I can't leave my little girl alone!" Whimpered Cara into Spero's chest, her tears coarsely drenching it. "I want to be with my baby girl! My poor Lia!"

"You'll see Sophilia again, Cara." Assured Spero, as he tightened his grasp upon her, willing every ounce of sympathy into the grief-stricken mother. "You both have what Cera could never possess… love."

"Come to my seal!" Commanded Alaskia to the companions in haste. "All of you… if your wish is to survive this day!"

"Why *are* you singing the Spirit of Darkness' Hymn?" Spoke Cara through shivering lips, as she and Spero edged their way towards him with Firin held jointly in their arms. "Why, Alaskia… WHY?"

"To *empower* him!" Responded Alaskia firmly. The Spirit's child-like voice took on a sudden, ethereal dominance over the sacred platform. "Brother will need all his strength to break though Kanaan's seal, it will not be long now though… before he can."

"I'm not scared of Kufiah… not anymore." Whispered Cara proudly to Spero, their bodies ached greater now through dragging Firin across the Sanctum platform. "Are you still afraid?"

"What about Cera though, Cara… what if *she* confronts you?" Responded Spero in angst. "I'm more worried about that, than what you will do in confronting Kufiah. I do not fear any Spirit, but *I am* scared that you will lose yourself during this battle."

"I won't!" Cara sharply nodded her head to affirm this belief. "There is still good in Cera; my little sister should not be doomed in the same way my father was. I will right the wrongs of my bloodline, not matter how long it takes - for Sophilia's sake at least." Alaskia fought strongly against his obsidian restraints and the falling debris to look upon Eternamorrah's infinite cosmic lights above. The Spirit's eyes glistened in the reflection of countless galaxies and other heavenly bodies, absorbing part of them into his own divine existence to reach a new level of spiritual power. The Spirit of Light gradually focused his will on casting a protective seal over himself and the three companions, as they clambered towards him, their fate yet unknown.

"…There is light!" Declared Alaskia passionately, his wrists burning against their cruel manacles. "Shield us from the Eternal Darkness!" A raining beam of golden energy then burst into flow around the Celestial Spirit from Eternamorrah's portal on high; shrouding himself, Cara and her companions in its powerful ray. "Do not forsake us!" Cara stared at Alaskia's obvious torment in sympathy, though Spero himself felt nothing. The Spirit, despite being ancient in age and wisdom, appeared no older than Sophilia but to Cara looked still as vulnerable. She could sense his evident pain; it seeped greatly into her and wrought with it a sickening realisation.

"We don't need your help, Alaskia." Muttered Cara in a gentle voice. "You need ours. Father's malice grew at such a young age… this must have weakened you so much?"

"I am Impartia's Eternal Light…" Countered Alaskia, though could the Spirit could barely speak and the spiritual connection he was now undertaking drained him immensely. "I… am…"

"*Teach us with your isolation…free us with your love…*" Sang Cara softly. Alaskia smiled in relief on hearing the familiar words of his own hymn being sung, for they strengthened his power into an even greater affluence. "*Cast aside the fear and pain…sleep beneath the stars above…*" Alaskia's pure light swiftly proceeded to surround the entirety of his Sanctum platform; creating an air of peace within it, whilst also deflecting the falling crystals from above.

"Thank you, though there is no need to be so afraid." Said the Spirit compassionately to Cara. "You are all safe inside this barrier of light, for as long as I will it… no darkness can penetrate." Spero discreetly glanced along Firin's draining skin colour; his friend's blood still pooled beneath them, taking with it what lifeforce remained. It was a poignant fact to him, that Spero was watching Firin die slowly and he had little power to do anything about this. Cara herself was trying not to acknowledge her friend's last moments. She instead desperately clung into Spero's embrace, praying for this horrific event to pass and for Firin to leave their company peacefully and without any further pain.

"Cara," whispered Spero to her nervously. "I want to… I *need* to ask you something. I don't know if I'll get another chance to…" He exhaled heavily, lost in apprehension to what response may meet with him. Cara sniffled and then lifted her head awkwardly to look up.

"What is it, Spero? What is it that you want to ask?" She had an inclination, though could not dare utter it herself. "Go on…"

"Maybe you don't remember… or maybe… you have chosen to block it out, like some of your other painful memories?" Stammered Spero, though his fear proved to be unnecessary. Cara merely continued to smile back, which helped to alleviate any risen tension between them. "When you fled from General Nira that night, ten years ago, with Sophilia; it was *me* that rescued you." He gulped heavily in apprehension, as did Cara in realisation. "I doubted it at first, but not long after I saw you again, those treasured memories quickly came back to me…of meeting you both." Cara clasped tighter onto Spero on hearing this. She had blocked so many harrowing moments in her life to cope with them; it was the only way she could, though this devastated her now to know that she had wilfully forgotten how brave Spero had been - in rescuing herself and Sophilia from Nira's clutches. "I never forgot, Cara… and I never want to. I'm just glad to know, that you and Sophilia had so many happy years together spent in freedom… away from harm… away from Magmorrah." Cara shed some joyful tears and then stared into Spero's eyes affectionately, never wishing to break this loving connection.

"I'm so sorry, Spero. I've been through so much over my life; it was easier just to block it all out." She gently stroked at Spero's face in adoration, which he himself met with a tender smile. "I'm so grateful for what you did for me and Sophilia back then - without you, we would have both most-likely been held as slaves to Kufiah…or worse."

"It's okay, Cara. I honestly understand." Said Spero sympathetically. "I can't imagine what Kanaan and Cera must have put you through together; I'm not surprised at all that you've attempted to block out such painful memories…you're so very brave."

"I didn't forget you on purpose," Responded Cara, held deep with remorse. "Somehow, I've known all along this journey with you - that there was something more meaningful between us. I'm so sorry… I'm so sorry, Spero." She stumbled over the last few words spoken, whilst Spero wiped away her dwindling tears with his gentle fingers.

"Cara!" Jolted Spero suddenly, his face stricken with fright. "Your mark… it's faded… it's…barely visible now!"

"What? It *can't* have gone!" Wailed Cara fearfully. She placed a hand over where Cerebrante's mark had previously been, praying to feel the scar that had wrought itself there since her birth. "Alaskia, what is happening to me...I can't feel Cerebrante's Mark...What does this mean?!" The Spirit of Light convulsed violently towards Cara, almost tearing the flesh away from his wrists where Kufiah's obsidian chains constricted them. Alaskia's mediation had reached its ultimate height, and the toll this was taking on his physical body was truly immeasurable – nearly fatal. Through his increased spiritual insight, Alaskia could now look outside of Skynah's mountain walls and what he saw truly astounded him, though it also brought the Spirit much grief.

"Kufiah!" Screamed out Alaskia in agony. "He is in pain... so much pain! There is too much power building inside of him... he cannot hold it for much longer!"

Outside, Kufiah unleashed a prolonged cry that spread far across Impartia's many nations, though it was solely aimed against Skynah's mountain and particularly at his counterpart hidden within.

"Render this mountain to the sea!" Growled Cera with a perverse and satisfied grin. "Fulfil your prophecy, Kufiah! Make *me* Impartia's Empress... Make *me* immortal!" Commanded the deranged Queen. The Spirit of Darkness shook and howled with agony as his body slowly deformed. His will now completely corrupted beyond any redemption, and his attained dark energy seemingly infinite - in all its destructive potential. Under Queen Cera's most-begotten of commands, Kufiah released a mighty display of decimation against Impartia's most-sacred mountain. The Dark Spirit cast out from his demonic mass a crimson shockwave that instantly rippled towards Skynah, tearing through its ocean waves and airspace like a sharpened blade through silk. A gargantuan halo of scarlet fire proceeded, vaporising all in its path and eventually Skynah's earthly shell itself. All that remained afterwards were Skynah's foundations, a choking black mist and Alaskia's golden beam of light centred within them all.

"What's going on?" Gasped Cara and Spero in unison. They could not see beyond Alaskia's shielding light, though they could hear the crashing of waves as pieces from Skynah's shell plummeted into them outside.

"...Kufiah..." Mumbled Firin, his voice wavering catatonically. Cara and Spero looked to him in shock and smiled fleetingly, both lingering on in a hope of their friend yet surviving from his grievous wound. "Don't die, Cara..."

"HE is here," spoke Alaskia contently, showing no fear in his eyes whatsoever. "The Spirit of Darkness... Impartia's unlikely saviour has finally come."

"Let Kufiah through your barrier, Alaskia!" Commanded Spero in a brave stance. "We are ready to face that beast!" He stood himself protectively in front of Cara and Firin, hoping to defend them from any possible threat that could now come their way. "...Let's finish this!" The radiant light from Alaskia's barrier flickered ominously around Skynah's inner-platform, its sporadic flashes only intensifying the terror already present within it. A sense of death and despair rapidly crept in; it swarmed around Cara and her friends like a predatory menace, filtering a perpetual sorrow deep into each of their hearts. A horrifying roar then suddenly entered the space within Alaskia's shield, as the foreboding figure of Kufiah now menacingly walked through it towards his spiritual counterpart, his malignant demeanour overwhelming.

"Kufiah..." Spoke Cara reservedly, as she glared towards the imposing Spirit. "Father was wrong to imprison Alaskia; in a sense he imprisoned you too...with that accursed amulet of his." She paused for a moment to catch an anxious breath. "You don't have to be a slave to my sister's will any longer...oh, Great Spirit." Kufiah gave a looming sigh in response; seemingly aware of Cara's repenting words - on behalf of her family, whilst the dense smoke that emanated from his tattered robes increased tenfold, and all light within the Sanctum now appeared to diminish.

"I am...The Eternal Darkness... Where there is Light... I shall destroy it!"

Chapter Thirteen: The Sacred Balance

The Spirit of Darkness glared upon Cara with his fearsome eyes, consumed by rage and an urge to see her life taken swiftly; it was an overwhelming emotion - albeit it one that was natural to Kufiah, though was solely being fed into him through Queen Cera's malignant possession and innate hatred towards her sister.

"I do not fear you," declared Cara assuredly to Kufiah, as she tightened her fists in anticipation towards the Dark Spirit's next move. "I pity you…."

"Foolish…Mortal!" Roared Kufiah. The Dark Spirit strangely appeared to be choking on his own smoke plumes, as they swept away from his towering mass to filter across Skynah's Sanctum platform entirely. The Spirit of Darkness then gradually motioned towards Alaskia; all the time sweeping his fiery eyes across Cara, Firin and Spero, whilst they looked back to him in defiance. "Infidels…" Groaned Kufiah in a tormented and drawn-out voice.

"You heard what Cara said!" Spero rose his voice in confidence, himself no longer dreading Kufiah's innate evil. "Should you attack us… we'll make sure that you'll regret it!"

"Are you *so* brave… to challenge me, Son of Hydrania?" Taunted Kufiah, with an unnatural growl aimed harshly against Spero. "'Tis you, that would regret such a futile move. I *will* fulfil my Queen's destiny this day!" The Spirit of Darkness then looked upon Firin's lifeless body with a perplexed expression, sensing the residual energy left within from Illuminecia's inflicted wound. "Death shall find you all soon enough… it will not be long for him!" Cackled the Dark Spirit cruelly.

"Don't you *dare* touch Firin!" Screamed Cara. She turned her head swiftly to Alaskia, praying that now would be the moment where he would intervene somehow. "Do something, Alaskia! Aid us…like you said you would!"

"Where there is darkness…there is light." Mumbled Alaskia incoherently, with his trance-like state continuing to overwhelm each heightened sense. "…Kufiah?" Alaskia lifted his head and fought at his obsidian chains to gain a closer look.

"Brother…" Whispered the Dark Spirit in a cautious response. Kufiah's aggressive stance had now faintly changed; he was beginning to grieve from seeing how his counterpart appeared so vulnerable - being locked within his own cruel restraints. With a swift action of his ashen cloak, Kufiah moved Cara and Spero aside so that he could face Alaskia more intimately. "Brother! Alaskia!" The Spirit of Light forged a sincere smile.

"I knew, that one day we would be reunited again." Responded Alaskia with a hopeful smile. "*The Sacred Balance*… cannot be undone!" Gleamed the Spirit of Light.

"I will destroy you! I will destroy Cerebrante!" Declared Kufiah proudly, though his flaring eyes seemed distantly vacant now. "I will fulfil…"

"You need not be a slave anymore, as Cara said." Interrupted Alaskia pleadingly, desperate to break Kufiah's unwilling possession. "Stand before me…Let me free you, Brother!"

"My Queen shall reign eternal!" Continued Kufiah, his voice firm and unwavering. "Queen Cera must be an Immortal!"

"It's no use, Alaskia!" Cried out Cara despairingly. "Cera's hold is too strong over Kufiah now…" She knelt herself again beside Firin, wishing to bring him some kindly comfort. The two Celestial Spirits silently stared upon one another, observing their own differences and it seemed as if both for a moment shed a single tear.

"You've changed so much, Brother…you look…so old!" Remarked Alaskia coyly. "Kanaan's venomous soul has truly impacted itself on you, it's such a shame." He pulled against Kufiah's restraints to hold a hand out to the Dark Spirit, who himself instantly recoiled away from this unprecedented action. "What have you become… Spirit of Darkness?" Kufiah snarled in dismissal to Alaskia's peculiar show of affection.

"You look just the same as *I* remember you… meek and feeble!" Mocked the Dark Spirit. Kufiah then tenderly stroked his skeletal fingers across Alaskia's obsidian chains to sense their restraining energy; they were powerful and everlasting, just as King Kanaan had intended. "It is necessary that you die now…Do not defy me…Do not defy Queen Cera!"

"No! I won't let you do this, Kufiah!" Screamed Cara, as she snatched herself away from Spero's reaching arms to stand before the eminent Dark Spirit. "You'll have to go through me first!" Kufiah released a terrifying roar that initially shook Cara to the bone, though it had no lasting effect on her brave resolve. Another haunting cry entered the space between Cara and Kufiah, however it came from neither and sounded far more blood-curdling.

"As always… you would stand in my way, Sister!"

Queen Cera suddenly burst out from within Kufiah's billowing mass, her withered body trembling in hatred, her eyes radiating with an incessant rage which she quickly fixated upon Cara. The Spirit of Darkness stepped away from Cera to immediately bow in subservience before her, with an agonised expression still present on his face.

"Your very existence is an insult to our regal Bloodline, Cara!" Scorned Cera cruelly to her. "Father always said that you were a mistake… that he should have had you terminated years ago!" She snapped coldly.

"Cera…" Cara could barely speak, her emotions overwhelming. "Father was a monster! How can you idolise him after the way he has treated us both?" Cera tilted her head and gave to Cara a judgemental stare.

"Idolise…Kanaan?" Cackled Cera sadistically at this notion. "Cara, it was *I* that imprisoned Father, and then usurped his throne from under his very nose!" She boasted. "I alone convinced Magmorrah's population that their begotten King had fallen into lunacy!" Cera's intermittent laughter rose louder and more aggressive. "Father is still alive… from a certain point of view. He started this war and I, with Kufiah as my slave now, shall finish it!"

"No, Cera." Responded Cara in a stern voice, as she tried to process the harsh fact that her father had not actually died. "It's not too late. Together, we can end this horrific war! All you need to do, is take off that cursed amulet and free Alaskia! Reform Impartia's Sacred Balance and be worshipped as a benevolent ruler… not one who reigns with evil!"

"Are you just going to stand there and do nothing, Kufiah?" Seethed Cera, as she violently shook her father's amulet towards the Dark Spirit. "Kill Alaskia NOW! Slaughter them all!" Alaskia and Kufiah were still locked in one another's gaze. The Spirit of Light smiled graciously to his counterpart, whilst Kufiah kept his fingers held firmly around the solid chains attached to Alaskia's wrists, tightening them with each passing second. "Destroy the Light!" Screeched Cera, her voice frantic and coarse. "Do it…I Order you…Slave!"

"If you do, Kufiah… then you yourself would be imbalanced!" Said Cara pleadingly. "Your powers would be beyond any control…they would destroy *you*!" Kufiah struggled against the arrogant will of Queen Cera, realising that what Cara was saying indeed held some truth. The Dark Spirit managed to slowly lift a hand towards Alaskia and on touching his face, released the obsidian chains away from their holdings – to Cera's immediate horror.

"What are you doing, Kufiah?" Stammered Cera in fright. "Kill Alaskia… don't free him!"

"Brother…" Whispered Kufiah, as he gradually removed his freezing hand away from Alaskia. "I…must…obey!" Cera cackled again in delight, her possession over the Spirit of Darkness now her only joyful element.

"Yes, I *own* you, Spirit!" Laughed Cera menacingly. "You are mine to control!" She kissed her amulet endearingly, then looked again towards Kufiah. "Now, kill them…or I will have you destroyed also! Nothing can stop me now!"

"Daughter of Magmorrah, I am afraid that you are mistaken." Assured Alaskia with a serene smirk. "You have no power over us Celestial Spirits... not anymore." Cera hissed and carefully stepped away from the central seal, recoiling in dismay as Alaskia now stood himself proudly upon it. The Spirit of Light was minute in size compared to Kufiah's foreboding figure, though he still radiated power equal in magnitude to him. "You freed me, Brother...now permit me to do the same for you." Said Alaskia, as he focused on Kanaan's amulet to hastily feed his own spiritual energy into it. The amulet's golden metal burned painfully against Cera's chest, causing her to fall and writhe in a never-ending torment. She howled pitifully whilst her precious adornment blistered the flesh beneath it, all the while Cara observed in reluctance, praying for Cera's suffering to end.

"Alaskia!" Cried Cara with an anguished look. "Stop it... you're hurting her!" She pleaded.

"Your sister's suffering *will* pass." Countered Alaskia, in a reassuring manner. "Where there is darkness...there is light!" The Spirit then stretched out his arms and with a blinding flash, Kanaan's amulet suddenly burst into several pieces. The shattered remnants landed heavily around Cera and where Kufiah's dark energy had once lain, it now vanished – along with the Queen's possession.

"What have you done...*what have you done*?" Grieved Cera bitterly to Alaskia. In utter desperation, she tried to join the fragments of Kanaan's amulet back together, though with each attempt made they only disintegrated more. "No...No!" She screeched with all her might. "This isn't fair! *I* am the strongest being in Impartia - not you filthy Spirits!"

Kufiah gasped in relief from the freedom Alaskia had brought to him; his soul reawakened, his free-will now granted once again and rightfully redeemed. The Spirit of Darkness turned his head slowly towards Cera and then passed by Cara and Spero, without uttering a single word to them. He stood himself before Magmorrah's Queen in dominance and in retribution, judging Cera just as she had done to countless others - during her tyrannical reign.

"You... are mine!" Quivered Cera, as she gradually looked up Kufiah's foreboding stature. "You are mine to control! You... belong to me!" For the first time in her privileged life, Cera felt both powerless and vulnerable. She stared at Kufiah defiantly, though inside Magmorrah's Queen dwelled in an unfamiliar sorrow and dread.

"I am no *slave* to you... nor any other mortal!" Declared Kufiah in a terrifying growl, his smoke-laden mass increasing with every breath taken. "I am the Spirit of Darkness and you... Queen... will suffer for your Bloodline's decimation of Impartia's *Sacred Balance!*"

"I only used you, Kufiah… to *bring* balance to this wretched world!" Implored Cera remorsefully, whilst holding her arms out fearfully as she fell to the ground. "It was Father that created so much chaos… not me! All I wanted to do, was to right his wrongs!" Cera shuffled awkwardly away from the nearing Dark Spirit, his presence truly overwhelming now. She lay herself close to where Cara stood and looked to her sister with innocent eyes, showing in them a faint sadness which had never been presented before. "I…don't want to die." Kufiah roared scornfully; his beast-like voice pierced those stood around him but seemed to have no effect on Alaskia, who merely continued to observe in silence. The enraged Dark Spirit swiftly fed out a series of smoke-plumes from his robes, that then wrapped themselves around Cera to lift her up in mid-air towards him. Magmorrah's Queen writhed in vain to free herself from this horrifying hold, though with every ounce of struggle made the plumes only tightened around her body more fiercely. "Let me go!" Begged Cera, her body shaking frantically for its freedom. "Let me go, Kufiah!"

"YOU will suffer for your sins, Mortal Queen!" Responded the Dark Spirit with a terrifying bellow, as he wrapped his plumes further around Cera's throat. "Beg… Beg for my mercy, INFIDEL!" Cara looked to Spero tearfully, her every emotion now conflicted and clouded by what to do next in aid of Cera. She then glanced upon Firin, who still lay motionless and seemingly lost – their quest had come at too-high a price for her.

"Please, Kufiah… don't hurt Cera…I beg you!" Cara knelt herself lowly before the Dark Spirit, though she knew that there was little that could be done - in changing his abhorrent resolve. "I know that she has committed many crimes, but she is *still* my little sister!" She fleeted her glance towards Cera, acknowledging her dread with a faint smile. "Please, all-mighty Spirit of Darkness…don't kill her… show some mercy."

"Cara…" Whispered Spero to her, as he held out a wanting hand. "It's too late, there's nothing we can do." He clasped onto Cara's shoulders, hoping again that this would bring some comfort to her.

"Very well, Princess." Spoke Kufiah in a sadistic tone, his risen smile haunting. "If it was not for your actions, then I could have not freed Alaskia and in turn, he could not have released me from my own chains." A sudden, rupturing flame surrounded the Sanctum platform. "I shall grant you your request, Magmorrah's Queen will not die… this day." Kufiah wrapped his fingers forcefully around Cera's throat, constricting it and robbing her from taking any immediate breath. The Dark Spirit then released a chorus of guttural noises from deep within his demonic mass, as he moved to declare his dire judgement over Cera.

"Alaskia, do something!" Screamed Cara despairingly. "How can you just stand there and do nothing? You are the Spirit of Light." Her genuine plea however, was only met with a vacant stare in response from the Celestial Spirit.

"Cera Til-Magmorros – Queen of Impartia's Ash Lands! Daughter of Kanaan – Cerebrante Incarnate…" Snapped Kufiah with a commanding swipe of his muscular arm. "You have wrought an imbalance upon this world and aided in your father's corruption of Cerebrante! Such a blasphemy must be punished in accordance with the magnitude of your sins and crimes!" The Dark Spirit joyfully paraded Cera in mid-air before Alaskia, basking in the humiliation this caused her. "I will grant thee a lengthy existence upon this plain… as you have so desired for so long! You will age in your flesh, though shall diminish in your mind… as slowly you will become a prisoner within your own crippling body, forced to rely on those whom you have deemed so unworthy!" Another horrifying roar left from Kufiah's lungs, aimed solely against the defeated Queen. "Your memories will fade away, and anything else that you cherish… I will now gladly rob from you!"

"Kufiah… No!" Begged Cara tearfully. She fought hard against Spero's restraining hands to reach Cera but soon collapsed in grief. "Don't… *Please*… Don't!" A powerful impulse of dark energy flowed from Kufiah's fingertips into Cera's entire body, violently forcing her to convulse in submission as a result. The Queen's limbs twisted in an unnatural manner, her eyes rolled back into their sockets and the amber radiance that once lingered in them remarkably dwindled. Cera motioned to beg for her life, though she somehow could no longer speak coherently and all that was sounded were a series of demented gurgles. "What have you done to her?" Cried out Cara in trepidation. Spero wrapped his arms around her but not in restrain this time, only to ease her obvious suffering. "Monster! You are evil!"

"I am a necessary evil; without my dark sanctity… Impartia's Sacred Balance would fall!" Responded the Dark Spirit coldly. "I am no slave! I am free!" After enacting his brutal will upon Queen Cera, Kufiah then violently cast her body upon the Sanctum platform. She landed in a vegetated state just before where Cara now knelt, weeping and lost for words.

"Cera, Sister… Can you hear me?" Stammered Cara, as she rested her brow gently on the fallen Queen's. "It's Cara, please speak to me!" She was met with a harrowing guttural noise at first in response. Cera lifted a hand to place it upon Cara's cheek, a strange smile then formed on her face.

"Mother…is that you?" Questioned Cera with an innocent voice, a tone previously so foreign to her. "Mother… is alive?" Cara grimaced and instantly looked towards the Dark Spirit in detest of him.

"You have turned my sister into an empty shell…is that not a fate worse than death?" Cara struggled to remain calm with all the anger now coursing through her veins. "What kind of life is she now to have?" Kufiah kept silent, feeling no need to justify his wicked actions.

Alaskia suddenly appeared beside Cara, placing a gentle hand upon her in attempt to disperse any residual hatred. The Spirit of Light then looked over Cera's frail body and sighed; it was an act that only his counterpart could have achieved, and it wrought him so much resentful anguish.

"Daughter of Magmorrah…" Whispered Alaskia cautiously to Cara. "There is nothing that I can do to undo this curse."

"You are the Spirit of Light…of Hope…" Wept Cara into her shaking hands. "How could you have allowed for this cruel punishment to be made?"

"What is done - is done, Cara." Explained Alaskia frankly; his youthful voice brought to her no respite. "You speak of death as if it is a wantful ending, one of which you would so freely wish upon your sister?" The Spirit of Light gently ran his fingers across Cera's hair, swiftly recoiling on sensing the dark energy that now flowed through it. "She is still alive and still has thoughts and feelings of her own, though they are now hidden away from our sight."

"How is *this* living?" Countercd Cara scornfully, as she pointed to Cera's crippled body. "She is only existing… Cera's life is no longer her own!" She punched at the Sanctum platform hard, the physical pain afterwards was nothing in comparison to her emotional heartache.

"If your sister was to die by Kufiah's hands, she would only be cast into the Void; where she would suffer for an eternity…" Said Alaskia, as he met his gaze with Kufiah's flaring eyes. "Now finally, Cera will experience what true love is…"

"Both of you are monsters!" Cara strained to scream out, her expression unified with Spero's own look of intent towards the Celestial Spirits. "Cera…" She whimpered sorrowfully.

"We mortals will never understand the workings of you Spirits, will we?" Said Spero in a sarcastic tone. "People say, that you all act as Impartia's mighty Guardians…what a joke!"

"Death is not the end; it is a transcendence." Declared Alaskia firmly. He lifted his arms and then encircled the Sanctum Platform with them, emitting a renewed burst of spiritual energy into the protective light. "I will show you!" As the glaring light gradually decreased, it revealed to each person stood upon Skynah's inner-platform a set of shadowy images - visions of their lost loved ones.

"Alaskia, what are these shadows that walk towards us now?" Asked Spero in uncertainty, recognising the eerie atmosphere to be like what he had experienced earlier. "Have we not been tortured enough by you Spirits?" An abrupt calm quickly entered him thereafter, as he saw his fallen family move through the raining light - as if they were all still alive.

"Stevian…Mother…Father…" Spero's family smiled back to him, showing no signs of discomfort at all in their realistic expressions.

"These are no willed images of my own doing, Son of Hydrania." Alaskia bowed in acknowledgment to his new guests and then to Spero. "They are the souls of loved ones; those who have passed on into the realm of Eternamorrah. I am merely acting as a vessel, so that you can communicate with one another." The Spirit of Light formed a gleaming smile, as he saw what joy this reunion brought to Spero. "Their physical bodies may have gone, but your family's love for you will always exist…"

"Spero…" Whispered Cara, whilst relinquishing him of his grasp upon her. "Go to them."

Spero anxiously nodded to Cara and then moved with caution towards his family's ghosts, unsure of what to say to them, being that he was still so riddled with guilt over their horrific deaths.

"If you can hear me… I'm sorry." Muttered Spero, as he gazed across to his little brother first. "I should have come home early that night, then maybe you wouldn't have died… maybe, I could have stopped that man - somehow?" Spero's mother then moved in closer to gently caress his chin with her fingertips, her touch as warming and real as it had ever felt. She then raised her son's head to greet him, wiping the tears away from both their eyes with a serene smile whilst doing so.

"Do not feel any guilt for our deaths, Spero." Spoke his mother reassuringly. "What pain we had felt is long-gone, and any resentment held towards that man with it. We're so proud of you my strong boy, my brave… grown-up son." Spero gasped joyfully, his pleasure in this moment immeasurable.

"I miss you all… don't leave me again." Spero threw himself into his mother's waiting arms, which were then quickly joined by those of his brother and father. "I love you…"

"We are always with you, Son." Uttered Spero's father proudly, as he tightened his embrace around him. "You have brought honour to our family; to help Cara and her child so selflessly, despite all the threats this brought to you." He scuffled at Spero's hair affectionately and then moved away from him back into Alaskia's light, along with his mother and brother.

"See you soon, Big Bro!" Cried out Stevian enthusiastically. "…Miss you!"

"Don't go…" Spero fell to his knees in dismay. He gave out a short chuckle and then looked up again to Stevian. "I'll will see you again, someday, Little Brother."

Cara reluctantly stared towards Firin; hoping not to see him standing within Alaskia's light himself, though was met with the image of an old man that leaned over her friend's wounded body. Firin gained enough strength to whisper some words to the blurry shadow lingering above him, though now gravely fatigued he struggled to raise his head as wanted.

"Grandpa?" Coughed Firin, blood trickled from his lungs into his mouth painfully as he spoke. "Is that you… does this mean that I'm dead now as well?" He blinked his eyes wearily to focus them on the aged figure, who himself was laughing heartily back to Firin – strangely enough. The old man shook his head disappointedly and then held out his hands to clasp onto Firin's own, the whole-time cackling like a wild animal.

"You're not dead, yet…though you've looked a lot better!" Jested Firin's grandfather, whilst shaking their hands in enthusiasm. "How do you always end up in these bad situations, my boy? You should have stayed at home, but then again… what a boring life that would have been!"

"Grandpa…" Spluttered Firin. "Always the joker!" He laughed faintly.

"Don't speak, just listen for once, Firin!" Said his grandfather sternly. "I died because I was old, it's as simple as that... it was *my* time!" He brushed at Firin's hair coarsely, just as he had always done when scolding him. "Remember all the good times we had... all the capers we shared in?" Firin nodded slightly in agreeance. "I'm so proud of you for what you've overcome and, dare I say it, honoured to be your grandfather. Stay strong my lad and you'll be okay...You'll see!"

"Grandpa..." Firin suddenly fell back into unconsciousness. His grandfather stayed for a few more moments longer by his side and then vanished, back into Alaskia's raining light, back into Eternamorrah.

"You see?" Said Alaskia, with a charming smile aimed at Cara. "Death... is not the end. Life continues to exist...just on a separate plain."

Cara wept heavily over the moving scenes being played out before her. She turned to face Alaskia's light, feeling apprehensive and in doubt of whom she herself may yet see. A tall, dark figure began to move towards Cara through the golden rays, though unremarkable initially in appearance, their distinctive walk wrought an instant terror in her.

"Not you, anyone...but you!" Seethed Cara, as she backed away into the centre of the Sanctum platform, greatly reluctant to look upon this revealing image for a second longer. "Go away...be gone...vile beast!"

"How dare you address your father and King with such...insolence!" Growled the imposing figure hatefully. "My time on this plain will be short...you must listen to what I have to say, Cara."

"Never!" Cara defensively stepped herself closer towards Alaskia, as the familiar and haunting stance of Kanaan came into being before her very eyes. Appearing as his more-mightier self once did, King Kanaan had upon his head the Magmorran Royal Crown and was wearing his regal robes; all a façade created by the king's yearning lust to hold onto power. Kanaan slowly gestured a hand across his heart and then bowed before Cara – a truly perplexing to behold for her. "Go away, Father! I do not wish to speak with you!"

"Cara, please... you *must* listen to me!" Ordered Kanaan, though in a pleading voice which was unlike his usual-aggressive manner. Cara continued to move away from him, shaking her head in disgust which each step taken, evermore sickened by his malignant presence. "Cara!"

"I have nothing more to say to you, Father! What you did to me and our family; what you did to the innocent people of our nation and the others in Impartia...is beyond any forgiveness!" Screamed Cara. This was a conversation she and Kanaan had gone over on numerous occasions before, each time they only grew apart further. "Go and rot in Kufiah's Void...that's where you belong!" Kanaan cackled again cruelly in response.

"I do not wish for your forgiveness...for there is nothing to forgive, Daughter!" Exclaimed Kanaan boldly, feeling no remorse at all towards his daughter's infliction. "That is why, I am Magmorrah's rightful ruler; there is no weakness in *my* heart."

"Nothing to forgive?" Snapped Cara, with a shocked expression. "What you did to me when I was a child; the sordid legacy you have left for your daughters… you're still as callous - even in death!" She turned ardently away from her father, having already spent so much of her built-up anger on him. A new concern then raised itself in Cara's troubled thoughts, regardless of Kanaan's mocking laughter. "If you are dead, then why has Cerebrante not bonded with me…why are Alaskia and Kufiah still in these forms?" She breathed heavier, her body shaking in agony as this realisation grew. "Ven told me that by having Cerebrante's mark on my face, it meant that I would be chosen as their new host…but it's gone. Alaskia is free now and our connection should have been made, I don't understand!" Kanaan shook his head disapprovingly against his daughter's naivety and then hastened himself towards her with a risen smirk.

"Are you so blind, Cara?" Beseeched Kanaan. "You cannot be Cerebrante; that *would* be Impartia's undoing!" He sighed, gently stroking his crown with a sorrowful touch. "I have relieved myself from Cerebrante's sacred duty. I have chosen a new and far-worthier vessel to replace me…" Kanaan's breathing increased rapidly, his anticipation for Cara's response rose even swifter.

"…A new host?" Stammered Cara in dread, as she clenched onto one of Spero's hand firmly. "What do you mean…What have you done, Father?" The outer-edges of Alaskia and Kufiah's robes started to fade, as did their likeliness to Kanaan. Together, the Celestial Spirits looked upon Cara with a knowing smile, and then bowed to her father respectfully – their connection now dwindling.

"You will understand one day, Daughter; the reasons behind what actions I have taken during my life." Said Kanaan bluntly, his expression vacant. "*The Sacred Balance* is corrupt; in its present form this world would have fallen into chaos…I had to do something!"

"So, you slaughtered thousands of innocent people; desolated our nation and imprisoned Alaskia, all in the aim of bringing peace to Impartia?" Sneered Cara, her hatred now lain out bare towards Kanaan. "You will only ever be known as the ruler that decimated Magmorrah – your home nation!"

"Impudence!" Blared Kanaan in frustration. "I took control over Kufiah, only because our bond was greater than Alaskia's. My amulet had the power to possess *any* Spirit…not just the Spirit of Darkness…"

"You possessed Kufiah to spread your dominance over Impartia…stop lying!" Countered Cara wearily. "Your words are venom, Father!" Her anger was oddly no longer reflected in Kanaan; his composure changed to display a man who, in truth, did feel remorse, though not to his past endeavours.

"I should have been honest with you and Cera, then perhaps you could have both understood - why I imprisoned the Spirit of Light?" Sighed Kanaan, as he removed his crown to look upon it. "There is an ancient force, far worse than anything I could have ever been capable of, festering in Impartia. My plan was to subvert its rise; to end a war that has been plaguing our world since the dawn of time, a war the Elemental Guardians have allowed to endure!" He replaced his crown slowly, then looked to Cara with pleading eyes. "After Cera took Magmorrah's throne from me, I began to muster a new plan. I knew that someday, someone worthy of Cerebrante's power would come to me…eventually my prayers were answered. Thus, I have granted my greatest gift of all…" Kanaan moved himself aside, revealing to Cara's instant grief the faint image of Sophilia lying motionless within Alaskia's heavenly light, appearing as if asleep in mid-air.

"My Baby!" Howled Cara, her cries blood-curdling. "You foul, *evil* monster! I hate you…I HATE you…and always will!" She collapsed into Spero's arms, despairing, disbelieving over what was now revealed. Kanaan lowered his head solemnly, as the vision of him started to fade. "You've killed my little girl…haven't you, Father? Coward! You murdered my sweet Sophilia in order to fulfil your wicked legacy! She was too young to bond with Cerebrante, you should have known this!"

"Why do you grieve so, Mortal Princess?" Interjected Kufiah. Despite his form diminishing, the Dark Spirit motioned himself gracefully towards Cara. "The child is not dead, though her life-force *is* wilting. Transferring Cerebrante's power from their host to another can cause a fatal strain upon both, this is what you are witnessing in Alaskia's light – the transcendence of Cerebrante." Cara desperately clung onto Kufiah's tattered robes. She gradually stared into his fiery eyes for further answers and hoping that he may in some way intervene. "This *cannot* be undone!"

"Save her mighty Spirit…bring back my only child!" Implored Cara frantically. "I *know* that you can cheat death - as well as cause it! For once in your existence…do the right thing!" Kufiah placed his hands upon Cara's head, the coursing negative energy from her torn emotions immediately flowed through him. He then turned to Alaskia for the Spirit of Light's own guidance.

"Such an unnatural act has not been achieved before, Brother…Can it be done?" Questioned Kufiah eagerly to Alaskia. "I have kept death at bay in mere mortals during my existence, but to disturb Cerebrante's Transcendence…alone…may ultimately destroy me." Cara threw herself upon Alaskia now, pulling at his robes like a ravaged creature.

"Help Kufiah save my baby-girl!" Ordered Cara in a commanding voice to Alaskia, her eyes flaring intensely. "You are the Celestial Spirits…You are Impartia's hope!" Alaskia sighed softly and then placed his hands upon Cara to comfort her.

"Brother speaks the truth, though it pains me to tell you this." Mourned Alaskia sincerely. "We are very limited; in what we can do to save your child." Cara aggressively snapped herself away from Alaskia's presence. "I am *truly* sorry, but Kufiah and I are not permitted to intervene in the ways of our Balancing Spirit. Sophilia will live on forever, without feeling anymore pain or ailment, when she finally reaches Eternamorrah. In that sacred realm, Sophilia *will* be safe, your loved ones will care for her…"

"Cara!" Shouted Spero, as she ran back towards her father's depleting vision.

"I HATE YOU!" Cara tore her hand viciously through the air to strike it against Kanaan's face, discovering to her instant pleasure that it did inflict him. Kanaan cackled in a shocked response, replaced his dishevelled robes and crown, then with a satisfied smirk vanished into the light behind him.

"Farewell, Daughter..." Said Kanaan tearfully, whilst looking to both Cara and Cera. "To Eternamorrah…I must go now." He smiled, sensing his nearing closure, then vanished completely.

"Forget him," whispered Spero into Cara's ear, as he willed another embrace between them. "We'll find a way to save Lia…trust me." Cara leant herself into Spero's muscular chest, his heartbeat soothing, his tender touch greatly welcomed. Through her tears, Cara continued to look upon her daughter's floating body, she longed to give Sophilia one last kiss – an impassioned desire that sadly could not be accomplished now.

"What about…a sacrifice?" Muttered Firin, his voice distant, worn though also absolute. "What if, you could transfer someone's lifeforce into Sophilia…is that possible?" He slowly tilted his head to glare upon the Celestial Spirits. "Don't let her die…"

"Yes!" Roared Kufiah lustfully, yearning to experiment with this supposed ability. "However, Mortal…your own life-force is almost gone. Brother and I would not be able to ensure that the child could be spared…"

"I'll do it…I'll do it for you and Sophilia, Cara." Declared Spero, his voice empowered and resolute. "I have lived a wonderous life…Sophilia has barely started hers."

"You would sacrifice yourself to save my Lia?" Gasped Cara. "No, Spero..." She said in reluctance, though her maternal instinct was overwhelming. "Would you really do that for us?"

"I have no regrets, Cara." Said Spero, whilst pressing her more firmly against himself. "My only one would be…that I will never feel your touch, nor hear your laughter again." Suddenly, Cara leant herself up to share in a delicate, passionate kiss with Spero. It would be a treasured moment that she would never forget.

"So be it, Son of Hydrania." Growled Kufiah, his face grimacing at the affectionate sight being displayed. "Stand within the central seal so that we, Impartia's Celestials, may perform this mighty act and do so with haste!" The Spirit of Darkness and Alaskia reached out a hand to Spero, willing him forwards, away from Cara's wanting arms. Spero knelt beside Firin to shake his hand with sincerity, then as he stood patted at his shoulder in a sign of respect to him.

"It has been an honour to journey with you, Firin." Said Spero endearingly, and with a humorous smirk to suggest otherwise.

"Too right it was…" Spluttered Firin in response, with a fleeting smirk. "The honour was mine…friend." Spero then lay himself within the central seal; making sure to take one more glance upon Cara, whom he had wished to spend more of his life with.

"Don't be sad, Cara." Assured Spero. "I'll be with my family again." He nodded his head in reassurance to her, as the divine Celestial Spirits finally moved to unify their powers against him. "Farewell…" Alaskia and Kufiah stretched out their arms together, afterwards the entire Sanctum platform began to shake violently. "I'm not afraid to die!" A dazzling ray of purest light fell from the cosmic portal of Eternamorrah, directly into Spero's body. It passed through his flesh, into the depths of his sentient soul, though it filled him with no apparent pain or fear. Spero now only felt a peaceful release come over his consciousness, as he fell slowly into a deep sleep, passing on into the endless realm, where his family duly waited to welcome him with open arms.

"Spero!" Cried Cara, whilst watching her friend's body gradually disappear upon the central seal. "Thank you…" Spero's body was swiftly replaced by that of Sophilia's, who herself entered the seal's light still lying as if asleep and without any sign of movement. "Sophilia?" Gasped Cara. "Lia, my sweetheart! Wake up! Mummy's here!" She sprinted towards the child, hoping to stir Sophilia from her endless slumber. "Please wake up, my darling…" The Elemental Seals suddenly activated in their radiant colours. Within them, stood their respective Guardians, who each entered the Sanctum platform in apprehension and ready again for battle. Ven and Levia immediately rushed towards Cara and Sophilia, whilst Aira and Pahoe stared upon the haunting visions of Impartia's Celestial Spirits.

"Are you alright, Cara?" Asked Ven briskly, his lips trembling. "Tell me, what has happened here? When I tried to connect with Skynah's Seal, all I could see was a golden light – that of only Alaskia's making." In the corner of his eye, Ven suddenly saw Sophilia gently breath and his anguish soon lifted. "Sophilia?" He gasped with relief. Cara gave to Ven a harrowing look, one that would forever haunt him.

"Kanaan…he severed his bond with Cerebrante." Said Cara, as she ran her fingers through Sophilia's hair, savouring this moment in case it would be their last shared together. "Sophilia and the Spirit of Balance are now connected…Kanaan's severance with Cerebrante nearly killed her – my baby!" Cara's temperament intensified with each coursing emotion now arising in her. "Spero sacrificed himself to save Lia, but she won't wake up, Ven… Sophilia won't wake up!" Ven placed a steady hand on both Cara and her child, feeding his spiritual energy into them, though on sensing Sophilia's heightened aura he defensively recoiled.

"Alaskia...Kufiah!" Exclaimed Ven in his excitement to the Celestial beings. "Behold, your Guardian of Balance is being reborn...Cerebrante *is* one with Sophilia!" The other Elemental Guardians fell into silence, their prayers seemingly answered. Cara however, remained subdued as she knelt against her daughter, feeling no joy or relief from this momentous event. "Sophilia needs your help!" Commanded Ven, whilst glaring upon the Celestial Spirits with a desperate expression. "Awaken her with your combined powers...or allow for chaos to reign eternal – it is your choice!" He stressed firmly, his eyes radiating intensely with their mighty spiritual power.

"Yes..." Roared Kufiah in ecstasy. "It *is* our choice!" The Spirit of Darkness then turned to Alaskia with a sadistic grin. "Brother, for the first time in our immortal existence, *we* can choose our Guardian's host and whether they are worthy or not!" Alaskia held his calm composure, though he too appeared enlightened by this notion.

"Yes, Brother." Smiled Alaskia. "I sense a wonderous future for Princess Sophilia...our *Lady Cerebrante*. She is truly worthy to govern us." Together, Alaskia and Kufiah held their arms over the motionless princess to focus their unified energy within her. The Celestial Spirits proceeded to fuel their might into Sophilia's body and soul, replenishing them and awakening a power that had lain dormant within her since birth. Sophilia awoke with a sudden gasp and instantly clenched onto her mother, a reunion both had greatly longed for. It seemed like all past woes had now left them, as Cara and Sophilia looked at each other with hopeful expressions, knowing that no force on Impartia could ever again tear them apart.

"Lia, my beautiful girl!" Exclaimed Cara heartily, whilst she wiped away the tears from her face and then did the same for Sophilia. "You're safe now...Mummy's here...Mummy's here..." She rocked the stunned child from side-to-side lovingly. "I'm so glad that you're okay!"

"Mummy!" Cried out Sophilia, in a strained voice. "You're...choking me!" Cara immediately loosened her grip and the two then laughed together merrily. "I'm glad you are okay too, just stop squeezing me!"

"What an honour it is, to witness such love." Said Levia, his radiant eyes glimmered as he spoke. "It was worth almost dying to reunite them...wasn't it Pahoe?" Pahoe tutted and instead turned her attention away from Levia to Aira.

"Sister, our purpose here is done." Declared Pahoe without expression. "It is time to return to our Sanctuaries; there is much work to be done in restoring our home-nations." The Guardian of Fire was never one to dwell in sentiment.

"Let us just savour in this moment for a while longer, Sister." Responded Aira, as she gave a humoured wink towards Levia and Ven. "This should remind all of us what our true purpose is...to preserve life and its precious events within Impartia."

"Well said, Sister." Said Ven, whilst bowing in respect towards Aira and his brethren. "Long may she live…Lady Cerebrante." The Spirits of Darkness and Light both sighed in exhaustion, their present time upon Impartia now coming to its end. Alaskia slowly released his hold over the heavenly rays beaming down from Eternamorrah. As the golden hue vanished, it revealed the immense devastation which Kufiah's attack had left upon Skynah; he had rendered the great mountain into its foundations, leaving only a surrounding peninsula and the Sanctum platform hovering above the Void below. Impartia's sun began to rise over its eastern horizon, shimmering like gold upon the surface of Skynah's ocean and lightening the darkness left from Kufiah's ruin. Ven and the other Elemental Guardians knelt respectfully before Sophilia, each placing an open palm across their hearts as a sign of adoration to her.

"It is so good to finally meet you, Sophilia." Said Ven with a genuine smile, as he moved to formally shake her hand. "May you bless Impartia, with your divine powers…" Sophilia stared back at Ven in perplexment, still unaware of what she had just been through or who these strange-looking people were that now surrounded herself and Cara. "It's alright, I understand all this must be very daunting for you."

"What's going on, Mummy?" Questioned Sophilia anxiously. "Who are these people and why are they bowing to me?" Cara brushed aside her hair and laughed back to show that there was nothing now to fear. "He's wearing robes like Jenny!" Ven's smile fell instantly, the grief for his fallen acolytes still painful and enduring.

"Well, I don't know who this *Jenny* is… but these people are our new friends and they will help to look after us from now on, okay?" Replied Cara innocently, blissful towards Ven's hidden anguish at losing his beloved Acolytes. "We must help to look after them in return though, Lia…they are strong but will need you in darker times."

Alaskia and Kufiah rapidly morphed from their masculine appearances back into small, vulnerable-looking orbs of light. Alaskia's orb shone white at its centre with a dark atmosphere encircling it, where as Kufiah's was a deep abyss with a white light surrounding the infinitely dark orb. The Celestial beings danced around Sophilia's head playfully, then soon returned to their respective seals upon the Sanctum platform without any further pomp or celebration. Sophilia looked curiously upon the peculiar orbs and their mystical departure, wandering why they had acted the way they did to her, as she then gasped in shock on seeing the injured torso of Firin lying not-too-far away.

"He's hurt!" Cried out Sophilia to her mother, hoping for her usual wisdom. "We've got to help him!" Before Cara could stop her, Sophilia quickly sprinted across to Firin. She selflessly wished to aid him in some way and was undeterred by the pool of blood seeping out from beneath. "Why is he bleeding, Mummy? There must be a way to help him! He can't die *too*!" Cara hesitated in revealing the truth behind Firin's dire injury, nor the death and destruction that had taken place upon the very mountain of which remnants they now stood upon.

"His name is Firin…and he is a new friend of mine." Explained Cara in a meek tone, knowing that her companion was greatly suffering through his last moments. "I don't think that there is anything we can do now to save him. All we can do, is to make sure that he is as comfortable as possible…" Suddenly, Ven brushed Cara aside to stand before Sophilia in prominence, with a genuine and loving smile on his face.

"My dear, sweet, caring child!" Exclaimed Ven excitedly. "There *is* something that you can do…to help this poor soul." He knelt again courteously on one knee beside Sophilia and then placed both of her hands directly over where Firin's weakening heart lay. "All you must do, is believe in yourself and focus all of your thoughts and emotions into healing him… try it, Sophilia! I know you can do it!" Sophilia glanced at Cara and then focused solely on Firin, just as instructed.

"Please… don't die." Muttered Sophilia, her thoughts turning back to the harrowing deaths she had witnessed at Ven's Sanctuary. "Let him live…take away his pain…" She silently prayed to herself, all the time her new powers flowed into Firin. Suddenly, Sophilia felt a strange, though satisfying, energy course through her arms into her trembling hands, subconsciously directing this flow towards Firin's heart and open wound.

"Amazing!" Breathed Pahoe heavily. "I can sense the power of Cerebrante in them both!"

"Silence, Sister!" Commanded Ven impatiently, with a swift gesture of his hand towards Pahoe and the other Guardians. "Sophilia needs to concentrate!"

"Come on, sweetheart…I know you can bring him back." Whispered Cara into Sophilia's ear. "*Teach us with your isolation…Free us with your love…Cast aside the fear and pain…*" She sang again softly, this time with the help of Impartia's Elemental Guardians.

"Cast aside the fear and pain!" Screamed Sophilia, taking all those stood around her by utter surprise. "Heal him!" Her eyes slowly opened and as they did a radiant-gold light burst out from within them, her voice magnified and became mighty in its tone. "Where there is darkness…there is light…where there is light…there is darkness…in-between…I now exist!" She declared with a strange, ethereal voice. The blood which had pooled out from Firin miraculously began to flow back into him; the flesh around his wound renewed itself and where Illuminecia's scarring infliction had been now completely vanished. Firin blinked his eyes against the piercing sunlight, not knowing if he had entered the realm of Eternamorrah or not. His expression quickly rose upon seeing the angelic face of Sophilia, who herself smiled back to him in amazement over this astounding recovery.

"Cara?" Questioned Firin, genuinely confused by what was transpiring around him, for Sophilia looked so much like her mother. "What are you doing? You're starting to freak me out!" Sophilia and her fellow onlookers laughed happily together in euphoria, as Firin righted himself against his previously dire condition to observe the child more closely.

"My name is Sophilia, though you can call me 'Lia'... Cara is my mummy!" Jested Sophilia, whilst looking back to see her mother's proud smile. "I helped to save you with my magic powers, you should be okay now!" Firin wrapped his arms around her passionately, grateful though astonished at how such a young girl could have managed to achieve this unlikely feat.

"Thank you so much, Sophilia!" Rejoiced Firin. "I'm very sorry, that I mistook you for your mother... you're far prettier!" He joined in with the immediate laughter and then set his sights upon Cara, who thankfully appeared to have suffered no harm, along with the four Elemental Guardians. "Hold on, where's that Hydranian sea-rat gone? Where's Spero?"

"Firin..." Cara took in a deep breath, as she fought back at her pressing tears. "Spero, he didn't make it. He gave his life to save ours and is at rest now with his family in Eternamorrah." She smiled briefly, trying to convince herself that her own words held some truth and then moved beside Ven solemnly. In her heart, Cara did not wish to divulge any further into their fallen companion's fate. "We will always remember him."

"Sorry, Cara..." Muttered Firin ashamedly. "I forgot; that Spero and I had shared in our last farewell...I was barely conscious." He knelt himself lowly upon the Sanctum platform, wishing to look out alone across Skynah's shimmering ocean waves in a quiet reflection of all that had transpired. "Every day that we now live...is a blessing. I hardly knew Spero, none of us did, but I will not forget the sacrifice he has made to save Sophilia - not to mention the rest of Impartia." Cara, Firin and Sophilia; along with the Elemental Guardians, all looked to the cosmic realm of Eternamorrah above and smiled – sensing their friend's presence and the start of a new era for Impartia.

Chapter Fourteen: A Chaotic Resurgence

Skynah was no-more; its mountain completely rendered by Kufiah, leaving only its foundations and Sanctum platform - which itself hovered precariously above the Void and below Eternamorrah's infinite realm; that still lingered somehow within its swirling clouds.

"Cerebrante has been reborn, thus so has *The Sacred Balance*." Said Ven with a content smile. There was joy in his voice, though with it lingered a sadness, that he now had to part ways with Cara and specifically Levia – his oldest friend. "We Guardians shall return to our Sanctuaries now; there we will assist in the healing our nations; our duty is once again to sanctify the elements and to protect Cerebrante's new host - Sophilia." Ven winked adoringly to the child, who herself remained oblivious to the true nature of her attained powers.

"Must you go?" Asked Cara to Ven. Her concerns now lay on how to leave the Sanctum platform, being that it was hovering perilously above an endless abyss. "How are we going to get back home…wherever that may be for us now?" Ven tilted his head in sympathy.

"Cara, I believe that Magmorrah and your subjects will be waiting for their new leading Queen." Smiled Ven. "That is your home, your rightful place within Impartia, and always has been…" An understandably horrified gasp came from Cara in response. "Have faith in yourself, my dear friend, as you have done throughout your trials in reaching Alaskia and saving Sophilia. I know that you will be a truly magnificent queen, and Sophilia a majestic princess – it is in your blood."

"I *am* a princess, Mummy?" Rejoiced Sophilia, as she curtsied to her mother. "Queen Cara of Magmorrah…I like it!"

"Shhh, Lia!" Scolded Cara, with a fairly mild look of annoyance to her child. "It's a lot to take in; I've never dreamed of taking the throne away from Cera…*Cera*!" Through all the turmoil, Cara had become side-tracked towards her sister's weakened state. She ran over to Cera and immediately fell back into a despair; the amber light that had once emanated from her eyes had now dwindled, her mouth foaming and body frail-looking as if she were elderly and infirm. "Oh, little sister…what has Kufiah done to you?"

"Aunt Cera?" Sophilia formed an instant frown against her wicked captor. "What has happened to her?" A swift relief grew upon Cara's expression, as her daughter moved in closer.

"Lia, my darling daughter, a nasty Spirit has cursed your aunt…" Cara's voice fell into a frantic plea, for a diseased desire had emerged through it. "Can you please use your magic again…to save Cera?" Sophilia continued to frown; seeing her aunt again, even in this pitiful state, did not change how she felt towards her.

"I don't know if I can, Mummy." Sighed Sophilia. "There is a dark cloud hovering above her body that I don't want to go near...can you not see it too?" She moved herself hastily away from Cera on sensing the now-familiar dark power of Kufiah that lingered inside of her.

"Kufiah is the nasty Spirit your speaking of...isn't he?" Cara's jaw dropped in shock, she could not reason as to how Sophilia knew of the Dark Spirit – particularly by name.

"It's okay, darling...I understand." Said Cara softly, as she caressed Sophilia into her bosom; just as she would always do in times where both needed one another's comfort. "Cera is not your burden; I will make sure that she is well cared for, and that no harm will ever come to either of you ever again."

"...Mother?" Gurgled Cera. Magmorrah's fallen queen could hardly muster the strength to speak, let alone move her body. "You're...alive?" Cara hid her sadness from Sophilia, she had been through enough already.

"A wise move, if I might say, Lady Cerebrante!" Declared Pahoe unreservedly, her words were wrought instantly by a succession of displeased stares from the other Guardians present. "What's the matter with you all? The last thing Impartia needs is for Cera to be brought back into power...her fate has been sealed...let it stay that way."

"Show *some* compassion, Sister...for goodness sake!" Scolded Levia, as he gestured towards Cara's mournful expression. Pahoe shrugged indecisively, and then without further word stood herself back upon the Sanctuary of Fire's seal. "Come, let us return to our Sanctuaries..." Ushered Levia. "It looks like *your* transport home has arrived, Cara?" The lead-vessel from Weissamorrah's United Fleet now approached, aiming itself against Skynah's peninsula with an increased speed and tenacity, showing no sign of diverting from its steadied course.

"That is our signal to go, I guess?" Commented Ven disparagingly, whilst placing himself upon his own seal. "Farewell, Cara and Sophilia...Farewell, Firin! Till we all meet again...someday." The Elemental Seals burst once more into activation, immediately teleporting the Guardians back to their respective Sanctuaries, leaving only the three mortals to ponder at what trial next faced them.

"Those Guardians like landing us in the thick of things, don't they?" Bantered Firin, his wound apparently had no infliction on the strange humour he had. "Only problem now is, how the Hell are we going to get off this platform?"

"That's easy!" Countered Sophilia with a proud smirk. "Walk into the light..." She playfully flicked her hand towards the central seal, soon igniting a golden beam within it. "I've asked Alaskia if they can get us on that boat...aren't I clever?"

"*Very* clever, young princess!" Laughed Firin in relief, trying not to show too much adoration for Sophilia's impressive skills. "Ladies first!"

"*Really*, Firin…this again?" Scoffed Cara amusingly. She lifted Cera into the protection of her arms with ease, and then gestured for Firin and Sophilia to walk into the ethereal ray of light. "I hope this works, Lia."

"Of course, it will, Mummy!" Said Sophilia. She hastened herself to walk into the light first. "Alaskia is a good Spirit, she will take us to safety…*she* promised!"

"She?" Remarked Firin, as he laughed with a beleaguered expression to Cara. "I can't say, that I'll miss the towering brute Cera had control over!" As they each ventured into the central seal, it suddenly transported them to land upon the deck of Weissamorrah's lead-vessel, its crew frantically rushed towards their unexpected guests with their guns and swords at the ready.

"Don't move!" Ordered one of the naval officers. "Stay where you are!"

"Thanks, *Alaskia*!" Mumbled Firin under his breath. "Some help you were!" The ship's captain curiously approached Cara, and at first retaliated on witnessing the undeniable figure of Cera being held within her arms. "Magmorrah's Queen lives!" He cried out to his crewmembers. "Take them below deck! They are, without any doubt, Magmorran spies!" Sophilia bravely stepped forward. In defiance, she displayed the radiating mark of Cerebrante upon her hand to the captain and his crew, instantly forcing them into a shocked state of silent surrender.

"A Spirit Mark? I've read about these; though surely…it can't be?" Queried the Captain, excitement quickly rose in him. "Those amber eyes!" He looked across Cara and Sophilia, and then to Cera, establishing what relationship they indefinitely shared. "Magmorrah's lost Princesses…what a day this has been!"

"I'm related to Talam's Royal Family, you know?" Quirked Firin confidently, though the Captain merely brushed this aside from his vagrant appearance. "Charming! Just for once, I'd like to be addressed appropriately!" He scoffed.

"Firin!" Scolded Cara again, trying not to laugh at her boisterous companion. "I have something important that I wish to declare to all here present." The Captain silently nodded in agreeance to Cara, then moved further back to allow for her proclamation. "Cera is no longer a threat to anyone, nor… is she Magmorrah's reigning Queen!" Cara attempted again to withhold her grief from view; it was strong, though her devotion to Sophilia was greater. "From this moment forth I, Cara, first-born daughter of King Kanaan, shall take rule over Magmorrah and its sovereignty! Let all nations know, that *my* reign will be one of peace!" The Captain and his crew members cheered rapturously at this news. "I promise to redeem Magmorrah's reputation, and to help rebuild the other nations of Impartia from the desolation my bloodline has cast upon them!"

"Long live, Queen Cara of Magmorrah!" Shouted the Captain joyously. "Long live, the rightful ruler of the Ash Lands!" His cries were met in unison with the fellow crewmembers, their instant adoration towards Cara truly astounded her.

"Please accept my sincerest apology, your Majesty." Said the Captain, as he bowed before Cara in respect. "Forgive my harsh response to your sudden arrival and pardon my insensitive approach to this burden, which you now hold in your arms." The Captain gave a fleeting look of detest towards Cera, then returned his subservient smile back at Cara. "I am Captain Jardiah and whilst you are a guest upon this vessel, she and my fleet are yours to command. We duly await your Orders... Queen Cara."

"Yes, Queen Cara!" Interrupted Sophilia innocently. "What are your Orders?" Cara threw herself into a silent moment of reflection. Despite always being addressed to as a princess during childhood, the notion finally hit her that she was now an actual, reigning monarch, and this duty filled her with much dread. Cara pondered how her and Sophilia's life would now be so dramatically changed, once they returned to Magmorrah, once she was coronated officially.

"I would be much obliged; if you could take us to Magmorrah and at once." Spoke Cara in an anxious tone, authority was never her strongest point. "My subjects must be told that I am their ruler, though they must never discover the truth behind what has happened to Cera."

"Very good, your Majesty!" Said Captain Jardiah with glee. "To your stations!" He commanded to his fellow crewmembers. "Make haste to Magmorrah's Capital, on the double!"

"We're going back to Magmorrah?" Whimpered Sophilia nervously to Cara. "I hated it there!" She stamped her feet to display this disbelief.

"Magmorrah *is* our home-nation, Lia..." Replied Cara, equally as nervous. "You will learn to like it - eventually."

It had reached nightfall by the time Cara's vessel docked within Magmorrah's northern-most port; only on account of the many detours she had requested, so that Sophilia could see Hydrania and Talam in person. The party of weary travellers and crew members cautiously alighted from their Hydranian ship, all wary of what response their unexpected presence may bring. To Cara's horror, hundreds of Magmorran citizens were waiting along the entire length of the dock for her; the news of their Queen's mysterious illness and sudden dethronement had already reached them by this point.

"Firin," whispered Cara apprehensively. "There are so many people, I don't know what to do."

"Look, Cara, you've stood up against Celestial Spirits and won...not to mention General Nira!" Exclaimed Firin, with a dismissive flicker of his hands. "There's not *that* many, maybe a couple of hundred or so?" His expression clearly showed that Firin himself did not believe his words.

"They look happy, Mummy." Sophilia suddenly appeared beside Cara and Firin, taking both by surprise. "I don't think they are here to hurt us..."

"Your Majesty," said the Captain Jardiah, his stance proud and bold. "Magmorrah awaits your gracious presence."

"Fine. I'll go first!" Snapped Cara, furious at her own reservations, as she looked to Firin anxiously. "Instruct the crew members, that they must bring Cera to the Royal Palace in *total* secrecy…not a single soul must know that she is aboard this ship."

"Don't worry, Cara." Said Firin with a serious expression, for once. "I'll make sure of it, that Cera is kept safe…just as you wish." After pacing the deck for a few moments longer, Cara then took her first free steps back upon the native soil of Magmorrah. She looked nervously over the gathered crowd; each citizen longingly in search for their Queen's anticipated appearance, each also hoping to see a glimpse of their fallen monarch. Cara tried to prepare herself mentally for any possible reprisals whilst she walked towards the sea of unknown faces, as memories from her first departure tore away again then swiftly retreated, only because Firin and Sophilia continued to shout their adoration for her from aboard their ship.

"Here goes nothing…" Muttered Cara to herself, whilst trying to hasten her steps forward so that she did not have to be at the centre of attention for too long. "This is…bad."

"Mummy!" Screamed Sophilia, against Firin's fleeting restraint. "I love you!"

"I love you too!" Said Cara passionately in return, praying that these would not be her last words to Sophilia. A loving moment then followed, as mother and daughter stared into one another's eyes passionately, releasing any doubtful tensions while the calming power of Cerebrante flowed between them from Sophilia.

"Noble Citizens of Magmorrah, I am Cara…first-born daughter of King Kanaan, and rightful heir to the throne of this great nation…" Cara stuttered momentarily, then once again took possession over her words. "My sister, Queen Cera, has succumbed to a grave illness on her recent travels. Therefore, she is no longer able to continue as Queen…I now take this honourable duty from her." A tense atmosphere lifted but quickly ceased, as Cara displayed her amber eyes to those stood around. "I promise, to every citizen here, and to the each of the other nations, that we *will* recover from the scars that have been inflicted! Together, we *will* create a brighter future for Impartia's next generation!" An elevated roar of cheers and chanting immediately met with Cara. Magmorrah's citizens hailed their new Queen and soon descended upon the Hydranian vessel, welcoming each of its crewmembers with open arms. Through the ensuing chaos, Cara called out for Sophilia and Firin to join her. Once they did, she held onto both tenderly, never wanting for this precious release to ever end.

"Long live Queen Cara! Long live Queen Cara!"

"I told you, Mummy…they love you!" Screeched Sophilia joyously, as she tightened her fingers around Cara's hands. "If you're a Queen now, does that mean we can live in a big palace?" Her smile grew wider in anticipation.

"Yes, Lia." Said Cara wearily, after taking a few breaths to regain herself. "That is where we are heading to now." It did not take long for Cara, Firin and Sophilia to reach Magmorrah's Royal Palace. The grand structure was situated directly within Magmorrah's
capital city - a mere few miles or so away from the northern docks. They were escorted by Queen Cera's Elite Guards, who had duly sworn their oath to Cara, without any need for persuasion. They entered through the Palace's towering gates to look upon its grand architecture, a sight both daunting and inspiring.

"This is our home now?" Gasped Sophilia, as she shook at her mother's arms ecstatically. "It's huge!"

"Yes, Lia...this is our home." Responded Cara, with a hint of dread in her voice. "It hasn't changed at all." She looked upon the Palace's obsidian walls fearfully; they were so alike to Kufiah's Sanctuary that it sickened her. "...Home."

Cara's old servants and court advisors met with her within the palace's magnificent entranceway. Each appeared to be surprised, though also greatly excited, as they celebrated the sight of their rightful monarch and lost princess. Their expressions however saddened somewhat, on observing Cera's frail body being carried towards them by Firin; her body cloaked with a thick, coarse sheet and her crown no longer adorning her head, all a sight so unfamiliar and undignified to behold.

"Your Majesty, it is good to have home again." Rejoiced the leading-servant, as she knelt herself respectfully before Cara. "Do you remember me, Majesty?" She grinned with an anxious twitch.

"Yes, Helena...I remember you very well and I'm not officially 'Queen' – yet." Cara instantly wrapped her arms around the servant, whom had been the only one to have ever shown her affection. "I've missed you very much."

"We have missed your gracious presence, also." Grinned Helena pleasantly. "The plans for your official Coronation are being drafted as we speak. The Palace and its grounds are yours to explore; for the first time...dare I say?" Cara then rolled her eyes back sympathetically.

"Thank you, Helena." Said Cara. Her immediate attention soon turned back towards the Royal Carriage, in which was carrying her vulnerable sister. "Please take Cera to her room and ensure that she is cared for...no one else must know of this; only those who serve inside the palace."

"As you wish, Majesty." Helena curtsied again, followed by the other servants and guards stood present. She then rose herself with a gaunt expression. "General Nira has not returned; she has been presumed dead and your first duty will be to anoint her replacement...I'm afraid." Cara showed no displeasure in being reminded of Nira's downfall. Instead, she smiled back to Helena with a hopeful glint in her eyes.

"I have the perfect candidate in mind, though I'm not sure if she is still a serving member of Magmorrah's Elite Force?" Commented Cara with a knowing smirk. "...Your sister."

"Katrinia?" Gasped Helena. "Yes, Katrinia is still a member of Magmorrah's Elite Force. Queen Cera did not take too kindly towards my sister's more merciful approach to her enemies...she is currently stationed as a Palace Guard here."

"Good, then have her come over to visit me as soon as possible." Commanded Cara firmly. "Magmorrah requires a valiant warrior to lead her army, not a sadistic murderer...like Nira was." She grimaced resentfully.

"I have no doubt that Katrinia will accept this honourable duty, though there are a few other issues which you need to address before your Coronation." Sighed Helena, knowing that this would be the last thing Cara would want to hear. "The remaining leaders of Magmorrah's Army are waiting for you in the throne room...there is much to discuss."

"Firin, if you would be so kind...could you show Sophilia the stables around the back?" Whispered Cara carefully to him. "She has always wanted to see a horse; they are her favourite animal...and there should be several in the stables."

"Okay, Cara...I'll be your babysitter!" Laughed Firin discreetly, he then turned to catch Sophilia's fleeting attention. "Lia, come with me...your mum has a surprise for you in the palace stables!"

"Firin!" Dismayed Cara. "You just can't keep a secret, can you?" Firin shrugged unashamedly and then joined Sophilia to freely explore the palace grounds. "Well, I presume that I should be getting on with my royal duties then, Helena?"

"Yes, my Queen. I would sincerely advise that you do." Responded Helena with a wizened smirk, laughing faintly afterwards as to not break from her formal role. "Magmorrah's Army...is now yours to command."

Cara's first Order, as Queen-in-waiting, was to withdraw her remaining forces from their invasive positions within the other lands of Impartia. She proclaimed, that they were to journey to the Sanctuary of Darkness, and once there arrest its corrupted guards and free any unfortunate prisoners hidden inside – that is, if they were still alive. As time drifted on, Cara and Sophilia slowly began to adapt to their new lifestyles, growing accustomed day-by-day with the strange, regal formalities which they now had to abide by.

Soon, the welcomed news reached Cara that her forces had returned from Kufiah's Sanctuary; though sadly fewer in number, as the guards who waited there fought bitterly until meeting with their own violent deaths. The surviving prisoners were either too disturbed or frail to leave, forcing Cara's soldiers to struggle in their rescuing efforts. Magmorrah's benevolent ruler raced through her palace's vast hallways, into its tremendous entranceway, to stand solemnly in waiting for the fragile souls from Kufiah's Sanctuary to appear – as was strictly instructed.

One-by-one the weakened guests and their liberators sauntered into Magmorrah's Palace. Cara bowed her head to each of them respectfully, fully understanding what torturous ordeals they had each endured - having shared a similar experience herself in the Vault of Loss.

"It gives me great pleasure to welcome you all here." Said Cara in a brave voice. She made certain to look across every face as she spoke. "You are free! Magmorrah is again your home…not your prison!" An awkward silence reverberated throughout the palace entranceway, swiftly taking a hold over Cara's resolute stance. She took in a deep breath and then continued with her address. "I know that it will take a great deal of time for you all to adjust, but I *will* ensure that each of you are well-housed and granted the freedom of which you deserve. Your liberation shall be long-remembered and cherished by every citizen."

Sophilia sneakily appeared from the one of the stairwells that led into the main entrance hall. She proudly watched her mother address the liberated prisoners, herself sympathetic towards their suffering and need for peaceful solace.

"Who are all these people, Mummy?" Bellowed Sophilia, without any concern of reprisal.   "What are they doing here?" She was hoping not to offend the already-disheartened figures with her curiosity, though they were too fatigued to even notice the small child's presence.

"They were prisoners at Kufiah's Sanctuary, Lia." Explained Cara in a displeased voice, though she was keen to promote Sophilia's empathy. "We are going to look after them all, that is, until they are well enough to start their new lives…just like we have." Sophilia nodded her head in agreeance.

"That's very kind of you, Mummy." Said Sophilia endearingly. Her intrigue rapidly moved towards a small boy, who himself was barely visible amongst the other prisoners. He was of a similar age to Sophilia, though his emaciated body and wiry blonde hair made him appear far older. She immediately ran up to him. "Hello, my name is Sophilia…what is your name?" Sophilia was so excited, that she hardly gave him the chance to respond. "Don't be shy!"

"My name… is Airan." Said the boy in a faint whisper, fighting against his exhaustion. He slowly reached his gaze to meet with Sophilia's; her angelic features emanated an empowering warmth that both entranced and excited him instantly. "It is a pleasure to meet you, Princess. I have heard a great deal about you." Sophilia clapped her hands frantically at the boy's cute response. Suddenly she noticed a similar birthmark to her own upon Airan's left hand, though very different in its design compared to Cerebrante's on hers. "Oh, that…" Muttered Airan dismissively. "It's…nothing."

"It's just like mine!" Exclaimed Sophilia. "You have a mark just like me…see?" She quickly held out her right hand in front of Airan, displaying to him the strong radiating mark of Cerebrante. "It means that you're special!"

"They *are* alike…" Breathed Airan despondently, as he steadied his marked hand beside Sophilia's to compare them. "Mine looks like a bursting star, doesn't it?" Sophilia nodded bashfully to agree. "The lines move on it sometimes, depending on what mood I'm in." Airan eagerly ushered for Sophilia to inspect his mark with him. Within its centre was a solid dark circle, that had several outreaching lines stretching away from it. The lines slowly shifted like dancing rays of sunlight, moving more-so as the pair concentrated harder on them.

"Amazing! That's one the greatest things I've ever seen, Airan!" Declared Sophilia, as she giggled shyly. "That must mean that we're both special…isn't that right, Mummy?" Cara smiled, though also stared in dread at Airan's mark. "Come and take a look, it's so pretty!"

Cara cautiously approached Airan, trying not to display her fear.

"How very unusual, Airan." Commented Cara in a polite tone to him, whilst still looking with dread to his mark. "Where are you from…might I ask?" The shifting birthmark now seemed to be reaching out its lines towards Sophilia, concerning Cara even-more, though she sensed no immediate threat coming from the small and frail-looking boy. "I would greatly appreciate it, if you could tell us."

"It's okay, Airan." Remarked Sophilia, as she nudged at his side playfully. "Mummy is kind, she won't hurt you…she's just nosey!" Airan stumbled over his words at first, then found courage once looking into Sophilia's eyes again.

"I can't remember much, honestly." Implored the boy in a pleading voice. "All I can remember, is being in a very dark place with nothing around me…I wasn't scared though. because I felt safe somehow." He forced an awkward smile to Cara, who herself granted the same gesture back in response. "All I know, is that I woke up to find myself in a small room, surrounded by people who all looked very sad and none of them ever talked to me." Sophilia rubbed at Airan's marked hand, hoping to comfort him. "Not long after, your soldiers came to rescue us all and for that…I thank you."

"You are most-welcome for that, Airan." Said Cara in a wavering voice. "You are free now and that's all that matters." Despite his youthful appearance and naïve mannerisms, Airan wrought a terror in Cara. She was certain that the boy had just described the Void at Skynah, fearing that there could be no other likely explanation. Cara planned to keep a close eye on him. "I believe that it would be fitting for you to stay here, in Magmorrah. I shall make the arrangements for your housing and provisions - immediately." Gulped Cara anxiously. "I pray, that this offer pleases you?"

"Mummy! Mummy!" Screeched Sophilia enthusiastically, she then tugged at Cara's robes to emphasise her desperation. "I want Airan to stay here with us! I haven't made any new friends yet and he seems like such a good boy!"

"I'm not too sure, Lia?" Cara hesitated initially, her eyes still fixated upon the shifting birthmark. "I'll have a think about it, okay?"

"Please, Mummy!" Begged Sophilia. She flickered her eyelashes pitifully to induce a guilt in Cara. "He's my friend now!" The doubts Cara had regarding Airan's story still troubled her, but soon she gave in to her daughter's wanting request. Cara, from the depths of her soul, could not bear to make Sophilia suffer the same loneliness that she herself had needed to endure throughout her own youth in Magmorrah's Palace.

"I promise, your Majesty…I won't be a nuisance." Interjected Aira wearily. His fellow prisoners rallied around him to display their own wish that Sophilia's request be granted. "I have been through so much toil, to be accepted into your palace would be a great honour."

"I never said…" Stammered Cara, deeply shocked by Airan's assumption. The prisoners cheered louder for Airan's royal induction, giving Cara little choice to act otherwise. "Very well, you can stay here with us." She looked to Helena anxiously. "Please prepare the necessary arrangements for Airan to be made a Prince of Magmorrah, Helena. From this day forth, he shall be known as my adopted son…if that is what Airan wants?" Helena froze in shock, as did Cara, with only her children and the liberated prisoners celebrating this brash decision.

"Bless you, *Mother*…" Replied Airan, his display of joy immediately shared in Sophilia. "We won't be alone ever again, Sophilia!" He cried to her. "We're going to be the best of friends!"

"Yes!" Screamed Sophilia in delight. "Thank you, Mummy! I love you so much!"

"I will make the arrangements for you, Ma'am." Uttered Helena reservedly, as she nodded to some of the other servants; signalling for them to inform the Palace secretary of this brash decision.

"Please ensure that Airan is inaugurated before my Coronation." Spoke Cara discreetly to Helena, her expression gaunt and overwhelmed. "I can't say that I'm looking forward to that either."

"All will be well in the end, Ma'am." Assured Helena. She and Cara then proceeded to inspect the liberated prisoners, while Airan and Sophilia were escorted to their separate rooms. "I dare not imagine what awful conditions they must have been living in," sighed Helena. "I've heard so many horrific accounts from those who suffered under the Acolytes of Darkness…they were nothing but evil."

"Most of them were," stammered Cara, as she thought back to Moah and his courageous actions. "That is in the past now, let us focus on rehabilitating these poor souls." She quickly turned to address her soldiers again. "Assist our guests to their rehabilitation complex and ensure that it is guarded - at all times."

"Yes, Ma'am!" Responded her soldiers with a deafening yell. In a relatively organised manner, they then escorted the weary prisoners away from Cara's palace. "Attention!" Bellowed the Staff Sergeant. "Follow out in single-file! Move it!" His harsh manner greatly displeased Cara. She swiftly concluded however, that under General Nira and her malicious control, the Staff Sergeant would have known no other way to act.

"I hope the children are behaving," sighed Cara to Helena, hoping to distract herself from the day's turbulent events. "Lia can be so boisterous at times, though she has taken an instant liking to Airan…there is definitely something peculiar about him."

"Ma'am…you have *nothing* to fear." Besought Helena with a dismissive smirk. "Airan is but a child; a vulnerable little boy, who *you* have given a new lease of life to." She could see from Cara's unresponsive demeanour that it would be wise to change this subject, though tactfully. "I will keep your children entertained over the next few days. As for yourself, Ma'am…you *must* concentrate on your Coronation."

"It is the sole thought in my mind at this moment, Helena!" Chuckled Cara, in trying to convince herself of how foolish her concerns really were. "I just never thought the day would come, where I would be crowned 'Queen of Magmorrah'…it still sounds strange."

"Get some rest, your Highness." Helena gestured Cara towards the grand staircase, obviously hinting that she should make to her bedchamber. "I will take care of every fine detail…you have nothing to worry about."

If only it were that simple. The days fleeted by too quickly and before Cara knew it, her Coronation day had arrived. Outside in the streets of Magmorrah's Capital, echoing sounds coming from the gathered crowds filled the city's air; it's streets vibrant with various carnivals and music festivals. Situated within the palace grounds was a mighty cathedral, that Queen Karolheid herself had built in honour of Kanaan's birth, it was soon to play as the setting where Cara would finally be crowned. Numerous leading figures and other dignitaries from across Impartia gathered in Karolheid's Cathedral, all eagerly waiting to meet in person Magmorrah's new reigning monarch. The sun that day had risen with a golden hue.

"You can do this, Cara…You can do this." Cara had seated herself before Karolheid's worn bedroom mirror, an antique even when she had purchased it. "Becoming a Queen won't be so bad, you've lived through worse." Her heart and breathing paced, the whole world around Cara felt like it was collapsing. "Your ancestors were all rulers, if they could do it…why not you? Don't be as heartless as they were though…What I am I doing?" She whimpered resentfully.

"Your Majesty?" Helena slowly peered her head around the bedroom's door. She presumed to have heard Cara talking with Sophilia. "Oh, good!" She exhaled in relief. "It is custom that you should be alone before your ceremony…" Helena's smile fell on seeing Cara's distress. "Old ways *can* be broken though, Ma'am. You will have the power to do that now."

"I would very much like to break that archaic custom…if that is okay, Helena?" Sighed Cara pleadingly. "Are Sophilia and Airan ready…are they behaving themselves?"

"The children are dressed and well," assured Helena. "However, they are already at Karolheid's Cathedral awaiting your entrance." She moved behind Cara to loosen the grips upon her hair. "You though, Ma'am…are far from ready!"

"Sorry," whispered Cara thoughtfully. "There has been so much plaguing my mind of late. I keep having flashbacks…"

"Flashbacks?" Questioned Helena, her face filling with dread. "Would you like to share them with me…perhaps alleviate their infliction on you?"

"No." Cara replied with a firm tone, which Helena worryingly had not heard come from her before. "They involve friends being killed and wicked spirits chasing after me; hardly an enlightening topic to share."

"Very well." Helena twitched nervously, not knowing how to react with such unprecedented issues. "I almost forgot!" She jolted excitedly. "Your dress is here, and the servant-girls are ready in-waiting to help you with your adornments."

"Thank you, Helena. You may be dismissed." A pleasant grin rose on Cara's face, she was enthusiastic to see for herself the dress that had been specially made for her. "You may come in, girls." Cara's dress-maker entered first, as Helena exited, and had within her hands the named dress which she had only a week to make. "Good morning, shall we get started?"

"Good morning, Your Highness." Responded Cara's dress-maker, in apprehension. "I hope you like it?" She held out with tremoring hands, what looked like, a lengthy sheet of scarlet silk. Cara had specifically instructed that it be lighter than Cera's Coronation dress, which indecently appeared more like the robes worn by Kufiah's Acolytes. The dress was fully laced with designs that were inspired from Impartia's varying nations, as a deliberate display of unity; a point of devotion which Cara dearly wished to promote as Queen.

"It's perfect!" Exclaimed Cara, as she held the dress up to inspect its finer details closer. "Congratulations, this dress is *absolutely* beautiful!" She embraced the dress-maker, to the immediate shock of her servants, themselves still haunted by Cera's crueller nature. "We must make haste!" Gasped Cara, the sun was signalling that it was almost midday. "My Coronation ceremony will be starting soon!" The servants and dress-maker rushed to prepare Cara, their hands shaking in a cocktail of excitement and anxiety as they did. Not long after, Cara looked again at herself in the mirror; something was missing, an adornment which she was truly dreading to wear.

"All you need now is your crown, your Highness…then you, yourself, shall look perfect…a true Queen of Magmorrah." Commented one the servant-girls naively. "Princess Sophilia will be so excited when she sees you wear it."

"Quite right!" Responded Cara in sharp voice, her tone bitter and resentful. "I shall wear Magmorrah's crown this day only. In a way, it still belongs to my sister…that horrid thing is more of a burden than an adornment." The servants briskly made their exit, sensing their master's angst, leaving Cara alone again to dwell in her thoughts. "Perhaps, there is still time to visit you…before the carriage arrives?" She thought ominously.

Cara traipsed her steps along the vast corridors of her palace, towards its main entranceway that felt so far away now. The hallways were eerily barren and silent, except one room where a series of harrowing cries originated from. Cara placed herself before the room where the shrieking howls were sounding, compelled beyond measure to visit her incapacitated sister, still desperate for her salvation. Cara knocked at the door in reluctance at first, as a steady sensation of sickness began to rise in her stomach.

"Password!" Commanded a stern voice from inside the room. "Password, or you may not enter!" They shouted forcibly.

"*A light in the darkness…*" Replied Cara begrudgingly, her lips tremoring as she spoke to fight back the pressing tears. "It's Cara, please permit my entry." A set of hurried clanking noises followed from the door's lock, it soon opened with an embarrassed-looking guard stood present behind – keys still in hand.

"Majesty, please forgive me." Said the Guard bashfully. "Of course, you may enter, Your Highness."

"Thank you, there is no need for forgiveness or such formalities; you were only following your Orders correctly." Replied Cara with a forced smile. "How is she?"

"I think it's best, you look for yourself…" Replied the Guard in a strange, cowardly manner. "We shall give you both some privacy." The other guards heeded their key-master's call and immediately left the room, leaving Cara though this time not alone.

"Sister?" Whispered Cara cautiously as she entered. "Cera…" The once-imposing and tyrannical Queen of Magmorrah was now nothing but a lifeless shell of her former, malicious self. Cera could hardly move or speak and each of her daily needs had to be met by devoted servants, each sworn to secrecy and of whom Cara had managed to persuade in looking after her sister's fragile body. "Cera, it's me…your big sister, Cara." Cera howled like she was in an insufferable form of agony, her flailing limbs contracting to display this tormented existence. "Cera, I've come to see you again… just like I promised." She placed a gentle hand upon her sister's, hoping to bring some comfort at the least. "I know you can hear me…"

"Mother!" Screamed Cera hauntingly, before falling back into an expressionless stare that she aimed against her grief-stricken sister. "You're…alive…alive…you're…alive."

"It is my Coronation today, Cera." Said Cara sombrely. "I wish, that things were different and that you could be there with me; despite all that has happened between us." She sighed glumly, then glanced around Cera's room; taking in every grotesque decoration which she had once lovingly adored. "I can't believe you kept that old tapestry - it's hideous… Nevertheless, I will leave it there…maybe it can remind you of happier times?" Cera continued to glare at Cara in a forced silence, her body compelled against its own involuntary movements, her life no longer her own. The cruellest twist in Kufiah's curse on Cera, was that she could hear everything going on around her, though she could not answer back coherently; she was cursed to forever dwell on her sins, held inside the prison of her own body. Cara wept softly as she moved away from Cera to leave the room, only glancing back one more time to grant her a remorseful look. "I will make you proud, Cera." Said Cara firmly. "I will do everything that I can to become a righteous ruler, and shall make sure that no harm will ever come to you again… I love you."

Cara finally arrived at Karolheid's Cathedral, a great deal later than expected and with a far calmer demeanour - thankfully. Cara's loyal advisors and handmaidens swiftly greeted her and then, with even more haste, escorted their queen-in-waiting towards the gargantuan cathedral doors.

"Sorry I'm late!" Said Cara in humour, thought it was not met kindly by her advisors who had grown impatient in their waiting. "Where are Sophilia and Airan?" She questioned frantically. "Where are my children?"

"They are inside, Ma'am!" Exclaimed a burly advisor, whilst trying not to choke on their struggling breaths. "The Prince and Princess shall follow you from behind, please hasten yourself, Ma'am! The ceremony has already started!" Cara had never set foot inside Karolheid's Cathedral before; it was ridiculously huge and was entirely fashioned from obsidian; appearing more like Kufiah's Sanctuary than a holy place of worship. An ancient pipe organ burst into song, a chorus of gut-wrenching sounds followed, as Cara began her procession along the vast rows of pews and strangers sat upon them.

"There are so many people here..." Thought Cara anxiously, not recognising barely any face around her. "There must be *someone* familiar here?" To her relief, upon the cathedral's grand altar stood Impartia's four Elemental Guardians. Each raised a prominent smile on seeing their unlikely friend again, though the radiance that had once lingered in Ven's eyes seemed somewhat weaker, almost sorrowful. Beside the Guardians stood Firin, now Cara's own personal bodyguard, himself gleaming proudly with joy. The various dignitaries seated nodded politely to Cara, whilst she looked back to them awkwardly in return.

"All rise!" Ordered the cathedral's Service-Master to his guests. "Please be seated...Princess Cara." He gestured towards an aged, wooden throne which had been situated centrally before the grand altar. "'Tis a glorious day for Magmorrah and her people!"

As her Coronation ceremony played out, Cara deafened herself from the tedious formalities which now had to take place, as the Service-Master performed his necessary and tedious proceedings. Cara's immediate thoughts were flowing back through all that she had been through recently; from her unfortunate capture by General Nira, to losing Spero in his selfless act of which ultimately saved her daughter's life. In the corner of her eye, Cara suddenly saw Sophilia. The child waved happily to her mother, disregarding the stringent customs such a ceremony enforced, then quickly approached the altar to stand beside Cara, who then enthusiastically lifted her child to sit upon her lap.

"It gives me great honour, to place this symbol of Magmorrah's sovereignty upon you!" Declared the Service-Master gleefully, as he lowered Cera's heavy crown onto Cara's delicate brow. "May your reign be righteous, and may you bless Impartia with your gracious wisdom and love!" Cara carefully adjusted the crown to fit her head more comfortably, though no matter how hard she tried it still hurt. "Princess Cara Til-Magmorros! From this day forth, let it be known, you *are* the anointed Queen of Magmorrah - Long may you and your divine bloodline live!" A deafening echo corresponded to the Service-Master's words, reverberating the love felt for Cara in all present.

"Queen Cara..." Repeated Sophilia in excitement. "I love you so much, Mummy! I've always wanted to be a Princess!"

"Try to be quiet, Lia!" Said Cara sternly. "The Ceremony is not over yet..."

"...Sorry!" Snapped Sophilia playfully, as she continued to look at her own reflection in Cara's crown. "What's that?"

"What's what, Lia?" Cara's frustration with her daughter's mischievous antics was now starting to grow. "Please sit still, the Ceremony will be over soon and then we can go to a party...okay?" She implored awkwardly.

"There's a pretty purple light in your crown...and it's not a jewel!" Urged Sophilia through a strained whisper. "Look, Mummy!" Cara tried to keep her composure whilst contemplating what it was that Sophilia had seen. "Mummy...it's Airan!"

"Airan?" Gasped Cara. She frantically searched through the sea of faces to find her adopted son, it did not take long to accomplish this. "Airan..."

The newly-anointed Prince of Magmorrah had seated himself in plain sight, rightfully within the first few rows, amongst some dignitaries from Talam. He stared intently upon Cara and Sophilia, interchanging his glance between both, seemingly expressionless and emanating an unceasing presence that drew in Cara's fearful attention instantly. Airan's eyes now glimmered with an amethyst light that radiated softly towards the startled Queen, they were piercing yet beautiful to behold.

"Airan..." Cara actioned her words across to him silently. "Are you alright?" Airan then responded to her in the same manner, his face still expressionless as if under a powerful possession.

"Long live...Queen Cara." A disturbing smile began to forge on Airan's face that unnerved Cara, giving further rise to the concerns she already had with him. The Prince of Magmorrah then turned his sights to Princess Sophilia again. "Long live...Lady Cerebrante." Karolheid's Cathedral suddenly erupted into a chorus of cheers, its service-master had completed Cara's ceremony and she hadn't even realised it.

"How are you feeling, Cara?" Questioned Levia sympathetically, as he placed a steady hand upon her shoulder. "All this must seem so foreign to you, but I know that you're going to be a fantastic ruler...without any doubt." He laughed faintly, though soon sensed Cara's growing fear. "What is the matter...did I startle you?"

"No, Levia...*you* didn't scare me." Replied Cara despondently. She then turned her head slowly to look upon the Guardian, whom always seemed so full of hope. "It's Airan...look at his eyes." Levia discreetly lifted his gaze to search for the elusive prince.

"What about them, Cara?" Questioned Levia dismissively, though the faint purple flicker in Airan's eyes soon changed his humorous tone. "...Airan?"

"Look at them, Levia!" Snapped Cara back in a desperate voice. "Tell me...what do you see?" Levia quickly stared into Airan's radiant eyes. The Guardian too felt an immense power emanate from them, and one he had only witnessed in his most-terrifying nightmares.

"What I see, Cara...is an ancient entity; a force that we Elemental Guardians have considered to be forgotten for almost five-thousand years." Faltered Levia anxiously, as he stared towards the entrancing amethyst light. "I am not certain; but we shall need to keep a close watch over Prince Airan...and Princess Sophilia." Airan continued to glare at the Queen and Guardian contently, his eyes radiating their light even greater now.

The End

It would be greatly appreciated, if you could leave a review on Amazon and/or Goodreads.

Thank you...

Cerebrante: The Forgotten Guardian

Scheduled for release – Autumn/Fall 2018

The Sacred Balance has been reborn in Princess Sophilia of Magmorrah. Her mother – Cara, now Magmorrah's ruling monarch, has spent the past eight years helping to rebuild Impartia from the desolation her sister – Queen Cera, had inflicted upon it during her tyrannical reign.

Before her official Coronation, Cara had adopted a young orphaned boy named Airan, who had been held as prisoner within Kufiah's Sanctuary of Darkness until Queen Cera's fall from power. Airan's history was strangely clouded and mysterious, his future as Prince of Magmorrah proved uncertain and filled with fearful judgement by many.

Chaos is steadily rising throughout the wounded lands, many still torn apart and falling further into disarray, with no end of this in sight. The once-formidable Elemental Guardians themselves, still healing from the haunting events that took place both before and after Skynah's destruction, struggle to adapt in their newly-formed world.

All the while, an ancient nemesis has secretly emerged within Impartia that could both destroy "The Sacred Balance' and all sentient life upon it…**Zolkiah**.

Appendix: Name Pronunciations

Impartia is an ancient world of varying cultures, which are ultimately comprised into six nations: Hydrania, Magmorrah, Skynah, Talam, Viridia and Weissamorrah. These lands share in one tongue, though differ in their pronunciations. In 'Cerebrante: The Sacred Balance' the names, as written, are pronounced in their mother-tongues and are desired to be read as so.

Airan: *Aye-rah-uhn*

Aira: *Aer-rah*

Alaskia: *Ahl-ask-ee-yah*

Cara: *Karh-rah*

Cera: *Szee-rah*

Cerebrante: *Seh-reh-brah-uhnt*

Danaki: *Dah-nah-kai*

Elona: *E-hul-oh-nah*

Eternamorrah: *Ee-tuhr-nah-mohr-rah*

Firin: *Fi-rihn*

Hackranom: *Haa-krah-noh-uhm*

Harryn: *Haa-rihn*

Helena: *Hel-leh-nah*

Hydrania: *Hai-dray-nee-yah*

Illuminecia: *Ill-uhm-ihn-ee-shee-ah*

Impartia: *Ihm-pahr-shee-yah*

Jardiah: *Jahr-dai-yah*

Jenayan: *Jehn-ay-yahn*

Jendoro: *Jehn-doh-roh*

Kanaan: *Kah-naan*

Karolheid: *Kah-rohl-hai-duh*

Katrinia: *Kaht-rihn-ee-yah*

Kufiah: *Koo-fhee-yah*

Lenya: *Leh-ehn-yah*

Levia: *Leh-vai-yah*

Magmorrah: *Mahg-mohr-rah*

Mirtziah: *Muhrtz-ai-yah*

Mandalaur: *Mahn-dah-loww-uhr*

Moah: *Moe-ah*

Natara: *Naht-arh-rah*

Nira: *Nee-rah*

Pahoe: *Pah-hoe*

Rosira: *Roh-sai-rah*

Silvra: *Sihl-vuh-rah*

Silvran: *Sihl-vuh-rahn*

Skynah: *Skuh-ai-nah*

Sophilia: *Soe-fee-lee-yah*

Spero: *Spea-roh*

Stevian: *Stehv-ee-yahn*

Talam: *Tah-lahm*

Ven: *Veh-uhn*

Void: *Voi-duh*

Viran: *Vai-rahn*

Viridia: *Vih-rih-dee-yah*

Weissamorrah: *Vuh-ai-sah-mohr-rah*

Zeddah: *Zeh-dah*

Zolkiah: *Zohl-kai-yah*

About the Author

Andrew John Bell was born and still lives in County Durham, England, UK. From 2010 onwards, Andrew has been working professionally as a Senior Care Assistant at a local EMI Nursing Home; this experience made him question his own moral and spiritual beliefs – both good and bad. Andrew met his wife whilst working with her at this Nursing Home, then over the next eight years they married and had two daughters together – his 'light in the darkness'. It was in 2017, that Andrew decided to accumulate his moral and spiritual questions into, what would eventually become - *Cerebrante: The Sacred Balance*. Andrew has plans to make a 'Cerebrante' Trilogy, which will specifically follow the life of Cara and her daughter Sophilia. There are also plans to develop a 'Cerebrante Series' to coincide with the main Trilogy; these books will focus on individual characters, delving into their pasts and other specific events.

Books by Andrew John Bell

Cerebrante Book One: The Sacred Balance (released - November 2017/July 2018)
Cerebrante Book Two: The Forgotten Guardian (release - Autumn/Fall 2018)
Cerebrante Book Three: The Divine Chaos (release - Winter 2018/2019)

Also…

Where Has Grandpa Murray Gone? (Released December 2017) – A poetic reflection of sharing in a loved one's Dementia.

Printed in Great Britain
by Amazon

33060105R00178